Retrieval
The Elifer Chronicles Book Two

Julie Boglisch

Published by Rogue Phoenix Press, LLP
Copyright © 2020

ISBN: 978-1-62420-556-9

Editor: Sherry Derr-Wille

Published in The United States

Dedication

This book has been a long time in the making and, for a while, I was worried that it would never get a chance to see the light of day. However, thanks to all of your support, and for everyone who has been looking forward to this second book even as the years passed, I am immensely grateful to each and every one of you. This book is for you guys and for the people at Rogue Phoenix Press who were so willing to take this series and give this book a chance. Stay strong, everyone who has supported me to this point, because this is for you all!

Chapter One

Lex leaned against the balcony, staring at the leaf-cluttered garden floor. Wind blew through the trees, ruffling his long black hair. His thoughts turned to the past few weeks, wondering why he decided to stay in this wretched place that was once home. While it contained all the luxuries anyone could ever dream of, it was oppressive and cold. He didn't want that. He wanted freedom, which was why he ran away all those years ago. Now he was back and why?

He shook his head, unable to hide his amusement. He knew why. Those kids who randomly showed up in his city without knowing a thing were the reason. Twins without any knowledge of the outside world and how messed up it was. He pushed away from the white rail and walked back into his room. He moved to the door and opened it to peer outside. Two guards stood on the other side, watching the door stoically. One nodded to him but did nothing else. Lex frowned and pulled his head back in. He moved to the couch and sat down.

He was glad that the two managed to escape. He didn't want them here anymore than he wanted to stay. He stared out the window from his seat on the couch, watching as a light breeze blew the branches back and forth. He lifted his hand and spread his fingers, looking at the pale digits. To think, just a week ago, he had been slowly dying from an epidemic the likes of which this country, the United States of America, had never seen, and now it was like he had never been sick. He let his hand drop as he leaned his head back and followed the patterns dotting the ceiling.

He stopped in his thoughts as he sat up and turned to the doorway. The handle clicked, and his brother stepped in. Lex furrowed his brow but stayed silent. His brother closed the door behind him and sat across from Lex, his expression nonchalant. His blond hair curved over his cheeks, emphasizing his chiseled features and intelligent grey eyes. They sat in silence, his brother looking him up and down little flickers of emotion flashing across his face, to be hidden just as quickly.

Lex felt a hint of sadness to think that the one person who had seen him as a person was now so cold. He wondered what would have happened if he stayed, if he never left this place to begin with. The idea frightened him.

"So, little Leo, what are you going to do now? Because of that little stunt you pulled with the fire alarm, they're watching you more carefully. They're still trying to salvage the pantry, by the way." Caym paused as he looked out the window. "Oh, and Dad is coming home."

Well, he wanted that, but still. He shivered at the thought. "I don't see why you are asking me," Lex said after a moment. "It shouldn't matter to you."

Caym shifted his gaze to Lex, sizing him up before he responded, "Of course it does, you're my little brother. I'm only making sure you are all right."

Lex quietly scoffed before he stood, stepping away from his brother and toward the window. He leaned against the opened glass doors, crossing his hands over his chest. "Caym, what's your real reason for being here?"

Caym gazed after him, his expression indecipherable, before he stood and let out a sigh. "Well, I wanted to let you know that Dad just called, he should be home in a few hours. I also came to salute you. It was fascinating how simply you executed the escape plan to get those two away from here. However, I don't understand why you did it. There was no reason to go through with something like that."

Lex growled softly.

Caym stepped toward the doorway before he paused. He looked like he was debating about something. He shook his head and continued out the door.

Lex walked back to the couch and slumped into his seat. He let his head rest in his hands. After a few moments, he stood and shuffled over to the balcony once more. He stared at the tree Karina used. The branch lay there, invitingly. He knew he wasn't as good a climber as the forest-grown female, but he was decent enough.

However, he also knew he wouldn't be able to get anywhere that way. He knew it would be a challenge to leave if he focused on the twins, but he couldn't let his father meet them. He needed to see his father and confirm something. He peered over the edge to the ground a floor or so below. He could see people working in the gardens as his thoughts wandered.

How was he going to get out of here?

~ * ~

Karina looked up, peering around the fairly empty train station. It was small, with only a wooden structure near a set of tracks and a ticket booth, being manned by a bored older man. Black hair dangled into her eyes as she shifted on the bench to look down at her twin, Maxwell. He was sleeping soundly, resting his head on her shoulder as brown hair fell into his face. He wore the new outfit, ah, sorry, she mentally chuckled, clothes she got him. It was a pair of faded jeans, a black zip hoodie, left undone, and a white undershirt.

She wore cargo pants and a long-sleeved t-shirt. She needed to find time to get more clothes, especially since the weather was still chilly as noon approached.

She turned and examined the station. She could see the train tracks curving into the distance to either side. Houses sat across the street, blocked off with a tall crisscrossing metal fence. The sun shone down, but following their long night she wasn't surprised her brother was still sleeping even now. Still, it had been two days since they escaped from Lex's house.

Lex promised he would meet them here a few days later. She was starting to get worried. She turned her head toward the sky as her brother shifted in his sleep. She couldn't believe that it was only a little over a month ago when she had been forced to leave her home with Maxwell, running from the very government itself. To think that she and her brother could be...her thoughts trailed off as she heard shuffling. She looked down to see Maxwell slowly blink his eyes open and let out a little yawn. Green eyes blearily looked up at her before a mumbled "morning" sounded from his lips.

Karina chuckled. "I was wondering when you would wake up. Come on, let's get something to eat."

Maxwell nodded and pushed himself off her shoulder. He stood and stretched, reaching toward the sky. Karina grinned and stood. Maxwell dropped his hands to his sides and gazed sidelong at his twin. "So where are we eating this time? I'm getting sick of fast food. I mean, it's not bad but I miss home-cooked food."

Karina had to agree. The place they frequented reminded her a bit too much of the nasty sandwiches Lex first gave them when they met the older teen. Unfortunately, fast food was the cheapest and one of the few things available close to the station. Plus, with so many people going in and out, they weren't really noticed, a good thing in her opinion. She probably wouldn't have minded the place, if she ate it as a treat or something but to eat it every day made her feel a little sick. Unfortunately, they had to save on money. They took turns sleeping in different places, either the wooded areas nearby or the church that Karina found the second day.

She walked down the platform, followed by Maxwell, who yawned loudly and trailed after her. They stepped off the platform and walked a little way down a short stretch of road before arriving in a quaint little shopping area. They were grateful it was right next to the train station. They peered into the different places, trying to figure out prices and such. Karina felt her stomach growl and pursed her lips in distaste. She needed to find something to eat soon.

"How about there?"

Karina turned to her brother, then followed where he was pointing to see a little pizzeria. She felt her mouth water. She hadn't had pizza in a long time, and it sounded good, especially with all the spices." Sure," she said.

She peered up and down the street. Cars meandered to and fro as pedestrians crossed back and forth. She was glad that the epidemic wasn't too bad here. What had Lex called it? The SS Phenomenon, that's what it was. It was amazing to think that such a devastating disease dwelled in the country. On top of that, the country was blocked off from the rest of the world, so they couldn't even get help from outside. Isolationism really wasn't helpful sometimes.

She examined herself before looking at Maxwell. To think that the two of them could be the cure to the disease itself, was it a fluke? Either way, she didn't want to think of it. If it was, then they were the reason their mother was taken from them, as well as their father. She felt sick at the thought. She didn't want to think about it. Her brother wasn't too fond of talking about it either, or so it seemed.

They stepped into the pizzeria, and Karina barely managed to stop herself from salivating at all the smells. Maxwell didn't look to be doing much better.

"What can I do for you?"

Karina turned to a young woman.

She had on an apron stained with flour and wore the white doctor's mask that most citizens desperately sought after. She seemed kindly, smiling behind the mask. "Uh, yeah, how much for a pizza?"

"What size?" she asked as she moved behind a counter.

Karina stepped toward it, alongside Maxwell, who was looking around the small place in curiosity. They went a little farther out today, and now she was grateful. This place smelled good, and she was hungry.

Maxwell seemed to pull himself from his observation to answer her question. Karina let him, deciding to let herself examine the restaurant. It was a small diner-style location with an older man next to a large oven. There was glass in front of it allowing people to watch, yet still being separated, away from the heat. It was cute. She turned back in time to see her sibling smile and hand over some money. The young girl nodded and moved to the back to place the order.

"Come on. Let's sit down. It'll take about ten minutes."

Karina nodded and sat on one of the plastic chairs across from Maxwell. He tossed her a water bottle and Karina took it gratefully. Maybe she should have paid more attention, when did he even grab one? She peered toward the counter, only to roll her eyes. Of course, there was a fridge right there. He probably just grabbed it. She opened it and gulped the drink down with a pleased sigh.

"Kari?"

Karina peered toward her sibling as he swished his bottle back and forth. He hesitated for a moment before he looked up at her. He opened his mouth, and then closed it.

"Yeah?"

"What should we do if Lex doesn't show up?"

Karina stared at her brother, then looked toward the back. She watched as the man prepared the pizza. She stayed silent for a little while before she turned back to Maxwell. "What do you think?" She was curious as she respected her brother's opinion. She knew her own, but she just wanted to see what he had to say.

He obviously was thinking the same thing. He sighed and leaned back, taking a sip before he responded, "We're going to have to leave. We can't stay around here much longer, the locals are getting suspicious, and the more we linger around the station, the more likely someone will say something and I don't think either of us want that."

He really didn't need to say more. Karina understood and agreed whole-heartedly, yet she waited for him to continue.

"We'll give him one more day, but after that, we have to take the train to Collern. We need to get to Mom before..."

"Before anything else happens?" Karina finished for him as he seemed to hesitate.

Maxwell nodded.

Karina let out a long sigh and took another sip of water. "That's basically what I'm thinking as well. The sooner we leave, the better."

She stopped as she heard footsteps. She looked over to see the young girl return, pizza in hand. She placed it down before walking away. Karina stared at it, before digging in. The cheese melted in her mouth as she chowed down on the meal. It definitely was better than that fast food crap they had been eating up until now. Why Lex liked it, she had no idea. So what if they paid a little extra? She wanted to feel somewhat satisfied for once. She watched her brother who was stuffing the pizza in his mouth with the same fervor and chuckled before taking another bite and looking out the window toward the street.

They would wait one more day, but after that they had to leave, with or without Lex.

She realized, with a hint of surprise, she did actually want to meet and have Lex journey with them again. She hoped he made it in time.

~ * ~

Lex looked up as the door opened to reveal Machael, his butler, step inside and bow. "Sir, your father requested your attendance at dinner."

Lex nodded and stood. He followed Machael as they headed toward the dining room. He felt nervous, annoyed and unsure. Had he made the right decision?

It didn't take long, much to Lex's consternation. Machael stepped to the side and bowed. Lex nodded toward him with a weak smile before stepping through the doorway. He hesitantly took the last available seat.

Next to him, on his right, sat his mother who had her hands placed gently in her lap as she peered at the group, her usually smiling face rather stoic. Caym sat across from him. His expression was a mixture of cold and professional, much like his own, Lex thought. Finally, he turned his gaze on the last member of the table who arrived only an hour earlier, or so he could assume. His father wore an impassive expression; his blue eyes were cold. He was still in uniform, Lex noted. The black uniform sat taut on his rough frame, and a silver medallion hung on the breast pocket. Black hair fell over a stoic face. "Leonard."

Lex for once didn't argue the name. He gulped but didn't say a word as the man peered at him.

"I wondered where you were. A child like you…" he paused and leaned back in his chair as he crossed one leg over the other. "No, I can see you are no longer a child. A pity."

Lex saw Caym's expression flicker for a second. Was that worry?

"Father, I don't think—" Caym began, only to be cut off by Father's look.

"Silence."

Lex looked over to see Caym wince slightly. It was barely noticeable, but it was enough. Their father turned his gaze from Caym to Lex's once more.

Lex mentally prepared himself. "Father," Lex managed to say, his voice surprisingly level.

He waited as his father stared at him before gesturing. "Well? Go on, I don't have all day."

Lex mentally winced, yet continued, "I wish to ask you a question, a small one, if I may?"

"You have already, but yes, you may."

Lex took in a breath before he leaned forward, hands in his lap. "Father, where were you four years ago? I remember you came home all flustered and, well, some incidents as of late have reminded me of that occasion. Do you recall? I believe you said you were on a business trip?"

His father leaned his head back, confusion flashing across his face for the barest of seconds before his eyes narrowed and he responded, "This came out of nowhere. Why do you ask?"

"Curiosity."

The man stayed silent for a while, as if debating what to say, or thinking over what the answer might be before he continued, "That is none of your concern. However, I do believe I know of what trip you speak. If it is, then it was to do with my corporation, nothing more, nothing less. Now, is that all?"

"Dear, surely you can explain more thoroughly. I think even I recall that time. You're usually so cheerful after your trips." Mother spoke up, leaning forward the slightest bit.

Cheerful wasn't the word Lex would have used, and Caym's split-second expression indicated that Caym thought that was a misnomer as well. At least it was Lex's assumption, as his brother turned to the window, facing Mother and away from Father's gaze.

"My dear, you know I must keep some secrets. Imagine if the outer community learned of some of these things? No, it's best if our son doesn't get involved any more then he already is."

"If you believe so…" Mother trailed off before clapping her hands, a little smile on her face. "Enough of this, though. I believe this is the first time in years the four of us have been together. Let's enjoy this time and eat. Oh, and Leonard dear, please make sure to sit properly. You are starting to slouch."

Lex found himself quickly sitting ramrod straight, Caym eyeing him quietly with an unreadable expression. "My apologies, Mother," Lex spoke up, keeping his voice even.

Father looked at him for a moment before turning to his food.

"Well, she is right. Come boys, let's dig in."

Lex hesitated before he nodded. The man picked up his silverware once more and cut into the chicken fricassee as silver clinked and servants moved. The servant's footsteps were soft over the wood floor, barely heard over Mother and Father's pleasant, if shallow-sounding conversation.

Lex tentatively went to pick up his own fork, trying to remember what he could.

"It's the second one."

Lex peered up toward Caym, making sure to keep his head bowed. Caym barely gave him a glance as he picked his fork off the table. He picked up the middle one of the silverware.

Lex was reaching for the first. He nodded subtly and picked up the appropriate one.

He heard a sound and looked up. His father looked at him, eyes narrowed and silverware suspended. "Pathetic. I thought you would remember your manners, but it seems not and Caym, it is none of your concern whether your brother knows his manners or not."

Lex grimaced as his father resumed eating. He heard a soft sigh from his mother and saw Caym's brow furrow. Caym caught his gaze and mouthed a quick sorry before continuing his food.

Lex looked down, feeling his stomach churn. He didn't have much of an appetite anymore, but if he didn't eat, it would look even worse.

After he finally settled into the rhythm of eating, being much more careful of what he did by following Caym, he let his mind analyze what he just learned. While it wasn't much, it was enough to confirm for him. He knew well enough his father worked for the government. The kids explained how the one who took their dad was a man in uniform with a cold expression and black hair. Usually that description wouldn't be enough, but if he calculated where his father would have been during that time combined with his father's affirmation that he was working for the corporation, it seemed all too certain that he was in fact one and the same. *So, I was right to help the twins,* he thought. *I have to get out of here. If Dad's leading the investigation, I need to get them gone before he realizes.*

After dinner, Lex stood from the table. His father gave him a passing glance before he continued in his conversation with one of the servants, demanding a cup of coffee. His mother sent him a worried look. He gave her a quick smile, then turned. He heard the scrape of a chair and peered back to see Caym also stood.

"Caym, where are you going?"

"Father, if I may, I wish to attend to something. I will be back in a moment."

Lex walked out the door, followed by Caym. Caym stepped up beside him as they walked down the hallway. "Caym, what do you want?"

"Why did you ask that question?"

Lex peered sidelong at Caym who was looking at him with a complex expression, one he couldn't quite name. He faced forward once more. "I was thinking back to around the time I left and happened to remember that was one of his longest absences and, as Mother said, he actually came back frustrated. Why?"

Silence enveloped the hallway as wind blew outside, limbs gently tapping on the glass windows. "That was stupid." This time, Caym was looking ahead. "You know as well as I what could have happened. You were lucky he was in a good mood." Frustration flickered across Caym's face. A moment later, it was gone and Caym turned, smile once more in place. "Well, as I said, the prodigal son has returned." Caym headed back to the dining room before pausing, staring toward the doorway. He looked back, expression level. "I hope you got your answer." He turned and continued on his way.

Lex stared at Caym's back. For a split second, he saw his brother as he had been. Those moments were so fleeting, he thought he missed them, but no, not this time. His brother wasn't entirely lost, something was left. He wondered how so much of it was lost. He paused and looked around as a memory tickled at the back of his mind. Wasn't there something missing?

"Hey, Caym."

Caym stopped and glanced over his shoulder, silent and curious.

Lex turned fully toward him. "Where are Ariel and Kiera? You are usually always with your wife and daughter."

Caym stiffened. "They're… Don't worry about them. You have other things to worry about anyway."

Before Lex could get a word in edgewise Caym was gone, back through the dining room door.

Lex frowned. What did that mean? Yes, he felt a little bad that he'd forgotten about Caym's wife and child, but in his defense, he had a lot on his mind up until now. Yet now, as he looked around the halls, he realized how empty they all seemed. That wasn't right. Usually he would at least hear a hint of Kiera's laughter or Ariel's singing practice, however off-key it was.

He turned and peered out the window. Clouds hung low in the sky and his thoughts drifted away from the two missing people, since it wasn't his concern, and toward the twins. Were they okay? Were they somewhere warm? Were they waiting for him? He knew Maxwell might, but with Karina he wasn't sure. He saw something drip onto one of the window frames and watched as more and more drops of rain hit the glass pane. They trailed down, tracks merging with one another as the sky outside darkened. He was glad it was only raining, though he suspected it was probably cold. Was it cold enough yet for snow? He didn't know. He peered up at the clouds for another moment, watching as they moved across the sky. He turned and walked toward his room, listening to the thrumming of the rain on the windows and roof. He could hear footsteps and looked back to see two guards, different from last time. They must have been following him and Caym. He shouldn't have been surprised. Of course, they would have someone watching him, especially after setting the pantry on fire to distract everyone so the kids could escape.

He peered ahead, scanning the surroundings with a practiced eye. During the storm would be a good and bad time to leave. It would be good because it was harder to see someone when it was raining, but it would be bad because of the same problem. He knew where the exit was, and he didn't particularly care if he got wet. No, he dealt with worse while in the cities, and those times, he was sick.

If anything, he hadn't felt this healthy since before he left home, when he first met Allen. He grinned. Decision made. He changed direction and headed toward the servants 'quarters. He was grateful the guards didn't say anything. He really wasn't in the mood to deal with trying to convince them that, no, he didn't need to go straight to his room. He opened the door and stepped into the servants 'quarters. It was a simple set-up with a hallway lined with doorways, all leading toward different rooms big enough for one person to sleep and change.

The problem was that the hallway was short and each room held two beds, thus two people.

They thought this was good, if not better, compared to outside? To be stuffed together like pigeons in a cage and treated worse than some of the poor outside the gated community? Who were the disillusioned ones? He was glad he could keep Karina and Maxwell with him for the few days they were here. He knew Karina would be positively pissed if she saw this. He stepped down the hallway as the rain thrummed on the ceiling and knocked on one of the doorways. After a moment, it opened to reveal Machael. He was still in his butler's uniform. He must have just returned.

"Sir?"

"Machael, can I speak to you for a moment?" The man peered past Lex, toward the two guards before he nodded. Lex smiled before he looked back at the two. "It'll only be a moment." The guards gave him a narrowed gaze but stayed still as he walked in the door and closed it.

Lex turned to Machael, knowing he didn't have much time. "Machael, I need your help."

Machael smiled softly before he took a seat. Lex stepped farther into the room. It was spartan with two beds, a desk, a chair, and that was it. He took the chair, sitting on it sideways. "You have been around the longest. You should remember—"

"Sir, I remember well. You have changed much in your time away. You seem much happier. You do realize what will happen though?"

Lex grimaced and looked down. He knew. He already got Machael in trouble once, when he was really little. He decided to try to climb one of the trees because he accidentally got something caught in the branches. He couldn't remember what it was, but Machael was watching him at the time.

Either way, he fell and broke his arm. His father demoted Machael from personal servant to just regular. Only Lex's insistence actually allowed Machael to continue working with the family. He didn't want to imagine what would happen this time if they discovered Machael was one of the ones involved with his escape. Especially if Father realized who it was that Lex was watching. "I know. That's why all I'm asking is for you to send a couple servants to my room with some things. Make sure they are in my mother's good graces, then go to work with Mother or Caym. If you're working with them during that time, they can't accuse you of anything. Please?"

Machael chuckled softly and nodded. "Sir, you are as strange as usual. Now, what would you like me to tell the servants?"

Lex grinned.

~ * ~

Maxwell peered up at the sky, mentally cursing its existence as rain fell down. His sister stood next to him, huddled under the overhang of the station's platform. Pedestrians moved on and off the train, opening and closing umbrellas or pulling up their jackets before walking out of the station.

"Why is it always raining?" Maxwell muttered, and Karina shrugged next to him, one arm massaging the other as she shivered.

"I want to know why it's always cold."

"Sis, it's winter, of course it's cold."

"You know what I mean."

Maxwell chuckled before he nodded and looked back at the clouds. It was getting late into the day and he was getting nervous. He grabbed his backpack and opened it before pulling out a photograph depicting his mother, father and twin. He stared for a moment, holding it carefully before pushing it back into the bag, buried as deep as it could go. He wished he still had the plastic bags from when his sister and he first left Claremore. He dug around and pulled out another bag. This one was one he found a couple hours after they arrived at Liberty Station. It held some money as well as goods. He wasn't sure where it came from. When he asked Karina about it, she had no clue either.

He could only suspect that it was from the last house they were at before they were taken unknowingly to Lex's home. There was no one else still living in that home besides the husband. Why did he do it, considering they caused his wife's death? He wasn't sure, but he mentally thanked him and felt bad, remembering the state the man was in. He wondered what would have happened if they just went up and knocked instead of sneaking in. Would he have turned them away? Would he have slammed the door in their faces, handed them their bags and pushed them away?

He didn't like the idea that his sister had to actually break into a house. While it wasn't technically stealing—they were just recovering their own stuff—it still felt like theft. He wondered what else they would have to do before they even got to Ma. What else his sister would have to do?

He didn't want to think beyond getting to Ma. It already worried him. He didn't want to imagine thinking of the cure, or the country. He would think of things one piece at a time. If not, he would be overwhelmed. He turned to his sister who puffed out her cheeks in annoyance.

"He better get here soon or else I'm hopping on the first train outta here. It's too cold."

Maxwell chuckled. In other words, his sister was worried about Lex as well. Karina sent him a glare, and he only smiled. It made him feel better, knowing his sister was no longer against having Lex's help. She was finally beginning to trust the man again. He hoped it would work out. He munched on some leftover food in the bag before he stuffed it back in his backpack and slung it over his back. He reached into his pocket and pulled out a ticket and looked at it. They should have gotten a later ticket, but there wasn't much he could do about that.

The ticket listed the six o'clock train. While that was admittedly in three hours, it felt worrying.

He knew it was already pushing it, but he wanted to give Lex as much time as possible. Who knew if they would meet again if they hopped on a train? There would be no way of knowing and Maxwell hadn't thought of getting Lex's number even though he had his cell phone on him. Whether it still worked or not, he wasn't sure. He put the ticket back into his pocket and reached into his other and pulled out the phone. He threw it on the charger earlier, so now could actually turn it on. He powered it up and flicked it open, waiting for the screen to do something other than show black. A large part of him wished to see that there were missed calls or messages from his mother or anyone, for that matter. He waited, sighing in a mix of relief and resignation as the insignia appeared before the phone turned on to show it was empty of any calls.

"I didn't even know you grabbed that."

Maxwell peered back at Karina, who was gazing at the phone with a raised eyebrow, before he looked down at the phone once more.

"I had forgotten, too. I hadn't really thought of it. I mean, who could I call? I didn't think of getting Lex's number, even though he brought out his cell phone quite a few times." He peered at the screen, noting the time to be three forty-eight.

"I guess you couldn't really call anyone from home, could you?"

Maxwell shrugged, flipping through his limited contacts. He had his mother's number, Karina's and, not much else. He never really was one to exchange numbers. He preferred talking to people face to face and, if he needed to contact them, he would just send an email. He was starting to regret that decision now. He flicked out of the contacts and flipped it closed. He looked at Karina who stared out toward the train tracks as another train pulled away, sending a whistle into the air.

~ * ~

Lex tapped on the window of his balcony, feeling urgency bubble in the pit of his stomach. It was already day three: he needed to leave. He heard a knock on the door and turned. "Enter."

The door opened to reveal two female servants. They curtseyed, holding their trays delicately with their free hands. They stepped inside and closed the door. They placed the trays on the table. "Sir, your tea and cookies." Lex smiled as they exposed the things, it was exactly that, tea and cookies, artfully arranged in a pile. He walked over and sat down at the table. He turned to the servants as they moved about, tidying up his place. One woman stumbled, dropping clothing on the floor next to him. He purposely ignored it, even though part of him wanted to bend over and help her like he usually did. He saw her kneel down and watched as she dropped a bag to the floor, unseen by the camera due to the angle. He used his foot and pulled it under the table. The maid, once she saw, smiled softly and stood, things in hand. "Sir Lex, enjoy, we will return in an hour to collect your things."

"Thank you. You are dismissed." The two nodded and left.

He pulled the bag closer and started to munch on the cookies and pour himself some tea. He looked at the tea bags and pulled out a small white one. He looked at it, then reached for another, keeping it in the palm of his hand as he grabbed the second and put that in. Once done, he opened the first under the table.

It was a quick letter, written neatly in script. "Sir, everything you asked for is in the bag. As you know, it wasn't much time, but everything should be there. We wish you luck and hope that one day, we can see you again." It was signed by Machael and a few other servants that Lex knew well. He smiled softly and stuffed it into his pocket before he took a sip of tea and picked up another cookie. He dropped it and cursed before ducking down under the table. He smiled, grabbed the bag, as well as the fallen cookie. He pulled the bag up, out of view of the camera and placed the cookie back onto the table. He knew it wasn't as discreet as he would have liked, but he was kind of limited in what he could do.

Now to wait.

Luckily, he didn't need to wait long. The servants returned and collected the items. He stood and walked away to watch, slipping the bag onto his shoulder. The servants collected the tea and cookies and left out the door. He heard a sound, followed someone yelling. He felt bad, but he knew his mother was very forgiving, especially for the female servants. He did specifically ask for two in her good graces. Accidents happened, and that's what he was using as he hurried to the tree. He slipped out and onto the balcony, over the commotion of the guards yelling, he doubted he was heard.

Now to get out of here.

He peered over the edge and at the tree. While it wasn't nearly as safe as when Karina used it, he really didn't have much choice. He grabbed the bag and dug out rope before wrapping it around the balcony tightly. He stepped over the edge and used the rope to slide to the ground. He left it there and ran, backpack firmly on his back. He wore a set of hefty new hiking boots he'd changed into earlier. He moved over the muddy ground, his clothes soaked through in seconds from the deluge. He could only imagine that this was what it was like for the twins when they left home. He suddenly felt empathy.

Luckily, he didn't have a forest to run through like they did, and he noted the rain was already starting to let up, changing to ice, he did hate hail. He moved into the back garden and continued forward. He wondered if his brother noticed. He figured he would, but what he wasn't sure of was how he would respond.

Chapter Two

Caym looked up from his paperwork as a servant stepped in, finding his annoyance still hadn't died down. Why had Leo asked that? It wasn't his business. He shook his head and turned his gaze on the servant. It was Machael and he looked a little shaken. "Sir, your father wishes to see you."

"And Lex?" Caym asked as he placed his pencil down and pulled off his reading glasses.

He placed them down as Machael responded, "A different servant went to get him. Your father said it's urgent."

Caym frowned, yet stood and followed after Machael, wondering what it was. To send two servants was rare, even in this family. His frown deepened as he realized where they were going. It was the recording room.

Machael bowed and left.

Caym straightened his posture and stepped inside, only to wish he hadn't. His father sat at the computer, fury emanating from him in waves. He turned his head toward Caym, then turned back to the monitors. There were two up. One showing the boy from before, what was his name again, Maxwell? He was holding a set of papers. His head was tilted up toward the doorway, showing worry. The papers looked like they were about to slip through his fingers. The next one was of the girl, Karina, talking to one of the servants as she carried a garden rake, probably going out into the backyard to help the ground workers.

Caym looked back. Even though he was used to his father's different emotions, even he was worried.

"Caym, do you know what you did?"

Caym stayed silent, figuring if he wanted to survive, he might as well.

"Well, these two? These are the damn brats I've been looking for since they escaped my men months ago. Do you know why?"

Caym waited, feeling his unease and worry increase. He saw his father slam his hand on the table as he stood. He turned and stepped toward Caym. Even though they were about the same height, his father looked down at him, fury in his eyes before he suddenly lifted his hand and backhanded Caym across the cheek. "You idiot of a son. Those two are more valuable than you can even fathom. They are what are going to get me to the top. Those two brats are the key to ruling this country."

Caym kept his head tilted away, feeling the painful throb of his cheek. He let his mind analyze what his father said. Ruling this country? How?

"The cure. You let the cure get away. You were there when they escaped. You just let them waltz out. How disgraceful."

His father turned and stepped up to the monitors. He placed both hands on the desk and leaned forward, eyes glued on the two. "Your brother was more helpful. He actually found them and brought them here. After all this time and betraying the family, he was the one who got them almost in my grasp. The very cure, the very thing that can control this country, control its very people, all at my fingertips. I could have been the one who decided life and death. Do you realize how much power that is? How much we lost because of your stupid arrogance? Your brother. Maybe he is better suited to leading. We'll have to reteach him, of course, but that shouldn't be too much of an issue."

Caym felt anger surge into his veins. His younger brother had done no such thing. He brought them here. He's the one who found his brother in the first place. His brother never even intended to come back. Even now, Father was still praising him. Caym ground his teeth in frustration before he threw on an impassive expression. Why was he so upset, isn't that what he originally wanted? To allow his brother to escape from this hell?

His father stared at the monitors for another moment before he peered over his shoulder, the glow of the multiple screens casting his face with harsh lighting. "I'll send these pictures in to the police. I'll make sure the government gets them one way or another. We will fix this mistake."

Caym pursed his lips as he turned his gaze toward the two kids. Now he understood why they were so special to Lex. He felt his cheek throb and finally deigned to put his hand up to it. His hand felt cool against the heat of his cheek. It was definitely going to make a nice bruise. Sadly, he was used to it. He closed his eyes as they waited in silence.

He could remember something like this happening a long time ago.

They were still young, he remembered that much. The suit felt stiff and all too hot as they sat to one side of the ballroom. The two-story-tall monolith was filled with partiers in fancy dresses and black suits. It was an impressive display as dancers twirled around and the sound of violins and cellos sang through the hall.

All Caym wanted to do was go back to his room and maybe sleep. His brother stood beside him, fidgeting. He was tugging at his tie which was obviously a bit too snug. His long black hair was pulled back into a low ponytail. His brother hadn't been thrilled with that idea, but it was either that or get it cut.

Caym gazed over the dancers, spotting a pile of presents off to one side. He saw Leo glance toward it before looking away, face falling. Caym pursed his lips as he spotted a newcomer put another present down, a present that should have been meant for his brother.

His brother was just turning twelve and yet the presents laid down were things no twelve-year-old would ever want or need such as fancy wine, high end clothing more fit for Mother and other such oddities which seemed to be more to appease Mother and Father. All those presents laying there and Caym knew that not a one was for his little brother.

He could tell that Leo knew too if his solemn expression was any indication. He could see Mother off to one side, socializing with a couple of the other woman while Father talked with some company president or another.

It didn't really matter to Caym. He glanced sidelong at Leo. "Hey, Leo."

"Hm?" Leo looked up, his eyes wide. It was the only real conversation they had all night. Most of the partiers ignored them. If they did see them, they would walk over, pinch their cheeks to say how cute they were and promptly get distracted by something else.

Caym glanced around the room once more before he turned to Leo with a small grin. "What do you say about getting out of here?"

Leo's eyes lit up at the prospect and Caym had to withhold the chuckle. His little brother was so cute sometimes. However, that chuckle died before it even started as Leo's face fell and he looked around worriedly. "What if Father notices?"

He hesitated and Caym couldn't blame him. He held out one hand.

Leo looked at it for a moment, then toward the crowd before he grabbed it. They wove through the party-goers, careful to avoid their parents 'eyes. He knew Mother wouldn't make too much of a fuss, but Father...

They slipped outside of the stuffy interior into the moonlit garden. Pristine hedges were pruned into perfect shapes with flowers waving gently in the breeze. The fresh air felt blissful after the overwhelming heat and perfumed smell of the ballroom. The music was faded, no longer ringing in his ears.

Leo sighed with relief as they walked deeper into the garden, finally being hidden behind some taller maze brush. Caym let go and Leo looked back.

"It's so much nicer outside." The statement was a fact, but Leo seemed to ask it as a question.

Caym nodded. He felt nervous. Usually, they had a butler or guard around them, but with most of the focus on the party, it was the first time the two of them could be by themselves since a long time ago.

He was also anxious about his father finding out again, but he quickly brushed it away as Leo turned to him, as if waiting.

Caym stared back, unsure what to say before he grinned. "Want to play a game?" Caym could see Leo's reluctance before he grinned and nodded.

They hadn't meant to be out as long as they were. They really hadn't, but it was fun, a lot of fun. It had been a long time, years actually, since Caym felt so carefree and he knew his brother felt the same way. It was such a simple game—Hide and Seek—and with a big garden to play within, there were so many places to hide. Of course, his brother wasn't very good at it, but Caym was fine with that.

It was Leo's turn to be seeking. Caym remembered hiding near the entrance to the garden. He knew it was a dangerous move, what with the party, but he figured he was enough out of sight to be fine.

He hadn't realized how late it was. The music faded from his hearing long ago.

He heard the doors bang open as footsteps headed his way. Caym glanced back to see his father, looking downright pissed. He gulped and glanced over to see Leo looking around, almost in sight of Father.

He didn't even debate as he darted from his hiding spot, grabbed his brother, who stared at him in surprise, and raced away. Leo seemed to realize, for he stayed silent, face paling as they hurried into a new hiding space, breathing heavily. Caym looked through the branches, hoping his father hadn't seen them.

To his relief, the man hadn't. His father gazed around, before stepping forward. "Boys. If you do not come out this instant…"

He let the threat hang and Caym shivered. He glanced at Leo, who was watching nervously, his hands twitching to hold on to something. They were in trouble, and they both knew it.

Caym took a deep breath and looked Leo straight in the eye before gesturing toward the doorway briefly.

Leo froze before he vigorously shook his head.

Caym glared. He was used to it, but his brother was not. He wouldn't subject his brother to this. He reached into his pocket, feeling the small lump in his hand. He cradled it for a moment before he gently pulled it out and laid it in his brother's palm.

His brother stared, eyes wide as Caym held up three fingers and slowly started counting them down. Leo's jaw tightened before he looked away, fist clenching over the gift. Caym finished his countdown, took a steadying breath and stepped away from his hiding place. After moving as far away as possible, he stepped out of the brush into his father's line of sight.

His father took one look at his messy outfit and his face contorted into one of utter disdain. "Where's your brother?" was all he said.

Caym shrugged. He saw his brother moving in the brush and made sure he had his father's attention. Caym looked away, crossing his arms over his chest. His father growled and stalked up to him. The sinister, yet seemingly innocent movement sent a chill up his spine.

Better one than both.

Caym didn't dare glance toward Leo as he ran into the ballroom, out of sight.

His father grabbed his hair and tugged. It hurt, but he wasn't going to do more than grimace as his father pulled him back to the ballroom. "You and your brother. Haven't I taught you never to leave or disobey commands? I told you to stay at the ball until it was done, there were important events to discuss. Your brother and you are supposed to know how to deal with them."

"Even though it was supposed to be for Leo's birthday," Caym muttered under his breath before grimacing once more as his father yanked sharply. He stumbled, but caught himself, half-tempted to reach his arms up to release his father's grip.

It wasn't easy to walk with someone wrenching your hair after all.

His father dragged him inside and past the pile of presents lined up on one wall with a happy birthday sign on top.

To his relief, Leo was nowhere in sight. He just hoped he escaped. "Now. What were you doing?"

Caym peered up at his father who didn't even spare him a glance as they passed out of the room into the inner area of the mansion. "I was outside for fresh air," Caym said bluntly. It was the truth, after all.

His father stopped, let go and, faster than Caym could connect the dots, slammed his loose fist into his face. Caym stumbled back, hand snapping to his cheek before he forcefully pushed it back down.

"Try again. What were you doing?"

Caym glared and went to respond, only to stop at the sound of footsteps. Caym and his father looked over to see Machael and Leo. Leo was cleaned up with Machael right next to him, hand gently sitting on his back. "Good sirs. It seems that my lord was a little tired and fell asleep when he went to the toilet. It was not intentional."

Leo flushed and looked away, whether in embarrassment for lying, or just how ridiculous the lie was, Caym couldn't tell. Caym kept a straight face even as he just mentally shook his head. Still, it was safer then saying they were playing hide and seek outside.

His father looked at Leo, whose flushed face paled.

"Father, it is late, is it not best that we all just go to bed?" Caym interrupted as he saw his father's narrowed eyes and the twitching hand.

His father stared before he turned. "I will speak with you both tomorrow about your actions."

With that, he walked off toward the opposite end of the room. Servants were already busily cleaning up the mess left behind. Once he was out of sight, Caym turned around in time to see Leo slam into him. Caym stumbled back as Leo let go and looked at his cheek.

"He hurt you." It was blunt and to the point, but Caym could hear the hurt and worry in his brother's voice. It made the stinging of his cheek noticeable and he winced, once more placing his hand up to his cheek. "Why do you always do this?"

Caym looked away, unable to respond and Leo sighed.

"Sirs, it's best that we head to bed."

Caym looked over to Machael and nodded gratefully. He was glad the butler was able to stay in the family. He was loyal to Leo and that was enough. Caym dropped his hand before looking at Leo.

Leo gazed back at him, his eyes searching before he looked away.

Caym noticed his hands stuffed deep into his pockets and gently asked, "Did you open it?"

Leo shook his head.

All three stayed silent as they walked through the moonlit hallways, the sound of servants hurrying about faded into the distance until it was just the three of them.

"Open it," Caym stated matter-of-factly.

Leo peered at him sidelong before he nodded. He dug into his pocket and slowly pulled the item out. It was carelessly wrapped and small, but it was something.

Leo opened it and his eyes widened. Suddenly, he started trembling, his footsteps faltering to a stop. Caym turned to him, then stepped in front of him, leaning down just enough so they were eye level. Leo quickly looked away, holding the item close to his chest.

"Sorry it took a while, but happy birthday, Little Leo."

A small, handmade pendant sat in Leo's hand. It was nothing like the extravagant gifts supposedly for his brother in the other room, but it was designed beautifully and held its own unique charm.

Written in an elegant cursive was the word "freedom."

"I found a way out of here, out of this whole place. Let's get out of here, all right?"

Leo nodded, holding the pendant close to his chest, as the quiet whisper of thank you slipped from his lips. Caym nodded, grinning widely.

They would get out of this hellhole. If not him, then at least Leo.

Unfortunately, Caym hadn't been able to show his brother the way out the next day, nor the day after that. It was a year and a half later before he got the chance.

Caym was pulled out of his thoughts as he heard running footsteps and turned as the door was flung open. A servant stood in the doorway, panting heavily and face pale. "S-Sir."

"What is it?" Caym asked, he didn't want his father's fury on one of the unfortunate workers. Even if he would rather it be diverted to someone beside himself for once.

"Sir Leonard. His room is empty. He's gone."

Maybe he shouldn't have. He felt his father's anger double and winced as his father turned toward the worker, eyes narrowed dangerously.

"Look for him. That brat has some explaining to do."

The servant nodded quickly and raced out the door.

Father turned to the monitors and flicked it off the freeze frames, switching to recording. Leo was nowhere in sight.

Caym pulled his hand away from his throbbing cheek as his father turned and headed toward the doorway. "Don't just stand there like a dolt. I won't have this family looked down on anymore, by either you or your brother's actions. Get that boy back and capture those two." He stepped out of the doorway and closed the door with a sharp click behind him.

Caym stood in silence, feeling his body shake in anger and frustration. His father, his damn father, no matter what he did, his father… He closed his eyes and slowly breathed in and out, loosening his fists and letting his body relax. He knew getting angry now wouldn't do anything. That was proven long ago. After a moment, he opened his eyes and stared at the screen, thoughts running through his head. His mind, once more in the present, focused on this issue at hand.

He was sick and tired of it.

Ever since his brother's escape, he'd dealt with it, before that, he thought he could handle it, that he could protect his brother. Maybe he was a fool for thinking such things.

He turned to the doorway and whispered, a quiet rage entering his voice unbidden, "It's time this ended, dear Father."

Chapter Three

Maxwell looked at his phone and then sidelong toward the road. He could see policeman moving about, stepping onto the platform and asking questions. They couldn't stay. He turned to his sibling who looked just as worried and upset as he felt. "Let's go."

She nodded. Maxwell closed his phone and stood, hefting his and Lex's backpacks onto his shoulder. He stepped toward the train, watching as the police guarded the entrance of the station. They stared out into the street as if looking for something. Whether it was them or not, he honestly couldn't tell, and he didn't want to know. One looked to be walking in their direction, so with purposeful steps, they moved onto the train. Maxwell handed his ticket over, getting an approving nod from the attendant. He hurried into the caboose of the train, closely followed by Karina, who was gazing over her shoulder with a mix of worry, anxiety and sadness. He could understand why. The train was about to depart, and Lex was nowhere in sight. He turned away from the doorway and moved into the main part of the train. It was a long metal contraption with seats on either side with rectangular windows beside the seats. There was a door up front, connecting to the next car of the train, but that was it. Passengers were already in their seats, talking, on their computers, or napping. All of them had on masks.

Maxwell peered at Karina who took a seat in the back, seated next to the window. The seat across from them was placed backward so as to face them. That was the way it was for all of the seats. Maxwell took a seat next to Karina as the whistle blew through the train. He heard hail slamming against the windows and peered past his sister to see the icy

Julie Boglisch

particles smash against the glass. He felt a jerk and then heard the churning of a motor. He watched sadly as the platform moved away. He continued to stare as the trees started to blur. They shot forward. Karina sat next to him, her expression strained as she stared out the window as well.

"He didn't make it."

Neither of them had to say anything else. Lex promised he would meet with them in three days. This was the third day and he was nowhere in sight. Maxwell leaned back and stared at the curved ceiling as they raced smoothly over the tracks. He didn't want to think about it. They were on their way to get their mother. He should be happy, but honestly, he wasn't. He knew his sister wasn't either.

Lex was important to them, even more so now. He listened to the drumming of the hail as he closed his eyes and slowly was lulled to sleep.

He awoke a while later, blearily blinking his eyes open to see Karina slumped against his shoulder, fast asleep. He peered out the window to see the train was still moving along, a little slower paced than before, perhaps because of the hail. It seemed pretty bad outside. He was just glad that they managed to get on this train. The next one wasn't till eight-thirty. He wouldn't have wanted to wait outside for that extra time. He peered out the window and then blinked as the train started to slow. He could see a city past the gray skies and rainy hail. The city blended in with the cloudy sky with its gray spires, and so he wasn't surprised he didn't notice them right away. He watched as the train pulled closer before gently waking Karina.

His sibling blearily opened her eyes before rubbing one eye and sitting up. "Are we there?"

Maxwell nodded. Karina sighed. They looked out the window as the train slowly came to a halt. They waited for the go ahead, then got off with everyone else. "When is the next train?"

Maxwell pulled the second ticket from his pocket to look at it and then at the clock on the wall. He almost dropped his ticket. "It's in two minutes!"

Karina almost dropped her own things as she whipped around to

Maxwell. "You're kidding? There should be more time."

"The train probably got slowed down by the hail, come on, let's go." They dashed around the people, Maxwell hurriedly looking around for a sign to their platform. There were shouts of annoyance, but he ignored them as they dashed down the hallways. The station was bigger than Liberty, much to his chagrin. He finally spotted a map and cursed. The train would be on the opposite end of the station. The two raced down the staircase and up another before turning a corner and coming to a halt. The track was empty.

"This is the right one, right?"

Karina nodded as they stepped onto the platform, but there was no one there. Their panting echoed in the chamber-like area as they tried to catch their breath. "Maybe we're early?"

Maxwell sent his sister a deadpan look. She sighed and shrugged. "I'm just guessing." She looked around, then seemed to spot something. She stepped forward. Maxwell followed and tilted his head back, seeing the time sheet.

The two just stared and Maxwell couldn't quite wrap his head around what it said. Finally, he understood, and he felt annoyed beyond belief. "It already left, and there isn't another one until this time tomorrow."

Karina cursed loudly as Maxwell sighed. Guess they were staying in this city until tomorrow. "Well, let's change our tickets for tomorrow. We should be able to exchange them if we explain the situation."

Karina frowned, but nodded. They stepped away from the platform and back into the tunnel-like hallway. They moved down the walkway over the ceramic floor and beneath annoying bright fluorescent lights. He let Karina lead. They finally arrived at a large atrium-like room. People were moving in and out past turnstiles and talking on phones or to ticket agents. The two looked around before spotting an open desk. They hurried forward to find a bored-looking woman sitting behind the glass. She perked up at their footsteps before letting out a sigh and slumping back down.

"What do you want? Where are your parents? Are you lost?"

Maxwell glanced at his sister before looking back at the woman. The woman's eyes narrowed.

Maxwell frowned as Karina's eye twitched, obviously annoyed at what the lady thought they were. Maxwell couldn't argue. They were young, but that didn't mean they were naïve or stupid. He smiled. "They sent us ahead. Actually, we were trying to get to Collern City. However, our train was delayed and got in too late to catch the next train. Can you exchange our tickets for the one that comes in tomorrow?"

The woman peered through the glass, looking at them critically before reaching a hand down. "Is that so? Do you have some way to contact them so that I can verify?"

Shit, Maxwell thought before he shook his head. "Sorry, they don't have a phone on them."

The lady stared at them for a moment before she said, "Tickets?"

Maxwell pulled his ticket out and handed it over through the little space. He felt a blast of air, a disinfectant? She picked it up and examined it for a moment before she nodded. "You're right, this left a few minutes ago, and which station did you say you came from?"

"We didn't, but it was Liberty Station."

The lady nodded and typed into a computer set next to her. How Maxwell missed that, he wasn't sure. "Ah, yes, it came in around the same time as the one to Collern left. Not much we can do about that, hand me both your tickets and I'll update them."

Maxwell looked at Karina who continued to glare at the lady, but tentatively pulled her own ticket out and handed it over. The lady took the ticket, looked it over and then turned to them. "Now get outta here, I can't have little child thieves stealing any more tickets. I won't be the one breaking protocol by letting you through, even if everyone else is lax about that law."

"WHAT?" Karina shouted as Maxwell blinked.

The lady frowned in annoyance as she tapped the tickets on the counter. "You're too young to be traveling by yourselves, especially during this time, what with everything going on, and these tickets are expensive. You can't give me proof of the contrary. I can't do anything if I can't contact anyone. Also, there's no way two kids could buy these tickets. Now I'll be lenient and let it go but get out of here before I call security."

Maxwell frowned before he sighed and turned to Karina. "Come on, let's hope we see Lex. He'll have to stop here anyway."

"How are we supposed to do that?"

"Excuse me?" Maxwell called, once more getting the annoyed lady's attention. They obviously picked the wrong person to talk to. "Can you tell us where the bathroom is?" The lady sighed and pointed. Maxwell smiled. "Thank you."

He turned, grabbed his sister's wrist and pulled her along for once. She followed as they headed toward the bathrooms. Maxwell looked around, back to the lady, who was watching them carefully, then looked at his sister. "Go inside and then come out with someone else, go back to the station we arrived on, we'll mingle with the crowd. If we leave, we won't be able to get back in." Karina nodded, then walked into the girl's room. Maxwell walked into the boys. He washed his face and stared into the mirror for a moment. He looked worse for wear. He fingered a lock of hair, criticizing it as it fell into his face past his eyes. He frowned before he dropped his hand and eyed the people leaving. After some hesitation, he joined a father and son duo. He smiled and joined in their conversation about the weather. He eyed the desk and stepped out. She was watching, but he was on the other side of the father. He walked a few feet, said goodbye and hurried around the corner, sighing in relief before he stared up at the sign pointing toward the different platforms. He walked down the hallway and arrived back in the one from before. People milled about, chattering into cell phones and hurrying past the gates. He looked around then took a seat. He stared up at the ceiling and waited.

~ * ~

Karina cursed vehemently as she slipped onto the platform, out of sight. *Stupid lady, stupid age, stupid trains and their stupid schedules,* she thought before letting out a sigh. She looked around the busy platform before spotting her twin. She hurried over and took a seat next to him. He tilted his head down to look at her and smiled.

She chuckled. "That was pretty smart. Luckily, the lady wasn't that attentive."

Maxwell nodded and looked toward the platform. "We just have to hope Lex takes the next train that was supposed to come. He can get us out of this mess."

"Ah…" Karina trailed off as she peered toward the tracks as another train pulled in. Pedestrians moved on and off as tickets were collected. Suitcases sounded over the ceramic as chatter filled the air along with occasional music. She was hungry, but there wasn't much they could do. They used up most of their money getting the tickets to Collern City, which meant they had enough money for food and maybe cheap shelter, but not nearly enough to buy another set of tickets. They just needed to hope that Lex would have the money. She looked down at her hands and clenched them into fists. Honestly, she shouldn't be surprised at the woman's reaction, even if it was a bit extreme. While they were teens, as Maxwell would say, they were still a bit too young to be traveling alone, or to have the money to do so. They had no way to prove that their parents said it was okay or any guardian to confirm that this was planned. Her lips narrowed into a thin line in agitation.

"Kari, you need to relax. There is nothing we can do, so just wait."

Karina turned to her brother to see him once again smiling, but this one was soft and comforting. Karina sighed and relaxed her hands before turning back to the railway. She just hoped that Lex got there in time, or else they would get caught in this city with all of two cents on them and the things in their bags, which wasn't much beyond that.

~ * ~

Lex looked around Liberty Station and frowned. They must have already left. He could see policemen moving around, which was probably part of the reason. Hopefully, his father hadn't noticed yet or notified anyone. He stepped up to the ticket booth and looked at the man behind it. "Sir, did you see two kids earlier, a black-haired girl and brown-haired boy about this height?" He raised his hands to a little below his shoulders before he dropped his hands and leaned against the frame. The man nodded.

Lex felt himself smile for a moment before it returned to neutral. "Can I have a ticket to Collern City?"

"It takes two trains, the next one doesn't come in to here until eight-thirty and the one to Collern already left until tomorrow."

"That's fine. I have money to stay in the city. How much?"

After some haggling, Lex managed to get the tickets and, within an hour stepped onto the train. The hail finally dissipated, and the clouds were slowly breaking up, although there wasn't much change. Everything was still dark as night hung over the country. He peered out the window, wondering about the pair. Did they make it on the second train? If not, were they comfortable in the city? The ticket was expensive. Would they have enough left over for lodging? He sighed and shook his head. He shouldn't be thinking about it.

He tugged at his clothes, pulling off his raincoat and slipping it over the seat. His clothes lucked out, only getting semi-soaked from the deluge before it changed to hail. He looked in the bag for the first time since leaving the house, browsing through the items. There was money, enough for all the traveling that would be necessary at least to get the twins' mother out and a little extra. There were his knives. He picked one up, not actually pulling it out of his bag. He felt the weight and smiled. He went to place the knife down, only to freeze. Underneath the knife was a small paper-wrapped item. He picked it up, feeling its weight before carefully unfolding it. His eyes roved over the words.

My lord,

One of the maids found it in the garden after you left, it was a little broken, so we cleaned it up and repaired it in case you returned. We figured you would like it as a keepsake. You were quite distraught when you found it lost the last time you returned to us before leaving. Do not worry, everything will be taken care of here.

Have a safe journey, and do not hate your brother too much. He's gone through a lot.

Your servant and friend,

Machael.

Lex stared at the paper before turning his gaze onto the little pendant sitting in his hands. The leather band and the wings were as nice as the day he got it. The cursive underneath was still as solid and real as he remembered. He gently flipped it over and saw the writing on the back. It was a simple two letter signature, his brother's initials. He clenched his fist over it and looked out the window. Once again, he wondered.

What made his brother change?

After some time, he pulled his thoughts back to the present and stared at the pendant, debating. He clenched and unclenched his fist around the cool metal before letting out a long sigh. He slipped the pendant around his neck, pulling it under his clothes so it wouldn't get ruined.

He carefully continued his search through his bag. There was a blanket as well as some bread for traveling. He hadn't asked for that, but he greatly appreciated it.

He closed the bag once more, then looked out the window, watching as the stars started to appear through the clouds.

It was an hour later when the train finally arrived. He stood and slipped off onto a busy platform. He looked around, then headed toward the exit, only to stop short. He turned to see Karina and Maxwell seated on one of the small benches near the edge of the station, leaning against each other with backpacks in their laps and one set between them. It almost looked like they were sleeping on the other's shoulders. He shook his head and walked over. "Idiots."

Maxwell blinked his eyes open and looked up before a wide grin appeared on his face. "Lex."

That seemed to startle Karina out of her daze. She sat up and looked at Lex before rolling her eyes, an amused smile on her face. "You made it."

"What are you doing here? How you could fall asleep in a place like this is beyond me."

The two looked at each other before Maxwell gave him a sheepish look. Karina just looked away, a tint of embarrassment showing on her face. "We weren't really asleep…" Karina trailed off, probably noticing his unamused expression. If they weren't asleep, they were out of it enough to practically be anyway.

Maxwell sighed. "Well, we didn't really sleep much when we were at Liberty Station since we were staying in random places around the town there, like the church. Sleeping on wooden pews is not comfortable."

Lex sighed, then gestured. "Come on. Let's get a room for tonight, then catch the train tomorrow. It's late enough already."

Once more, the two looked at each other. This time, anger flashed across Karina's face, along with frustration, Maxwell just looked annoyed.

"What happened?"

"That woman took our tickets. Said we stole them because people our age couldn't possibly pay for those tickets and that we should be glad she didn't report us."

Lex sighed. He should have expected something like that. He had hoped that no one would say anything, but the twins' luck just seemed to like to prove him wrong, since they found the one person who would actually enforce that rule. Go figure. "I'll take care of it. Just tell me which teller and we'll get this cleared up." The two sighed in relief and stood.

Maxwell handed him a backpack. "Here, this is yours." Lex took it and flipped it onto his shoulder.

"I'll take a look at it later, now lead the way."

He followed them as they walked down the hallways. They arrived into the entranceway. Glass windows decorated the walls and the glass doors opened to a city street, but his main focus along with the twins, was on the row of booths set off to one side before the turnstiles.

He followed the two as they walked up to a woman, who seemed aghast and annoyed.

"I should call security."

"That won't be necessary," Lex interjected with a smile.

The woman paused to look at him in surprise before looking at the twins.

"I'm their guardian on the trip. However, my train got a little waylaid. I heard you took their tickets when they asked you for an exchange?" He left the sentence hanging as the person paled slightly before nodding. "If you wouldn't mind, I'll pay for any extra fees necessary to change the tickets accordingly."

"No, no, don't worry about it." The woman waved it off before printing out two tickets and handing them over sheepishly. "Sorry, protocol."

"It's fine. Thank you for your hospitality." Lex turned and walked toward the turnstiles.

They passed through and out the door before he turned to the two and handed them their tickets. Maxwell took his while Karina grabbed her own and looked at it before stuffing it in her pocket.

"Thanks," Maxwell stated before he put his own into a pocket.

Lex nodded, then turned, looking around.

Now where could they rest for the night? How expensive would the hotels be around here? He stepped onto the pavement and walked down the sidewalk, followed by the duo. After a few moments, he found a decent-looking hotel and stepped inside. It took no time at all to get a room, though he cringed at having to pay for two nights, considering check-out would be way before noon and he knew none of them would be up for that time.

They took the elevator, the twins leaning against each other with the energy of a sloth. He bet their sleep was probably pretty sporadic at best over the past few days, so he didn't mind. He watched the numbers click upward before stepping out and walking down the hallway. He opened the door and led them inside before handing the key to Maxwell who took it and slumped over to the bed. It only held two beds, but that was fine. They both took a bed, flopping down unceremoniously. Well, he corrected himself, Karina did.

Maxwell sat down, blinked, then seemed to notice Lex still in the doorway. "Where are you sleeping?" he asked.

Lex smiled and held up another key card. "I got a separate room. Now get some sleep, I'll see you tomorrow."

Maxwell nodded before pulling his shoes off. He seemed to notice his sister and groaned before pulling hers off too before finally settling into bed.

Lex shook his head and closed the door before going to his room across the hall. It was much the same as the twins with a single bathroom and shower, a dresser, two beds and windows on one side. He closed the door, showered and sat on the bed, staring out the window to the streets below.

He forgot that they were still only fourteen. It reminded him a bit too much of his own life. To be so young and yet to be chased by someone like his father, or more likely the entire government, was not easy. He looked back toward the doorway before his attention drifted down to his hands. He was positive now. The only way he could have been cured was during the blood transfusion; it was the only time something happened that was different. If they were the cure to this country's sickness, then they carried quite the heavy burden, didn't they? Life and death. Which would they decide?

He shook his head and lay down. Now wasn't the time to think about it. Now it was time to sleep. He closed his eyes and snuggled into the stark sheets. For once, he fell into a deep and desperately needed sleep.

Chapter Four

Maxwell blearily blinked his eyes open and looked around. The room was spartan with wide beds, a window and a dresser which sat between his and Karina's beds. He looked over to see Karina slowly waking herself. Light gleamed high in the sky, falling into his eyes. He covered them and slowly sat up. His clothes clung to his skin and he wouldn't be surprised if he needed a shower, a bath, or both. He shook his head and realized with distaste, as his hair fell into his eyes, that he needed a haircut too.

"Maxwell, what are you doing?" Karina's voice jerked him out of his observation. Karina stared at him, one hand waving in his face. "Oh, you finally see me. You were completely zoned out. You okay?"

"Yeah, fine, just thinking," Maxwell said as he swung his legs over the side of the messed-up bed.

Karina nodded before she stretched to the ceiling and sighed. "Well then, I'm going to take a shower."

Maxwell stood and headed toward the doorway as Karina walked into the bathroom. "I'll go see if Lex is up and where we can get some food."

"All right. See ya, little bro."

Maxwell huffed before he stepped outside and closed the door, key safely in his pocket. Now that he thought about it, which room was Lex's? He reached into his pocket and pulled out his phone. He needed to recharge it soon. He noted forlornly that it was afternoon. Man, he must have been tired. He slipped it back into his pocket before looking up and down the hallway. He padded down the rugged path, enjoying the carpet against his socked feet. A sound made him stop. He turned back to see the door across from their room open. Lex stepped out, cleanly shaven, wearing a jacket with a gray shirt and black pants, tucked into much cleaner and newer boots.

Lex noticed him watching and turned. "You're up."

Maxwell walked back over. "I wasn't sure which room you had."

"You were just going to walk around for a while?"

Maxwell nodded. Lex shook his head and walked forward. "Karina?"

"Shower."

Lex didn't seem particularly surprised. "Well, we have a couple hours until the train leaves. There's no point in rushing anything. I was going to grab lunch and clean up myself."

Maxwell went to respond when his stomach growled loudly. He felt a blush move onto his cheeks as he mumbled a quiet, "Lunch sounds good."

Lex chuckled. "All right, let's get some food. We can bring some back for your sister as well, unless you want to wait for her?"

"Nah, she'll probably be in there for a while."

Lex just shook his head in amusement. "Well then, get some shoes on. I'll wait here."

Maxwell looked down at his feet before hurrying back to the room. He threw on his shoes and then stepped toward the doorway. He paused, then turned toward the bathroom. "Kari?"

"What?"

"We're going out to grab some lunch. Anything in particular you want?"

"As long as it's not that fast food junk, then I don't care."

Maxwell scoffed. "Yeah, yeah, I'll see you later." He waited for a response, not getting one except for the sound of the shower turning on and a soft humming. He turned and walked out the door, closing it behind him.

He met up with Lex and the two walked down the hallway to the elevator. The journey was quiet as they moved out of the lobby and onto the busy streets of the city. Maxwell shivered in the cold air as he peered around at the metal skyscrapers piercing the sky and the packed sidewalks filled with masked pedestrians. The place reminded him of Reinmark. Maybe it was a city where the epidemic was still somewhat under control? How? Utilizing their father's blood? That obviously wasn't enough if they were now after Karina and him.

He shook himself from his thoughts as Lex led him toward a restaurant not far from there. They stepped inside and he mentally sighed in relief as warmth washed over him. They took a seat. Maxwell looked around, noting that the restaurant was one of the slightly more expensive ones, an actual sit down and order restaurant instead of a fast food or pizzeria joint. "Can we pay for this?" he muttered softly before peering toward Lex.

Lex nodded. "You need a decent meal. When we get to Collern, we won't have the luxury to do things like this."

Maxwell nodded and looked at the menu. He decided on something simple, not sure what else to do. He also perused the menu for his sister, then had to hold back a laugh. "That's definitely something she would enjoy." He chuckled as he read the name of the dish: Ultra-Spice Skewers with Jalapeno. His sister would love that.

They ordered before Lex leaned back, peering at Maxwell curiously. "Now, would you mind telling me what happened after we went separate ways?" Lex narrowed his eyes as Maxwell hesitated.

He took a breath and started. "Well, it began with…"

~ * ~

Karina pulled herself out of the shower and changed into her clothes, frowning slightly at the smell before she sighed. Not much she could do about that at the moment. She looked at the clock on the wall as sunlight streamed through the faded red-dyed curtains. It was around two in the afternoon. She hadn't really checked the clock, so she had no idea when she woke, but it was nice to know they only had to wait four hours. She would only be bored by that time, not bouncing off the wall bored.

She dried her hair, humming quietly as she looked around the room. Their bags were slumped on the floor, side by side. They were ragged and worn from use. Maxwell's looked worse for wear: dirt and other stains marred the black lapels, causing some of the lettering on the bottom to be lost. She wasn't surprised though. The backpack wasn't exactly made for travel, especially not for this long. She peered out the window, staring down at the people walking through the streets as her thoughts wandered.

Admittedly, it was kind of nice just being by herself, for at least a moment. She loved her brother dearly but being around him so much lately was making even her feel a little annoyed. She was glad her sibling decided to go out with Lex for a short time. He would be safe with Lex at least. Karina fell onto her back and stared at the ceiling as she placed her hands behind her head, thoughts churning. She needed time to think, something she had been ignoring while showering and even before that. She only thought of their travel and safety, pushing the letters to the back of her mind. However, she couldn't ignore them forever. She sat up and reached into her bag. She pulled out the letters and shuffled back so that she was pressed against the headboard. The wood creaked as she leaned against it. She opened the letters, looking at the curling script once more. After a moment, she pulled them close to her chest and just sat there. Her eyes stung, but she didn't cry.

It was too much, too much to handle, to think about. They rarely talked about it. Not since Maxwell managed to convince her where to go. She never saw how much he changed until that moment. When his eyes sparkled with hope and his voice conveyed a confidence she didn't even feel. Her little brother had changed so much. She bent her head down and closed her eyes and let out a breath. What about her? She wanted to protect her sibling, but she was in just as much danger as him. They were a thing of life and death. Lex was proof enough of that. Not only that, but what about other people? Would they have the time to make the cure and save them? Would they be too late? What about Mom? Would they be able to save her? Get her away from the very people after them? Wasn't that just suicide, running right into the arms of the people who wished to take them? She didn't want to imagine what would happen if she and her brother were captured.

Suddenly, she wanted to see her brother again. Maybe she wasn't so fond of the idea of having alone time.

As if on cue, the door swung open revealing Maxwell standing in the doorway. He took one look at Karina, then stepped inside. He closed the door, walked over to the bed and sat down right next to her, head on her shoulder and bag on his lap. He pushed the bag over to her and closed his eyes.

Karina felt a smile cross her face as she took the bag. She opened it and looked inside and chuckled before circling her arm around her brother's shoulder and squeezing. She didn't have to say anything; he seemed to understand.

Maxwell opened his eyes and grinned before pushing himself off the bed and stepping toward the other, plopping down on it and staring outside. Karina picked up the plastic fork and chowed down on the spicy jalapeno chicken skewers, drizzling a little hot sauce on occasionally. She didn't realize how hungry she was until she devoured the whole plate.

She shook her head and placed the food next to her. She stood up and joined her brother in looking out to the street. They stayed silent for a moment before Maxwell spoke. "I told Lex about the letters..."

Karina looked over as Maxwell continued to stare outside, expression solemn. He tilted his head toward her before looking back outside.

"I see," Karina replied softly as she looked down. She let out a long breath before she felt herself smile. "Well, that's good. We need someone else on our side, after all."

Maxwell turned back toward her once more. This time confusion flickered onto his face as he waited for her to continue. Karina smiled. "We can't really do this ourselves. Just look at what happened with the stupid ticket lady, even if she was an exception."

Maxwell rolled his eyes.

"Still, I guess I trust Lex. He's helped us this far and I have a feeling he will do whatever he can to help us get to Mom, and we'll need that."

Maxwell chuckled, this time causing Karina to be confused. He seemed to notice her confusion. He leaned back, hands placed on the bed to hold him up as his feet kicked out playfully. "It's nice to know you finally trust him. I told you while we were in the house and a couple other times."

"Well, I don't know, maybe you're just very trusting," Karina snapped back, pushing her finger into his face.

Maxwell rolled his eyes and pushed the finger away. "Uh huh, sure. Believe whatever you want. Now I'm taking a shower."

"I was wondering where that smell was coming from. Then again, I thought boys don't like showers."

"That's a joke, right? Not funny." Maxwell frowned.

He stepped into the bathroom and within seconds, Karina heard the shower turn on. Karina chuckled.

She turned back to the letters, sitting nestled on the pillow next to where she was sitting earlier. She walked over and picked them up. She folded them carefully, then found a still usable plastic bag. She slipped the letters inside before she put the whole thing back in her bag, pushing them deep so as to protect them. She zipped up her bag and sat back down, bag in her lap and head against the backrest once more. She just waited quietly as Maxwell finished his shower.

A while later, the shower turned off, and only a few minutes later, Maxwell walked out, hair still dripping. "We really need more clothes."

Karina was definitely not going to argue with that assessment. She nodded and stood, tossing Maxwell's bag to him. He stumbled for a moment before catching it. He sent over a glare as Karina grinned.

Maxwell sighed, shook his head and slipped the bag over his shoulder. "Now come on. Lex wants to talk to us, then we should start heading toward the station. Even though we just had lunch, we should probably grab something small for dinner before we get onto the train."

Karina nodded. Maxwell turned and opened the door. Karina hurried after him. She watched as he stepped into the hallway and knocked on the door across from them. After a moment, the door opened to show Lex, freshly cleaned as well. He let them in and they all took a seat.

Karina sat next to Maxwell as he leaned against the headrest of the bed. Lex sat opposite them, legs crossed as he leaned forward, chin in hand and elbow on his knee. "Can I see the letters?"

Karina hesitated for a moment before she dug into her backpack and pulled out the letters. He perused them. One was from their mother, the other their father. He only glanced at their mother's before focusing on their father's. He muttered a few sentences aloud as he went.

"My dear Veronica, I'm sorry, but this will be my last letter to you. The epidemic is spreading fast, they're getting desperate. I've seen more officials lately. There's talk that they might try our children soon. But, if this is the last time I can send a letter, I had to warn you and the children. No matter what, don't let them get them. I don't want our children to get mixed up in this. This country's government is ruined, but I can't stop it, so please, just protect them. Karina, Maxwell, I just want to tell you... it's actually pretty hard, but you've probably realized by now. You may or may not know that an epidemic is destroying the very heart of this nation. People die and suffer almost every day and it's only getting worse. I had immunity, but it wasn't a full one. You two have the full immunity. In your blood, you hold the cure that can save this nation's people. It's up to you what you decide to do with it.

"This is the hardest thing I'm going to have to ask for, but please help this country. Their goal, if they obtain you two, is a complete and utter genocide. Anyone that doesn't fit the bill, those too weak, old, frail or sick will perish without a second thought. I wish I was lying, that this wasn't the truth, but it is. I've managed to get this letter to you safely, so that they don't know what I wrote, or that I wrote it, but this will be the last time. I pray that, for the sake of the country, you two stay safe. You are our hope. Don't forget, even if you don't believe everything I've written here. Please believe that your mother and I truly do love you and wish that this never had to happen..." he trailed off and sighed before he handed the letter back.

Karina took it carefully, peering down at the letter for a moment before cautiously putting it back in her backpack once more.

"Admittedly, I already guessed most of that." Lex let out a long, drawn out breath before looking straight at them. "Part of the reason I stayed back was to verify something."

"You never did tell us why," Karina said as she leaned back onto her hands, Maxwell nodded.

"I didn't feel like it would be necessary, however since it does pertain to you two, I might as well let you know. I actually stayed to meet with my father. You might know him."

Karina narrowed her eyes before shooting a look to Maxwell, who just shook his head before turning back to Lex. "How is that possible?"

"It's more than possible, especially if it has to do with what happened to your father four years ago."

Karina stiffened and leaned forward, Maxwell reacting practically the same way. "What do you mean?" Karina asked. Her tone harsher than she intended.

Lex didn't seem to mind. "My father works for the government as a head of Enthrope. You should know of it."

Karina nodded, feeling disbelief well up.

Maxwell's expression was contorted into one of dismay.

"He was higher up than your mother, one of the heads. He's also the one whom I suspect came to your home four years ago and took your father from you."

Karina felt her mind slow to a halt before it suddenly snapped to attention as she tried to remember, the details from four years ago. The man had been big, black hair, bearded. Now that she was actually trying to think about it, he had the same eyes as Caym and features of Lex. She stared at Lex, frozen, as Maxwell slumped next to her, disbelief obvious on his face. "You mean—"

"We were that close to our father's kidnapper?"

Lex's expression said it all. He winced and looked out the window past their shoulders. Karina leaned forward, placing her hands in her lap as she traced the pattern of the faded rug decorating the hotel room. Her thoughts were whirling.

Lex was the son of their father's kidnapper? The one who started all of this? She looked up to her brother who was staring at Lex with an odd expression. She turned to look at Lex, noting his stiff, uncomfortable posture. She'd never seen the older boy so nervous. His hands twitched in his lap as he waited for the two of them to respond.

She let out a long sigh. How could she do this? She'd finally come to trust Lex and her brother trusted him from basically the beginning. Even though he was the son of the one who started this he was still their friend.

"I had to get you two out of there. There was no way you could have met my father. He probably would have realized as soon as he saw you. There were no other options," Lex stated as he leaned back, appearing relieved.

Karina and Maxwell leaned forward, listening. She would trust him. This would be the last time she would doubt Lex, considering just how much he'd sacrificed for them. "Now, I think our best option is just to keep heading to Collern City, but first, we should get you two new clothes. We still have two hours before we leave."

Karina nodded. Maxwell let out a breath before shaking his head. "Any other surprises? We seem to get a lot of those, don't we?"

Karina could only agree.

Lex watched the twins cautiously as they walked down the street. They were both wearing a new set of clothes, their originals stuffed haphazardly into their bags. Maxwell seemed to have decided to keep his black zip hoodie, a new pair of sweatpants and a heavier coat. Karina also grabbed a heavier coat, a t-shirt, and sweatpants. Rather simple and good choices, in Lex's opinion.

He turned back, only to stop, grabbing the twins' arms and pulling them behind him. Near the train station were a group of Enthrope employees, dressed in black and examining each person coming and going from the train. He frowned. That limited their options. "Well, we can't leave by train."

"Great, so now what do we do?" Karina's sharp voice cut through his thoughts and he sent the girl a look before letting them go and stepping back.

"Honestly, I think it might be best just to lie low. We could try to move onto the next city. But the easiest and quickest way is by train."

"So, are you saying we should stay here until they leave?" Maxwell leaned forward, and Lex nodded.

Annoyance and uncertainty shone on the twins' faces. Lex felt the need to groan. "In all honesty, I would rather stay here for another reason. If we go right to Collern City it would be the same as leaving a trail of breadcrumbs for not only my brother, but also my father. I know you two don't like that idea, but our best bet is to stay here, wait it out and not rush ahead."

Maxwell and Karina exchanged looks before reluctantly nodding. "How long?" Maxwell asked, voice uncertain.

Lex looked them over, hesitant. "About a month or so."

"What?" Karina shouted before pulling back.

Lex looked over his shoulder before having them follow him, continuing down the street, away from the train station. "I'm going to go online and change our tickets. Don't worry. I have enough money to keep us fine for the month. We'll just stay in a local hostel. It'll be expensive, but I'll see if there is a room for us to share alone."

"All right."

It didn't take much to read the kids' mood in order to realize Maxwell really wasn't too keen on saying that.

"If you think that would be the better option. Neither of us are in the mood to deal with those guys anyway."

Lex felt a hint of relief, a small smile flickering onto his face. He was worried they would protest more than this, but he was glad they hadn't. Thankfully, he did have a fair bit of money and he knew a nice hostel around here that was fairly cheap and well kept. He led the way to a small building quite a way from the train station. It was what one might qualify as a cute little place. He stepped inside to find a clean entranceway with a young lady sitting at the counter. She looked up and smiled.

It didn't take much to get their rooms and it seemed like the twins were actually a little relieved. After all, they were able to relax a bit. They weren't stressing about being captured or how to find their mother. They were literally in the interlude period.

Lex was just glad to get a rest himself. He knew he needed it.

Chapter Five

"What? How can you not find him? He wasn't gone that long. Get the brat back, now."

Caym watched in silence as his father slammed the phone back down onto its place, the phone getting slightly off balance from the recoil. His father's expression was furious as he pulled his hand away and paced around his office. Caym stood off to one side, a safe distance away.

Caym admittedly found himself slightly amused. His brother wasn't an idiot after all. No matter how much he despised him at times, his little brother could be incredibly resourceful when he needed to be. Case in point: his father couldn't find hide nor hair of him.

His father sent out pictures the day before, but he knew they wouldn't get out until the day after tomorrow at best. By that point, his brother could be anywhere. Travel was exceptional now in days, no matter which way you went. His father finished pacing and turned to him sharply, standing straighter, as if trying to tower over him. Caym wasn't cowed, although he knew that he should be, but he felt more disappointed than anything. He still couldn't hold in the wince as his father stepped forward. A rabid beast is dangerous, just like a wounded one, but it's still a beast and doesn't have the intelligence except to lash out. He'd seen it enough in his childhood. Yet he didn't say anything as his father pursed his lips and turned. "Why are you just standing there? If you don't have something to say, then leave. I have to find your wayward brother and those treasures."

Wayward? Treasures? Interesting choice of words, Caym thought in annoyance. "I know—"

"If you know, then leave."

Dammit, why doesn't he ever let me finish. " I wanted to tell you that. Wouldn't it be more prudent to check out any traveling locations, such as trains? He would want to get as far away as possible…"

"Of course…trains." The father turned and picked up the phone.

Caym narrowed his eyes.

"I knew I would think of it eventually."

Caym resisted the urge to spit in disgust. He turned and left. This wasn't going to work. Obviously, his father was going to take the credit, no matter what he did. So why keep up this charade? He walked into the monitor room and shut the door. The camera lights flickered over his face as he locked the door and stepped up to the computer monitors. His fingers flew over the keys. He let his eyes rove over the pages, looking and searching. After a while, he paused and grinned. He stood, went to the door, and left.

He walked toward the entranceway, pulling out his phone. He dialed a number and waited as it rang, only for it to be picked up a second later. "Bring my car to the front, I'm heading out now."

He didn't wait for a response as he snapped the phone shut. He stuffed it in his pocket as he stepped out the door and stared down the paved road. He took a few steps down and waited a moment. It didn't take long for a car to pull up to the front entrance. He stepped inside.

"I want to check a few places out. Here are the locations." He passed over a map to the driver and then sat back to wait.

The night lights glistened off the fountain and pearly white granite and marble buildings. He heard a creak. *Guess the gates need to be oiled,* he thought and looked forward.

While he managed to narrow it down, he still had quite a few to check. Still, a hands-on approach was always better. This also gave him a chance to breathe and think, away from his father's and mother's overbearing influence. He leaned back and crossed his legs. *Little brother, I will find you and I will bring you home.* He could feel the dark memories try to invade and quickly pushed them away. Now was not the time. Even as a small part of him jumped in joy at his brother's continual escape, the larger part was adamant to get him back.

For what reason, he wasn't entirely certain himself.

Chapter Six

The month passed without much actually happening, to Lex's great relief. The twins were able to rest up and, while he knew they were deeply worried about their mother, they needed some time to just relax and process things. It was also a good time to make sure they got a good set of clothes and haircuts which they badly needed. He tried to keep in contact with Antonio, but the informant didn't have much to add and his brother was surprisingly quiet. By the end of the month, even he was getting a bit antsy to move on and if he was antsy, he could only imagine the twins. Thankfully Maxwell was able to keep Karina entertained. It could have been worse.

Speaking of her, he chuckled, recalling one morning. He never knew Karina was a prankster. Then again, it did fit with her personality. Unfortunately, Maxwell hadn't found it funny when he woke up and went through part of his day without realizing that Karina decided to make him look like her, hair dye, hair clip and all. Lex admitted, he thought Maxwell's reaction was pretty funny when he finally realized why everyone was giving them double-takes. The boy ranted at his sister for a good half hour as he tried to rub the dye off in the sink with Karina chuckling the entire time.

At least Karina hadn't gone so far as to put makeup on him. She wasn't that cruel— Lex hesitated at that thought before grimacing. Actually, it was probably more she didn't have time now that he thought about it. Poor Maxwell. Though, he had to admit, it was interesting to see just how similar the two could look. Actually, for some reason, Maxwell ended up keeping the clip Karina had put in his hair, though whether that was because of Karina's very much stubborn insistence that he keep it, or that he could ignore how girly it looked and see the usefulness of it, Lex wasn't sure.

He pulled from that thought as they stepped into the heated entranceway of the train station. They moved past the turnstiles without a hitch and walked to the platform. It was packed as people waited for the train. He moved to one side, followed by the twins. They were chatting amiably back and forth, dressed in a new set of clothes more fitting for the cold weather. Lex shifted the backpack on his back as he leaned on one foot. He reached a hand up, gripping the pendant hidden under his shirt, thoughts flickering back and forth on his decision to keep it. Still, as he held it, he felt himself relax.

He would find out what happened to his brother. Even if he no longer could stand him, he would try to find out what changed him.

They sat in silence as people talked all around them, moving back and forth over the ceramic flooring as they hurried to and fro. Finally, the train pulled up. Lex stood and stepped on with Karina and Maxwell in tow. They handed over their tickets, then took a seat. Maxwell sat near the window with Karina next to him. Lex sat across from them. He peered out the window as the train filled up. After a few minutes, there was a chime and he felt the train slowly start to move. They were surrounded in darkness for a few minutes before it broke into the moonlit night. *It went dark way too early at this time of year. When was daylight savings time again?*

He was pulled out of his thoughts by a noise across from him. He looked over to see Maxwell and Karina leaning near each other, but he could tell from their expressions they were listening to something. He paid attention and stayed quiet.

"I heard someone managed to obtain guns, something about a revolt, it was squashed almost instantly. The poor—"

"Ssh! Be quiet! You know you're not supposed to sympathize with those rebels, or even speak about it, remember? Now stay quiet."

Lex pulled away from the conversation and sighed. Of course. He heard about the revolts; they were as common as protests, though the government made sure nobody talked about them at all.

He felt a set of eyes on him and looked up to see Maxwell and Karina watching him with similar expressions, a mix of confusion and indignation. "Yes?"

"Lex, I've been wondering this. I never thought about asking, but…" Lex waited as Maxwell seemed to debate on his words before he sighed and continued. "I remember, in history class, that America has the constitution…"

Lex paused, unsure how to explain it. He figured Maxwell would bring it up at some point. He honestly was a bit surprised the more curious twin hadn't asked until now. Then again, now would be one of the best times to ask, considering.

"…that was a self-repairing living word, or something, so why isn't…"

"Ah." Lex leaned back against the seat and peered out the window, noting as the city dwindled into the distance and stars began to glow softly in the sky. "People took for granted what they had, and the policymakers passed laws purposely in a way that the 'stupid 'American public wouldn't understand. By the time anyone realized what happened, it was too late. There's no voting, except in the upper class. No freedom of speech or press. There isn't even the ability to wield guns. We were too late to realize what the policies were that went through to the point where we can no longer revoke them." Lex watched as the twins ' expressions morphed from confusion to horror.

"Wait, nothing? No freedom of speech or…"

Lex shook his head as he peered around him. He noticed a few wary eyes glance their way and wasn't surprised. They were probably worried about being overheard, especially on a train such as this one. Their hands covered their masked mouths as they subtly leaned away, as if to move away from the one who would dare say anything against the government on a government-run train. Maxwell and Karina also seemed to realize. Karina narrowed her eyes as Maxwell's brow furrowed. He turned his gaze on Lex before slumping in his seat and peering outside.

Realizing that the conversation was over, Lex turned to look out the window, eyes following the plains and loops of the hilly area around them. He relaxed into his seat and let his mind wander, wondering just what they were going to do.

~ * ~

The train ride felt long as Maxwell drifted in and out of sleep, constantly jostled whenever the train wheels hit an uneven patch or took a turn. The night dragged on as hills slowly flattened out. Long strands of something blew gently in the breeze as stars sparkled in the sky. The moon shone down softly as the train sped along.

Lex slept quietly across from them, his head leaning against the back of the seat, having been bumped one too many times when next to the window.

Karina sat next to him. Her eyes were closed as her head drooped to one side, hair falling into her face.

All around them were people either trying to sleep or something else. Their expressions were wary as they occasionally glanced in their direction, even though it had easily been over a couple hours ago when they last said anything, at least of significance.

If he recalled, the trip was supposed to take most of the night, if not the whole night and quite a bit into the next day. He sighed and leaned back, closing his eyes. He got comfortable in the seat as the lights remained dim. He could hear the train wheels rattle softly over the rails and the soft snores of those already asleep. Wind whistled past the window as clothing rustled. It was oddly comforting yet worrying. Would something happen? Was his mother okay? Would they be able to save her? Weren't they a bit over their heads? He shook his head and opened his eyes to stare at the metal ceiling. He watched the curve before letting his head fall sideways to stare out the window. The stars sparkled in the sky, shining brightly as they moved over the changing landscape.

"You should get some sleep."

Maxwell turned to Lex to see gray-green eyes staring back at him. The smallest of smiles sat on his face. Maxwell nodded before once more peering outside. He knew he should, but he slept a lot earlier and now, he wasn't tired.

He almost wished he was.

He heard a long breath flutter from his friend and peered sidelong toward Lex as he leaned back in his seat to get more comfortable. "You're not tired, are you?"

Bullseye, Maxwell mentally groused.

Lex chuckled before his expression grew serious. "I'm guessing you have a lot on your mind?"

Maxwell could practically hear the question, but he ignored it. He smiled and shook his head. Lex stared at him before he let out a soft amused huff and nodded. "Well then, why don't you just try to relax? There's nothing else to do at the moment."

Maxwell agreed. The trip was already boring, and they still had a long way to go. He pulled out his phone and stared at the time. It was a little after midnight. He looked toward Lex. Lex waited.

"Can we share phone numbers? In case something like that happens again?" Maxwell asked.

Lex paused, glancing at the phone before he nodded. He pulled out his and they quickly exchanged information.

"That reminds me. Have you gotten any notifications?"

"Notifications?" Maxwell asked as he slipped his phone back into his pocket.

"You haven't gotten a voicemail or anything regarding payment?"

Maxwell glanced at his pocket in thought, then shook his head. "No."

Lex peered out the window, fiddling with his phone for a moment before shaking his head and turning back to Maxwell. "I see. I wouldn't be surprised if it's an electronic deposit…" Lex trailed off, as if in thought.

Maxwell stared at him for a moment before glancing to his sister, who shifted slightly in her seat to slump closer to him.

"Hey, I have another question," Maxwell proposed softly, finding himself hesitant. Lex looked up from his musings as Maxwell peered back at him. "You're cured, aren't you?"

A neutral look fell onto Lex's face, as if he was lost in thought. He leaned back in his seat, phone idly in his lap as he stared out the window. A small smile formed on his lips. "Who knows? Anyway, get to sleep," Lex reminded, finally putting his phone back into his pocket.

Maxwell grudgingly decided to take Lex's advice even as a small feeling of relief made him want to smile. He snuggled down in his seat and tried to get comfortable. Even then, his thoughts kept racing, there was so much to think about and Lex seemed to add more to it each time.

~ * ~

He wasn't sure when he fell asleep, but he awoke to light shining brightly on his face and a heavy weight on his shoulder. His eyelids flickered, heavy from sleep. After a moment, his eyes adjusted to take in the warm glow of the sun, shining softly through the windows. It hung low in the sky, gleaming over grains of wheat and barley, their golden hues almost red in the spilling light, spinning in the gentle breeze as they moved past. Lex was slowly waking though Karina was still out of it, her head leaning on his shoulder and a bit of drool trailing from the corner of her mouth. He grimaced in slight disgust as he gently pushed her back against the seat. She shifted, before getting comfortable again.

Maxwell shook his head before he looked out toward the fields. He hadn't been able to figure out what they were before, with it being so dark, but now he could tell. He could see so far, and it was astounding. He was used to things towering over him, whether it was greenery or steel. To see this wide-open expanse was stunning, especially in the light of the rising sun. Yes, they still passed quite a few trees and homes, but for the majority it was just flat land.

He knew he hadn't slept much, but he was glad he got to see this. He felt a smile cross his face. *Maybe it would be all right.*

~ * ~

Or not. He groaned as they stepped out of the train to be met with snow. Lots and lots of snow. He huddled tightly in his jacket as he watched his breath flutter into the sky, only to be blown away by the wind within a second. Karina huddled next to him, burying her hands in her pockets as Lex moved ahead, cutting through the snow with only a slight shiver as indication of the cold. Pedestrians crowded around them as they hurried off the platform onto the main road. It was bustling with cars, stuck in the blizzard conditions and taxis honking loudly through the gale.

Maxwell peered through the snow, feeling himself slip and slide over the ice as they walked through the new city, Karina didn't seem to have much better luck, but at least she could stay on two feet. Still, this city was very much like the previous cities. Though this one was organized in neat rows with older architecture and brick buildings. As they were walking, he heard the sound of thrumming and looked through a bank of stumpy trees to see a low building, set into the golden gates of the Richie section. He stared, surprised to see as people from this side moved into and out of the building. What was it even used for? Connected to it, he could see another building with a thin, heavily guarded pathway leading to the other building, almost grand and menacing compared to the squat structure on their side.

"That's rare."

Maxwell jumped before turning to Lex who was staring at the building with a slight frown. He must have noticed Maxwell's look. He turned away and continued down the street. Karina grabbed Maxwell's wrist and pulled him along, catching up. "What's wrong? Why are you hurrying?"

"There aren't many buildings that connect to the gated community like that. The only ones I know of are government agencies. Something we don't really want to get close to if we can help it."

Maxwell glanced over his shoulder, letting a frown grace his face as they continued through the streets before reaching a squat building. It looked like it had seen better days, the wood creaking as they pushed at the door and the paint peeling off in thin strands. The entranceway, thankfully, was well lit, though still sad compared to the last hostel Maxwell was in. Drooping trees lay on either side of the doorway as they entered. A table stood off to one side, with a woman sitting behind it, casually reading a magazine. Well, at least that was consistent, but the shabby, slightly unkempt appearance of the place was a bit of a shock after having stayed in the first brightly lit and homely hostel.

The woman at the counter looked up as they entered. Maxwell winced at her piercing gaze and found himself slipping behind Lex with his sister as their friend moved forward to speak. "We would like rooms for one week, please."

The woman looked at him and nodded before reaching under her desk. She pulled out three keys and handed them over. "Your rooms are on the second floor at the end of the hall. Make sure not to go into the wrong hallway, all the information and rules are written on this pamphlet." She slapped three onto the desk, they weren't that thick, but Maxwell could almost hear his sister's groan. "Girls are on the left, boys on the right."

Lex nodded, taking the keys and reaching into his pocket. Maxwell tuned out the rest of the conversation regarding payment and examined the place. The entranceway was small with two staircases on either side of a large door. He could smell the faintest hint of food and so guessed it was the cafeteria, well that was also the same. He glanced at his sister as she looked toward the left staircase. It was kind of worrying, to know she would be in another area all together, but he highly doubted either of them wanted to make a scene right now. He heard clattering and looked over to see Lex had taken the keys and was turning to face them, handing one over to Karina. "Here, go drop your stuff off, then meet us in the cafeteria."

Karina nodded, taking the key and, hefting her bag, headed toward the stairwell.

"Will you be all right?" Maxwell found himself asking as he glanced at his sibling.

"What do you think?" She saluted, giving him a cheeky grin. "See you in a few."

Maxwell frowned, but accepted it as he watched her turn and hurry up the stairwell. He followed Karina's example and hurried up the right-hand stairs with Lex a bit behind. The hallway was narrow, but well-lit with doors on either side and another staircase that wound its way up to the higher floors. He ignored it, heading down the hallway with Lex following. At the end of the hallway, there was only one door set on the right.

"This is it." Lex nodded toward the door, stepping forward and inserting the key. He pushed it open. Maxwell peeked inside as Lex stepped in. The room wasn't anything special, but it was packed with bunkbeds lining both sides of the room. He could see a few boys of differing ages sitting around. Some slept on the bunks, some played cards and a few were just doing nothing. Though, even this display made him miss the other hostel with its mixed rooms, bright lights and, though a bit more expensive, clean sheets and bedding. Eyes glanced their way before returning to what they were doing. Others lingered, and one boy waved, giving a small smile before returning to his game of cards. Maxwell followed after Lex and quickly chose his bed. There weren't many open beds, so he was a bit limited in his choices. Lex didn't seem to care, throwing his bag on the top bunk. Maxwell grabbed the lower bunk on one of the others, finding that the lower bunk of Lex's chosen bed was already occupied. He glanced up to the top bunk, seeing sheets trailing over the edge, but no person, so they must be out. He slipped his backpack off and let out a sigh of relief as the weight left his shoulders. The room was tight with one window at the end and barely any room to walk, but it was warm and, while the sheets weren't the cleanest, it was still a bed. He would take that over a hard floor any day.

Under each of the beds, he could see what looked like a cage with two doors. Some had locks on them. Others were open with stuff inside anyway. He slid off his bed and slipped his bag into one of the cages before closing it and standing up. Lex was already done, stuffing his wallet into his pocket before heading toward the doorway. Maxwell took one last look at the room and scrambled after him.

~ * ~

Karina pushed the door open, feeling a lot more nervous then she let on in front of her brother. She took a deep breath and stepped inside. It was a small room with a thin window near the top of the far wall. It almost looked like a little nook for storage more than a room. Still, it fit three bunkbeds, all of the beds except one taken up by girls. They looked up and one of the girls snorted, looking unimpressed before turning back to painting her nails, or whatever she was doing. Karina huffed and stomped right past her. She threw her bag onto the lone bed and sat down to organize her things. She knew she was supposed to meet her brother and Lex, but she needed to make sure everything was in place. She felt a couple eyes on her and looked up to see the girls glance away.

"Did you want something?" she asked, feeling a hint of annoyance creep into her voice even as she tried to keep her words polite. From a quick glance, all of the girls seemed to be older than her. A strange substance coated their faces, the make-up Mom talked about before; it made them look much older than they probably were. Though she suspected that had something to do with hiding the signs of the epidemic more than anything. She saw the girl who'd given her the unamused look click her tongue before standing and putting her hands on her hips.

"You're new around here. By yourself? That's pretty daring."

Karina gave her a look and shrugged. "My brother is staying here as well. I don't see a problem with it. Now if you'll excuse me, I need to meet up with him." She shifted around the girl and headed for the door.

"Wait."

Karina let out an annoyed sigh and looked over her shoulder. "What?"

The girl's eye twitched. "At least tell us your name. The name's Abby, by the way."

"Karina." Karina waited to see if the girl would say anything else. When she didn't, Karina turned and left. At least, she tried to leave.

A loud thump met her ears and she jumped as one of the girls let out a shriek. She turned around to see that one of the girls had fallen on the floor, legs twitching. Karina found herself frozen as the twitching subsided and the girls let out a breath of relief.

"Gab, you okay?" Abby spoke up with a nervous voice, no longer paying attention to Karina.

The girl on the ground, Gab, nodded hesitantly. "Yeah. Sorry. This stupid disease."

Karina whipped around and hurried out the door. She didn't want to think of what she'd just seen. That was another part of the third stage, wasn't it? She shivered. She probably should have stayed, and made sure everything was all right, but she didn't think it would do anything. She didn't know them, and she would prefer keeping some distance. After all, they were only staying for a week. Part of her wondered how they would get to Mother and get her out so quickly. She pushed the thought away as she stepped into the kitchen. Well, common room was a better term for it in her opinion. The kitchen was set off to one side through a doorway. She could just see Maxwell over there, scrounging for some food. Lex sat on one of the couches, leaning back and relaxing. A couple girls and boys sat around the place, chattering away. Karina glanced into the far corner, seeing movement, and winced. She did not want to see people making out, no thank you. She quickly looked away and stepped up to her brother.

He looked up, curious eyes spotting her before he grinned. "Hey, Kari, how's the room?" he asked as he leaned back, closing the fridge with a pack of yogurt in his hands. To none of Karina's surprise, it was orange-flavored.

"A little tight." Karina shrugged. "But why did you just grab yogurt? I smelled something earlier that seemed pretty good."

Maxwell let out a sigh and shrugged helplessly. "They hadn't actually cooked it here, it was takeout. There really isn't much here for cooking." Maxwell shook his head before stepping over to Lex. He stopped and turned his head to face her. "Oh, that reminds me, Lex wanted to talk with us. Grab something to eat, then come over, okay?"

Karina nodded, reaching for the cupboards. They were fairly barren, but she managed to find some leftover cereal and poured it in a bowl that she quickly cleaned. She passed on the milk and walked over to sit beside her brother, spooning down the dry flakes. It wasn't the best tasting thing, but she preferred that over watery oatmeal, the only other option there." So, what did you want to talk about?"

Lex looked up and adjusted his cap before sitting up. "Couple things, really." Lex waved his hand and Karina glanced around as a boy hurried by and two girls giggled off to their left. "It's a little packed in here as you can tell. So, once we situate ourselves, I want to take a look around town. I'm going to have to find us someplace to stay that's a bit more permanent."

"Huh?" Karina blinked, placing the bowl between her legs. "What do you mean? I know a week is quick, but…"

Maxwell frowned as he glanced at Lex, who winced. Maxwell sighed, as if realizing something and glanced at Karina. "I think what he means is that it won't be that easy to find Ma and get to her. After all, all we know is that she's here, but it's a big city. Look how well we were able to look around the other cities."

"Not at all," Karina muttered, placing her spoon down. "So, the week thing was only to get us situated in the city. How long do you think it might take? In that other place?"

Lex looked a bit surprised before a weak smile crossed his face. "I honestly don't know. It could take anywhere from a month to a couple. I don't think more than a year though. It's too dangerous to stay in one place for that long."

Karina almost dropped her bowl, eyes wide. *Wait, that long? But she'd already been searching for so long.*

Maxwell looked as upset as she felt, his body slumping into the couch. "So…" he trailed off, obviously unsure of what he had been even trying to say.

"I know that will be difficult, but that's all I can say. We can't just charge in, even if we do find her right away, keep that in mind."

"I know that." Karina bit her lip, brow furrowing. "But, it's still hard to think that she's so close and yet…"

Maxwell nodded and let out a long sigh. "So, what are we going to do?"

Lex glanced to him before looking toward the doorway. "I'm going to look for a place to stay. I want you two to start doing research on any suspicious areas within the city. Just be careful, okay? I would advise starting at some local libraries and doing some research on the computers there, then get a layout of the city. Find different routes, different places."

"That shouldn't be too hard." Karina shrugged, pulling herself from her worried thoughts. She needed to stop worrying about how long it would take and just do it.

Her brother rolled his eyes. "Easy for you, I'm lucky I still remember the routes around town in Claremore."

"That's because you were always in your room, reading or whatever." Karina waved it off.

"No, I wasn't. You were out of the town half the time anyway," Maxwell pointed out, annoyance clear on his face.

"Yeah, then why did I always find you in your room every time I got home? I know you have some books stashed away in your closet."

Maxwell blushed and glared. "I thought I told you not to look in there."

Karina playfully stuck out her tongue and Maxwell huffed, crossing his arms over his chest, the last of his yogurt cup dangling in his hand. Lex chuckled and pushed himself to his feet. "It's almost the end of the day. For now, get yourselves cleaned up and ready for bed. Tomorrow, we'll head out and start exploring."

Karina frowned. How late was it? She looked around, trying to find a clock. Maxwell beat her to it, pulling out his phone and wincing. "Oh." Karina glanced over, spotting the bright glow of the time.

Lex reached over, flicking through the phone before handing it back to Maxwell. "Unfortunately, it didn't look like it automatically updated. Here, this is the time in this city." Karina leaned over her brother's shoulder to take a look and frowned. Oh, she'd forgotten about there being an hour time difference, it was still pretty late even with it being earlier.

She shook her head. She was just confusing herself now. Needless to say, it was a lot later than she thought. That snowstorm really threw off her timetable, then there was the whole fact that they were in a different time zone. She remembered her brother once mentioning it, along with Mom. It had been part of her mom's stories regarding how disorienting it was to be miles away, yet you arrive around the same time you leave, according to the zones. Karina shook her head and pulled away. "All right. That sounds like a plan."

Lex grinned and headed toward the doorway. "Why don't you two stay and talk? I'll be in the room." With that, he left, disappearing through the closing doorway.

Maxwell watched him go before turning to Karina. "So tomorrow, how do you want to start?"

"I think we might want to just get our bearings first." Karina shrugged, finishing up the last of the cereal. "Even though I joked with you, I don't want you getting lost either."

"Makes sense." Maxwell placed his cup onto the coffee table before him and leaned his elbow against the arm of the couch. "I agree with Lex we need to start looking into suspicious places but figuring out where everything is would probably be best. Plus, we need to be careful. What if there are those officers around like in Reinmark or New London City?" Maxwell shook his head and let out a sigh. "Well, let's meet up here tomorrow morning, nine sound good?"

"Should be late enough for you, sure."

Maxwell sent her a look before he stood. "I thought nine because then it would be light enough out for us to see and give us time before it gets dark again to explore the city."

"I'm just joking, geez."

"I know." Maxwell shook his head, seemingly amused before heading toward the doorway. "Anyway, see you tomorrow."

Karina watched him go and let out a sigh before getting up. She patted herself down before heading up the stairs to her shared room. She opened the door and stepped inside. She found herself relieved to see that everything was still in order. She looked at her bag and frowned. The top looked like it had been opened. She looked around the empty room before stepping over to it and opening it. Nothing seemed to be out of place.

She dug around and pulled out her clothes and felt around in the bag. Her climbing gear was there, bottles for water, purifiers, her mother's Bible with the letters from her parents hidden inside, but—

She froze as she pulled out the last item. Where was the money? The money she'd gotten from Martha and what was left from Mom?

Her search became more desperate as she looked through her bag, trying to find those envelopes. She let her hand drop, staring at the bag in frustration. Where could she have put it? When did she lose it? Did she give it to her brother? She knew the answer to the last one was a no. She growled in frustration and started piecing through the items, putting them away as she went. She checked in the locker and in the sheets. After a while, when she'd mostly put everything away, she heard the sound of odd laughter. She looked over to see the door creak open and the girls from before stride inside. They were swaying, cheeks flushed and a bottle in hand.

"Man, to leave your wallet just hanging around, idiot."

"Don't say that, what if she hears you?" Another girl giggled, before they all stepped through the doorway. Karina's eyes widened before she jumped to her feet and stomped over to the girls.

One of the soberer girls looked her over with clouded eyes and raised an eyebrow. "What do you want?"

"You took my money, didn't you?" Karina growled, sticking her finger forward. "What did you do with it? Give it back."

"What?"

The girl Karina saw earlier, Abby? Karina thought that was her name, stepped forward and looked down at her. All the girls were a bit taller than her, Karina noted. The girl leaned forward, and Karina barely moved, glaring right at the hag. Her breath stunk, and the make-up looked even worse up-close, all smudged.

"What are you talking about?" A glimmer shone in her eyes as one of the girls giggled. "You left it right there. What did you expect? You're living with us, deal with it."

"Hell no." Karina slashed her arms sideways, not intimidated by the girls, even as she found the doorway crowded. She couldn't help but take a step back as one of the other girls got right in her face.

"That's no way to treat your elders, little girl."

Karina almost wanted to snap, but she could very well see that would just end badly. She straightened up and glowered. "I'm not dealing with this." She turned and scooped up her bag and marched past the girls to leave. "I'll see if I can room with my brother at this rate."

"Oh, the little one has a brother, eh? I bet he's as ugly as you, if not worse, though I highly doubt that's—"

Karina whipped around so fast, she almost had whiplash. But it sure as heck felt good when her fist connected with the stupid bitch's jaw. The girl that dared slander her brother let out a cry as her butt hit the floor and the other girls stiffened. Karina held up her fist, trembling in anger. "Don't you dare say anything like that about my brother. You hear? I was going to let you go for stealing my money because I don't want anything to happen, but you ran out of luck."

Karina was pissed and she full well knew it. She hadn't done anything to these girls, so why the hell were they acting so...ugh.

The girl that fell slowly pushed herself up, massaging her cheek. Karina wondered if she even felt it, considering how much she was swaying and how drunk she probably was.

"Ah, the ugly little kitten has fangs."

Karina bristled, but decided it was high time she left. She turned to the doorway and pushed through the crowd, gripping her backpack tightly. She descended the stairwell, shaking as she went, her footsteps sounding harsh against her ears. She stopped when she got to the bottom floor, and it was only then she felt water sting the corner of her eyes. She frowned, annoyed that she'd been so bothered by those girls. She quickly wiped at her eyes and headed toward the side doorway that read "Matron's office". She knocked and waited.

The door opened after a moment to reveal the lady from earlier.

She blinked a bit before tilting her head. "Hello, dear, did you need something?"

"Do you have any other rooms I can stay in? It doesn't matter, but I can't stay in the room I have right now."

The woman looked at Karina for a bit, examining her up and down before she let out a sigh and stepped up to her desk. She dug through it before pulling out a key. She looked it over before nodding. "Hand me your key."

Karina handed it over and waited as the woman gave her a new one. "This is for room 306, third floor on the right-hand side, okay?"

Karina couldn't help the smile that spread on her face. "Thanks, and I would like to report thieving. The girls in that room stole—"

The woman raised her hand and Karina's expression fell. The woman gave her a look. "This is a hostel, girl. You need to protect your own things. You don't have any proof that they stole anything, and the police won't believe you over the five of them, so I wouldn't even bother."

Karina pursed her lips. She wanted to argue but decided not to push her limits. She was already taking a lot of liberties to switch rooms. "Right, thanks."

She turned and hurried up to the third floor and found the room in question. It was also quite crowded. Thankfully, everyone was asleep and there was room for her to walk. She stared at the lone bed, set into the corner, the top bunk was once again taken. She let out a sigh and slipped into the lower bunk after quietly closing the door.

She pulled her shoes off and got changed, thinking through what the matron said. She wanted to go over to her brother. Maybe he and Lex would figure something out. Still, she didn't think she could. It almost hurt to think that they hadn't even been here a day and she'd already lost something so precious. On top of that, there were those stupid rules. She didn't want to get them kicked out because she couldn't wait to speak with them. There was nothing she could do, was there? Even though they joked about it, she didn't have any proof besides that, and she was supposed to be keeping a low profile, so she couldn't just go talking to the police. She clenched her fists, digging into the dirty sheets. She ignored the disgusting feeling as she closed her eyes.

Luckily, those girls don't know him and the two of them looked almost nothing alike with different hair and eye color and, well, Karina sighed once more, curling around her bag in a protective embrace. She guessed she should just be grateful for what she had and that they'd only taken money.

Money that Martha gave her even though she was struggling.

Karina felt that frustration well up and quickly pushed it down. There was nothing she could do now. She wasn't sure how long it took, but she had a feeling the sun was almost on the verge of rising by the time she managed to finally fall asleep.

Chapter Seven

Maxwell looked around the dining room, worried. Karina was nowhere in sight and Lex decided to leave after about a half hour of waiting. Maxwell tapped his finger against the seat, watching the door quietly.

"Damn, that bitch punched me hard. What was with her? Ugh, I can't remember."

Maxwell sighed and looked over to see a group of girls chatting away at one side as they passed by his couch. The one at the front shrugged, holding her head. "Ugh, shut up, it's too bright in here."

"Yes, yes, Abby. Still I wonder…" The rest of the sentence faded as the girls slipped into the kitchen.

Maxwell turned his focus back on the doorway. It was barely five minutes later when he saw his sister step through the doorway. He shot to his feet and hurried over. "Kari? Are you okay?"

Karina hefted her backpack more solidly on her shoulder and sent him a sharp glare that caused him to back off. His sister usually wasn't one to be this moody in the morning. What could have happened? Why was she carrying her backpack? Shouldn't she leave it in the room?

Upon seeing his reaction, Karina let out a sigh before waving it away. "It's nothing, I'll explain later. Sorry I'm so late, ready to go?"

Maxwell returned his sister's glare before finally letting out a groan. "Yeah, come on. But first, get something to eat."

"Not hungry." Karina shrugged, and Maxwell furrowed his brow, feeling a hint of worry creep in. *She wasn't sick, right? No, she couldn't be, and she did say she would explain.* He shook the thought away and walked out the door, staying even with her as they moved outside into the brisk wind. He was glad he'd gotten better winter equipment than just the sweatshirt he left home with. He pulled the jacket closer around him as he looked around the streets. They were crowded with people. Karina stayed at his side, holding back yawn after yawn. He couldn't stop from examining his sister. Did she get any sleep last night?

"Hey, Kari?"

"Hm?" His sister hummed, taking in the surroundings like they were supposed to be doing.

Maxwell opened his mouth before finding that he wasn't sure what to say. He turned away, surveying the area. To one side he could see a group of teens walking down the street, talking avidly to each other. Right next to them was a husband and wife, or so he could assume, swinging their clasped hands back and forth while their faces were practically plastered to each other. He quickly looked away. "What do you want to check out first?"

"I figured we would just walk around today. I'll get an idea in my head of how the city operates, then we can go from there." Karina shrugged before biting her lower lip. He could see indecision on her face. She wanted to say something but was she not sure how? What was wrong?

He turned to face her, leaning forward slightly. "Kari?"

She shook her head and gestured, glancing back toward the hostel before stepping around him.

Maxwell conceded reluctantly, watching as they passed another alley and continued down the street, having taken a left upon exiting the hostel. Considering they'd come from the right, this was all new territory. The tall buildings hovered over them, as imposing and cold as ever. The smell once more hit his nose, a rancid odor he knew would fade over time as he got used to it once more. The streets were organized, he noted as they took a turn and then another.

"Maxwell?"

Maxwell glanced sidelong at his sister, surprised to see her rubbing her eyes. She seemed to be struggling to think. She really must not have gotten much sleep at all. "What's wrong?"

Karina blinked and glanced at him, eyes slightly teary before she let out a sigh. "I just had some trouble with roommates last night. They…" she trailed off.

Maxwell slowed himself to a stop and turned to face his sister. It took her a moment before she also stopped as well.

"Karina?" He nudged, trying to get her to speak. This wasn't like her, to be so silent.

"I was careless. The girls in the room stole all of Martha's and Mom's money. I ended up having to switch rooms and couldn't get to sleep."

Maxwell stiffened as he felt anger surge up. Someone did that to his sister? Karina must have seen the anger on his face because she winced. Maxwell curled his hands into fists and turned to her. "Kari, why didn't you tell me right away? When it happened?"

Karina rolled her eyes, trying to push it away like normal. "Because I didn't think it was that big of an issue, and there's not anything we can do about it. We can't exactly contact the police now, can we?" She shrugged.

Stop being so stubborn about this, Maxwell wanted to scream at her but held back as she continued.

"Plus, I got out of that room. My roommates now aren't that bad. They leave me alone and I leave them alone. Not only that, but you were sleeping, and I didn't want to wake you. You know, in the boys' dorm?" She sent him a sidelong look and he looked away.

Okay, that last bit was a good point, but still." You know you could have told us. Lex or I, we could have figured something out. They didn't use all the money, right?"

"I honestly don't know." Karina huffed, arms over her chest. "They stank of alcohol and a couple were high, I think." She shook her head. "I just don't have any proof and you two can't just barge into the girl's dorm. Last time I checked we *needed* to stay here for now."

Maxwell winced, realizing his sister was right. Especially now that they lost all that money. Neither of them would know where to even look and, while he could ask Lex, he wasn't sure how much that would help. He would still have to talk with him though. It would be stupid to keep this under wraps. Maxwell pursed his lips, cautiously stepping up to her. "What if those girls try something else?"

"I wouldn't worry about that." She flexed her fist, curling her hand inward.

Wait, don't tell me... He glanced at his sister, examining her quietly. There was a little bruising on her knuckle which meant... "Kari, what did you do?" He placed a hand to his face, letting it trail down before giving her an unimpressed look. "You attacked them, didn't you?"

"Like they would remember. They were completely drunk." Karina looked away, somewhat sheepish.

Sister, you are too reckless. Maxwell shook his head and dropped his hand. "Well, that's happened."

"Whatever." Karina shrugged before turning to continue down the road. "Now come on, before night descends on us already."

Well, at least that explains why she has her bag with her and why she was so out of it. It probably also hurt her pride, and considering his sister, that was bound to be painful. He hurried to catch up to her as she took long strides ahead. "Karina, what are you going to do now? We still have another week here."

"I'll be careful. Plus, they don't know about you and Lex. At least, not much, what can they do in a week?"

Maxwell wasn't sure, but he had a feeling that he didn't want to know.

His hair blew into his face as he stared up at the slowly shifting clouds. Karina was strong, he knew full well she could take care of herself. They walked down the street in silence, looking at the different buildings as they passed. The roads were crowded like usual with cars and pedestrians, but it was easier to move about, now that they were more used to it. Around lunch, they stopped near one of the stalls and Maxwell pulled out some bills Lex gave him. He felt bad, wasting Lex's money now that he knew how much had been lost, but they still needed to eat more than yogurt and cereal. Karina seemed to agree, even though she was just as hesitant.

He grabbed the food and took a seat with Karina across from him. She slipped the backpack off her shoulder and set it next to her.

They finished up their food in no time and continued going around before finally heading back to the hostel. Right before the doorway, he stopped. His sister took a few more steps before realizing and turned back to face him. "Kari, please be careful." It was all he could say right now. "I'll talk to Lex and see if we can find a way to deal with this, but…"

"Thanks, little brother, but I'll be okay, you know me." She pumped her fist, giving a cheeky grin.

Yeah, he did, which was why he was worried. He let out a sigh and gave a weak smile back. "All right." He waved bye to his sister and headed up the stairs, meeting up with Lex as he stepped out of the side door at the top of the stairwell, the bathroom.

"Hey, Lex, any luck?"

Lex shook his head. "Sorry, it's not exactly easy to find what I'm looking for."

"Shouldn't it be? After all, you're just trying to find an apartment, right?"

"Yes and no." Lex opened the door to their room and stepped inside, throwing his bag into the cage before pulling out a lock and closing it. The room was empty, all the other customers still out partying or something. Maxwell wasn't sure and didn't want to know. Lex glanced at him.

"I need to find something that is cheap that we can stay in for a long period of time and has enough room for the three of us. It should be close to areas that might be suspicious regarding where your mother is, but not so close as to be dangerous. Something that's not falling apart at the seams and that is safe enough that as long as we are careful, we can avoid any mishaps."

Lex let out a long-tired sigh and Maxwell couldn't help but feel a little sorry for his friend. Yeah, that sounded difficult, he almost didn't want to burden his friend more but…

"Lex, about money."

Lex's face grew impassive, as if he already suspected something. Maxwell couldn't hide the grimace. "My sister had a run-in with some girls. They stole all her money."

Lex cursed under his breath, causing Maxwell to take a step back in surprise. He knew Lex would be frustrated, but he hadn't expected that.

"I need a smoke." Lex's voice was weak as he stepped toward the doorway. "Don't worry, I'll think of something. Just make sure your sister is all right."

With that, he left. Maxwell watched him go, feeling himself sink. This was not going well at all.

~ * ~

Karina sighed in relief as she awoke to a room full of quiet chatter. The girls weren't bad. They sent her quick smiles before resuming their own conversations. Like she told Maxwell, they left her alone which helped.

She met up with Maxwell and they explored the city some more, though she could see Maxwell would occasionally send her worried looks. She knew her brother had a right to be worried, but she was glad he didn't say anything. After all, what could he say? She was just glad they were able to talk normally, and she knew full well Lex knew.

She could tell because when she went downstairs the second day, she found him standing outside in the freezing cold, cigarette in hand and staring listlessly toward the sky.

"Lex?"

Lex glanced over to her and let out a sigh, stubbing out the cigarette before throwing it in an ashtray next to him. "I heard what happened from your brother."

"I figured…" she trailed off. She bit her lip before she muttered a quiet, "Sorry."

Lex looked as if he was zapped, his eyes shifted to her, worry shining clear through them. "I didn't expect that." He shook his head, fingers fiddling with another cigarette before thrusting it in his pocket. "Idiot. I should have warned you to keep that stuff on you. So, I am partially to blame." He shrugged and pushed away from the wall. "Just don't do anything reckless, we'll be out of here soon."

The only thing Karina could do was nod. After all, what could she say to him?

~ * ~

The third day of their stay dawned, and Karina found herself trudging downstairs after getting changed. It was still early, and she knew her brother probably wouldn't be up for a little while. She let out a yawn and stepped into the kitchen area. She spotted some girls off to one side, whispering as they glanced at her. She frowned, but ignored it, digging inside the fridge.

"Hey, sweet cheeks."

Karina gagged. Who says things like that? She shook it off, grabbing something in the fridge before standing up and turning, only to stumble as she ran smack into an older boy's chest. She yelped and backpedaled, glaring up at the boy.

"What are you doing?" she growled, and the boy whistled, examining her a little too closely for her taste before placing his hand beside her head against the fridge.

"What a cutie. I heard from some of the lovely ladies here that you were looking for a good time?"

Karina blinked once before she ducked under his outstretched arm and pushed past him, causing him to yelp. "Hell no," she said, taking a bite of her yogurt as she stepped through the doorway, spotting a sputtering and confused boy standing behind her.

What was that all about? Who uses lines like that anyway? Was he trying to hit on her? She shivered. *That was not a pleasant thought.*

"Oh, hey, Kari!"

Karina looked up at the sound of her name, seeing her brother step up to her. He had a soft smile on his face. Karina couldn't help her own smile. Part of her was worried the girls would realize Maxwell was her brother, but she hadn't really seen those girls since then, so that worry was starting to fade.

He'd cleaned up and pulled his long hair back, away from his face with that plain brown clip she'd gotten him, keeping his bangs out of the way. It blended well with his hair, so it didn't look too out of place. He was dressed in the clothes she gave him in New London City and he had a wide grin on his face.

"Hey, bro."

"It's good to see you're feeling better this morning. Looks like Lex is busy again today, though he seemed to be muttering something about leads." He seemed to hesitate before shaking his head. He waved his hand, leaning on one leg. "Where do you want to go today?"

Karina raised an eyebrow, hand on her hips. "Leads?"

"Well, you don't think Lex would just let *that* slide, right? I think he might be looking into seeing if we can salvage some of it. Though it has been a few days now, so I'm not sure what he might get out of it." Maxwell seemed a bit disheartened for a second, glancing away from her as his shoulders slumped.

She rolled her eyes, lightly smacking his head, causing him to yelp and his hands to dart to his head. He glared at her as she gave him her cat-like grin. "Is little bro worried?"

He dropped his hands, giving her such a heavy glare that she almost burst out laughing. She couldn't help the snort that escaped at his expression and he just shook his head, a hint of amusement playing on his lips.

She heard rustling and some whispers from behind. She saw her brother lean to the right slightly to peer past her as she glanced over her shoulder. There were a few guys eyeing her in a way that sent shivers down her spine, but she didn't let that show, instead glaring at them and turning sharply back to her brother. "Let's go."

"What are they...?" Maxwell frowned before looking at her.

Karina waved her hand, "Don't know, don't care, now let's get going." She grabbed his wrist and walked toward the door, causing him to stumble after her.

"Kari. Would you let go?"

She rolled her eyes but loosened her grip enough where he could retract his hand and massage it. Oops, had she really grabbed that hard? She clicked her tongue before heading past the matron and out the door, her brother hot on her heels.

"What's going on? Are you okay? I'm not stupid, those guys were obviously looking at you. Did something happen?"

Concern was clearly heard in his voice as he managed to catch up and peer toward her. His eyes shown in worry and a hint of anger, though from what she could only guess. Maybe he saw the actual looks, though how he interpreted them, she wasn't sure.

Karina peered sidelong at her brother. Had he grown a bit? It looked like it now that she was looking closer. She shook it off and grinned. "Nothing I can't handle."

The deadpan look he sent her made her cringe, this one not as amusing. Okay, maybe not the best line, considering what happened the other day. "Really, it's not a problem. For some reason, people are starting to look at me strangely, I don't know why."

Maxwell looked like he wanted to argue, his hands clenched, and he huffed. "Strangely wasn't really the word I would use." He seemed to scan her, as if searching for something, hesitating before loosening his grip. "They looked, well, like those people we saw when we first arrived in Reinmark, remember? Before we met Lex?"

Karina grimaced, remembering all too well. As much as she hated to admit it, the hungry looks weren't that different and considering what Lex mentioned about that area it didn't help. At least here she wasn't as worried about being kidnapped. She wanted to believe she was a bit more knowledgeable than back then. "Well even so, they aren't doing anything and we're leaving soon. So why don't we just not worry about it, all right?"

She placed her hands on her hips, glancing sidelong to Maxwell. Only then did she realize they must have stopped walking at some point, pedestrians passed around them as the walk signal beeped above.

He looked her over before slumping his shoulders. "If you say so." He definitely wanted to say something else, she could see that plain as day, but she smiled anyway.

"Thanks, little bro, now let's get going. We still have quite a bit of information gathering to do, can't get lost now, right?"

She turned, crossing the street. Maxwell scurried after her just as the walking sign turned to red. Cars zoomed behind them as they continued along the path, passing store front after glass store front. Karina sniffed and found herself grateful to realize that they were in a shopping district, a food one at that. "Hey, Max, want to grab something to eat?"

Shaken out of his thoughts and his brooding mood, Maxwell glanced up and shrugged. "Sure. What are you in the mood for?"

Karina walked down the street, looking over the items with her brother tagging along. After some time, they found something and got it to go, walking as they ate.

"This place doesn't seem too hard to figure out." Maxwell swallowed a bite of his orange chicken and glanced sidelong toward Karina. "Where do you think we should start looking for Ma?"

"Don't know." Karina shrugged, crumbling up her empty package, she'd been hungry. "I mean, they wouldn't make it obvious where she was kept, and we do still need to be careful, what if those police are around?"

Maxwell grimaced, probably not too happy about that thought. "Well, for now, we might as well make sure we know the whole city. Maybe grab a map as well so we can better keep track of everything."

"Probably a good idea." Karina gestured. "That way, if we find any place suspicious, we can mark it down."

With that in mind, they grabbed a map and continued on their way.

Karina was admittedly glad when they returned to the hostel. While the hostel wasn't necessarily comfortable, it was warm, and she knew her brother was tired. She let out a yawn and, after ruffling her brother's hair, causing him to squawk in protest, she returned to her room. She stepped inside to find the girls gathered around, whispering quietly to each other. They stopped as soon as they saw her, giving her wary looks. She rolled her eyes. *What was up with everyone?*

She grabbed the lock and clicked it open, pulling out her backpack and checking through, just to make sure she had everything. She picked up a water bottle and, after sliding the bag and lock back into place, left to go to the kitchen.

Even though she and her brother had lunch, they both decided to save money and just grab something small for dinner at the hostel. She descended the stairs and stepped inside the kitchen to grab some water, passing a custodian who seemed to be on his way out. She hummed quietly as she filled the bottle, hearing the soft gurgling and rattling of the pipes. The water was cold, some of it spilling over the lip of the bottle.

She heard movement and certainly did not let out a screech when something touched her. She whipped around, some of the water splashing on the person standing behind her, who cursed. It was a scruffy, taller boy whose hand migrated way too close. He looked startled, eyes wide as she held the bottle in front of her, almost as if it was a projectile or something. Part of her didn't think he looked that bad, but she squashed the thought down, more annoyed that he'd touched her. She glared at him, hands squeezing just slightly around the water bottle, watching water dribble out.

He eyed the bottle and her stance hesitantly before raising his hands. "Sorry, just grabbing something to eat, didn't mean to bother you." He slowly backed away until his back reached the doorway. He made a very hasty retreat after that and, as the door swung shut, she finally found herself relaxing a little, looking down at the water bottle.

"Pervert," she growled, both annoyed and a hint worried.

That was the second time in just as many days. She shook her head before turning back to what she was doing. She'd wasted some good water, so now she had to refill, what a pain.

~ * ~

Maxwell let out a yawn as he descended the stairs, rubbing the sleep out of his eyes. It was the fourth day, a day after they picked up the map, and he and his sister decided to go out separately to see if they could find anything different. His sister wasn't back yet, but he wasn't exactly worried, there was still a decent amount of light left and he knew she could take care of herself. After all, she was a lot healthier than everyone else here. He got back early, but he was tired. The nap helped, but he quickly found himself letting out another yawn. He hadn't gotten much sleep last night and he noticed Lex looked just as tired and frustrated as him. Must be hard, it was a new city, after all. Lex was almost in the same situation as Karina and himself were in, with the added bonus of looking for someplace for them to stay and, from what Maxwell could gather, trying to find out what happened to the money. Maxwell let out a sigh as he stepped into the kitchen area. A light flickered off to one side, the bulb dying. Looked like the matron would need to get that fixed.

"Oh ho, if it isn't the little brother of the ugly kitten."

Maxwell blinked. *Who?* He heard movement and glanced over his shoulder to see a couple of girls. Make-up adorned their faces and cruel grins turned their lips upward viciously. Were these the girls Karina mentioned? He vaguely remembered hearing them talking a few days ago when he was waiting for his sister. He turned fully, feeling a hint of anger at their harsh words.

"Did you want something?" He figured he might as well be polite, even if they were rude, calling his sister ugly and him a little boy. For one, his sister was anything but, just because he was her brother, didn't mean he couldn't see that.

One of the girls snorted. "Definitely the little brother, even saying the same thing as an introduction."

Really? Huh, no wonder Karina was annoyed. He frowned. "I'm sorry, but I don't know you, and I don't think my sister does either, so is it really necessary to say such rude things?"

One of the girls giggled, he vaguely wondered if they were drunk, but pushed the thought aside. He shook his head and glanced at the cabinet, no point wasting time with these girls. He quickly reached up to grab something when one of the girls grabbed his wrist. He let out a sharp cry as the girl spun him around, trapping him against the counter, one hand on his wrist the other near his waist on the counter.

"Hey!" He wrenched his arm from her hold. "What are you doing?"

The girl grinned and backed away, letting him breathe. "Seeing how you would react." The girl shrugged. "After all, your sister is quite stubborn, even with some of the guys making advances on her, she doesn't even move an inch."

Making advances? "What have you done to my sister?" He'd never heard his voice sound so cold and he wasn't surprised when he noticed one of the girls wince.

The main girl shrugged and flipped some hair over her shoulder. He noticed a thin scar down her neck, a sign of the epidemic. The makeup was probably hiding a good portion of it too, considering how thickly it was layered on. "Nothing, nor are we doing anything to you." The girl examined him with a smirk. "We don't need to. Others can do it just as well."

Others? Maxwell frowned, hands curling tightly, fingernails biting into the skin of his palm. "What did we even do to you?"

"You made a mockery of us." The girl glared. "That prissy little girl with barely a scar, healthy and pretty, of course we'll be pissed. She doesn't even look like she cares, and she can hold herself like she's some princess."

That was the first time Maxwell ever thought he would hear his sister called princess, he never wanted to hear it in that tone again. Yet she continued, as if no longer paying attention to him.

"She doesn't need to wear makeup and has the audacity to punch one of us." She trailed off, only to lean forward sharply, causing Maxwell to almost bang his head against the overhead cabinet when he was backing away. "Neither of you look sick. You must hide it well, but it's angering. After all, how could two low-lifes like you avoid it?" The girl placed her hands on either side of him. Now, he might not have been completely against this situation, if it wasn't for the fact that this girl was not only getting on his nerves but wasn't even playing fair.

She gave him a solid look-over before a mischievous gleam shone in her eyes. A smirk slowly crawled across her face as she pushed away, walking away with the other girls. It was only then when Maxwell realized he had been holding his breath. He made himself take a sharp intake of breath, trembling hand going to his chest.

That was dangerous, for multiple reasons. He could feel his legs shaking as he pushed himself away from the counter. He quickly grabbed a cup of water and, making sure it was filled, downed it in one try. What were those girls up to? The reasons they brought up seemed petty, but it shed light on a good point. Neither Karina nor himself looked sick, and lately, Lex seemed to be faring better as well. There was also the fact that almost no one around wore masks. Part of him wondered about that, but another part didn't want to know. After all, wasn't this area close to the quarantine zones? Either way, it could be dangerous. They would have to have some means of showing that they might be sick, or in the third stage, but how?

He let out a long sigh and, shutting off the tap, he turned and headed out the door. The girls were gone, but he could still see people whispering off to the side. He wondered, what were they going to do next?

Three days left.

Chapter Eight

Lex walked down the street quietly, examining the crumbled buildings and shady characters, in another rundown part of town. Much to his chagrin, there were a lot of those, including the area where the hostel was located. He let out a sigh. He couldn't help but to take a puff on the cigarette sitting between his lips; the warm smoke filled his lungs and calmed his stressed nerves. Ever since Maxwell made mention of what happened to Karina, he'd been trying to keep an eye out for them, find out where the money went, while also looking for a new place to stay. Finding the money was like trying to win a game of chess against Caym. He knew it wasn't going to happen, but he still tried anyway. Though he never was much of a fan of chess and, contrary to the way Caym acted lately, neither was he.

He'd gotten a few leads that only turned up dead, both figuratively and literally in one case. It had definitely been an accident, but still set his nerves on edge. He'd tried to follow those girls, from what Karina told him, but with his time restraint and keeping an eye on the twins it was nigh impossible. He was trying to do too much at once and it was burning him out.

Yet, he knew he needed to. He needed to get the twins out of there.

He wasn't naïve, like the twins. He could hear the lewd conversations and spreading rumors. What he could gather from the girls wasn't really encouraging either. They were analyzing the twins as much as Lex was analyzing them and it made him deeply worried. How could he stop it though? He couldn't kill them, and he didn't have the means to shut them all up. He could see how one of them was an obvious leader and he figured he could try talking with her. The one time he tried, however, she just twirled her fingers, said she wasn't interested and walked away.

Of course, he hadn't been too keen on that, but he ignored it. After all, he knew right now, it was Karina being most affected. However, the perpetrators weren't dumb. Given how often they dodged topics or stayed under the radar, even with him watching. If anything, they probably already realized that trying to go after Karina wouldn't do them any good. For some petty reason, they wanted to humiliate Karina and, while he wished he could find a way to stop it, he didn't realize soon enough. Even if he stopped the girls, it didn't mean he could stop the ever-escalating rumors, or their impact.

He wasn't there twenty-four seven. He couldn't be with the twins while also trying to get them a place to stay.

He let out a sigh and took another puff of the cigarette before throwing it on the ground and stubbing it out in frustration. He was honestly more worried about Maxwell. The kid was too sweet for his own good. While Lex knew both of them were strong, it was different types of strengths. He couldn't stop the long groan from slipping through his lips as he pushed a hand through his hair.

He took another corner, realizing he'd gotten side-tracked. He looked around and slowed to a halt. While the previous neighborhood left much to be desired, this part of town wasn't that bad. He spotted brick and stone buildings. Little gates surrounded some of the snowed-in lawns. He walked quietly down the street. This would be a good area, if he could find something here.

He heard a sound and looked over to see a police officer. His blue uniform, an indication of being a regular police officer instead of an Enthrope officer, shone in the afternoon light. He was talking amiably with a young boy around the twins 'age. The young boy held a wide grin and put his arms up. "Don't worry, Dad. I'll watch Mom while you're gone."

The policeman chuckled and, after saying good-bye, hurried

down the street. A police officer's abode, and a non-affiliated one at that: that could be both helpful and hindering. He looked at the boy, just as the boy turned to see him. His eyes widened, and he tilted his head. "You're new around here."

"I'm sorry, I'm just trying to find an apartment," Lex started walking up to the boy, who nodded. Lex had to admit, part of him was impressed, while the boy seemed to have a casual air around him, his sharp eyes and readied posture indicated otherwise.

"Well, I know some rooms just opened up in my friend's apartment complex, just down the street."

Lex bowed his head slightly. "Thank you." He continued on his way.

This might actually be what he was looking for. Now just to find out how much it was, and see if he could scrounge up the necessary money. It was in that moment he wished he'd managed to find what remained of the twin's money. He figured it was all gone now, having probably been squandered over the past few days, but the thought was nice. Of course, being realistic, he already knew the likelihood of finding it was low, but he had still wanted to try. He would have to give up on that for now and just bite the bullet and contact his uncle. It would be dangerous, but if he could get his uncle to transfer some money to a brand-new account, it could work. He would need quite a bit, considering how much they lost, but that would take at least a day, if not two. Once he contacted his uncle and spoke with the owner of the apartment, he should have enough time to get what he needed to done in time to get the twins out of there.

He hoped the twins would be all right and hold out just a little longer.

~ * ~

Karina awoke to the sound of creaking. Her eyes snapped open and she looked up to see Abby. She was holding what appeared to be a knife in her hands. Karina shot up and pushed her away, stumbling out of bed. A pair of arms grabbed her, and she cried out, wrenching at the hands holding her upper arms.

"Hold her still, we don't want to cut that ugly head of hers," Abby called.

Karina growled, tugging at the hands that bound her arms and waist. She heard movement and looked over just in time to see her brother thrown on the ground. He winced, managing to protect his head with his arm. He sat up and shook his head before looking at the scene.

His eyes widened, and he mouthed her name. One of the girls stepped forward and squatted behind him, holding his mouth and nose. He reached his hands up to pull her off but was quickly stopped.

What was going on? Why was Maxwell here?

She heard a quiet chuckle and looked over to see Abby twirl the knife with way too much ease. "We'll start with yours and then move onto him. I wonder what kind of tattoo I can make on his skin with these."

She reached forward, wrenching at a piece of Karina's hair, Karina didn't even have time to think before she heard the sharp cutting sound of the blade. Black locks fell to the floor and, out of the corner of her eyes, she could see her brother's fearful gaze as another knife, held by one of the girls holding him, drifted closer to his cheek.

"Let go!" Karina fought, feeling the grips tighten more and more, knuckles white.

The girl who'd just cut her hair stepped in front of her brother, silence filled the air for one moment, and it was all Karina could do not to strain, breaking something, just to see her brother, hidden behind the girl. Her heart stilled as a sharp-pained scream shot through her to the core.

Plop... Karina slowly looked down to see blood dripping to the ground and quiet whimpers. *No...*

*Plop...*more blood dripped, and Karina slowly moved her eyes upward, away from the red slowly staining the ground as the girl stepped away.

"Kari."

Karina screamed.

Hard ground met her face and Karina groaned, head smarting and throat aching. She blearily opened her eyes to see that she was laying on her side, sheets so tightly wrapped around her upper arms they were trapped. She heard the lights flick on as one of the girls hurried up to her. She sat up, untangling herself.

"Are you all right?"

"I'm...I'm fine. Thanks," she managed to mutter. She could feel herself trembling violently and let out a breath. "Sorry."

The girl shook her head, then looked at the surrounding girls. "No worries, just a nightmare, it seems. Everyone get back to bed."

The other girls sent Karina one more look before hurrying back to their beds and falling asleep.

Karina didn't have the strength to be embarrassed, the nightmare playing through her mind over and over. She let out a sigh and sent the girl a weak smile. "Thanks."

"No problem, now can you get up? You took a nasty fall."

Karina nodded and pushed herself shakily to her feet. She felt her hair, matted to her head, trail around her shoulders, still its normal length. "I'll be back." She turned and headed out the door. She needed some water and she needed to see her brother. She needed to make sure he was okay. She hated that her dream involved him.

She descended the stairs slowly, using her hand to lean against the wall. The hallways were dimly lit, and she could tell it was late. The moon shining through the curtains set at each level was high and bright. After some time, Karina found herself in the kitchen, water spilling down her chin as she drank it down.

She placed the glass down and leaned against the counter with both hands. She let her nerves calm before she slowly pushed away and headed toward the entrance. She briefly glanced at the boy's dorm and hesitated, seeing the camera's red-light beam at the entrance. She would be taking quite the risk, but when did that ever stop her when she was honestly trying?

She climbed quietly up the stairs, keeping close to the sides and listening intently. Eventually, she reached the second floor and hurried down the hallway. She could faintly hear the sound of snoring and the occasional murmur. She shook her head and, finding the last door in the hall with a familiar number, cautiously pushed at it. It wasn't locked, much to her relief.

Then again, the boys didn't necessarily have as much to worry about. She slipped inside and looked around. Moonlight shone into the messy room, splashing across sleeping faces and shifting figures. Within no time, she spotted her brother, curled into the sheets. She stepped carefully over a pile of clothes and knelt down beside her brother's bed. If she wasn't careful, this could be a huge problem. Though she knew she was probably already in trouble if anyone looked at the cameras, at least if no one saw her, she might be able to get away with it. She looked him over, seeing his chest rise and fall and his eyelids flutter in sleep.

She let out a sigh and went to stand.

"Kari?" a familiar groggy voice spoke up and she barely stopped herself from jumping and banging her head against the top bunk. She squatted back down just as Maxwell sat up, rubbing his eyes. He looked drowsy and only half awake. "Wha' are you?" his words were slurred as he looked at her.

"Sorry, little bro," she kept her voice soft, placing both hands on his cheek, turning his head side to side to make sure everything was okay, that he wasn't bleeding.

He blinked, putting a hand up, before shaking his head and pulling her hands away. He seemed to be waking up, his eyes a little sharper and full of worry.

"What are you doing here? You could be in trouble," he hissed quietly, looking around. Karina nodded and quickly pulled away. Maxwell looked up at her and then sighed, rubbing his head. He threw off the sheets and slipped out of bed.

"No, you don't have to…" Karina found herself unable to complete her sentence as Maxwell sent her a glare.

He threw a sweatshirt on over his pajamas, grabbed another one and gestured for his sister to follow him.

Karina grumbled under her breath and slipped out the door.

Maxwell looked up and down the hallway before hurrying away, Karina right on his heels. Within moments, they were back in the lobby and Maxwell let out a sigh before turning to Karina and flicking her in the head. "What were you thinking?"

Karina winced, placing a hand to her head. "I was thinking I was worried."

Maxwell looked at her, glancing over her quietly before he let out a breath and closed his eyes, deep in thought. "Let me guess. You had a nightmare like when we were little after Dad—"

"Maxwell." Karina interrupted her brother, not wanting to get on that subject.

Thankfully, he seemed to understand. He opened his eyes, a faint encouraging smile on his lips.

They walked into the dining room and sat on one of the couches. Maxwell handed over the sweatshirt and Karina gratefully took it, noting how cold she was now that she was no longer shaking.

"So, what was the dream about?" Maxwell crossed one leg under the other, letting the other trail over the couch as he leaned back.

Karina huddled into the sweatshirt, pulling both her legs onto the couch and curling her arms around them. She could feel her back dig into the arm of the couch. "It was just a stupid nightmare."

Maxwell stayed silent.

Karina sighed. "It was about those stupid girls. They captured me and you. They had these knives, they cut my hair and then turned to you and…there was blood and you screamed. I don't get it. Why do something so stupid to me and hurt you?"

Maxwell peered sidelong at Karina. Karina could feel the gaze, knew he was watching, but…she closed her eyes, straying from the look. She didn't really want to see him right now. Over something so stupid.

"I think I understand."

"Huh?" Karina turned to Maxwell, who was staring at the ceiling, as if tracing the cracked pieces and listening to the quiet whispering that could sometimes be heard from the upper floors through the thin walls.

"I had a run-in with those girls yesterday. They mentioned—"

"What?" Karina sat up, leaning forward. They tried to do something to Maxwell?

Maxwell was only partially startled, as if he expected her outburst. "I wasn't hurt, they just mostly used intimidation tactics, but I don't like where this is going."

Karina pursed her lips and looked down. "What about Lex? Did he say anything?"

Karina could feel her brother shake his head, a heavy sigh leaving his lips. "Just…I don't know what to do, for either of us. I can't keep saying be careful. That's like trying to say not to jump into the fire when you're already standing in it."

Karina couldn't help but chuckle at the analogy. She stood up, drawing his attention. "I think we might have to start sticking close to Lex a bit more, just until we're out of here. You especially."

"Why me?" Maxwell stood, befuddled.

"Well…" Karina couldn't admit it out loud. She knew she could handle whatever came her way, but she wasn't sure how she would handle it if… "You know what I mean."

She could feel Maxwell's gaze at her back as she headed for the stairwell. She heard his reluctant groan. "All right, Kari."

Thanks, little brother. She ascended the stairwell, feeling a little better than when she went down them.

Still, she curled her hands tightly, shaking.

Two days left.

~ * ~

Maxwell let out a long breath as he returned to his room. The steps creaked as he went up.

"Wasn't that one of the girls?"

"Yeah, that really pretty one. I've seen her from time to time, she is beautiful. Too bad I heard she likes to sleep around."

"Well, then why don't you nab that?"

"Nah, not into those types, I wonder if her brother is the same way?"

"Oh yeah, I did see the two of them go down to the dining room. Was he going to meet one of the girls or…"

Maxwell frowned as he stepped down the hallway, catching the two standing near the bathroom off guard. The two spotted him and scurried away.

Damn, so they saw him and his sister. That wasn't good. What was this about his sister sleeping around? Was that what the girls meant by boys trying to make advances on Karina? He gritted his teeth, fingers digging into his palm as he walked back to his room. He thought it would be late enough, that no one would be up. Seems that wasn't the case, and he hadn't been able to see who the two were in the dim lighting. He wanted to curse but held it in as he slipped into bed, shivering as the cold bit into his exposed feet. He glanced toward Lex's bed, spotting him asleep.

Part of him wanted to wake his friend, the other part wanted to let him sleep.

He leaned against the wall, glancing toward the window as he curled up with the sheets around him. The wall felt cold, but he wasn't tired anymore, not after seeing his sister in such a state.

That dream must have bothered her. Yet he could understand. He let himself slump against the wall and closed his eyes.

The next thing he knew, he woke up with a crick in his neck. He cringed, blinking his eyes open. The sun couldn't even really be seen, just a thin coating of gray showed that it was starting to turn bright. He rubbed his eyes. He stretched, trying to unwind his stiff neck and shoulder muscles. He looked around and pushed himself up. He noticed Lex's bed was empty, he must have left early to get things done.

Maxwell frowned before he shook his head and decided to go downstairs. He would have to meet up with Lex later.

After getting changed, he slipped downstairs in time to see Karina's tired frame step through the doorway. She spotted him and sighed in relief. She was still wearing the sweatshirt he gave her. He wondered if she even noticed, considering how tired she looked, though she must have, considering she was no longer in pajamas.

She gave him a weak smile before stepping over. "Hey, where's Lex?"

"Already gone." Maxwell reached a hand to the back of his neck, trying to get rid of the crick, feeling it stiffen.

Karina sighed. "Do you want to just head straight out? I'm not that hungry and it'll give us more time to see the city."

Maxwell hesitated. "I'm okay with that. Are you ready to go?"

Karina nodded. They headed outside into the cool morning air. Snow drifted around their faces, clinging to hair and skin alike. The soft cold texture made Maxwell shiver, but he ignored it, along with Karina, continuing on in silence. Maxwell wasn't sure what to say to her and he knew she just felt uncomfortable, especially after revealing how afraid she was last night.

They grabbed breakfast, staying in the warmth of the little café they'd found. It was what one might call a cute place with comfortable chairs and a quaint atmosphere. The interior was made of wood and the baristas were friendly and pleasant. Plus, it had the added benefit of being a good distance from the hostel. Maxwell sipped at his tea, staring out the window as his sister downed what was probably a latte. He wasn't sure. The swirling snow gave everything a grayish white sheen.

"Hey, Maxwell, do you think we will have to deal with things like this the whole time we're searching for our mother? Do you think it will be like this at the apartment?" Karina's voice caught Maxwell's attention.

He turned and furrowed his brow. "I don't think so. Lex is working really hard to find us a place where we don't have to worry about that as much. I mean, yes, he's busy with other things as well, but you know Lex."

"True. So that's why he seems so tired lately."

Maxwell nodded, and Karina gazed out the window, hands tightening around the warm cup. Maxwell couldn't help but trace the wood of the table, trying to organize his thoughts. "Oh yeah, Kari, we should pick up some bandages."

"Hm? Why?"

"In order to make it look like…" Maxwell looked around before lowering his voice. "We have the sickness. It's already suspicious with the way things are. We might be in trouble if someone puts two and two together."

Karina frowned. "I guess. We'll do that on the way home."

"That's fine." Maxwell pulled back and took another sip of tea, sighing at the warmth.

They just had to wait a little longer, just a few more days and they could move on. He looked forward to it.

After picking up some bandages and finding that, as usual, there were no available masks, they decided they would apply the bandages when they got back. They continued with their perusal of the city. Maxwell glanced sidelong at the building he recalled passing when they first arrived. It was as busy as usual, people coming in and out of the double glass doors. From what he could see from the other side of the street, the inside looked warm and cozy, something he did not expect from a building that was attached to the gated community in such a way. He turned to Karina, who was gazing at the place as well.

"You know, it seems like a long shot, but that place really stands out."

Karina turned to him. "Do you think?"

"I think Lex has been looking into it when he can, but I think you might be right." Maxwell turned away, continuing down the street with his sister at his side. "It stands out the most, compared to the other things around here. Plus, there is just the fact it's attached to the gated community. We both know Ma was taken by Enthrope, who seems to have control within the communities, so it makes more sense. That is, if she is in there and not in the gated community proper."

"We wouldn't be able to do much if she is completely inside," Karina muttered, hand to her chin. "So, I guess, we'll just have to hope that she's there."

"Exactly. Yet I wonder, what are we going to do to get to her?"

Maxwell let that thought hang in the air. After all, even though they had a feeling they knew where she was, it was also one of the most heavily guarded areas in the city. It would be dangerous for the gated community if this side got through.

They returned back to the hostel with that thought in their minds. It was still early, and Maxwell knew Lex was busy making the final preparations for their move since they would be leaving the day after tomorrow, if not tomorrow. He glanced sidelong at his sister who seemed to be trying to center herself. She must have noticed his look because she grinned cheekily and waved it off. "I'll see you for dinner in a few minutes, okay?"

"All right, see ya, sis."

Maxwell watched her head inside with a frown, noting as she looked around warily. Karina was a bit more attuned to danger than he was, even if he was able to trust certain people more easily than she.

In this place, she must have felt completely trapped. He hated the idea of putting Karina through that. He shook his head to push away those thoughts and stepped through the doorway. His sister was already gone, probably having rushed to her room. Maxwell glanced toward the girls ' stairwell before heading toward the boys'.

Before even reaching the first step, he heard the sound of quiet whispering coming from the dining room, the words faint, yet he could have sworn he heard his sister's name.

Maxwell hesitated before slipping close to the dining room door and peeking inside. In the corner, he could see the same group of girls from earlier talking to a guy. What were they talking about? Part of him wanted to ask, another part wanted to just leave it alone, they only had one more day here, after all.

"Hey, you."

Maxwell jumped and turned to see a girl who looked like she could be part of the group with make-up and all. What was she doing out here? Is she the leader? He wasn't sure, but she had a worrying gleam in her eyes. "Ho ho, if it isn't the ugly little kitten's sissy brother."

Ouch. Maxwell glared at the girl, only to hear footsteps behind him. He glanced back, just in time for the door to swing open. He was surrounded.

He glanced sidelong toward the boys 'dorm then over to the empty front desk before turning back toward the girl in front of him. Her arms were crossed in front of her chest, as she appraised him.

Maxwell didn't hesitate, it would be foolish to stay here. He hurried toward the stairwell, only for an alarmed sound to escape as someone grabbed his arm in a rough grip and tugged him backward. He stumbled, finding himself being dragged through the dining room door. The hand let go and he fell back with a cry. His backside smarted as he looked up, seeing all the girls standing above him with one boy stepping away, off to the side, looking a little uncomfortable. Was he the one who grabbed Maxwell?

"Well, girls? What do you want to do? After all, the ugly little kitten should be here soon. We want to make sure she sees her poor brother humiliated, after all."

"What's with this long hair? You trying to look like your sister?"

Maxwell cringed as he was tugged by his arm across the wooden floor. He tried to struggle, pulling at the arms holding him, yet, even though he knew they were affected with the disease, they seemed to hold on with a death grip.

"Oh. Let's do that. Dress him up, cute little dress and all."

One of the girls off to the side giggled.

The main girl who'd spotted him outside rolled her eyes. She turned to Maxwell, who found himself in the same corner he'd spotted the girls conversing in. He slowly pushed himself to his feet, using the wall as support and watching them warily.

One of the girls stepped forward and leaned close to Maxwell, grinning widely. "You know, it's a good thing you're a guy."

Huh?

"Because we don't have to worry about any repercussions. After all, aren't you supposed to be the big bad man? The one who hurt us? You try to go to the police, guess who's going to be the one in trouble?"

Maxwell gritted his teeth. He didn't need this girl to remind him of his and Kari's predicament. "What do you want?" he growled, his eyes scanning the room to see if there was a way to escape.

It was true, though, if he actually tried to fight his way out, it would be their word against his, and there were no cameras in the dining room.

"I already told you, we're going to humiliate you in front of that prissy sister of yours, should shut her down a bit, wouldn't you say?"

Without preamble, he found himself stuffed in the corner, shoulders digging into the wall as the girl, probably Abby if he recalled the name correctly, stepped closer and pulled something from behind her back.

"Maxwell!"

A sharp startled voice rang out as the door opened. Maxwell looked over Abby's shoulder to see Karina standing in the doorway, another girl behind her. Karina must have spotted something in Abby's hand that Maxwell couldn't quite see, because she paled before darting forward.

"No. Let him go!"

Maxwell glanced down to the item Karina's eyes were on and felt the color drain from his face. *That was…*

A flash of Karina's scared expression as she told him her nightmare was enough to send his heart racing. The silver gleam of a pair of scissors shone in the weak light of the dining room. It wasn't a knife no, but in some ways, it was worse.

Using his position, he pushed off from the wall, aiming for his sister, he didn't care who he hurt, he had to get away. He felt hands grab his arms just as the boy grabbed Karina around the waist, tugging her back. She struggled, wrenching at the arms and kicking at his shins, but the boy was taller than her. She went to shout when one of the girls stepped forward and slapped something over her mouth.

Maxwell went to shout as well when he felt a rough hand cover his mouth with what felt like cloth.

Fear didn't so much trickle through him as pound through his veins. His heart beat loudly in his ears as he found himself dragged back into the corner. Karina's agonized gaze caught his from across the room. Two girls held her arms while the boy kept a firm grip around her waist.

He saw the girl with Karina step back out of the dining room and wondered what exactly she was doing. *A lookout? Maybe.* His thoughts were pulled from that when Abby stepped forward once more, unamused. He could feel two girls holding him down and could already feel the fatigue from his continued struggling.

"Well, now that everyone is in attendance." The girl's voice was cold as she glanced at Karina. "This is a little present to you from us." She sent Maxwell a parting glance before sifting through the small crowd of girls to Karina.

Karina had a cloth gag in her mouth which Maxwell could see she was trying to spit out. She stopped when Abby stepped close, slipping the scissors under her chin.

"How dare an ugly wench like you remain healthy. How dare you suffocate us with your presence."

Maxwell could see Karina stiffen as the girl leaned forward and said something soft enough even he couldn't hear. He glanced sidelong at the door before looking toward Karina. He couldn't just leave her there. He glanced down at the hands around his wrists.

He calculated the distance to his sister, the distance to the door and the crowd. He would barely have any chance, especially with that girl standing so close to her with a weapon.

He couldn't handle seeing Karina hurt like that.

He could see his sister's face become stark white and he could see her trembling as Abby turned around. Her struggles became reinforced and Maxwell could almost see the three holding her gritting their teeth. The boy's eyes flashed as his hand dipped and Karina stilled, horror shining on her face as she glanced over her shoulder. Maxwell stiffened. *Wait, that guy...*

He went to pull away, to reach toward his sister to get her away from that boy, when he felt something sharp dig into the side of his neck. He froze, glancing sidelong to see one of the girls holding him held a second pair of scissors. *Where the heck did they get all these scissors? Was there a knife shortage or something?* He quickly shut that thought down, focusing more on the impending problem and less on his semihysterical mind. He noted that the scissors were open, one blade pushing close to his throat. Footsteps drew his attention back to Abby, who stopped in front of him. "Now, shall we begin?"

Cold shot through his veins as Abby grabbed his wrist and wrenched him around. He cried out as his arm was bent behind him at an awkward angle. The scissors at his throat shifted away as that girl let go. He felt the peeling paint of the wall dig into his cheek as he was pressed forward. He tugged at the arm, trying to kick out, but he grew off balance. Abby kicked his legs out, causing him to crumble onto his knees. He couldn't hold back the wince, but at least the pressure on his throat disappeared. He felt a hand grab his hair. The hand not held in a tight grip shot up, trying to reach for the tugging fingers. It hurt! He heard a chuckle as he tried to see out of the corner of his eyes. He heard movement and then the thin snip of scissors. Snip, snip, snip. *How could...?*

His cheeks flushed red as he realized what was happening, how could he let this happen? Brown locks trailed around his face, hitting the ground in spools. His hands twitched, and he found himself shivering, the other hand caught in a death grip that almost made him want to whimper.

He faintly heard a commotion despite his ringing ears and heard the sound of the scissors stopping. There was a hum of confusion before the door was shoved open.

Maxwell glanced sidelong toward the door, barely able to turn his head with the sharp grip on his hair. He heard the sound of anger from the doorway as Lex stepped in, dragging the guard girl. Lex took one look at the scene before he glared at Abby, his free hand reaching toward where Maxwell suspected Lex's knives were. "That is enough, let them go."

Abby glowered at Lex before suddenly letting go of Maxwell's hair and arm. *So it had been another girl cutting his hair,* the thought flickered through his mind for only a moment. Not expecting the sudden release, Maxwell found himself landing on the floor, hands protecting his head. He pulled out the gag with a trembling hand, unable to see what was going on behind him.

He pushed himself up and looked behind him to see Lex pull Karina away. Maxwell couldn't see her face, but she was trembling hard, almost worse than he was. The boy holding her was on the ground, holding his head.

Maxwell wasn't sure who hit him, but Lex looked absolutely livid, so it wasn't too hard to guess. It was then Maxwell noticed the silver sheen in Lex's hand, the familiar knife he always had on him. Maxwell reached toward the wall and struggled to his feet. He wasn't necessarily hurt, just a little battered and bruised. He could, however, feel that the shock was catching up to him. No matter what he did, the trembling wouldn't go away. Abby gave him one last haughty look before shrugging and slipping out the door, followed by the rest of the girls. Lex watched them go, holding Karina back tightly.

Maxwell wasn't sure, but he had a feeling his sister was ready to about massacre everyone here. He watched them go before hurrying toward his sister, worry clouding his mind. He knew he should be more worried about himself, but…

Lex held up a hand, stopping Maxwell in his tracks. Maxwell looked at him, and it was only then that he could feel wetness in the corner of his eyes. He glanced away, feet trailing to a stop.

"We should get going, I would say grab your stuff, but I'll come back to pick it up later."

Maxwell found himself nodding as his gaze stayed strictly on his sister, who still wouldn't look his way, even now that it was over.

~ * ~

Lex heaved a heavy sigh. He had been afraid of something like this happening. It was just lucky one of the leads he'd been following had one too many drinks and mentioned about this little ambush.

He didn't remember moving that fast in a while. He glanced toward Maxwell, seeing the tears on the boy's cheeks as worry clouded his eyes. Bruises were already forming around his wrists and a thin trail of blood slipped down his neck from when the scissors must have dug too close. His hair looked like, well, Lex didn't think he needed to describe it. His attention drifted toward Karina. Her gaze was distant, the trembling still not having disappeared even as he led her out the door.

Out of the corner of his eyes, he could only see the boy, left dazed and alone in the room. He was almost amused to know Maxwell decided to ignore the boy entirely, considering the situation. Then again, Maxwell was more focused on his sister, so it was understandable. Lex turned and continued down the street. Maxwell stayed close to Karina, hands unsure what to do as they flitted around her frame.

After some walking, Lex could see a bit of something returning to the girl, as if the shock finally slipped away. She shook her head and then looked around before spotting Maxwell.

Tears. There were tears in her eyes, something he never expected to see from her. Maxwell was stunned, surprised as Karina suddenly pushed away from Lex and hurried up to him. Lex trailed to a halt, waiting as Karina checked her brother over. Her hands were shaking as she reached for his neck, arms and finally touched his head, pulling his head down as he let out a squawk of surprise. She examined him as thoroughly as possible before finally dropping her hands and darting forward, pulling her sibling into a tight hug. Maxwell stiffened before he let out a sigh and gave a tight hug in return.

"I'm fine." His whispered words seemed to catch Karina's attention because, after a moment, she pulled back, wiping at her eyes.

Her normal cheeky grin was back, even if weakened. "I know."

Lex let out a sigh. *These two were way too strong.* He gently placed his hands on their backs, feeling the remnants of trembling before he pushed them forward. "Come on, let's go. You two probably are looking forward to seeing the new place." Maxwell and Karina glanced at him and nodded.

Lex withheld the sigh of relief that threatened to escape. He was glad he got there when he did. He honestly hadn't expected to already have to pull them out of something. He was glad the girls didn't decide to go farther. He knew they could have and would have done much worse. There was definitely a reason why that boy was there, and it was abhorrent to think about. His mind quickly dismissed the words spoken by the girl he'd talked with who ended up mentioning about the ambush. He was not going to let his thoughts go down that route. He almost had to congratulate the girls on their cruelty, if they had actually followed all the way through with their initial plan, he doubted Karina and Maxwell would have come out unscathed. He was just glad they let him take Maxwell and Karina out of there. They must have gotten what they were after, either that, or they weren't in the mood to put up a fight with someone who very well could defend themselves. He glanced sidelong toward Karina.

As much as he could tell, Karina was keeping up appearances. He wondered just how badly this must have affected her and her brother. After all, the girl had been forced to watch, unable to really do anything.

The trip to the apartment was quiet, neither Karina nor Maxwell wanting to talk. Lex couldn't blame them. Thankfully, before too long, they arrived at the street he'd found the other day. He saw the young boy outside, clearing the driveway. The boy looked up and almost instantly, his gaze zoomed in on the twins. His eyes widened, and he hurried forward. "Whoa, what happened?"

Lex winced. Not really subtle, he'd been hoping they could get to the apartment first. The boy must have noticed because he backed off. "I would invite you guys in, but Mom's not home."

"Don't worry…"

"Oh, you must have gotten that room then." The boy examined them briefly before he hurried ahead. "Let me talk to Emma, she'll probably have something to fix them up." Lex watched him go.

"Who?" Maxwell asked, his voice quiet.

Lex glanced at him before responding. "A local. I believe his name is Arik, he's the one who helped me find this apartment, now come on."

He led the way toward the apartment complex, spotting the door as it swung shut. He chuckled weakly and hurried toward the doorway, being careful not to drag the twins. He slipped through the doorway and dropped his hands. The twins, who he noted were holding hands, stared at the room in slight awe. The downstairs was a cozy little place with a fireplace humming happily at one side. A brown desk sat on the other side with a little note on it saying that the landlady was out. Lex trailed up the stairs, followed by the twins. It didn't take long to come across the right hallway, as evidenced by the sounds of talking. He opened the door to their hall as the voices quieted. He could see Arik talking to a young girl with loose twin braids and darker skin. He vaguely remembered meeting her once. Her eyes shifted to the twins before widening. She turned to Arik, nodded, and slipped back into her room. Arik glanced at them. "Well, she said she would help. Might as well go to your room."

Lex nodded and led the twins toward a room across the hall. He slipped the key out of his pocket and opened the door, letting them in. He'd have done this sooner, but the last residents only just left that morning. He saw their eyes widen before Maxwell hurried in, Karina only a step behind him. Lex watched them take in the room as he turned to Arik. "Thank you. I'll take it from here."

"What happened?" Arik's eyes were cold, his voice soft. "They looked like they were attacked, was it…"

"Some people at the hostel. I don't think your father will be able to do anything."

Arik clicked his tongue, aggravation clear on his face. "Damn. Well, if it happens again, let me know, I know Dad should be able to do something if it's a repeat thing."

"I'm not too worried about that but thank you."

Arik nodded, his face neutral instead of the grin he was sporting as he talked with Emma. "If you say so. I'm heading home. Once they're settled in, let me know, I would like to speak with them myself."

Lex nodded as Arik slipped past him and out the door. He glanced over his shoulder before turning toward the room. Well, time to deal with what happened…

He was not looking forward to it.

He stepped inside to see the twins wandering around the place. They checked the two bedrooms on either side, the kitchen and dining room then returned to the living room entranceway.

He took a seat on one of the two couches and leaned back, legs crossed and waiting. They seemed to slowly get the hint, Maxwell a bit earlier then his sister. He tugged her just enough for her to glance over and realization dawned on her.

"So, you wanted to talk?"

Lex nodded, keeping his posture neutral. They both took a tentative seat on the other couch, still holding hands. His gaze flickered to their hands before he looked at each of them. "I'll start off." He closed his eyes and let out a long breath, organizing his thoughts. He needed to figure out how to make sure they calmed down. He opened his eyes, staring directly at Maxwell, knowing the boy would be able to tell his sincerity with the next words. "I'm sorry."

Those two words seemed to shock the twins, but he wasn't surprised. He pushed a hand through his hair using the ensuing silence to explain. "I'd been following leads on those girls since Karina mentioned them in hopes to find out what they did with the money. However, by the time I'd started searching, they'd dispersed it all amongst other people and groups that, to put it simply, are not so savory."

He couldn't help the flicker of disgust as he thought of one of the locations he'd found in his search. He wasn't averse to most of those places, but he may have let something slip to the police about that one, considering the chain marks and bodily fluids that permeated the place.

He pulled from that thought, shaking his head and turning his gaze back on them. "I'd planned to meet with one of the leads earlier, but she'd convinced me to wait until today due to circumstances. Of course, once I met with her, I figured out why." He shook his head, feeling a little disgruntled at having been played like that. "If..." he paused, well, he was explaining, so might as well continue. "If I hadn't gotten her drunk enough to spill, she probably would have made sure I was with her the whole time and you can imagine how that would have gone." His gaze flickered to Karina, who stiffened.

"Wait, did she tell you what they were going to do to us?" Maxwell's voice came out quiet as his hands clenched in his lap.

Karina sat up straighter, horror slowing dawning on her face.

Lex nodded. "Though I do not think you want to know, you have enough to deal with as is."

Maxwell shivered, but nodded in agreement. Lex sighed and pushed himself to his feet. "I know you two, idiots though you are sometimes, you two aren't dumb enough to let this bother you for long." He glanced toward Karina who looked up, her expression shifting slightly, and Lex couldn't hold back the small grin from flitting over his lips. "So, I figured I might as well let you two know that we all had some unfortunate hand in what happened, and now that we know, we can move on, right?"

"Right," Karina said as Maxwell pursed his lips but nodded anyway.

Lex slid a hand through his hair leaning on one foot as he let out a breath. That went a bit better than he thought, at least they didn't argue with his assessment. He dropped his hand and looked at them sternly. "Now, I'm going to head back to the hostel. The people who lived here just left, so I don't think there is anything in the fridge, but there is someone coming over soon who will help you settle in if I'm not back yet, understood?"

"Yeah." Maxwell's smile lifted Lex's spirits a little, reminding him, once again, why he was impressed by these two. His smile dropped slightly in worry as a thought seemed to cross his mind. "Lex, how are you going to get our bags? Karina's isn't exactly…" he trailed off.

Lex looked at him quietly before letting out a soft huff. "No need to worry. All right?" he opened the doorway and glanced back. "Shouldn't be long. I'll be back soon." With that, he slipped out the door and walked down the hallway, toward the stairwell. He needed to collect all of their things and collect some necessities, so that they could live there. Toilet paper, food, the list went on in his head as he hurried toward the hostel with a firm pace, not breaking from his even stride one bit.

~ * ~

Karina hadn't realized they'd clasped hands until now, as Lex left the room, but she was fine with it, thoughts swirling without going anywhere. Her brother must have sensed her worry, because he glanced over, green eyes shining as he squeezed her hand, not wanting to let go either. His brown hair fell haphazardly around his face, differing levels of strands catching her attention. Why did her dream have to happen? Why did she have to tell her brother? Why did Lex have to tell them?

No, she was glad their friend had been willing to tell them that he'd basically screwed up. At least he was honest, and, in that moment, she appreciated the honesty.

Those girls. She hated them, for deceiving Lex, for hurting her brother, for... Why did they do such a thing when Maxwell hadn't done a thing to them?

"It's your fault, you know. If you hadn't started this, then no one would have gotten hurt." The girl's voice rang in her head, piercing and haughty.

It's not my fault. Karina shook her head viciously. *It's those stupid girls' fault, for hurting her brother, for doing this all of this… for stopping her from helping him.*

She felt another sharp squeeze and glanced over to see her brother leaning closer to her, clearly concerned. She didn't want to see that, why was he so concerned over her instead of himself? He'd grown.

She squeezed back, forcing a weak smile on her face. He hesitated, uncertainty causing him to lightly bite his lip as he gazed over her. "Maxwell, I'm fine. Now why don't you go get cleaned up?"

They really just got a quick preview of their new home before sitting on the couch to rest and speak with Lex. Karina was grateful for his help and for the place he managed to get them.

Karina figured there were probably two bedrooms in this place, from what she was able to see, with bathrooms attached to each. Part of her hoped that Maxwell would be willing to stay with her tonight. She felt awkward though, hoping for something like that. Though, if he got too annoying later in the week, she could kick him onto the couch. The thought sent a weak chuckle through her, catching Maxwell's attention.

"Hey, Kari?"

Karina glanced over, watching him fidget under her look before he let out a breath and faced her. "I just wanted to say. I'm sorry."

Karina stiffened as Maxwell glanced away.

"I know I should have fought back more, but when I saw they captured you, well, I panicked and found myself unable to do anything."

He let out a sigh as Karina felt her stomach flip. *Why was her brother...? Why was Maxwell apologizing just like Lex? Why were they both apologizing for something they didn't do?* " I know you can take care of yourself, but I couldn't help but worry, after all, that boy was right there."

Karina shivered, remembering that touch. It hadn't gone too far, but even she could feel the intent was there. She was suddenly grateful for Maxwell's decision, even as she hated herself for thinking that.

After all, what would that boy have done? What was it that Lex heard? His expression was so filled with disgust that she found her tongue stuck to her mouth and throat dry. For once, she didn't want to know. After all, she wouldn't have been able to get away with all those girls there. The thought made her shake and she felt her free hand drift toward her arm that held her brother's, gripping it tightly as if to ward something off. She could tell her brother had been thinking the same thing. His bit lip was almost bleeding with how tense he was. Her hand hurt from the tight grip, but she didn't pull away.

She let out a breath. This wasn't getting anywhere. As much as she wanted to berate her brother for apologizing for something he didn't do, or to discuss Lex's words, she couldn't find it in herself to care. She stood up, letting go of Maxwell's hand. Maxwell started, looking up at her in surprise. She grinned, this one a bit more genuine to ease his worries. She reached up to his hair, hesitant. She knew they needed to get it fixed, but she was almost afraid to cut it. She shook herself from that thought. "Let's fix that hair of yours."

He blinked, then reached up, tugging at a strand that trailed into his face. The only thing that seemed to remain was that clip she'd gotten him. She knew it was probably seen as girly, so she was honestly surprised her brother kept it, and that those girls hadn't cut it out, especially since, in her opinion, it suited him. She tugged her brother up, only to jump when she heard a light knock on the door. She felt her brother stiffen beside her as she hesitantly stepped toward the doorway. Lex mentioned someone coming over, so could that be them?

She opened it to see the girl from across the hall. She seemed a little uneasy as she shifted before them. In one hand, she held a basket, neatly arranged, and in the other, a little box. "Hello, my name's Emma. I live with my friend Madeline a little down the hall. I was wondering if I could give you this." She reached forward with the basket which Maxwell took. He pulled part of the blanket up and then smiled broadly.

"Thanks."

The girl nodded, smiling in return as her posture relaxed. "Oh. I know this may seem weird, but I was wondering if you would be willing to let me fix you two up."

"What do you…?" Karina went to argue, but Maxwell cut her off.

"Thanks, we would appreciate it."

He sent Karina a look which she found annoying. It was that same look he had with Lex. She sometimes hated how her brother could trust some people and not others so easily. She almost wished she had that ability. Yes, Lex said to let her help, but she wasn't necessarily keen on the idea.

Karina stepped away, letting the girl in. The girl sent them both a grateful look before slipping inside. Karina closed the door as Maxwell walked past the little entrance living room into the kitchen. Two doorways on either side of the living room led to respective bedrooms with small bathrooms accordingly. The girl looked around and smiled. "Ah, it kind of looks like our place, though a lot cleaner, which makes sense." She turned to Karina. "Ah, sorry, I never caught your name."

"My name's Karina…" Karina trailed off as the girl nodded and stepped forward, looking her over.

"Karina, that's a pretty name. Anyway, why don't you sit down, and we can get you cleaned up?"

Emma took Karina's hand, surprising her enough so that Emma

could lead her onto one of the couches. Emma knelt on the floor, opening the box she brought with her. She pulled out some ointment and reached up toward Karina's face.

Karina winced as Emma touched the pad to her cheek. She hadn't even realized she got cut there. *It must have happened when she was struggling right before the guy*—she cut off that train of thought as she watched the girl work. Emma dabbed the ointment on then reached in, pulling out a Band-Aid before practically scanning her for any remaining injuries. After some time, she gently picked up Karina's wrists and examined them. "You don't look too bad. I don't think your wrists are sprained, which is good. You'll have a lot of bruising, but you should be okay."

"That's good."

Karina started, spotting her brother standing behind her. He must have slipped back in while she was paying attention to Emma, a cup of water in hand which he gave to Karina. He sent her a sheepish expression as Emma turned to him.

Emma gestured for him to sit down and he did, stepping around the couch and joining Karina. Karina scooted over to give him more room as she took a sip of the water. Maxwell sent her a grateful smile and then winced as Emma took his wrists and looked them over.

"Well, it looks like other than some bruising, and a light sprain that should heal in a few days, you should be fine too." She paused, examining them both. "I have a feeling that haircut wasn't paid for."

Karina grimaced as Maxwell shrunk backward. The girl let out a long breath and pushed herself to her feet, wiping away at her knees before turning to face them. "Do you mind if I clean it up?"

Karina stiffened along with her brother. What? She couldn't just let this girl do everything. She didn't like the idea of imposing on this girl anymore and she knew she could do it." No…"

"Karina," Maxwell spoke, catching her attention. "We both know it needs to get done, and wouldn't it be better to have someone else do it? I don't want you doing it."

Karina almost felt like she was slapped. Her brother seemed to realize what he said, and his eyes widened as he quickly went onto explain. "No, I mean, that's not what I meant! I meant that I don't want to force you to do it if you don't want to. I can see that you weren't thrilled with the idea, so…" he trailed off, flustered.

Karina couldn't help smiling as she chuckled quietly. "All right." She glanced over toward Emma, feeling her lips turn downward. "Listen, if he tells you to stop."

"Karina…"

"I will," Emma nodded, her serious expression cementing her words. Karina stood, patting herself down before helping Maxwell to his feet.

"So how do we do this?"

"We'll use the kitchen sink. There should be some nice-sized chairs in there for him to sit while we work, with a good amount of space as well."

They stepped into the kitchen and Maxwell, after pulling up one of the wooden chairs, tentatively took a seat.

Emma took the towel she'd used to cover the basket, which must have been a gift for them, and placed it around Maxwell's neck after making sure any loose hair was gone. Maxwell sat patiently, waiting, though Karina didn't miss the way his hand flicked back, reaching for her. She quickly grabbed it, taking a seat beside him after pulling up another chair and watched as the girl worked. Emma grabbed a comb from her kit and gently pulled it through Maxwell's messy hair as she turned to Karina. "Do you mind holding some things for me? It'll help it go faster."

Karina nodded, raising her free hand. The girl sent her a thankful expression. "Here, why don't you finish combing your brother's hair while I go grab a few things." With that, she slipped out the door. Karina watched her go before hesitantly letting go of her brother and reaching up.

Maxwell gripped the towel tightly, eyes staring out the window sitting over the sink. "Hey, Kari?"

Karina hummed softly as she trailed the comb through his hair, her fingers working to untangle the knots she found littered throughout. The fact that he wasn't arguing and was letting her do it said a lot. She was glad. She used this to calm herself. While the ragged ends were still bad, she could tell it wasn't as bad as she thought. She closed her eyes as she worked through the knots and smoothed his hair down enough to be cut.

"What now?"

Hm? Karina opened her eyes, finding herself confused. "What do you mean?"

Her comb stilled as Maxwell peered over his shoulder just enough to look at her. "I mean, what are we going to do now? We can't really go near the hostel at this rate. Lex must have spent most of his money and then some on this place and we have only just started. It's only been a week since we arrived in this city."

*Ah...*Karina furrowed her brow, biting her lip as she finished up with her brother's hair right as Emma returned, carrying more supplies. She let the question hang as Emma quickly got to work. Emma pinned up the longer pieces of hair and used the comb to measure out the lower pieces. Karina watched quietly, holding the supplies in her arms as she thought over what her brother said, keeping half an eye on Emma's work. What were they going to do now?

~ * ~

Lex padded down the street. The hostel stood in front of him. He looked it over in silence. He shook his head and stepped inside, opening the door with a creak. The matron looked up from her spot at the counter and nodded to him, a strange expression crossing her face for a brief moment. Damn, he wished she hadn't been here. It would have made things easier. He briefly looked into the dining room to see the boy was gone. It seemed to have been cleaned and swept, a few people meandering about. He pulled away and headed to his and Maxwell's room. It was easy enough to get his things, but Maxwell's were a bit harder. He looked around the room, glad to see it was empty, and squatted down, swinging his backpack off his back. He reached inside, pulling out a paper clip and a flat head screwdriver. With quick work, he heard the click of the lock. He never thought he would use this skill again, but lo and behold, he still found it useful. He couldn't even remember when he'd learned it. Whether he was still home, or after he left Allen's place for the last time. He wasn't sure. It was a handy skill either way. He reached inside and pulled out Maxwell's stuff, not even bothering to lock it back up. He walked down the stairs and looked toward the girl's hall before walking up to the Matron.

She looked up and placed the reading material down. "Ah, it's good to see you."

"Hello, ma'am. I was wondering if I can ask a favor."

He saw no reason in bringing up the attack. He doubted the Matron could actually do anything, considering how many people were involved and he didn't necessarily have proof, it was their word against a whole group. He knew that would get them nowhere.

"Favor?" The Matron sat up slightly and fully turned to him. "What would you need?"

"The girl who came with me, she left her stuff here and I came to pick it up. May I ask for assistance retrieving it?"

"She can't come herself?" The Matron narrowed her eyes.

Lex smiled gently. "No, something came up and she needed to return home. So, may I reclaim it?"

The matron looked him over, eyes scrutinizing. He frowned, spotting the hints of a burgeoning wound over her eyes. That wouldn't be good in the next few months.

"All right, I'll come with you."

Lex nodded and walked up the stairs, following the Matron. He ignored the occasional eye sent his way, noting that none of them were the girls that were involved in the ambush. It didn't take long to get to Karina's room, where he found her things locked away in the little cubby underneath the beds. The Matron looked at the lock before turning to him. "Wait right here, I will be back with the key." She gave him a stern look, then hurried downstairs. Lex looked around, spotting a few girls glance in his direction, uncertain.

They didn't seem too bad, mostly leaving him alone, since he was with the Matron. He leaned on one foot, tapping it gently against the floor. He was glad, as he looked over the room, that he got the twins out of here and into a new building. As expensive as it was, it was worth it. He noticed the door was wide open when he spotted a couple girls from before walking past. They noticed him and glared, talking amongst themselves, but they didn't do anything. Part of him was curious, but the other part didn't particularly care. He didn't have any reason to worry about those girls anymore, and the area the twins were in had no connection to the areas he'd found while investigating them. He was leaving soon anyway.

The Matron returned not long after that, key in hand. She unlocked it and handed Lex the bags. "You do know that I keep all payments, even days that aren't used, correct?"

"I am well aware of that, ma'am. You may keep the money."

The woman nodded and then gestured for him to come downstairs. He was all too happy to leave, not even giving the hostel a parting glance as he hefted the bags over his shoulder.

~ * ~

It was a while later when Karina heard what sounded like Lex returning, his boots clopping over the wood entranceway. Emma was almost done, finishing up the last strands that fell around Maxwell's face.

It was cut short around his face to make it a bit more even with the sections that had been wrenched out, though the back was slightly shorter still to clean up the worst of the damage. In the end he still ended up having a few bangs on either side of his face. Thankfully, the clip Karina got him still sat in his hair, to his insistence for some reason, pulling the leftover bangs from his face. The sound of the kitchen door opening caught Karina's attention. She looked over to see Lex enter the kitchen. She sent him a quick nod as Emma pulled away, laying down her equipment and wiping her brow. "All set."

Maxwell turned around, tentatively reaching one hand up. He smiled. "Thanks, Emma."

The girl beamed and shook her head. "It's no problem. It looked like you needed the help."

"Plus, Arik helped convince you, too." Lex's quip sounded more amused than anything.

Emma blushed and waved it away. "Well, that too." She coughed into her hand before turning to Maxwell and Karina. "I've done all I can for now. Why don't you two rest up? I'll let the others know not to bother you until tomorrow, sound good?"

Karina nodded along with Maxwell, who was taking off the towel. Emma quickly swept it up and nodded to them. "I'll see you tomorrow."

With that, she hurried out the door. Lex watched her go before shaking his head. "What a cheerful girl."

He turned to Maxwell and Karina, presenting their bags to them. Karina's eyes widened, barely hearing when he said, "Are you two feeling better?"

Karina reached toward her bag, only then realizing she was no longer shaking, the fear that had been stuck in her since the attack finally disappeared. She would have to thank Emma for the change. "Yeah," she murmured as she opened her bag at the kitchen counter, digging through it.

Maxwell seemed to be in the same boat. Digging through his own things, he sent Lex a quick smile. "Yeah, thanks." He finished going through his things and let out a yawn. "Why don't we get some sleep?"

"Sounds like a plan." Karina pulled away from her bag, glad to see everything was still in it and hurried to their room. She was grateful to find a queen-sized bed, with enough room for both of them.

She walked over and took a seat. Maxwell looked at her, then the bed, before letting out a sigh. "We just can't win, can we?"

"Nope." Karina chuckled at Maxwell's morose expression before she patted the bed. "That is, unless you want to sleep with Lex." Her voice trailed off, partly hoping her brother would deny it. She wasn't completely opposed to having her own room, but not right now.

Her brother stared at her for a bit. She leaned forward. "Hey, at least it's comfortable, and there's more room here then at the hostel. Plus, everyone seems a lot friendlier here."

"True," Maxwell sighed as he took a seat, surprisingly enough beside her.

Karina glanced sidelong at him before looking forward, feeling a relieved smile wash over her face.

"To answer your question." She felt Maxwell's gaze drift to her, but she continued to stare ahead. "I think the best thing for us to do is to find jobs. That way, we can help Lex take care of rent. I might try for a job at that café we found the other day." She glanced sidelong toward Maxwell. "After that, once we get a bit more settled, we can help Lex look for Mom."

"Hm…" Maxwell kicked his feet a bit before nodding. "I might try to get a job at that place, you know, the one we passed when we first arrived?"

"Are you nuts?" Karina shot up, turning to her brother, who looked up at her before shaking his head.

"No, I know it's crazy, but I think we should start from there. It would be best if we don't both work there. I could be wrong, and she might not be there, but it's worth a shot. Plus, I'm just going to apply, it doesn't necessarily mean I'll get in." He waged a finger at her. "Either way, we have to do something. While finding a job is great and all, we also have to look for Ma." He trailed off before letting his hand drop. "I get that it's probably very stupid to think of doing this, but what options do we have? We can't just transfer jobs halfway through. No employer would accept that."

True, she knew well enough from Martha's talks how difficult it was to get a job. Maxwell's assessment was accurate. Plus, the likelihood of him getting in was low, so why not take the risk now? When he's still new to the area than when the people there might be more wary of him?

She let out a sigh and Maxwell grinned, having probably realized what that meant. "Thanks, Karina."

"Don't thank me yet. If this doesn't work out, I'll bring you back myself to deal with you," Karina quipped, unable to hide the grin from forming on her face as she gently nudged her brother.

Maxwell chuckled before standing up. "Come on, let's get some sleep."

"Sounds good to me." Karina let out a yawn, glancing toward the window. It was getting dark out. It was probably still early, but…

She quickly got changed and slipped under the covers, stuffing as much of the bedding between them as she could, too tired to find some pillows from the other rooms. She would find a way to rearrange them tomorrow.

She hoped the nightmares would stay at bay with her brother's presence. At least for tonight.

Chapter Nine

Maxwell awoke to a comforting presence. He opened his eyes, realizing, as his brain took a moment to slowly process it, that his sister was curled toward him, her hands close to his chest and head bent forward almost on top of the pillow somehow still between them. It was something very different, but very much still her. She looked surprisingly peaceful.

Maxwell couldn't help but chuckle before carefully extracting himself from his sister's grip. Admittedly, he was thankful they were sharing a room last night. He knew his sister joked about him joining Lex. He thought about it, but he also knew both of them really just wanted to be together after what happened. He couldn't leave his sister alone. He had a feeling both of them would have had a restless night if apart. He reached a hand up to the clip in his hair. Yes, it was girly, but he kept it as a memento. His sister gave it to him and it was one of the few things that came out undamaged after the attack. He might get rid of it later, but for now, he didn't feel he had a reason to. Plus, it didn't particularly stand out, considering his sister was at least considerate enough to find one close to his hair color. Just because it was girly didn't make him less of a man. He thought he pulled it off pretty darn well.

He dropped his hand to his side, and slipped out of bed, arms reaching for the ceiling. It was rare for him to be up before his sister, though lately, it was becoming more and more common. He let out a sigh at the thought and, letting his sister sleep, slipped out the door. He could smell something faintly coming from the kitchen and glanced over to see Lex was making breakfast. It was just eggs and toast. He hadn't eaten much yesterday and food sounded great. He reached a hand up, feeling at the tips of his hair, barely trailing into his face, thanks to the clip. It felt weird. The last time he had it this short, Dad was still around. The thought sent a pang through him and he shook his head. "Hey, Lex, you're cooking?"

Lex glanced over his shoulder at the sound of Maxwell slipping through the door. He nodded, turning back to the food as he whisked the egg. "It's a simple enough dish. Luckily, there were some food goods in that basket Emma gave us."

Maxwell chuckled, remembering. The wide assortment of foods and the other items surprised and delighted him. He'd even spotted an orange in there. He was just glad his sister was willing to let her in. He understood his sister's wariness, but sometimes he couldn't shake the feeling that it was more paranoia than anything. He sighed and pulled himself from that thought as he dug into the fridge. The kitchen wasn't a large area, but it could comfortably deal with two people with a little room to spare. Windows let in the morning light. The sky was overcast, spattering everything in a grayish tinge.

"So, Lex, what are you going to do now?" he asked as he pulled out the orange and started to peel it.

Lex slid the eggs onto a plate with the toast and slipped the pan into the sink, letting the water run before turning to him. "I still have some things to take care of. I only made the payment for a month even though I was supposed to put a six-month lease on it." Lex rubbed a hand through his hair, turning the water off. "Beyond that, well—"

"Actually…" Maxwell spoke up, catching Lex off-guard.

Lex glanced at him, dropping his hand to his side.

Maxwell threw the peel away before turning back to him. "Karina and I decided we were going to get jobs." Lex appeared hesitant but gestured for him to continue. "Sis is going to the café nearby and I'm…" He bit his lip, before nibbling on one of the juicy slices. He was still a bit uncertain, especially with how much Kari argued against it, but… "I'm going to apply for a job at the corporation connected to the gated community."

Lex's eyes widened. Lex opened his mouth, probably to argue then looked away. A hand drifted to his face and he slowly shook his head, muttering something under his breath before turning back to Maxwell. "I'm guessing your sister wasn't too keen on that idea?"

Maxwell winced, and Lex leaned back, hands holding onto the edge of the counter as he stared up at the ceiling. "I can understand what you're doing. The only thing I can say is, give it some time. Collect more information before diving right in. Karina has a good idea to get a job right away, even if it's not much." He looked down at Maxwell. "However, I won't argue with your decision. After all, I was thinking along those same lines."

Maxwell blinked. Lex was thinking of doing the same thing? But...

Lex held up his hand before continuing. "However, since it is a two-way corporation, I planned to do some research first and then..." he seemed hesitant to say the rest, his hand drifting up to his chest, where he seemed to grip something through his shirt tightly.

Maxwell briefly wondered what it was but pushed the thought away when Lex dropped his hand. "I was thinking of going into the gated community."

"What!"

Maxwell jumped and looked over to see Karina standing in the doorway. Her arms were lax, her eyes wide. "Kari..."

Karina pursed her lips before looking toward Lex. "You're being as reckless as ever. It's stupid. Didn't you just get out of the gated community? Are you really willing to go back in?" Karina leaned on one leg, looking affronted. "You know what? I don't even know why I'm bothering."

Maxwell winced, understanding where his sister was going with that. He'd wanted to argue with Lex's decision as well, but he did understand why Lex was doing such a thing. He shook his head and turned back to Lex. "There you have it." He shrugged. "Though, we can't really say anything either. We're all restless, especially...m—" He cut himself off. "We're supposed to be meeting the neighbors today, right?"

The switch in topic caught both Karina and Lex off guard. Karina turned back from her perusal of the cabinets, probably in search of a cup, while Lex placed his fork down, where he'd been eating the eggs in silence. Lex chuckled, took another bite and placed his plate down. "Yes, so why don't you two finish grabbing something to eat and get changed. We'll finish this discussion later."

"All right," Karina muttered, having finally found a cup. She filled it with water and downed it like it was air.

Maxwell finished up his fruit, the taste not quite as good as he'd hoped, before he turned and headed toward their room. He wasn't sure what he was doing or how to feel. Part of him just wanted to forget what happened yesterday, partly for his sister's sake and partly for his own.

He was just glad neither of them was seriously hurt. He glanced over his shoulder toward the kitchen as he slipped into their shared room. He wondered how his sister must be feeling. Was she upset? With herself or with him? He knew how protective she was, and she was unable to do anything.

He shook his head vigorously. *His sister was strong, always had been. She would be fine.* He threw a grin on his face. Now, to focus on the next task. Meeting the neighbors and finding a new job.

Why did it sound like some corny sitcom Ma might watch when she had free time?

It was a few hours later when Maxwell heard a heavy knock on the front door, followed by multiple voices. He trailed up to it. Lex was still around, contacting people via phone. Right now, he was probably talking to his uncle, Maxwell wasn't sure. Karina was in the kitchen, trying to set things up so they were easier to reach. He had been busy organizing the entrance room so that it fit a bit better for him and his sister as well as Lex. The furniture had originally been just placed willy-nilly.

He opened the door to be met with two familiar faces and four unfamiliar. He jumped back as Arik grinned, pushing at the door.

"Arik?" Emma stammered, hurrying after the energetic boy. Arik waved, quickly apologizing for his intrusion.

Maxwell couldn't help but shake his head before pulling the door the rest of the way open. Emma sent him a grateful smile and, the next thing he knew, the whole group was piled into their main room.

He was glad he moved the couches around.

He closed the door and took a seat right as Karina slipped into the room, probably startled by how many people were there. He heard the sound of the door and looked over to see Lex flip his phone closed, glancing over the group. A short smirk splayed across his face before he stepped forward and took a seat.

"Sorry for the intrusion," one boy muttered. His short black hair was tinged red and spectacles sat perilously on his nose, causing him to push them up with his finger, only for them to slide back down, exposing slim eyes.

Another boy with brown hair and an eager smile sent Maxwell a sheepish grin. "Arik is a bit spontaneous, but thanks for having us anyway. My name's Mitchell, by the way. The boy who just spoke is named Leon, and it's amazing that he said anything, actually."

Leon sent Mitchell a glare, causing the boy to rub the back of his neck in an apologetic gesture. The third boy rolled his eyes and huffed. "The name's Andrew. Pleasure." His voice was curt even as a smirk slid onto his face. His hair seemed almost as dark as his tone, matching with his clothes which seemed to fit him to a tee.

Maxwell turned to the last girl, who hadn't spoken yet. She had brown curly hair and an uncomfortable expression on her face as she stared at him. The others seemed to realize her silence as varying expressions flashed across their faces. Mitchell looked surprised, Leon's expression drew into a small smirk, Emma looked happy, if the wide grin and nudging elbow were any indication and Andrew seemed annoyed, his arms crossing over his chest.

The girl quickly shook her head and reached her hand forward. "My name's Madeline. It's a pleasure to meet you. You're really cu—I mean. Nice place you have."

Maxwell hadn't missed what she'd almost said, and it seemed his sister hadn't either as a cat-like grin grew on her face, barely hidden by the hand that sat over her lips. Her eyes gleamed as she stepped forward. "Thanks," she chirped as Maxwell coughed into his hand, pushing away the feeling of a blush forming on his cheeks. *Why did girls seem to want to call him cute?*

The girl deeply blushed, stiffening before looking away. "Uh, sorry, I'm not good with meeting new people."

"Liar," Leon muttered. Madeline glared toward Leon as Mitchell chuckled and Emma rolled her eyes.

Emma turned to Maxwell and Karina, examining them quietly before nodding. "You two look better, that's good. So, why don't you introduce yourselves?"

Maxwell couldn't stop his hand from slapping his face, only to let it trail down with a sigh. "Oh, right. My name is Maxwell, this is my sis, Karina. The silent one over there is our friend, Lex."

Lex's expression swiftly shifted to unamused before he let out a sigh. "Don't mind me, just continue with your conversation."

"Really?" Karina eyed him.

He shrugged, "Honestly, I don't have anything to say at this point, you already pointed out everything I needed to do, but either way, it's good to meet you all again."

Maxwell watched them all look back and forth before Arik grinned. "Yep, sounds about right, now, where were we?"

Karina waved, still holding that cheeky grin. "Oh yeah, something about my cute little brother? Don't mind him. He's still getting used to—"

"Karina," Maxwell quickly said, glaring at her. *Ugh, she is being so annoying right now and I see that smirk, Lex.*

Karina stuck her tongue out playfully before returning to a more neutral expression and facing the group. "Seriously though, it is a pleasure to meet you all."

Madeline glanced between them, squinting her eyes and frowning. "You said little brother, but you two look like you're the same age?"

"We're twins," Maxwell found himself saying at the same time as his sister. That hadn't happened in a while.

Emma chuckled. "That explains a lot. You two are very close. Anyway, we brought some stuff as welcome gifts."

More stuff? Maxwell couldn't hide the surprise from flitting across his face. Emma already gave them quite a lot.

Madeline seemed to snap out of whatever daze she was in, because she coughed into her close-fisted hand and reached behind her.

Now that he thought about it, he remembered seeing the edges of a wicker basket when she walked in.

She pulled it out, placing the basket on the coffee table, set in the middle of the group. It was a large basket, much bigger than the one Emma gave them yesterday. He and Karina exchanged looks before reaching forward. Inside were all sorts of things: food, cooking equipment and even a few drinks like soda and juice.

"Sorry it's not much, but we figured a nice gift from all of us would make you feel more welcome. It's been a while since we've had a new face around here." Madeline's eyes were soft as she put her hands together, face shining.

"Thanks." Maxwell felt himself perk up, unable to hide his grateful expression. Karina's doing the same. Lex seemed amused, legs crossed and relaxed. That was rare to see from their friend.

"See, I told you they would like it." Emma nudged Madeline while Mitchell laughed.

"Precisely." Leon pushed his glasses up once more, and tilted his head, amused. Andrew just sighed, dropping his crossed arms and shrugging.

Arik, who had been mostly quiet up till this point, leaned forward, a curious expression on his face. "By the way, if I may be so rude to ask, what happened to you two yesterday?"

Maxwell stiffened along with Karina. Lex frowned, eyes narrowed, as if he was going to say something.

"Arik," Emma snapped, beating him to it and looking highly affronted.

"No, it's no problem." Maxwell sighed, waving it off. Though he winced slightly when he realized he used his bad hand. Right, it was still lightly sprained. He had to remember that. Karina looked away, arms crossing over her chest. He took a deep breath, centering himself before he began. "Some girls at the hostel had a bit of a vendetta against my sister and, as a result, I kind of ended up involved. They attacked us without warning." He shrugged. "It's over now, though. Nothing really happened, so it's nothing really to worry about."

Karina pursed her lips, but didn't argue, which Maxwell was grateful for. He wasn't sure he would be able to argue back.

Leon was watching with a curious look as Mitchell turned away. Madeline seemed uncertain of where to look and Emma's gaze avoided theirs, her fingers gripping her skirt tightly.

"Ah, I see." Arik's voice was soft, before he perked up. "Anyway, enough about that, let's have a party. I say we do Madeline's place."

"What?" Madeline yelped as the others laughed.

"You two are, of course, invited. Drinks and food on us."

"That's not what I said," Madeline cried as she hurriedly stood up and raced after the cackling Arik, who was already out the door and down the hall.

"I'll make sure Madeline doesn't beat Arik to a pulp." Mitchell waved before hurrying after them.

Emma shook her head, amusement clear on her face as she turned to them. "It'll take a while to set up the party. However, we should be ready around five. Want to come?"

Maxwell and Karina exchanged glances.

"You two should go."

Maxwell glanced toward Lex as he stood. "I…" Maxwell sighed. He was going to say yes anyway.

Lex looked at him and chuckled. "Ah, I spoke too soon. My apologies."

Karina harrumphed, definitely annoyed. Maxwell grinned before he turned toward Emma, Leon and Andrew. Karina nodded and turned to face them as well.

"We would be glad to." They spoke, their voices once more in unison.

~ * ~

Karina was glad they had the day to themselves. They went out to pick up some items like food and other necessities for the apartment before returning in time to drop them off and head to the party. She had to admit, the party was fun. Everyone was very relaxed and laid back, for the most part.

Arik came out of it with only a bruise on his arm from when he banged himself too hard into the wall while dodging Madeline's fury. Maxwell seemed content and even Lex joined in for a moment, just to make sure where they were. Of course, he ended up sticking around while talking with Arik. All too soon, they had to go their separate ways and Karina found herself returning to their shared apartment, brother in tow. He was giggling and looked a little red-faced. Was there something in the food? She wasn't sure, but he seemed almost a little drunk. She rolled her eyes as he stumbled with her onto the couch. She never thought she would see her brother, of all people, drunk.

"Sorry, Kari." He blinked, rubbing his eyes as another fit of giggles escaped him. Definitely the punch. Good thing Emma warned her. She hadn't gotten a chance to warn her brother before he got a cup for himself.

His face was flushed, even after only one drink. Made sense, she supposed. Neither of them ever had alcohol before so neither really knew what kind of tolerance they would have to it.

She sighed as she helped her brother onto the couch. He sat down pulling lightly on her shirt. She paused, glancing at him as he stared up at her. She rolled her eyes but took a seat next to him. He leaned his head against her shoulder and closed his eyes.

"Sis is warm." His voice was slurred as he hummed softly.

Oh geez." Maxwell." She frowned, not sure whether to shift away or just let him lay there. Instead she decided to let him be, staring up at the ceiling as she felt the heavy weight of her brother.

"You know?" His voice somewhat startled her, and she glanced back down. "I was worried. I didn't like that that dream came true for you. Yet I couldn't do anything. I was too worried. Then you went and smiled it off like you usually do. You are so strong and…" He blinked and stared up at her, looking dazed. "Sis is strong, but is she really strong? I don't know. I'm worried of worrying her. Hey, sis, should I be worried? I don't know if I should be worried or not." Maxwell mumbled the last part.

How much did he drink?

She sighed, trying to decipher what he just said. She bit her lip before finding herself hugging her brother gently. She felt his arms clumsily wrap around her waist. Damn, he was an affectionate drunk. She would have to tease him about it later, but she could tell right now wasn't the time. After all…

"Sis?"

"Hm?"

Maxwell sighed. His flush had gone down, but he still looked woozy. "I want to see Ma again. I want us to be a family again. So, can you help? I know you don't want me to go, but I think I should, I want to protect you, just like you've protected me. Is that okay?"

Karina opened her mouth, unsure how to respond. She felt a soft breath ghost over her collarbone and glanced down to see Maxwell's eyes closed, in a light sleep. He was slumped against her side, her arms around him being the only reason he was still up. She shifted him to her side, so he could lean against the couch.

Maxwell… She pursed her lips. She wiped at her eyes, calming her thoughts before she reached forward, pushing some hair from his face. "All right, now get some sleep, little brother, you have a long day tomorrow."

She looked up just as the door opened and Lex stepped in. He took one look and shook his head.

"Do I want to know?"

"Be careful which punch you get over at Madeline's. Where were you anyway?"

"Ah." Lex glanced at Maxwell, who was sleeping soundly against Karina's side. "I was checking out the area. However, it makes sense. You two wouldn't exactly have a good tolerance to alcohol."

"Did you have some?" Karina wondered, spotting the slight flush to his cheeks.

Lex grinned. "Yes, good observation." His smile dropped as he took a seat on another couch and leaned back. "Don't worry, I'm more used to it than you two. I'm fine." He glanced toward Maxwell. "Kid's out of it though. Idiot." His tone was fond as a small smile flitted over his face.

"Yeah." Karina's gaze flickered to Maxwell as he slumbered. It was nice, to see him so calm and comfortable. Her thoughts flashed to his fearful and tear-stained face and she curled inwards, almost seeking her brother's warmth. Her hands reached out to her brother's head, hand passing through his hair.

"I was..." she bit her lower lip, yet, at Lex's encouraging gaze she found herself speaking once more. "I was worried," she decided to say, seeing a flicker of something on Lex's face as she continued, "I couldn't do anything, and Maxwell was hurt. Then, once it was all said and done, he just—he was so calm about it." she felt her hand slow to a stop, looking down at the rug sitting under the warn wooden coffee table.

"So were you."

"Huh?" she looked up as Lex leaned back, arms dangling over the back of the couch and head facing the ceiling.

"I'm not saying you were okay with it, but I also know you two have already come to terms with it. It's happened and it's done. Your brother knows that, and I think you do too." He turned his head down, staring her in the eye. "You're just being an idiot and not realizing."

She stopped herself from snapping back at him for calling them an idiot again, because in some ways, he was right. There was no point in dwelling on what could have happened. They were already healing, and her brother was already feeling better. Enough so that he wanted to protect her. She wasn't sure how she felt about that but, she did feel a warmth at the thought. Her brother was growing up. She was both happy and sad at the thought.

"Come on, let's get him to bed."

Karina flicked her gaze toward Lex as he stood and stepped over. Lex slipped his arm around Maxwell's shoulder and tugged him up, Karina followed suit on his other side. The three of them stumbled to the twins' shared room where Karina gently placed her brother onto his side of the bed. She stood up and looked toward Lex. "Thanks."

Lex glanced sidelong at her. "It's no problem." He left the room while gesturing for her.

Karina took one more glance back, before following Lex to the other room. Karina took a seat with Lex across from her.

"So, enough with the previous topic. You've had the day to think. What are you going to do?"

Karina looked at him, realizing where he was going with that question and groaned. "You think I'm going to argue with your and Maxwell's decision to go to that corporation, don't you?" Lex gave her a sheepish expression before turning neutral. Karina huffed. "I understand why. I don't like the idea. I'm not exactly keen on being the only one who isn't involved…"

"Actually, I'm glad you're not." Lex's words caused Karina to glare and Lex quickly continued, "That way, we can have someone on the outside, watching out for the community. Maxwell and I will be looking into finding your mother. We won't be able to keep track if something's going on outside the gated community. That's where you come in. Plus, we can't have all our eggs in one basket. Your brother knows that full well. In truth, if you said you would be working there, he would have suggested that he work at a café or something."

Karina pursed her lips, looking down. She hated it, but she knew Lex was right. "I know. It's just hard." She shook her head and glared at Lex. "If he and you do get in, you better protect him or…"

"You'll pull me from the grave yourself and beat me back into it." Lex's grin was soft, yet genuine.

"Right in one." Karina couldn't help but smile. She was glad she'd come to trust Lex. He was a good friend and ally. "Still, thanks."

Lex waved it off. "No worries. I'll make sure he doesn't dive in head first. You focus on getting that café job. It'll be easier for you and we do need the money."

Karina stood and saluted. "My pleasure, leave it to me." She dropped her hand and placed it on her hip. "And thanks, for finding this place and getting us out of the hostel. As well as…" she found her voice faltering and instead waved her hand. "I think my brother and I both appreciate it."

Lex opened his mouth, surprised, before closing it, a soft expression on his face. "No problem." With that, he stood and trailed off to his room.

Karina stared at the ceiling, lost in thought. After some time, she walked into the kitchen, grabbing herself a glass of water. She downed half of it before gently sitting it back on the table, fingers curled around the cool glass.

She needed to apply for a job tomorrow, but what were the age limits around here? She forgot to ask Lex and she knew Maxwell wouldn't know. She furrowed her brow and, after taking another sip, turned and slipped out the door. She headed back to Madeline's room and, after hesitating a moment, knocked on the door.

It took longer than she expected, but it eventually swung open, showing an annoyed Emma. "If this is you, Andre—" She stopped and then straightened up, surprised. "Oh. Sorry, I thought Andrew was coming back because he forgot something again." She shook her head. "Anyway, did you need something?"

"I was wondering what the age limit is for working around here." She felt stupid for bringing this up, now that she thought about it. Why didn't she just ask Lex? Then again, he was probably sleeping. She wasn't in the mood to deal with that.

Emma watched her for a bit before she chuckled. "I see." She opened the door and slipped out into the hall before closing it quietly behind her. "How old are you two, anyway?"

Karina went to respond before she frowned. How long had they been journeying again? She knew their birthday was coming fairly quickly after this all started so… "What's the date?"

Emma blinked slowly and then laughed before quickly quieting her chuckles behind her hand. "I'm sorry, I didn't mean to laugh there." She shook her head and gave Karina a warm look. "It's November. November 5th."

Oh…OH! Karina slapped her face and let out a sigh. Their birthday was over a month ago and they hadn't even realized it. "We're fifteen." She decided not to mention that they turned fifteen exactly one month and a day ago. It wasn't exactly that important right now, and she was NOT in the mood for another party. She didn't want to worry about another drunken incident, even if her brother was careful.

Emma stared at her, then slowly looked her up and down. "Wait, fifteen?"

"Yeah, why? Is that going to be a problem?" Karina frowned, crossing her arms over her chest.

Emma's eyes widened. "Oh shit," she muttered. "I thought we were all of age." She winced. "Your brother was drunk, wasn't he? Oh, gosh, we thought you were both almost eighteen, if not at least seventeen."

Did they look that old? Well, that was a loaded statement, Maxwell definitely didn't act his age and lately, she didn't either. "Well thanks and all, but no, we're fifteen."

"Oh," Emma sighed. "Well, I'll just have to warn them from now on." She shook her head and looked sidelong. "Not that it would bother some of them all too much." She turned to Karina and examined her once more. "Hm." Emma put a finger to her lips, her brows furrowed in thought. "Well, to answer your question, that's not a terrible age. You can work with that. Where are you thinking of applying?"

"I'm thinking of applying to a café. I think it was called Café du Latte or something?"

"Ah, I know the place." Emma smiled, seeming relieved. "If you can get there at a good time, then you should be fine. The owner knows how difficult it is for people our age to live, especially nowadays."

"What do you mean?"

Emma stared at her like she lost an eye or something. "You don't know? I thought everyone knew." Emma shook her head. "The younger and older folks are more susceptible to the disease. So more often than not, there are quite a few orphans around our age on the streets and sometimes people our age are the only ones who have the ability to work. It's a bit of a vicious cycle. Anyway…" Emma trailed off before she looked toward Karina. "I think you should go for it. If you mention that Madeline recommended you it will help."

"Why?" Karina couldn't help but voice her confusion. Where did Madeline's name come from? It almost felt like it was out from left field.

"Madeline's mom has a good amount of influence around here. If we use her name you should be all right." Emma shrugged before she let out a yawn. "Why don't we head to bed?" She looked down at her wrist, then gave Karina a sheepish grin. "It is late."

Karina glanced at Emma's watch and grimaced, it was almost midnight. She hurriedly said good-bye and returned to her room. She needed to go to bed, especially if she wanted to be alert tomorrow to apply for that job.

She slipped into her room, making sure to lock the main door. Her brother was fast asleep, curled up in the sheets. She snickered before quickly changing, grabbing a few more pillows to separate them better this time. She slipped into bed, staring at the ceiling. Her mind lost in thought.

Even as she lay there, she found she couldn't convince herself to fall asleep. She felt the slight groan flutter from her throat and looked over to the side of her bed, spotting her backpack, which still needed to be unpacked. She reached over, almost falling out of the bed to get it before sitting up, the sheets curling around her legs. Near the top was Mother's Bible. The leather looked even more worn than when she'd grabbed it all those months ago. She reached in and pulled it out, letting it flip open toward the end. It wasn't that she wanted to read it, but it was more that she wanted to feel close to her mom, at least for tonight. Her eyes skimmed over the page, growing weary with the endless words.

"We ought always to thank God for you, brothers and sister, and rightly so, because your faith is growing more and more, and the love all of you have for one another is increasing. Therefore, among God's churches we boast about your perseverance and faith in all the persecutions and trials you are enduring." Karina trailed off as she read through it, before rereading it, silence enveloping the room in a gentle glow, her gaze flicked to the numbers. "Second Thessalonians, huh?" Karina closed the book and leaned her head back, letting the Bible sit in her lap, hand resting on the warm leather of the cover.

The moon glowed over her and her brother, feeling comforting, even when she knew it was a frigid night outside those windows. She turned to her brother, whispered a quiet, "Good night," and turned, placing the Bible on the side table before flicking off the light. She thought she heard her brother murmur something but didn't pay attention as her thoughts drifted off into slumber, even as she felt a smile flit onto her face.

Chapter Ten

Maxwell winced, hand darting to his head. *Ugh, why did his head hurt so much?* He shook it off, stumbling out of bed. Within no time at all, he found himself in the kitchen, downing glasses of water. He let out a sigh as the headache dulled. *What happened?*

He winced as a few memories flitted through his mind. He had a conversation with Karina last night, right?

He paled. *Oh gosh, had he really said all that?*

He put his face in his hands and let out a heavy breath. Ugh, talk about embarrassing. He should have paid closer attention to those punch bowls. There had been signs on them, why didn't he read them?

He let his hands fall, his head tilting up as he gripped the sink. He listened to the water run. Luckily, or unluckily, he remembered most of what he did last night. Thankfully, he hadn't had too much, so he wasn't completely drunk, but it was definitely enough to cause him to act up.

Why did he say so much to his sister? Well, it was out there now. He groaned. What did his sister think of what he said? Why couldn't he be a quiet drunk?

"Hey, Maxwell, good to see you're up." Karina's voice sounded from behind him, causing Maxwell to jump. and looked over his shoulder, only to find her familiar grin and relaxed posture, hand on her hip. "Seems like you slept well. Feel better?"

"Ugh." He looked away. "You're going to start teasing me now, aren't you?"

"Usually, I would."

Those words caught Maxwell off guard. He turned to Karina,

noticing her uncomfortable expression before she waved it off. "I'll hold off teasing till another time. No, I actually wanted to talk about something else."

Maxwell could tell from her expression that she didn't like what she was about to say. He turned fully to face her, turning the water off in the process, curiosity flitting across his face against his will. "Kari?"

"Well, it's two things, really." She grinned sheepishly. "Happy belated birthday, bro, it seems we both turned fifteen a month ago and never realized."

"You're kidding." Maxwell stared, feeling his headache increase as Karina just kept the same uneasy expression. *Crap, she wasn't lying.* "You're serious? Oh come on, how did we miss that?"

"Don't know, but I figured I would let you know."

Maxwell groaned, putting his head into one hand and letting out a heavy sigh. "Do I want to know what the other thing is?"

"It's not nearly as bad." Karina chuckled weakly and hesitated before she looked away. "You and Lex should get a job at that company. I'll help by watching the outside, all right?"

Maxwell's eyes widened. Karina was letting up on her protectiveness? What had he said to convince her? Well, other than the fact that they were both fifteen and completely missed it. That was just not right.

He tried to think over the night before, but he just vaguely remembered saying a lot of random stuff. Feeling embarrassed just trying to remember, he shook it off and sent her a relieved smile. "Thanks, Kari, it means a lot."

Karina waved it away with a sigh. "I know. Now why don't you get yourself something to eat then start helping Lex with the research? I'm going over to that café to see if I can apply for a job."

Maxwell nodded, watching as she slipped out the door. She was already well-dressed and cleaned up. She wore a nice blouse, a long-sleeved sweater and a pair of black pants she had picked up in the last city. It was too cold to wear shorts, after all, even though he knew she preferred them. Her hair was done up with a little ribbon he got her when she picked up the clip for his hair. Speaking of, it was kind of a nice reminder that she was still there. That something was still permanent, what with their mother's search and the disease. He fiddled with it for a moment, lost in thought before dropping his hand and stepping over to the fridge. He pulled out some eggs and bacon, glad that he had the chance to go out shopping yesterday before the party. He slid them into a pan, watching as they crackled and hissed, the bacon sizzling.

It didn't take long to finish cooking. He gobbled the food up, cleaned the pans and headed toward Lex's room, to see if he was out. He knocked on the door, hearing Lex call, "Come in."

He slipped inside, closing the door behind him as he moved across to where Lex was flipping through his phone, seemingly looking for something. Lex looked up and slid the phone into his pocket before standing. "You ready to go? I think I know where the library is, we'll go there first."

"That sounds fine."

Maxwell walked out the door after Lex, waiting as he locked the door before Lex turned to him. "When you get a chance, talk to the landlady, she'll give you a key to the room. All right? Just give her your name and mention my last name."

"Your last name?"

Lex nodded as he descended the stairs. "As long as it's not in the gated community, I don't have to worry about anyone knowing my last name and equating it to anything."

"No, I get that. I meant, what was your last name again?" Maxwell felt a sheepish expression bloom on his face. He couldn't quite remember if Lex ever told him his last name.

Lex glanced sidelong at him before he ruffled a hand through his hair. "Right," he mumbled. He dropped his hand. "Askren, all right?"

Maxwell quickly nodded as they passed through the lobby and out the door. Well, that was awkward. He shook it off, following after Lex down the street. The wind blew strongly, piercing through his clothes, even with the thick jacket. He hoped his sister was all right.

It didn't take long to reach the library. It was a multi-level building with granite stairs leading to double doors. They hurried up the steps and into the warmth of the library.

Maxwell gaped, staring up at the second and third levels, all filled to the brim with books. The library in Claremore looked like a school room compared to here. He didn't realize his mouth was open until he heard a quiet chuckle from beside him. He quickly closed his mouth, feeling a bit embarrassed.

"You two are something else." Lex just shook his head, amused. "Why don't you take a look around? I'll be over at the computers." Lex gestured to a line of computers off to the right side of the room.

The entrance area had a set of reading tables where a few people sat and worked quietly. Off to the left was what looked to be a reception desk. Maxwell thanked Lex in his mind as he raced toward the bookshelves. He could see all sorts of books, from Classical Literature to Musicology. Yet, there were a lot of repeating books and there wasn't much on history or on anything regarding American history. He frowned as he perused through the shelves. There was regular fiction, but non-fiction was surprisingly scarce. Did it have to do with the influence of the government due to the internal affairs? He slipped up the stairs to the second level before finally moving up to the third. The third seemed to be a children's area. Off to one side was a comfy-looking reading area with all sorts of beanbags on the floor and picture books littered on the tables. A few children were sprinkled about, reading. Maxwell couldn't help but smile at the wonder on their faces as they read, even as he noticed the oozing wounds.

He quickly looked away. How long would children like that last? He shook the thought away and sighed. He might as well check to see how Lex was doing. As impressed as he was with the size of the library, he was disappointed in the selection. He loved history and to see it practically non-existent within such a massive library was disheartening, and, if he was being honest with himself, scary.

He strode downstairs and over to the computers. He peered over Lex's shoulder just as Lex let out a slew of curses and sighed, reversing back as he found a site that was blocked by the government. The familiar eagle with lettering Maxwell remembered seeing on the Enthrope police medallions shone on the screen. Lex glanced around before standing up and stretching before walking down a bit to a corner seat, away from the librarian's line of sight. Maxwell glanced over his shoulder before hurrying after him. "No luck?"

"None." Lex's curt response was enough indication of his friend's frustration. "They're really cracking down on restrictions. I'm surprised there are even books left at this point."

"Most are fiction or repeat books. There's not much on history or religion or anything."

"No surprise." Lex typed at the screen, eyes flicking quickly over the letters, hands moving in tandem.

Maxwell leaned forward with one hand on the chair as the other rested on the table. Lex finished typing and scrolled down through the options. Maxwell could faintly see a list of websites, and, at the bottom, a list of sites removed by the government.

"Anything with an X mark at the end means it's only for authorized personal. Unfortunately, I don't have the PIN and it's military level coding. Even Antonio would have a tough time getting through."

Maxwell grimaced. If even that man, who had hefty ties with the black market and was the reason they found their mother's location, struggled to gain access, it must have been quite difficult. His eyes flickered over the sites, spotting X's on a good portion of them. After two or three pages of searching, he spotted a strange title.

Actually, scratch that. It wasn't the title, which was probably another news article, if Maxwell had to guess. No, he noticed the website underneath not only didn't have an X on it, but it also had something about E Corp. He pointed it out to Lex who raised an eyebrow, but clicked on the page, noting as it didn't automatically bring up the blocked screen. The design was simple, nothing more than a green and white background. Lex flipped down the page, humming in amusement until he found what he was looking for. Maxwell leaned forward as Lex's grin widened. "Gotcha," he muttered as he highlighted something at the bottom of the page. In small type was the name of Enthrope Corp. The page itself was a subsidiary company called L. J. Fox Inc. which seemed to deal in fertilizer. The main headquarters was within the city itself, not even a couple blocks away. The very same headquarters Maxwell passed almost every day lately, and the one he was thinking of applying to.

"Well, I guess we have our answer."

Lex pushed away from the table, quickly clicking out of the page and turning to Maxwell. "Don't sound so excited. That was the easy part."

Maxwell winced. "I know."

"As long as you do, good. Now let's get going. We still have to get some clothes and equipment to get you situated before you apply."

"What about you?" Maxwell faced Lex as they stepped out of the heated library.

"I'll deal with things my way. Don't worry about me." He smirked. "I've survived this long, I have no intention of making a mistake now."

"You're going into the gated community soon, aren't you?" Maxwell couldn't help the deadpan expression from crossing his face.

"I can't get anything past you two lately, it seems."

The words were brutal but said in such a joking and light tone that Maxwell found himself relieved. While it was worrying to hear his friend would be venturing into the gated community once more just to help them, he was glad to hear that Lex was at least optimistic about the outcomes.

"Right. Anyway, let's do a little more research then grab something to eat. I wonder how Karina is doing?"

"She should be fine. Though I suggest we eat first, then continue. Wouldn't you say?" Lex smirked as Maxwell's stomach growled. Maxwell couldn't hide the embarrassed blush as he looked away.

Lex chuckled as he headed down the street, Maxwell in tow.

~ * ~

Karina looked around the little café in wonder and worry. She was sitting off to one side, having just finished an impromptu interview by the resident manager. Supposedly, one of their staff just left, having lost their family to the epidemic, so the cafe had an opening. She was both glad at the good luck and couldn't help but cringe, rubbing her arm at the thought of another death. Thankfully, the interview was short and sweet and while she did mention Madeline's name, it only got a slight frown and an "oh" in response. She wasn't sure if it really did anything, but now she was sitting with a water cup in hand and pursed lips.

She felt her foot thump against the floor in an irregular beat as she waited. She could see some of the workers hurrying about, helping the customers and making drinks. Quite a few had bright smiles on their faces, or so it seemed.

It was hard to tell with half of them wearing masks.

She was just glad the woman who ran the store didn't particularly care that she didn't have a mask. Though she hoped that worked the same for her brother. They did try, at least.

She heard footsteps and looked over to see the portly cheerful woman lumber back to her, a bright smile on her face. "Well, dear, I'm sorry to keep you waiting."

She took a seat across from Karina who found herself sitting up straighter, tense. The woman must have noticed because her smile dipped slightly. Karina felt herself droop. That wasn't good.

"Don't worry, dear. It's nothing too bad." She leaned back in her chair. "Right now is our busy period, what with Thanksgiving and all. So, unfortunately, we can't hire anyone new, since we don't have anyone to spare to train you."

Karina winced and looked down. She hadn't even realized. Thanksgiving wasn't really much of a thing for them, so she hadn't thought too much about it.

She waited as the woman continued. "However..."

Karina perked up, glancing at the woman, who smiled. "In one week, the busy period will be over. I hope you don't mind waiting until then to start working."

A giddy feeling shot through her. "Really?"

The woman nodded, seemingly content with her enthusiasm. "You seem like you would be a good employee. Now, why don't I give you a quick tour at least? After that, I'll have to send you on your way. I'll have all your information set up and in the system in a week. So, I will see you then for training. Now the number I'm contacting…"

Karina could see her confusion because she quickly nodded. "That is my twin brother's. We're sharing a phone." She decided not to mention they would probably forgo ever getting a house phone.

"Ah, that makes sense. Though, eventually, you will want to get your own, so we can contact you if something were to happen, understand?"

Karina nodded, and the woman smiled. "Good, now." She stood and gestured for Karina to follow. "This is the main lobby." She walked to the right side of the room, where there was an employee only doorway. They stepped through to reveal a changing room and another doorway on the far side that said head's office. "This will be your changing room and break room, unless you want to go out."

She stepped out the door and moved left to where Karina could see the other employees working. Stepping behind the counter, Karina found there were all sorts of mixers and concoctions. She almost felt a little dizzy with all the different items. The lady pointed out each one, explaining what they did and how they worked.

With how busy it was, Karina found herself constantly dodging the employees, who sent her quick smiles before continuing on their way. She heard the manager telling her each of their names, but Karina found herself overwhelmed. If she didn't get them now, she would have another chance later. So, not worrying too much about remembering, she hurried after the woman as they slipped through another doorway that led to the kitchen area.

The door itself was a flip door, meaning it went both directions and was flimsy at best. Karina passed through and found herself in an older-style kitchen. She could see white fridges and gold and brown ovens. Tabletops lined the area and, was that a meat slicer? She had only ever heard of them. She found herself gawking at the items and appliances, both surprised and unsurprised. After all, stainless steel and such would be incredibly expensive. No wonder they had such outdated stuff, it was all most people could afford outside the gated communities. She quickly snapped her mouth shut and followed after her new manager.

"That doorway leads out to the garbage dump. Unfortunately, while we're able to hire you even with your younger age, we can't allow you to get near that, so ask one of the older workers to take care of that for you, understood?"

"Yes, ma'am." Karina almost forgot to add the proper terminology at the end, though to her relief, she remembered. With that, the woman led her back up front. Karina waved good-bye and slipped back into the streets, pushing away the cold as she bundled her hands in her pants pockets. She was both excited and nervous. She would be starting in a week. So that meant she had one week to kill before she could really do anything, and since she couldn't really get involved with her brother's side of things. She let out a sigh and slumped.

She was going to be very bored for the next week.

~ * ~

Maxwell couldn't believe how fast the week flew by. It was as if he just snapped his fingers and it was the next week. He gulped as he straightened himself, staring at the building in front of him, squat and menacing. He was dressed in a nice pair of slacks, a button-down shirt with a vest and tie. It felt a little uncomfortable, but they were probably some of the nicest clothes he'd worn outside the gated community.

Lex stood behind him, waiting quietly. He knew full well that Lex didn't want to do anything until they both knew Maxwell had a position. The last week had been focused on just research, and Maxwell was both nervous regarding some of the information they found on acceptance rates, and glad they decided to do all that research.

He let out a breath and stepped forward. He had applied a few days ago and received a call the day before for an interview. Now was the hard part. He decided not to glance back, stepping through the glass doorways that swished open upon his approach.

Inside was reminiscent of the building Lex's uncle worked at with potted plants, a few glass windows, and a back wall with tumbling water over white granite. The lobby was fancy and impressive. He gulped, then strode forward, trying to keep his head up. His sister made mention that more people their ages were being accepted for jobs, so it wasn't far-fetched to believe that he could have a chance. Though, it still mind-boggled him that they missed their own birthday. He knew they were busy lately, but still, that seemed a little ridiculous. He withheld the sigh he so wanted to let loose as he stepped up to the receptionist with a polite smile. "Hello, I'm here for an interview?"

The receptionist, a blonde woman with long flowing hair tied back in a clip with a mask over her face, looked up. She appraised him for a moment and then spoke. "Name?"

"Maxwell Eli." They both decided to go with a shortened version of their name, no need to be too dangerous, and, with the way things were now, no one would really know anyway.

The woman started typing at the computer in front of her, silence enveloping their little area of the room. Maxwell could hear the sounds of footsteps and chatter coming from all around and he felt the need to thrum his fingers against his leg to keep himself calm. He held off long enough until the woman looked up and, printing something off on a nearby system, handed it over. "This is your name-plate. Your interview will be with Mr. Jangos, on the right." She gestured to a doorway, leading to what was probably another hallway.

"Thank you." He gave a slight bow of his head before walking down the hall and through the door, trying hard to keep an even pace. He needed to get this job, both for his and Kari's sake as well as Ma's.

Within no time at all, he found the room in question and, bracing himself, knocked on the door.

"Come in," a rough voice called.

Maxwell's fingers curled around the doorway as he stepped inside. The inside of the room was Spartan. Two chairs made of leather sat near the doorway with a wooden desk in front of them, which led to a broad-looking man with an even broader expression. "Ah, you must be Maxwell."

"That's right."

"Come in, take a seat."

Maxwell, after a moment's hesitation sat down in one of the chairs, sitting forward a bit so he could keep his back straight. The man raised an eyebrow, seeming amused before his face grew neutral. "Now, I have a couple questions for you, answer them honestly, understood?"

Maxwell nodded, finding himself unable to speak at the moment. His tongue sat heavily against his jaw and he tried to swallow indiscreetly. He wasn't sure how successful he was.

"Now, what do you know about what we do?"

What an annoying first question. Maxwell felt a smile cross his face. He was glad Lex decided to do a lot of research to help him with this. "I know you are a company working in the fertilization of crops, specifically those used within the gated communities. Any excess is used for the purpose of keeping crops on this side of the company viable options and a way to give some jobs to the lower class."

"Eloquently put." The man seemed impressed, a small smile forming on his face. "So, why do you want to work here? You are young, fifteen, correct?"

"Correct." Maxwell felt a bit more at ease now, knowing how to respond. "I was fascinated in the use of fertilization and the widespread impacts it might have on a small community. Plus, if I recall, there are other opportunities within the company for advancement. I do aim to move up in the ranks, if that is a viable option."

"Huh, an achiever." The man leaned back, resting his hands in front of his chest with elbows on the table. "You seem to know what you are talking about. Now, tell me about yourself."

Maxwell kept the smile in place as his heart sped up. *Now came the fun part.*

~ * ~

Karina breathed a sigh of relief as she slipped out the doors of the store. Her first day had been… something. She swiped some sweat off her brow as she walked down the street. Her uniform was coming in tomorrow, but she already knew she wasn't going to like it. The tan pants and black collared shirt weren't her style at all. Plus, the fabric just looked uncomfortable. Still, she wasn't going to complain; she knew she had a job, which was good enough for now.

She hadn't realized how much of a travel point that café was. Even at the slow period, where she was able to learn how to make the drinks and take orders, it was always bustling. It also seemed like a lot of the waitresses and waiters knew quite a few customers, so they must have been regulars. She could only hope she didn't run into anyone from the hostel. It should be far enough away, but she was not going to push their luck.

Thankfully, the people she worked with were nice, but her mind was a bit distracted all day, wondering how her brother's interview went. She meandered her way home and, stepping through the door to the warmth, she ascended the stairs to their apartment. She was glad Lex found this place, it was cozy and inviting. She heard the sound of running water and blinked, walking into the kitchen. Her brother was standing there, staring at the running water, hand shaking as it curled around the glass cup. Karina stepped forward, pulling the cup from his hand, which seemed to garner his attention. He looked over and sent her a weak smile. "Oh, hey."

"What happened?" Karina put the cup down and reached around her brother to turn off the water before leaning against the counter, arms crossed. "You're distracted."

"Yeah." Maxwell looked out the window for a moment before turning to her. "I got the job."

Karina narrowed her eyes, wondering why he wasn't more enthusiastic about it. "And?"

Maxwell chuckled. "No, I'm actually happy about that…" He sighed. "Well, that's not entirely true." He pushed himself away and turned to face her. "Something about that place just unsettles me. It almost feels like I'm being watched, more than usual." He quickly admitted, before shaking his head. "Yeah, I know it's probably because of the fact the building is connected to the gated community, but it just feels like something else is the issue."

Karina frowned. "Will you be all right?"

"I should be fine." Maxwell nodded. "I already let my new boss know I'm aiming for advancement, so hopefully I can start exploring the place a bit more without standing out."

"Just be careful, will you?" Karina rolled her eyes. "I can't exactly do much for you in there."

Maxwell elbowed her lightly in the ribs. "Now that's just mean. I can take care of myself." He smiled and shook his head. "Thanks, I needed that."

"No problem, now where's Lex?"

"He said he needed to do something. He should be back in a few." Maxwell shrugged.

~ * ~

Lex wasn't sure what to feel as he returned to the apartment. He glanced over to see the twins talking quietly. They looked up upon his entrance. Karina seemed to straighten slightly, a smile playing on her lips while Maxwell grinned. "What took so long?"

"I was getting some things arranged before I go." He closed the door with a soft snip and took a seat across from them, pushing a hand through his hair.

As if sensing his unease and tiredness, the twins 'expressions shifted to worry as they both sat forward, attentive. "Lex?" Karina prompted.

Lex chuckled. "It's nothing too much to worry about." He waved it off. "Now that we know Maxwell is going to be working there, it wouldn't be safe to have him working alone. So, I'll be going to work on the other side. That way I can watch you and see if there is another way to get to your mother." He noticed their worry, and he couldn't blame them. Though they knew he was planning this, even he wasn't too sure about his decision. Thus, speaking for all of them he said, "I won't be in any danger, I will contact someone to make sure Father doesn't realize."

"Who?" Karina leaned forward, curiosity clear in her posture.

"Someone we all know." Lex grinned, deciding not to mention names. *The less they knew, the better and easier. After all, they would never let him go if...*he cut off his train of thought and reached into his pocket. "Anyway, I will contact you via cell phone. You still have my number, correct?" Lex looked over to Maxwell who nodded.

"How will you get to us if we need help?" Karina sat back, arms crossed. "It's not like you can just waltz back and forth through the gates. Someone is bound to notice."

"Exactly. No, after I leave, I'm going to be staying in there until we retrieve your mother."

"What?" Their voices rang out through the room.

Karina's arms dropped to her side as Maxwell pursed his lips, looking unsettled. They must not have realized.

"It's only reasonable," Lex continued, ignoring their mounting anger. "That's why I tried to get you two into a place with some protection. If you need anything, talk with Arik's father. The police brigade should be able to help a little."

"Police brigade? Are they different from those men..."

"They are two different entities." Lex nodded, assuaging Maxwell's concern. "The police brigade has its own problems, and many of them have disbanded in most cities, which is probably why you didn't see them that often." Lex closed his eyes and leaned back, trying to calm himself.

He heard shuffling and quiet murmurs before Maxwell let out a sigh. "Fine, I guess it's not completely stupid."

Lex chuckled and opened his eyes to see the twins 'annoyed and resigned expressions.

"Just don't be completely reckless." Karina rolled her eyes, finger pointing straight into his face. "That's our job."

"Kari."

"What? It's true."

Lex shook his head, feeling amused and saddened. After all, this would be the last time he spoke with them face to face for a while. Part of him almost wished he just left but he decided this was better anyway. He stood, dusting off his pants, even though he knew there was nothing on them, and turned to face Maxwell and Karina. "I'm not going to be bringing my bag. For now, it'll stay here. Maxwell, when you get the layout of the place, we'll figure out how you can get it to me, all right?"

Maxwell frowned but nodded.

"What are you going to do about clothes? The only reason we had anything last time was because it was your home." Karina leaned forward, elbow against her knees and gaze filled with concern.

"Don't worry. I do have a plan, it'll be fine." Lex smirked.

She rolled her eyes, pulling away as Maxwell shook his head.

"Well, I best be heading out. That's all I really needed to say."

"I understand, yet I'm still worried about whether it'll be okay or not. What will you have to do to get in? Are you going to use your name? Even with that contact?"

Lex stared at the door before he turned to face them. "If I told you, then I might dissuade myself. Don't worry, I believe it will work out." He could tell Maxwell wanted to speak and even Karina looked a little hesitant to see him go.

Finally, she let out a sigh and threw her hands in the air in such strong resignation he almost chuckled. "Well, get going, why don't you? We'll call you if we need anything."

He felt a smile cross his face before he nodded and turned, heading out the door. He just hoped those two would be all right.

~ * ~

"So, he's gone," Karina murmured, feeling sadness seep into her thoughts. "That was so sudden."

"I know." Maxwell let out a long breath before shaking his head and turning to her. "Not much we can do now. We said our good-byes and it's not like he'll be gone forever or anything. It just means we have to work harder to find Ma, for his sake as well."

"And not just because you're annoyed at him thinking he needs to watch out for you." She felt a chuckle escape as her brother huffed and crossed his arms over his chest.

"Geez." He groaned. "Anyway, how was your first day?"

"Ugh." Karina winced. "I mean, it wasn't terrible. It was just different. Did you know there's, like, fifteen different ways to make coffee, with one machine?"

Maxwell grimaced, sending her a sheepish look. "That bad, huh?"

Karina chuckled. "Could be worse. Plus, honestly, the conditions aren't too bad, and pay is good, relatively speaking. You?"

"Same." Maxwell shrugged. "I was anxious, though, but I guess we lucked out." He grinned. "After all, we both got the jobs we were aiming for and now, with Lex leaving, we'll be able to have separate rooms."

Oh, right. Karina pursed her lips, both glad at the prospect and saddened. She wasn't sure why though. After all, they both wanted their own rooms since this whole thing started. So why was she upset about it?

"True." Karina found herself giving a slightly amused grin even as she suppressed the stupid emotions. "Now, we just have to work hard. The next few months are going to be fun." She couldn't hide the sarcasm in the last sentence, even if she tried.

Maxwell laughed, his expression saying he agreed completely.

Chapter Eleven

Lex stared up at the golden gates, keeping his expression neutral. Honestly? He hated this, but he didn't have that many options. With a sigh, he stepped up to the guard gates. The guard quickly drew his gun, pointing it at him. "Stop. Who are you?"

Lex gave a curt smile. "Leonard. Leonard Askren."

The guard's eyes widened as he dropped the gun. He reached below his desk, padding through papers before bringing one up. He glanced between it and Lex before his mouth gaped open. "Sir. Where have you been? Your father has been looking for you."

No surprise. "I was doing some research. Now, would you kindly let me in?"

"We have to do a check first. I also have to contact your father—"

"There is no need for that." Lex reached into his pocket and, stepping up to the guard station, slipped a few hundreds through, and into the guard's hand.

The guard jumped and looked down. His gaze flicked up to Lex who tilted his head just slightly as he waited. A moment later the man pocketed the money and, placing the gun back into his waistband, turned.

"Give me a moment, good sir."

Lex waited as the guard slipped from his concrete protection and quickly opened the first gate, leading him through. On the far side was a small building, almost like an outhouse, except it was designed to appeal even to those within the gated community. *Not that it was ever used in such a way,* Lex thought. Lex stepped inside. He stripped out of his clothes, waiting as the spray washed over him, eyes closed. Within no time, it was done, and he was dressed in a spare set kept there for instances like this. They weren't his style, at all, but they would do until he could get something for himself. He stepped through the second set of gates, the guard leading him. "I wish to speak with my brother. Get me in contact with Caym Askren."

"Sir?" the guard hesitated, and Lex raised an eyebrow.

The guard gulped and nodded, grabbing his radio and speaking in hurried tones into it. Lex noted, out of the corner of his eyes, as another guard hurried over to take his guide's place. He was glad he was able to find a bribable guard. Though, he wasn't surprised. People from this side didn't have that kind of money except for the exception like his uncle, who wasn't from this side.

After some time, they arrived at another building, just through the golden gates. It looked to be a visitor entrance area. Lex stepped inside, feeling the warm air wash over him as his footsteps clacked over the granite floor, echoing around the pristinely clean environment. The lobby was empty, except for a reception desk off to one side with an elaborately comfy chair. The receptionist was nowhere in sight. They walked past the desk into a small side room, well, small for gated standards which was equivalent to the size of their whole apartment on the other side. He was led to one side, where he spotted a set of phones and large fluffy couches. He took a seat, crossing one leg over the other and arms back. The guard bowed and hurried away, probably to get the information, so Lex could make the contact, and to make sure Caym was even available. Lex glanced sidelong at the camera, set off to the side with its beady red light. He stopped the sigh from escaping and reached to his chest, fiddling with the pendant through the cloth of his shirt.

Thankfully, he didn't have to wait long before the man returned and gestured to follow. Lex stood and walked after the guard, finding himself in a small side room. This one was legit small, with only a desk and a computer, probably someone minor's office. He took a seat, seeing a booting screen show the circular update symbol, rotating in place. The guard bowed and stepped out the door just as the computer clicked.

"Who—" Caym stopped, looking on in interest as his eyes settled on Lex. "Leo."

"Caym." Lex spoke, eyes narrowed. He felt varying emotions rising to the surface at his brother's appearance.

Caym looked him over, a smirk forming on his face, though his eyes showed something else. Lex couldn't quite discern what it was and cursed, wishing Maxwell was there. He had no doubt the boy would have been able to figure it out. "It's a pleasure to see you are alive and well." Caym glanced to one side and a little frown flipped onto his face before he looked back. "What are you doing in Collern City?"

"My reasons—"

"Those twins." Caym spoke, expression sour. "You're trying to help them with finding their mother."

"Did Father—"

"Do you really think Father would figure something like that out? The cameras were pointed in such a way that he couldn't read the papers, no, he thinks they're just trying to get that cure of theirs out."

So how did Caym figure it out? Lex pondered as his gaze flitted to the surroundings. *From the look of things, Caym was still at home. What was he doing there?*

Caym must have noticed him observing the room, because his smirk widened. "No worries, brother, I'll be out of here shortly, just doing some last-minute things. Now, there's bound to be another reason why you're contacting me, besides just wanting to speak with me, as much as I or you might love it."

Lex stopped himself from clicking his tongue, but he was unable to hide the grimace from flashing on his face. Caym's smile dropped into an unreadable expression. Lex quickly cut in. "Well, you know full well why they're here. I have a proposition for you."

"Proposition?" Caym's eyes narrowed as he rested his chin on his hand, elbow on the table beside him.

Lex waited, but Caym didn't say anything more. "A trade. Let me get their mother out, however long it takes. After, I will return with you to the gated community."

Caym's eyes widened just a fraction and Lex could see him stiffen. "That's a daring proposition, and what about that freedom you so envy?"

Lex couldn't quite read Caym's expression. While Caym's face showed he was interested, something about his posture screamed why? Why would his brother do such a thing?

Lex wondered if Caym actually did have some of that protective older brother left in him that he remembered. Lex wanted, once again, to know what changed him. He shook it off and nodded. "It doesn't particularly matter. After all, I only promised to help them with their mother." Liar." Plus, it would be quite difficult for me to keep Father off their trail so far away. I might be able to bribe a guard or two, but you know as well as I how people talk."

"Then why don't you return now? I could—"

"Father would never relinquish their mother of free will, even for me, you know that." Lex gestured.

"No, you are right, he wouldn't." Caym examined him quietly. "All right, Leo, how long?"

Lex stopped himself from stumbling, surprised at his brother having accepted his offer so easily. "One year. Give me one year to get her out."

"Make that nine months." Caym leaned forward.

"No." Lex cut him off. "I feel you would prefer more of a challenge. Keeping Father off my back for one whole year should suffice."

Caym stayed silent, peering over him before backing off. "You are right." He looked Lex over, unreadable emotions on his face. "One year, once you retrieve their mother, you will come home. If not, I'll use everything in my father's and, if necessary, the government's power."

Lex winced. He didn't particularly want that. His father's agency was dangerous enough. To get the whole government involved would mean being unable to move without being spotted; he had to avoid that at all costs. "As long as you stay away from Collern until then. After all, Father would suspect something otherwise."

"You take me too lightly, little Leo. I have no reason to go to Collern at this time. No, I have other things that I need to take care of." The smile on Caym's face could put a shark to shame.

Lex couldn't hide the slight tremor, even if he tried. He gazed at Caym, square in the eye. "Then... Deal."

"It's good working with you, brother. I will contact you at a later time, and don't worry. Father will never know." With that, the connection died.

Lex stared at the camera before placing his face in his hands. The last deal he made with his brother hadn't ended well; what made him think this one would? He breathed out a long sigh as his thoughts flickered to years ago. After all, they were still young, and he'd been stupid enough to believe that he would be fine doing anything.

~ * ~

"You're crazy." Caym looked at him with an amused expression on his young face. He was barely thirteen. His eyes were alight with mischief and certainty. "I mean, that's usually my job, coming up with these plans and all."

Lex puffed out his cheeks, glaring at his older brother as the sun sank, delivering the last rays of light before moving onto the shadow. "I'm serious."

Caym's smile dulled as he looked at him, silent eyes gazing over him before he gave a soft expression. "All right, I'll help, but let's make a deal."

"Deal?"

"Yeah, if Father comes around, I want you to split and hurry back to the house, you got me?"

"What?" Lex glared at his brother, who shrugged, a grin forming on his face.

"Oh, come on, Leo, it's a challenge. See if you can get back to the house before Father finds you." Caym waggled a finger. "I bet you my dear Flaffy you won't be able to."

Lex narrowed his eyes. Caym's favorite stuffed toy? Oh, this was fun." Deal."

Caym's eyes sparkled, a hint of relief that Lex pointedly ignored. It took no time at all to slip out into the gardens. The finely cut grass swayed in a gentle breeze as the workers busied themselves with the last-minute additions as the moon slowly began to rise, bathing the area silver. A few smiled their way, giving them looks before hurrying about their business. Lex ignored it, alongside his brother. Once out of sight of the house, both let out a breath of relief before Caym carefully pulled out a jar. "I should never have told you about those fireflies." Lex frowned, earning a playful wink from his brother as he handed one of the bottles over. "So why don't we hurry and catch one? Father won't even notice since he thinks we've gone to bed. I made sure Machael told him."

"Won't that make it worse for Machael?" Lex found himself glancing down at his now-healed arm. The remnants of the scar were still a little visible, though rapidly fading.

Silence filled the air before Caym spoke softly. "You know he was aware of the risks of letting you climb up there. We both were, if only I hadn't distracted him then…" Lex saw the pain flash through Caym's eyes and he grimaced. It wasn't his brother's fault he'd been stupid enough to get his kite back and broke his arm in the process. He shook his head and held the jar tightly.

Caym must have noticed because he grinned, tossing one arm lazily back so the glass of the jar rested against his shoulder. "So, why don't we get going? It's been a while since it's been just the two of us. Let's see who can collect more, shall we?"

Lex and Caym found themselves at a little pond, still on their father's property. It was well maintained, like everything else, and sparkled under the moonlight. Lex was tired, but that tiredness disappeared as the area slowly lit up with small lights, flitting over the water and through the branches with ease. He could see Caym glancing at him, a warm expression on his face before he darted forward and, almost gently, caught one of the fireflies in the jar before covering the jar with his hand. Lex hurried over, staring at the jar as the little creature fluttered around, landing at the bottom. Light glowed a faint yellow from the tail as black wings settled into place on its back, antennae waving slowly. He noticed Caym's amused expression and he huffed before trying to catch one himself.

He ended up splashing into the water with a splat. He shook his head, water trailing down his skin and dripping from his hair. He sat up as his brother laughed, placing the jar down so the firefly didn't flee before stepping into the water to help him up. Lex glared, splashing Caym, who yelped and stumbled back, staring down at his soaked shirt. Lex chuckled and scrambled to his feet. Caym pursed his lips, bangs dragging into his face as he looked at Lex, gleam in his eyes. "Okay, that's it. Competition time."

Lex scrambled away, grabbing his jar before darting to the other side of the pond. He watched his brother scoop up his jar, quickly capping it with a metal cap with holes in it for breathing before darting after him.

It was a race, but it was fun, running around the pond while trying to catch the fireflies and avoiding falling into the pond as they both tackled and shoved at each other playfully.

It all ended when the sound of harried footsteps caught their ears. Caym shot up, blond hair dripping and clothes practically glued to his skin like Lex's own. His head snapped toward the sound. It was only a moment later when one of the servants burst through the undergrowth. She took one look at them and paled. "Masters. You must hurry. Your father is looking for you."

Lex felt fear trace up his spine, how long were they out? Caym's eyes narrowed and he nodded. "Hurry back, we'll follow. Can you distract Father for a moment?"

The servant hesitated a fraction before nodding and darting away. Lex felt himself shiver, the cold piercing through his clothes as much as terror at the thought of being caught by their father in such a drenched state. Even the fireflies were gone, most having disappeared earlier with their running around, but now the area was completely devoid of them. Caym gave a tch noise before turning to him. "Time for that deal." Lex went to open his mouth and Caym shook his head. "Hurry back, understood?"

Lex pursed his lips before he nodded and ran into the undergrowth, wondering just what his brother would do. He knew what would happen if he was caught. If Father was in his normal state of mind and if Mother wasn't around, or Caym… He rubbed his arm, as he dashed through the trees and back to the garden. He stopped, looking around before slinking up to the doorway. Were the cameras on? Oh gosh, he hoped not. He slipped in through the door, praying to all above that Father didn't find him or Caym. He clutched the little jar close to his chest, realizing it was Caym's once he saw the firefly nervously flitting about. After all, he hadn't managed to catch a single one.

When did Caym switch them? He shook his head and, to his relief, found himself back in his room. He placed the jar down on the side table and quickly got changed into drier clothes. Once changed, he should be all right, right? The childish thinking was one he quickly realized wouldn't work. He heard footsteps and looked over as Father slammed open the door, his figure swallowing Lex's small frame easily. He looked down his nose, eyes as cold as ever before he peered around the room. He spotted the little jar and his eyes narrowed. "Leonard, what is the meaning of that?" Lex's gaze snapped to the jar and he froze. What could he say? What was he supposed to say? He found his mouth opening and a tremble forming down his spine.

"Oh, Father."

Lex jerked as Caym's calm voice came from the other side. His father turned, exposing his brother, who was standing there, having also changed into pajamas. Caym's eyes darted around the room so quickly, Lex thought he missed it before Caym grinned. "Hello, Father, I wanted to ask you a question, it's about my studies. I was studying so much that I ended up waking Leo when I passed his room."

"Studying?" A strange light appeared in Father's eyes as he knelt down. "Studious as ever." He ruffled Caym's hair before stopping his hand, the fingers lightly tangled in the knots near his scalp.

Lex found his hands inching toward his shirt, trembling, more for his brother's safety then anything. "But how does that explain the jar that's sitting on Leonard's table over there?"

Caym's gaze snapped to the jar before turning back to Father and, if Lex hadn't been scrutinizing his brother, he would have missed the flash of panic for what it was. "I asked one of the servants to pick one up for us, you know, Leo is sometimes afraid of the dark and I startled him earlier."

Caym winced as Father tugged sharply before standing up and letting Caym go. "Fine. You said you had a question about your studies? I guess I'll have to make sure you get more tutoring hours. I can't have you waking your brother at godawful times of the night. Now come along." He sent one last look around Lex's room before ushering Caym out the door. Caym glanced over his shoulder and winked.

Lex didn't feel any better and it was a day later when he realized why. After all, now he never even saw his brother, and when he did, Caym was exhausted. He worked hours on end with tutors and studies to the point where he could barely string coherent sentences together. Still, he always kept up that easy smile and warm expression.

Lex glanced toward the firefly as the light slowly died, draining with the life of the little creature captured inside and at the same time, as the glow slowly died, he knew he was the reason Caym was now in the very same state.

Because he'd made a deal to catch a firefly and finally get some time away from the house, to be with his brother, who had to pay the price.

Lex slammed the memory away, pushing it to the recesses of his mind like usual as his hands clenched into his hair. *Why did that stupid memory have to pop up? Why now?* Still, it dredged up the question of what happened to get rid of his brother's warmth? One hand trailed down and tangled around the pendant, digging into the soft fabric of the shirt. He remembered that he hadn't fully gotten out of that one unscathed. His father ended up finding the dirty clothes and he could still vaguely remember the hands pounding against his flesh. His brother hadn't managed to spare him from everything, but he also knew Caym always endured a lot worse than he did. So, what happened during those three years?

What about Ariel? Lex pulled away, leaning back in the chair to stare at the ceiling. Caym always talked about his wife and, though Lex only met her briefly, she was as kind as he remembered his brother. So, where was she? Why did he react so strongly lately when Lex asked about her? He let out a sigh and pushed away from the desk. This wasn't getting him anywhere. He walked to the door and stepped out, grimacing in the light.

The twins were definitely going to kill him. If this deal didn't first.

Chapter Twelve

The weeks turned into a month without Maxwell or Karina even really noticing. Work was tough, and, for Maxwell, he found himself tired. After all, he'd gotten a heavy lifting job. The bags of fertilizer wouldn't store themselves. So, he was tasked with throwing them onto the machine to be put in place accordingly. It was hard work and it left him exhausted. However, it did give him the chance to get a feel for the layout of the place, if he could call it that. He mostly stayed in the outer portions of the building. In a way, the place kind of reminded him of an onion. He tried to keep an eye out for any way into the gated side, but the walkway there was always heavily guarded and locked.

He heard whispers and rumors, but they all sounded fake to him. Though that was probably because people believed the gated community housed devils and they used magic to whisk people away. He remembered snorting when he overheard that comment.

Other than that, he would occasionally manage to pilfer a printed document or glance at one of the screens as he passed into his work station. They always said the same thing. Dates of deposit, tendency, workers, reception. There was nothing outright incriminating and nothing he could use for anything to help him or Lex.

Since he was such a new worker, he didn't really have access to any places besides the loading bay and front entrance. Most of the people he worked with seemed to be in varying levels of decay from the epidemic. Some, like himself, were just slightly bandaged, while others looked like they would keel over if you blew on them. Yet they all came in from the outer community to work. It was quite fascinating, actually.

He knew his sister was in a similar situation with her job. Both of them were working almost all the time to help pay for food and other necessities after Lex left. She often kept an eye out for rumors and news articles, occasionally bringing home clippings that interested her, such as reports of an entertainer called Rose Thornfield who would be passing through town on tour during the summer and articles that spoke of the epidemic's increase. He could have sworn he heard that name before but didn't think much of it. There was even one article she found which detailed the report of the government debating on releasing some bombs in order to try to take care of the south and all the quarantine zones there. The report wasn't received well.

Yet, for the most part, things were quiet. He was just glad Lex paid at least a little ahead, so they didn't have to worry about those bills. He let out a sigh as he slumped on the couch, head tilted back. He could hear his sister's footsteps in the kitchen as she returned with two glasses of water, one for each of them. "Here." She handed one over and he took it, grateful, gulping it down before sitting up, cradling it in his hands. "So, anything?"

Maxwell shook his head. "I haven't really heard from Lex, though I know something must have happened. There was a sudden upheaval when I started, and I don't think it had to do with me." He let a quick cheeky grin cross his face before he groaned, flopping back against the couch. "I just hope Lex didn't do anything stupid. What can we do though?" He shrugged. "Anyway, the place itself is huge. I don't get a chance to explore much, so I can't say anything at this point." Maxwell could hear the frustration in his own voice and assumed his sister did as well.

She gave him a worried smile. "Well, if it makes you feel any better, I'm in the same boat. Not much is happening besides work."

"That could be a good thing," Maxwell pointed out, getting rolled eyes for his comment.

"Ha-ha. Anyway, I heard that Emma and Madeline are having a Christmas party…" Karina trailed off, biting her lip.

Maxwell grimaced. Neither of them was too keen on the idea of a Christmas party, but they both knew they needed the distraction. "When is it?" He leaned forward, placing the cup down and draping his hands between his knees.

"Next week sometime." Karina shrugged. "I've been wondering where they've been. Emma's been around, but most of the others are gone during the time when we're around. Thankfully, that also seems to be the case at work. I never see anyone from the hostel."

"That's good." Maxwell pursed his lips.

What his sister said was pretty accurate, on both accounts. Over the past month, Maxwell barely saw any of the neighbors besides Emma and when he did, they only said a quick greeting before hurrying on their way. He wondered whether they all worked night shifts, but decided not to pry. After all, it wasn't his business. It wasn't like he was living with them, necessarily. He and his sister did become good friends with Emma though. The girl was kind and thoughtful and surprisingly patient, though he suspected that had more to do with the people she hung around with more than anything. Karina actually came to like her, which was a relief to Maxwell.

"So, do you want to go?"

Maxwell started, realizing he never gave his sister an answer. "Yeah, sure. I just need to make sure to read the labels this time." He couldn't help the sheepish grin from crossing his face.

Karina's eyes flashed in amusement. "Yes, let's avoid that, shall we?"

She chuckled as Maxwell frowned. *Not fair, sis, not fair.* "Oh, by the way, do we need to bring anything?"

Karina shook her head. "I asked, but Emma said not to worry about it, it will probably be something small, like just a game day or something."

"I guess. I feel a little awkward since they've already helped us quite a bit." Maxwell furrowed his brow, unsure.

Karina seemed to be thinking along the same lines as she bit her lip. "I know what you mean, little bro. Unfortunately, I can't think of anything to do for them."

Maxwell tilted his head back in thought, staring at the cracked ceiling. They didn't really have much they could do. "I guess we could just make them something, like a dessert or something?"

"That could work." Karina grinned. "I've gotten better at baking, at least a little."

"In other words, you've learned how to not burn toast?" Maxwell teased, causing his sister to huff, annoyed.

"Yeah, yeah, just because you know how to cook…"

"I watched Mother." Maxwell rolled his eyes.

It was more that he felt he needed to help Ma cook. After all, she was always so tired after work and Karina was almost never home.

"Fine." Karina looked away. "Still, that sounds like a good idea. Cake?"

"Cake works." Maxwell shrugged. That wouldn't be a problem, and cake was always a good choice.

The days leading up to the party were a blur to Maxwell. He worked and helped his sister. They bought ingredients and, a day before the party, got together to bake the cake. His sister proved that she was learning something at her new job as she worked carefully on frosting the top. Maxwell had to admit, it was fun, working with his sister on something so menial.

Maxwell picked up the cake, sister in tow and headed toward Madeline's room. It seemed like Madeline had the largest apartment room of the group, so the most space. Karina knocked on the door, startled as Arik wrenched it open. He took one look and his eyes glimmered upon seeing the covered cake in Maxwell's hands.

"Oh, dessert." He grinned. "Anyway, come in." He swung the door wide and slid behind them, pushing them in.

Maxwell heard Karina yelp quietly as he stumbled forward, barely keeping a hold on his gift. He placed the cake down on a little side table decked in a thin white tablecloth.

Most of the group was already there, with the exception of Andrew and Mitchell. Leon was off to one side, playing a chess game against Madeline, who was mildly cursing as she lost a knight. Emma looked up from her seat, watching the game, and smiled brightly. "Hey, guys, you made it."

"Of course," Karina called, waving and walking over to Madeline. Maxwell followed with Arik close behind. "I also made sure to remind—"

"Karina." Maxwell knew full well just where his sister was going with that statement. She gave him a sheepish look, showing she'd gotten caught before turning to Emma, who chuckled.

Arik held a fanged grin on his face, entertained. "By the way, is that fella Lex coming?"

"No, he's busy." Maxwell glanced toward Arik, who nodded, as if verifying something. He didn't ask anything more.

It wasn't much longer until Mitchell and Andrew arrived. They came through the door with Andrew in a huff and Mitchell chuckling. Maxwell yawned before focusing back on the party, making sure to avoid the punch with alcohol in it, deciding instead just to get water from the tap. Within no time, the party went into full swing with them playing games like BS and other card games. Maxwell was glad to see the delighted expression on his sister's face as she won another round or was cheering for him on the sidelines. He was concerned that, since she wasn't involved with Ma's search, she would be a bit depressed, but that didn't seem to be the case.

The cake was delicious, and Madeline looked almost star-struck when she realized Karina and Maxwell made it. Emma seemed highly amused by that fact and Mitchell just grinned. Arik scarfed it down like it was air and even Andrew held a small, if reluctant, smile.

Honestly, he was glad to celebrate Christmas with someone. It hurt, not having Ma around to spend Christmas with. So, the change of pace was appreciated.

Clean-up wasn't bad and eventually, Maxwell found himself and his sister back in their room. He glanced at his bag. He'd managed to get his sister something but he wasn't really sure when to give it to her. He would have this morning but…

"So, remember Lex said it might take a year? I wonder if we'll be staring at this same ceiling next year around this time without Mom."

Maxwell turned his gaze to Karina, who was staring at the ceiling with a sad gaze. He pursed his lips but didn't respond.

She gave a morose laugh that held no mirth and glanced sidelong at him. "No surprise, I'm getting way to pessimistic lately…" she trailed off and shook her head before going over to her bag. "Here, I got you something."

To Maxwell's surprise she pulled out a small gift-wrapped box with a little bow on it. It wasn't anything extravagant, but it was a gift nonetheless.

He couldn't help the fond expression from crossing his face. "We think alike way too much sometimes." He reached over, pulling out his own gift to Karina's amusement.

"Nothing wrong with that." She whistled and accepted the gift before ripping it open. Maxwell took his time, undoing the bow as he watched his sister open the lid to her gift. She stopped, staring down before her gaze softened. "Thanks, Maxwell." The sincere words were so full of warmth that Maxwell ended up looking down at his own gift.

He hadn't been sure what to get his sister, but, as he peeked up, he could see her carefully pulling on a pair of fingerless gloves with a flip top in case she needed it and a long wrist band that extended to her elbows for extra warmth if she wanted. Considering Karina's usual attire, he figured she wouldn't mind.

He glanced down at his own and stopped. Under the gift wrapping was a pair of headphones and a book. A book he remembered hearing about when he was younger. He gently picked it up, flipping through the aged pages.

"How did you manage to find one? Even the library didn't have any."

Karina seemed proud, even as she finished pulling the gloves on. "I got Lex's help. Remember when you'd finally figured out how to get things from Lex?"

"Yeah, and I'm still frustrated that it doesn't work both ways," Maxwell groused, remembering as an orderly brought him the box, saying it was from an employer. He was still a little peeved that he couldn't send anything back through the same channels.

"Well, he'd managed to find one in one of the bookstores in there."

Maxwell shook his head, now feeling bad. He hadn't gotten anything for Lex and while Karina seemed to be pleased with his gift, his gift felt weak compared to hers. It was a book detailing World War II and the following era. Even in school they only ever glossed over this. He'd first read something like it a few years ago, so he found himself stunned. After all, he didn't think this country still held any historical books, especially one this detailed about everything leading up to the closing of the borders. He flipped through the pages, seeing the content. There were pictures of grainy black and white people and places, words in print that he didn't even know were used and information that, now that he'd seen what became of America, sounded so accurate it was scary.

He closed it and placed it back into the box before looking up at Karina. "Thank you."

"No problem," she reached over and, before he could stop her, ruffled his hair before pulling back.

He definitely did NOT pout, but he did let his gaze flicker to the window, feeling a little down. "I wonder how Lex is doing."

"Don't know," Karina slumped into the headboard, following his gaze and eyes dim in thought.

Maxwell could hear other people partying, but in this room, with his sister, it was calm and peaceful. Right now, with his emotions in a tumble regarding his Ma and his thoughts periodically going back to the disease, it was nice to have peace and quiet. Now, if only it would stay that way.

~ * ~

"Merry Christmas, little Leo."

Lex cringed. *Why, oh why, did he pick up the phone?* The restraints regarding the deal with Caym were...tough. Caym worked quickly, having set up a landline that led directly to his mobile. There were also cameras in the building in which he lived, reminiscent of home. Was Caym paranoid he would renege on the deal? Probably.

"Same," Lex muttered, feeling uncomfortable.

The first call he got was a Merry Christmas from his brother. He wasn't sure whether he was glad Caym was staying out of his life for the moment, or annoyed that the only call he received was to say that. "Did you want something?"

"Can't a brother call to say Merry Christmas?"

"No."

"Ouch." Caym didn't sound hurt, but Lex could faintly hear the sound of shifting papers before he spoke again. "Then again, I can't get much past you, right? No, the reason I called was I need information."

"What type?" Lex didn't really want to give anything away, at least not to this person who seemed completely different from the boy he remembered.

Caym sounded slightly hurt, as if sensing his intentions. "Uncle. Uncle Hugh? I wanted to speak with him, since he was the last one you interacted with after leaving us. Care to disclose anything so I can speak with him?"

"I have nothing to tell you." Lex replied, voice monotone. He leaned against the headboard, legs crossed over the silk sheets and arm draped over his stomach. "It's not like you to ask."

Caym sighed. "Well, you know our uncle. He's a stubborn one and he hates Father, for probably a very good reason."

Lex blinked, surprised as Caym continued, as if ignoring the small bomb he just dropped. "I figured I would speak with you to find out how best to meet with him. After all, you promised to come back to the family, and I know you won't stay without good reason. Can you blame me? Plus, I have a few other things to ask him as well."

"Just use your contacts. I highly doubt he will ignore you completely." Lex frowned. No matter what he said, Caym would find a way to deal with his uncle. However, it was interesting to hear him say that there was a good reason to hate Father, considering what he was like when Lex returned home. Still, he felt bad for his uncle, but there wasn't much he could do. A thought slipped through his mind and he frowned. "Caym, why aren't you with your wife and child? It is the holidays."

Silence enveloped the other end of the phone for the longest time, which deepened Lex's confusion. This wasn't like Caym, old or new. His thoughts flashed to the last conversation he held with him face to face. A deep sense of worry flooded his veins and he frowned.

"Leave it, Lex."

The cold tone startled Lex about as much as the use of his nickname. Caym never used Lex, just Leo. It caused him to stiffen and sit up. "Caym, what happened? You just kind of pushed it off last time we spoke, but—"

"LEX. LEAVE IT." The tone was sharp, and Lex could hear a slight tremble in Caym's voice. Whether that was anger or anguish, he couldn't tell. He pursed his lips before letting out a groan.

"Fine." Lex dropped the subject. "I'll talk to you another time. Good day." He put down the phone, knowing quite well that it would cause Caym to fume, but he didn't particularly care. He slid a hand through his hair, fingers catching in the tangles. *What happened? To hear Caym like that...* He rubbed his eyes tiredly. He wasn't going to find out this way. He just hoped his uncle would be okay.

He slid his legs sideways, grimacing at the feel of the silk, and stood. He quickly got changed into a set of clothes he picked up within the gated community. Considering he needed to deal with the snotty folks of the interior, he figured he might as well dress the part. Plus, he couldn't get away with wearing his old clothes, comfortable as they were. He debated on whether to call the twins or not to give them a Merry Christmas and, some part of him, wanted too. Unfortunately, he didn't have the time.

He would call them after this farce of a party, when he would need something to lift his mood.

His room was large with a king-sized bed and all the amenities to live a daily life. A wide-open kitchen to cook or have a maid cook and a bathroom that would put the twins' shared apartment to shame with way too many soaps and shampoos for any single boy in his teen years. Lex walked past the walk-in closet and out the door. The long hallway, which led to glistening elevators, was lit with a gentle light and wide windows opening out into the snowy back fields. He stared past the window, toward the golden gates, with chagrin. It had already been a month and he was no better off. He knew there would be a challenge in coming into the gated community, but he didn't doubt he made the right choice. Father would never put the twins 'mother on the outside and he doubted Maxwell would be able to find out any information on the outside either. Besides maybe a way to sneak to the gated side, but it was too dangerous for the teen to do that by himself. He didn't expect it to be quick and easy, but it sure would have been nice if he was able to do something that actually involved looking for the mother and getting a bit more freedom. He shook his head at the last notion before turning and heading toward the elevators. After all, freedom. What did it even mean sometimes?

No, he needed to get his mind focused on the task at hand, going to a business Christmas party and seeing if he could enhance his status, which was not going to be fun.

He heard the ding of the elevator as it hit the ground floor and he stepped out. He saw a couple maids and butlers scurry out of the way, and noticed as one man, a higher-up in the gated community, gave him a slight bow of his head, stepping to the side. "Ah, if it isn't Sir Leonard. A pleasure to meet you."

Lex gave him a half-hearted look. The wide grin on the man's face and the way his hands slid around themselves was enough to tell Lex that the man was looking for something from him.

"The pleasure is all mine, now is there something you wish to speak with me about?" The words felt forced and almost foreign on his tongue. He hated this formalized speech.

"Ah, yes. You see, my daughter is of marrying age, a beautiful young lass. I heard you are without wife, so I wish to inquire if you would be willing to meet with her."

Lex tilted his head up, forcing himself to look down his nose at the man. "I am busy of most import at the moment. I do not have the care, nor time, to ascertain a meeting with your daughter." He turned and walked toward the door, mentally cringing as he heard the scrambling of feet behind him.

"Sir, I would be most grateful if you could consider her as a bride. Here, a picture, if you will." The man stepped in front of Lex, handing him a picture. His smile was shaky and uncertain, quickly enveloped in a weak poker face.

Lex looked down at the picture. In all actuality, the girl in the photo was beautiful with long auburn hair curled in just the right way to reflect the sun, soft green eyes and honey-colored skin. Yet, Lex knew well what was going on, you could almost see the pained grimace on her face and the tense posture if you looked close enough.

She full well knew she was being sold to someone she didn't know, just so her family could live a better life.

Honestly, he knew something similar happened with Caym and his wife. However, that ended up working in their favor, since it saved her life from an abusive family and a dangerous second relationship. What was it again? Her second suitor was a man from the government, a fifty-year-old who had just lost his third wife and was on the look-out for a younger bride.

Lex mentally grimaced at the thought. That's why part of him wondered just what happened. From what he recalled, Caym was happy, and so was his wife. He never really saw them apart except when Caym needed to work. Right before Lex left, Kiera had been born.

Lex shook his head and looked at the man, who was waiting with an impatient and worried air, hand trembling. Lex took the picture and pocketed it, getting a sigh of relief from the man. "I will think about it," Lex spoke before heading toward the doors. He could hear the man bowing behind him, if the rustling of clothes was any indication.

He stepped out the doors and down the ice-covered sidewalk. Even with all the salt on the roads, it was still quite slippery if one wasn't careful. He tilted his head back to see his breath float up into the chilled air. Honestly, that was the third man to ask him since he arrived within the gated community. Now that he thought about it, it made sense.

Everyone here knew who he was but stayed quiet due to Caym's influence. That didn't mean they wouldn't still try their hand at getting one of the head agency's sons engaged to their child, just to get a little extra money and prestige.

Honestly, it was disgusting, the way the men groveled. He could understand though. For a gated community, this one seemed to be surviving simply due to L. J. Fox Inc. It was on the poorer side, so it was like having a celebrity living next door.

He groaned at the analogy. He wasn't some celebrity or prize. Why could no one understand that?

He shook his head as he passed more buildings and arrived at the meeting place. It was a building set off to one side of the headquarters, a banquet hall of sorts.

Honestly, if he had to deal with more people like that he might have to just lie and say that he already had a bride lined up for when he returned home. It would be easier for his sanity, at least.

He stepped inside the building and looked around at the high golden walls and hanging tapestries decorating the room. He could already hear the quiet chatter from down the hall. A butler, set off to one side, stepped forward and bowed, extending his arms. Lex noted he stayed in that position to accept his clothes. Lex wasn't exactly enthused at the idea, but he slipped his coat off anyway, handing it over. The butler draped it over his arm and hurried away to one side where Lex could see other coats hanging up.

He could've just walked over there himself.

He withheld the groan he knew he would be feeling for the rest of the night and slunk into the main hall. Chairs of pearly white and glass tables sat along the side walls with ceiling-high windows showcasing the beautiful gardens on either side, covered in a thin layer of snow. He heard a herald call out his name from one side and couldn't quite stop the wince as he descended the stairs, finding most eyes focused his way. Upon reaching the ground, a group of people migrated toward him, introducing themselves and, in obvious ploys, trying to get in his good graces.

"Ah, the main guest of the party." A voice rang from the other side of the room.

Lex looked over to see his employer, a scientist by the name of Finnien Gladius, or so Lex believed. It was a strange name either way. The man, both a scientist and a CEO, stepped forward and gave a gracious bow before straightening up and giving a welcoming, though curt smile. "It's good of you to come. I welcome you to our party. Come, sit, have a drink and some hors d'oeuvres."

The man gestured a waiter over and Lex glanced over the choices. He almost wanted to click his tongue or let out an annoyed sound, but held off, picking the less radical of the choice of dishes, what was probably a blue crab beignet. He grabbed the fritter with a toothpick and nodded toward the waiter before turning to his employer, placing the food onto a crystalline plate. "Now, how are you liking working with us?" The man placed his elbows on the table, chin leaning against the backs of his hands as he curled them over each other. "I bet it's quite different from home."

Lex looked sidelong at him quietly, examining the man he only really met once before. His salt-and-pepper hair was indicative of one too many experiments gone wrong. A permanent grin sat etched on his face, even when he gave the subtlest of frowns. Lex took a bite of the fritter and placed it back down before speaking. "You are correct. I'm still getting a feel for the layout of the company. Though you have not been very open with me exploring the premises."

"Unfortunately, even you have no access to some of those areas. That's just the way things are." The man shrugged. "Now, you've been with us for a few weeks. Any particular plans on what you want to do or where you want to go? After all, this is a dinky little community for someone so prominent."

That's saying something, Lex thought, glancing out the window in the direction of the city, *considering what it was like outside.* "Not particularly. I have my own reasons for being here, as I stated before."

Coming from outside the gated community, even with his name, hadn't been easy. People were reluctant to get near him. It was honestly a stroke of luck and annoyance which gave him the chance to meet

Finnien, the resident director and CEO of L. J. Fox, Inc. He honestly should have realized. Still, the man took Lex under his wing immediately and set him up with the occasional paper transfer or secretary job. Menial tasks even for the gated community, but something, at least.

"Now, I know a position opening up for assistant manager. It's not as prestigious as you might be used to, but it's better than what you have been doing up till this point."

"What would that entail?" Lex leaned back, crossing one leg over the other and placing his hands in his lap.

He noticed a couple eyes looking his way and quiet conversation surrounding their table. A waitress stepped up with some flutes of what appeared to be wine. He took one, along with Finnien.

"A 1998 Château Pétrus, quite delicious, no?" Finnien gently swirled the small flute glass and grinned. "Now, as for this new position. You would be working under me. It would give you access to some of our more private sectors. However, you are going to be acting as my go-between. You've been outside with those vermin, correct?"

Lex pursed his lips, barely stopping the glare from forming on his face, though if the expression on his employer's face was any indication, he didn't fully succeed. "Yes, that is the case."

"I see, something quite handy, considering my company works between the two. I need to have someone keep an eye on the vermin side as well as this side. If you would be willing to do that, I would be more than willing to give you more leeway within the company."

Lex narrowed his eyes. That was quite a good deal, almost too good. "The catch?"

The man chuckled. "Smart. The catch is that I think one of my employees on that side is being a little frivolous with the goods, sneaking more from this side out than agreed upon and selling it separately. I need you to look into it and bring that man or woman, I'm not going to be biased, to me. Understood?"

"So, you want me as a bloodhound."

Lex took a sip of the wine. Whoa. Definitely high end. The alcohol floated over his tongue, giving it a gentle buzz. He wasn't a wine connoisseur, but he could tell it was a well held and expensive wine.

"I wouldn't use those words." Finnien shrugged, placing his flute down, hand trailing over the table. "Now, what do you say?"

Lex stared at him for a long time before reaching his hand out, startling his employer. "As long as I see it in writing, we have a deal."

The man looked down at Lex's hand before taking it and giving it a firm shake. "Then, we have a deal."

Lex dropped his hand and stood, patting his clothes down to straighten them. He figured now would be a good time to get away from his employer with the ever-cheerful look. He had a lot to think about now. At least this way, he might have a chance to actually not only collect more information but also meet up with Maxwell.

He could only hope that this person wouldn't get Maxwell involved. That's all they would need. He turned and glanced over the crowd. He spotted quite a few people he didn't recognize, which seemed a little strange. He'd met everyone in the company on this side of the gated community simply because of all the running around, or so he thought. He noticed one of the men hurry up to him, seeming nervous. The man almost let out what would have been a very undignified sound as he stopped right in front of Lex. "You are Leonard Askren, right? The only person to come back from the outer community?"

"Yes?" *Where was this going?*

The man brightened and held out a pad and paper. "You're a celebrity around here, you know, the man from the dead. I'm usually incredibly busy with work so I never thought I would get a chance to meet you. Can you sign this for my wife and me? Our children will be delighted as well."

Lex wasn't really sure how to respond. Instead, his hand just moved automatically and, the next thing he knew, he was being bombarded by people, asking what happened, how he survived out there, even what he wore to blend in. He grimaced. This was the other reason he hadn't wanted to come. At least, for once, the beaming look on the first man's face was genuine as he pulled away. Such a rarity, yet, where did the man work? Lex never saw him before.

His thoughts were pulled away as someone tugged on his arm. He pulled his arm away, standing straighter and carefully fixing his features into their normal neutral appearance. This was going to be a long night.

He was now very glad he decided to wait on calling the twins. He would need a way to destress and talking to them, however annoying at times, was a great way to do it. They were usually pretty easy to talk with and, really, a simple Merry Christmas would suffice. He figured they would still be up anyway. Plus, it helped that both understood.

Still was going to be a long night though.

Chapter Thirteen

Caym paced back and forth, furious. What right did his Leo have to push him off in such a way? The reminder of his wife and child didn't help. He cursed under his breath and forced himself to sit down. Lex's words, especially today, did not help his mood. His wife left him behind, taking little Kiera and breaking their promise. That was that. Caym closed his eyes and put his hand over them, the back of his hand felt cold against his warm face. The heated room was just a tiny bit too hot for his liking. He could hear the quiet chattering from the maids as they passed his room.

Father was being a pain. It was more of a challenge than Caym expected to keep his father from finding out about little Leo. He managed to tap into his father's phone to redirect any calls from Collern and replace them with his own information. He had the servants help retrieve any paperwork that might slip through and managed to set up a direct link regarding the computers in Collern to his own system. It took a lot of effort and it only made matters worse when Father got suspicious in his sudden increase in workload. He was able to easily play it off, but it wasn't so easy to hide from then on.

He slipped out the door and down the hall toward the kitchens. As he passed, he heard his father's crude shouts and tapping feet. Out of morbid curiosity, he opened the door enough to peer in.

He could see his father, standing in front of his desk with one hand on the desk. He was chattering into a phone, back turned to the door. "I don't care what you have to do. Find the cure."

Caym slipped away, realizing the conversation was getting close to an end, if you could call it one. He continued down the hall, only to pause.

"Mother." His voice came out curt as he spotted his mother walking down the hall, delicate and trying to be refined.

She gave him the facsimile of a smile. "Oh, hello, Caym, dear. What are you doing around here?"

"Just some last-minute things, I will be heading out shortly."

"Oh, where are you going? You are staying for dinner at least, right? It's Christmas after all." She clasped her hands in front of her chest, worry shining on her face. "After, you'll be back with Leonard, right?"

"Yes, Mother, I'll be back, and he will be too."

He tried hard not to think of the dinner Mother already planned. She was so obstinate on retaining this farce of a family.

He missed when Leo was still there to help with the awkwardness, at least it was one of the few times he could talk with his brother with somewhat ease due to his father getting drunk, for once, off the eggnog and his mother 'spreading cheer', as she called it, to the servants.

Aka, giving them tips for once.

He pulled from that thought when he realized Mother was still waiting for a response from him. "Don't worry, Mother, I'll be at the dinner."

"Good dear. Now I will see you in a few hours, understand?" The relief on his mother's face was only shadowed slightly by the greedy gleam in her eyes. "When Leonard returns, he can finally settle down with a wealthy family. Oh, the benefits of having two sons."

Caym refrained from biting his lip or looking down at his mother. She was short-sighted, unlike his Leo, but he couldn't blame her. No, it would be a waste of time. "Now, I need to go, Mother."

"Yes, dear. I'll head over to make sure your father doesn't kill anybody."

The fact that she said that without a care should have unnerved him, he knew, but it was such a commonplace thing that he shrugged it off and continued on his way. Little Leo denied helping him, no surprise there, so that just meant he needed to spend time wearing his uncle down. The best way to do that would be to get to the gated community closest to him, but that would risk exposing Leo to his father. He would have to reroute Father's contacts to him and set things up in a way that Father wouldn't notice the change. In many ways, he needed to usurp his father's control.

Considering he was aiming for that even before Little Leo left, he wasn't too worried. That way, Father would be out of the way when little Leo came back, and they could be brothers once again, family again. With that goal in mind, Caym descended the stairs and checked over the luggage already set to be delivered to Reinmark's gated sections. He flipped through it and nodded. He had everything he needed to speak with his uncle and get away from his father. As much as he knew staying close by would benefit keeping Leo safe, he was sick and tired of his Father's presence and wanted out. Reinmark seemed like a good option, for two reasons, one being that the epidemic was under control there and two…that was the last place Leo lived before returning home with those twins. He wanted to know what happened to him there and how he'd changed. His uncle would know, plus Caym figured he might as well ask his uncle about Ariel. His uncle would know whether or not she was happy with her new husband. Caym stared back at the upper floors and furrowed his brow. Now, the hard part.

Getting his father out of the way long enough so that Lex had that promised year, and dealing with a Christmas dinner that he in no way wanted to attend.

Well, he never was one to back down from a challenge.

Chapter Fourteen

The holidays passed, and winter came and went, delving into the early layers of spring. Maxwell yawned. It had already been a few months since they arrived, and the April weather was just starting to hint to warmth.

With Lex's new position, Maxwell was able to see Lex a bit more often and finally managed to give Lex his bag. Which was a relief to both of them. Thankfully the outer side seemed to appreciate his hard work and smarts. He was actually moving up surprisingly quickly, but he didn't complain. At least now he could see a few more data sheets without having to watch his back. Still, that really didn't mean much. With Lex running back and forth between the two sides and having to deal with security both ways, it was a hassle and a half. Though thankfully for Lex's sanity, he didn't have to be cleaned every time, though he was being grilled to find someone who seemed to be undermining operations.

Maxwell couldn't quite recall seeing anything like that. He let out a groan, tilting his head back as he stared up at the ceiling of the apartment. It was still pretty barren, since they only really ever acquired enough money to buy food and pay for rent along with daily amenities. He pushed himself up, hearing a faint rap on the door.

"Come in, it's unlocked," he called, knowing that it wasn't Karina.

He looked back to see Emma standing in the doorway with Madeline behind her.

Honestly, he didn't really understand Madeline. The girl always seemed to be a little nervous around him. Both his sister and even Emma occasionally joked that Madeline might like him. Honestly, he wasn't sure.

No, he wasn't an idiot, he could see the signs, but it just seemed strange to him. He pulled himself from that thought and pushed himself to his feet. "Hey, Madeline and Emma, what's up?"

"Madeline here was wondering if you—"

"Emma?" Madeline yelped, pushing past her before stepping up to Maxwell. "I was wondering if you...if you wanted— Can you— Would you be willing to join Emma and me for dinner on Friday? There's this new dessert at the café that your sister works at that I really wanted to try and..."

Maxwell could hear flesh meeting flesh as Emma smacked her face and groaned. Madeline sent her a glare before turning back to Maxwell. "I mean, your sister is invited, of course. That is, if you don't mind."

"I'll have to talk it through with my sister." Maxwell shrugged.

He didn't mind the idea, honestly. The two girls were really nice, and he knew that his sister liked Emma as a friend. He did too for that matter. "She should be home soon."

"All right, then I'll just..." Madeline stammered and hurried out of the room.

"Honestly, she's completely different around you." Emma shook her head before turning to Maxwell with a relaxed air. "She's usually a lot tougher and more, get near me and I'll punch you to Saturn and back."

"I remember Arik telling me that once." Maxwell chuckled as he took a seat. Emma closed the door and sat across from him.

"Yeah, that sounds like Arik. Leon would probably say it too, but he's smart enough not to run his mouth." Emma shrugged before she leaned forward. "By the way, how is work going? I heard you were supposed to be meeting up with your friend in a few days for a 'Work interview.'"

Maxwell chuckled. *Oh right, that.* " Yeah, well, he's been going around, asking to interview all the employees. It's taken so long because,

I swear, he can only interview, like, two people per week at most. Whoever he's working for is keeping him busy. If anything, he looks frustrated, but we can't really talk. I think he changed phones and never got a chance to send me his number." Maxwell ruffled his hair. His hand knocked into the clip and he carefully tugged his fingers loose. "Anyway, what about you? Any luck with the job search?"

Emma slumped in her seat. "No, I so thought I had that position, even with the long delay, so I didn't really try to look for others."

Maxwell felt bad for the girl. Emma was so focused on a writing position at the local newspaper, that she forgot about everything else. Still, they didn't have to reject her so harshly." Well, you can always try elsewhere. Where were you thinking of looking next?"

"I heard a spot opened over at the hostel where you two stayed when you arrived." She looked up as Maxwell stiffened. She gave him a sheepish expression. "I know, probably not the best idea." She muttered something under her breath, something about getting enough money up to give Arik a gift.

Her blush indicated that was probably what she was saying, and Maxwell quickly turned away. Even months later, he wondered if there was anything between them. "I heard there have been some strange things happening there though."

"Strange things?" Maxwell furrowed his brow before shaking his head quickly changing the subject. "Oh yeah, did you want something to drink? I forgot to ask."

"A water would be nice." She gave him a soft smile before it shifted into a frown. "Yeah. A lot of strange rumors about disappearances." Maxwell frowned as he stood and grabbed a drink from the other room. Disappearances? "It got to the point that one of the cleaning staff left."

"You're not worried?"

Emma bit her lip, fidgeting in her seat as she fiddled with her hands. Maxwell chastised himself. Of course, she was. He placed the cup down as he heard a creak and looked over to see the door open. Karina walked in, rubbing her eyes. Her hair was falling from her ponytail and she looked tired, another busy day, it seemed. "Hey, Kari."

Karina looked up and grinned, closing the door behind her. "Hey, little bro. Emma, what are you doing over here at this hour?"

"Oh, right." Emma perked up, standing with the glass in hand, part of it already empty. She must have downed it when he wasn't looking. "I wanted to ask you if you would be available Friday. Madeline decided to chicken out."

"Really? I guess I'm not surprised." Annoyance flashed on Karina's face.

"Kari, were you trying to set me up?"

"Why would you think that?"

"Your face says it all."

"Of course not, I'm your sis, after all." Karina shrugged, a cat-like grin on her face.

"Ah-huh." Maxwell couldn't hide how unamused he felt. *Really, Karina was too much sometimes.*

Emma chuckled and turned to Karina. "We're having dinner at the café, is that all right?"

Karina frowned and then sighed. "Yeah, that's fine, just don't expect me to eat much. I'm a little sick of their food after eating it for the past few months."

"Hey, free food is free food," Maxwell pointed out and Karina glared. He raised his hands in defense. "At least you can get free food on breaks. I have to make lunch and hope it doesn't get squashed."

"True." Karina rolled her eyes and turned to Emma. "That's fine. What time?"

"Friday at six o'clock."

"Sounds good to me. I'll see you then." Karina watched her leave, seeing Emma wave good-bye before turning to Maxwell, hands on her hips. "So, what were you two talking about when I arrived?"

Maxwell blinked and then frowned. "You know the hostel?"

Karina's unamused look was enough to warrant he said something stupid. He winced. Rightly deserved there. "Well, Emma was thinking of applying for a job there." Karina pursed her lips but stayed silent. Maxwell was kind of glad she didn't say anything, so he could continue. "I'm worried though. She mentioned disappearances."

"Disappearances…" Karina trailed off, lost in thought. "Right. I've heard some mention of that the past few days, I didn't really think too much of it though." Karina's shoulder slumped as she took a seat on the couch. "I guess I got so used to working that I fell into a routine and since I never see anyone from the hostel, I don't really think about it."

He knew he probably wouldn't have noticed either. Rather, he probably wouldn't care to look into it. After all, other than Lex's new position, not much changed over the past few months, which was both relaxing and frustrating beyond belief. "Makes sense, but it is kind of worrying."

"Did you try to dissuade her?" Karina crossed her arms and leaned back, looking like she wanted to put her feet up, but decided against it. "Emma's not dumb, why take the risk?"

"Arik, probably." Maxwell shrugged, and Karina groaned in understanding. "Anyway, Lex contacted me. I'll be meeting with him in a few days to have my 'interview'." Maxwell didn't forget to put up the quotes. Karina snorted, rolling her eyes. Maxwell dropped his hands. "Though I'm not sure what Lex is going to do. He hasn't found anything yet and it's getting more difficult. He needs to get the employer's trust to go into the deeper areas of the building, but he has no idea who it is." Maxwell bit his lip.

"You don't know either, do you?"

"I'm not positive. Not really. I suspect, but…" Maxwell could only think of the person who hired him, and the same person who was allowing him to move through the company so quickly. The man always seemed a little different from the others to him, but he could never put a finger on why. Not exactly solid evidence to indict someone.

Karina pursed her lips and hummed softly in thought. "I see. I'm not sure I can help with that." She looked away, hands tightening on her arms before she let them fall and stood. "Anyway, we have to make sure you have something for that dinner date with Madeline and Emma Friday."

"Karina, really?" Maxwell grumbled at the wording and Karina smirked.

"Oh, come on, little brother, you're not that dense."

"No, I'm not, but I'm also not interested."

Truthfully, he wasn't. Madeline wasn't a bad girl, but he didn't know much about her, just what he heard from the others.

Karina stared at him in silence, face impassive. She let out a sigh. "All right." She reached her hands to the ceiling, stretching like a cat. "Anyway, don't forget to get Lex's number."

"Just like I keep reminding you to pick up a phone?" Maxwell recalled, glaring at Karina, who waved it away, a sheepish expression on her face.

"Yeah, I know, geez."

"Well, if your employer keeps calling me for you, she's not going to be too happy."

Karina groaned. "I know, it's just nothing is cheap enough."

Maxwell found himself frustrated, because he understood. He had the advantage of having his phone from home and, checking on the account, realized it had been receiving automatic deposits. Ma must have set up a separate bank account to pay for it. Though how long would that last? He had no idea how much money Mom had, nor how expensive it was. It was a lost cause trying to think of it, though it made sense that she would set it up that way, considering what happened to Dad.

Karina's was probably the same, but hers was still at home.

His thoughts drifted to home. What was happening to it now? He briefly wondered what happened to Mr. Parkin, the man who found them hidden in his shed when they'd fled the house. Did the black-clothed police do anything to him? What about the rest of the town?

He could still remember the state of his home, the pulled-up rug and blood-stained sink, the jagged doors and yet the upstairs, untouched by it all. He still remembered the note, how his heart had sunk into his shoes as he nursed a paper cut he'd received from it, how his sister thought he'd found Ma. To think that little note brought them all the way out here. He shook his head, pulling from his thoughts. There was no point thinking about it now. They couldn't exactly go back, not yet at least.

Maxwell heard movement and looked up as Karina stood. He scrambled after her as they slipped into the kitchen. They both grabbed something small to tide them over before going their separate ways. Maxwell walked into Lex's room while Karina took their originally shared room.

Actually, if not for the occasional contact, and the short call during Christmas which was basically just a few exchanged words, Maxwell would have almost thought Lex pulled a "Dad" on them. It was a disconcerting thought. He looked around his room. It was as barren as ever. The sun was dipping below the horizon and he yawned. Tomorrow should be interesting to say the least.

~ * ~

Maxwell grunted as he found himself shoving his way through the larger men heading for break. He lucked out and got an early break, but still. He slipped into the main hall and released a breath. Lex's interview time was coming up soon. Thankfully, he should be able to make it in time.

He glanced over his shoulder at the closed doorway before he continued down the hallway to a door at the end. It led to the bridge between the gated community and here. The room had a set of guards at the end, watching with machine guns strapped over their shoulders. Maxwell didn't even glance to them, taking a right toward the doorway off to one side where a third guard waited. The man looked at him, then looked at his name. "You may enter," he sneered before stepping aside.

Maxwell frowned, but moved past him, through the doorway.

Lex looked up from his pile of paperwork. A weak, but genuine smile flitted onto his face. "Take a seat." His voice was neutral as his eyes flickered to the camera set off to one side. Maxwell withheld a grimace. His friend could never seem get any luck. Lex must have noticed his look because he lightly chuckled, face clearly away from the camera. "Don't worry, it doesn't record sound, I've already checked."

Maxwell took a seat, doing his best not to let out a breath of relief. That would make things easier. He kept his back straight as Lex laid down his papers and faced him. "It's good to see you are doing well. How are you and Karina?"

Maxwell felt a smile wash over his face. "Good. I've gotten the hang of working here. Most of the people here are much older than me though. It makes working a little frustrating because they never really give me much credit. Just because I can't lift a one-ton stack like half of them," he muttered the last bit in annoyance.

Lex winced, giving him an amused, if apologetic expression. "So where are you working now?"

"Oh, you heard of the transfer?" Maxwell wasn't too surprised. It happened only recently, really. "I'm actually working with the receptionist at the front desk, delivering papers and letters throughout this side of the corporation which, by the way, is way too big." He frowned. "The docking area alone, I've gotten lost in a few times." Lex chuckled as Maxwell looked down. "The thing is, I haven't found anything about Ma. Have you had any luck?"

"No, not particularly." Lex furrowed his brow, frustrated. "I wanted to use the capture of some 'traitor' to garner attention so that you could slip through, but that isn't going to work for two reasons."

"I can probably guess what they are." Maxwell shifted in his seat.

"You probably could," Lex readily agreed, turning to face him. "I don't have enough trust from my employer and I'm starting to suspect that, even if I do catch the person, my employer is just going to have that person disappear."

"Disappear." Maxwell couldn't help but shiver at the word.

Lex, being his observant self, noticed. He gestured for Maxwell to continue.

"Emma was saying how people have been disappearing from near the hostel lately, no one knows why. Karina also heard mention of it."

Lex steepled his fingers and leaned his chin against them, lost in thought. After some time, he laid his arms on the desk. "That's worrying.

I'll call my informant and see what he has to say."

"You're still in contact?"

Lex nodded. "He calls me with the occasional updates. They are nothing really important, but it's still critical to know things are not a problem."

Maxwell concurred no news was never technically good news. "Right, do you think you can send a little extra money? Karina really needs to pick up a phone."

Lex gave a short chuckle. "Idiot." He shook his head and stood. "I can do that. Now, here is a folder I'm supposed to give you, now that I've authenticated your legitimacy with our conversation." At that, he gave a slight mischievous grin before his expression turned neutral once more. "Inside is my new number. I'll call you if I receive anything."

Maxwell took the folder gratefully, "Thanks, Lex. We appreciate it."

Lex's lips twitched upward as he gestured for Max to head out the door. Maxwell scurried out, folder in hand. The guard barely sent him a look, sending in the next person waiting to see Lex. Through the partially open door, Maxwell could see the neutral and unamused expression cross Lex's face.

He felt sorry for his friend. It honestly must be such a hassle, but at least he was sort of getting somewhere, unlike the two of them.

He walked toward the front and took a seat next to the receptionist, who sent him a relieved smile. "I'm taking a break. You came just in time."

"Already? Didn't you just get in?"

"You know how they are." The girl groaned and hurried off. Maxwell glanced at the computer. He didn't have authorization to touch it, but he could glance at whatever the receptionist had up, and occasionally, she would let him watch as they worked. It was a bit of guesswork, though, every time he turned around, he felt there was a new worker. Then again, he wouldn't doubt that the disease had a good amount to do with it.

There was another graph on screen of sales. It was quite

interesting, actually. In truth, he was surprised to find that more fertilizer actually went to his side than the gated community. The gated community seemed to get a special concoction that made it more expensive. According to the research that both Lex and he did, that wasn't the case. So why the disparity?

He couldn't think too much of it, noting as someone hurried up to him, saying they needed to meet with the head. Maxwell mentally groaned. Not again.

~ * ~

Lex felt his whole being collapse as he returned to his room, arms laden with pages of text. Honestly, he was very much starting to wonder just how much of a hand Caym actually had in all this, if any, simply due to the fact that his employer was treating him like a personal secretary, without the trust.

He dropped the papers down and got changed out of the stuffy clothes. He sat on the bed, running his hand through his hair. Three months and nothing. It was more than frustrating, it was insane. He knew, full well, that there were areas he still wasn't able to get into and he still was getting bombarded by people either asking for his hand in marriage, or for their daughters. Either that, or asking for a job with his father or something else just as crazy and stupid. He even had a few more people come up to him for an autograph from what Caym called the prodigal son. He was starting to see why Caym used those words. It was honestly straining his patience and, last time he checked, his patience was pretty good. It didn't help that so far only about two of the people actually seemed to care in any way. The man who first asked for his autograph and a young girl, whom he later found out was the first man's daughter. The irony.

He reached for his phone, an older model he managed to grab without Caym noticing. He attached it to his uncle's account so there wasn't as much connection to him. He flipped it open and placed it to his ear, hearing the quiet hum as he glanced toward the camera. He was at such an angle where the camera wouldn't be able to see what he was holding, which was a relief. He heard a click and then a gruff, "What is it?"

"Pleasant as ever, I see."

Antonio's voice was more than a little tinged in annoyance. "Of course, I am. That brother of yours is stomping through the area, incessantly pestering your uncle. I'm going to have to leave soon if I want to avoid the damn backlash that's ready to explode around here. Now why did you call?"

Lex grimaced, he was afraid of that. "I need you to check in with your contacts."

"Worried about the twins?" His voice was monotone, almost soft.

"Recently, I've heard there have been disappearances occurring near where we used to stay."

"Do you believe it's not some small-time punks?" Antonio's voice was a mix of curious and amused.

Lex leaned back, staring at the ceiling. "I don't know. However, I know that my charges live with a police chief nearby, and these disappearances are still occurring around that area. I just want to be on the safe side."

"That sounds about right. You say there have been multiple disappearances?"

"From what I infer."

Antonio hummed, before clicking his tongue. "I'll look into it and let you know if I find anything—Roxanne, what are you doing? Hey. Let go—"

"Hey, Lex." A soft feminine voice sounded through the phone and Lex rolled his eyes.

"Roxanne, did you wrestle the phone away from Antonio again?"

"Well, yes." Her voice was cheery and light.

Lex could almost imagine her shrugging it off, little grin on her face.

"You know how Antonio is. Anyway, hopefully, I'll be able to see you soon. Plus, it's good to hear you sounding better. You sound so healthy these days."

Lex paused, uncomfortable. "Well, trying to keep up with those two is a trial and a half."

Roxanne chuckled. "Anyway, I just wanted to check to see how you are doing. Plus, I wanted to say thank you for keeping your promise."

"So, you do still remember." He hadn't meant to say that out loud, but it came out anyway.

"Of course,," Roxanne said, sounding hurt and a little annoyed. "You told me to tell my stubborn older brother that, if he will stop his endeavors, you will try to pay each week. You promised me one day, I'll get better. I would say you kept that promise." Roxanne's voice seemed to have tried to imitate Lex's voice and failed.

He could almost imagine her wagging her finger as she spoke and chuckled at the image. He heard a shift before Roxanne spoke again, voice quieter. "Anyway, I'll make sure Antonio doesn't do anything reckless."

"I would appreciate that." Lex couldn't stop the tiny grin from crossing his lips. "I'll speak with Antonio later, take care of yourselves." With that, he hung up. He slipped his phone away and leaned back. Now he just needed to wait.

To his surprise, it was only a day later when he received the call.

~ * ~

Karina took a seat in the café and glanced over to Maxwell, noticing as he frowned at his phone in annoyance. "I swear, I need to get a new battery for this thing." He huffed, putting the phone back into his pocket before looking around the place. Karina leaned back, kicking hard enough to push the chair into the wall, leaning on two legs. The other two chairs were empty as they waited for Emma and Madeline to turn up.

Karina could see some of her fellow workers, glancing their way in amusement. Abigail, one of the waitresses, meandered over with a raised eyebrow. "Hey, Kari, this your twin?"

Karina nodded, tipping her chair back into place. "How did you guess?"

"He's giving ya an amused and resigned expression. Plus ignoring hair and eyes, ya two look a lot alike."

Karina glanced toward Maxwell, who had gained a few inches recently, then to herself, finding she filled out a little more before shrugging. "Not really."

Abigail raised an eyebrow before shrugging too. "If ya say so, dear. Now what are ya having?" She glanced toward Maxwell, who quickly mumbled some drink.

Karina rolled her eyes, guessing it was probably the orange tea. Abigail glanced at her and grinned. "And of course, the normal for ya?"

"Right in one." Karina saluted, watching as Abigail snorted before looking toward the door. Emma and Madeline stepped in, spotting them right away. Madeline's face reddened to the point of bursting. She looked really pretty tonight, and Karina could tell Maxwell seemed confused by that. Madeline was in a simple white dress with a scarf draped nicely around her shoulders. Her hair was done up and, was she wearing some makeup? Emma, who was in casual clothes like Karina, stepped behind Madeline and pushed her forward. They hurried to the table, taking seats. Abigail glanced between them, amusement shining on her face as she tapped her writing pad. Karina waved. "They'll just have water for now."

Emma nodded as Madeline stuck her head into the menu.

Abigail chuckled. "Right away." With that, she turned and hurried away. Karina glanced sidelong at Maxwell, who was looking at Madeline strangely, unsure, probably, how to deal with her. There was a faint blush on his cheeks, which almost sent Karina into a cackling fit.

"She's cute, right?" she whispered, causing Maxwell to jump out of his skin and glare at her, yet he didn't say a word.

Dinner was quiet, for the most part, with Madeline occasionally glancing up from the table or food. They hadn't ordered much, Madeline mostly mumbling some things so soft, Emma had to tell the waitress what it was. Emma and Karina exchanged annoyed glances before Emma jabbed Madeline in the waist.

"Ouch, what did you do that for?" Madeline glared, earning an eye roll from her friend. She took a deep breath, as if to center herself and looked toward Maxwell, who was glancing between them with a neutral, though curious, expression on his face. Madeline straightened, eyes directly at Maxwell's. "Maxwell. Do you have girlfriend?"

Karina, who was taking a drink, honestly not expecting the girl to be so bold, choked alongside Maxwell. Even Emma seemed flabbergasted.

Maxwell coughed to one side, as Karina wiped her mouth and Madeline stiffened.

Maxwell, the ever-observant brother of hers, noticed and quickly straightened. "Sorry, that caught me off guard." He grinned sheepishly. "No, I don't have a girlfriend, and anyway, I doubt that Sis would ever let me get that far."

"I'm not that bad," she mumbled but couldn't completely contradict his statement. If she didn't trust Emma, she wouldn't even dare trust Madeline. She took a bite of the cake the group decided to order, having already finished their dinner of chicken and vegetables. She'd honestly forgotten they had that on the menu. Either way, it was good.

Maxwell just sent her an unamused look which screamed he didn't believe her before facing Madeline. "Why do you ask?"

Well, that's blunt.

Madeline gulped, stammering out incoherent words. Karina shifted about as much as Emma, closing off any escape routes. Madeline glanced at them, a betrayed expression on her face before she faced Maxwell. "I was wondering...would you like to—" She bit her lip and went to open her mouth, when a scream cut through the room.

Karina jumped and turned toward the doorway, standing along with the other three. The other residents cut off their conversations and looked over, trying to figure out what happened as well.

Shouts filled the air and Abigail, who was heading to their table already, hurried over. "It seems the epidemic struck." Her voice shook as she gestured for them. "Come on, everyone's being led through the back entrance, this way."

Karina glanced to the rest of the clientele, noticing the other waiters and waitresses doing the same. Karina nodded. "I'll lead them, you focus on another table." Abigail sent her a grateful smile before hurrying off. "Come on." She gestured, pulling Maxwell to his feet.

A frown sat over Madeline's face as she examined the situation with surprisingly critical eyes. Maxwell's gaze was locked on the doorway, uncertain. Karina didn't even need to guess what he was thinking. She tugged sharply, catching his attention. He looked over and she shook her head enough for him to see. He gritted his teeth, yet joined her and the rest of the guests as they moved out the back door.

The worst part about this, Karina thought, was it wasn't the first time she had needed to do this. She grimaced as they finally slipped out the back door.

Madeline turned to them, eyes sharp and posture straight and proud. "I need to check on something. I'll find out if anyone else got afflicted. You three, hurry home."

Emma nodded, while Karina and Maxwell exchanged glances. What? Why would Madeline get herself involved in that? Before they could argue, Madeline was gone, lost in the departing crowd.

"What?"

"We should return home," Emma said, giving them a weak smile. "It's cold today."

"I'm still hungry though." Maxwell sighed, earning an apologetic look from Emma.

"Well, there is a place down the road with some quick food, why don't we stop there on the way?" Karina spread her arm out, gesturing down the road.

The little alley they were in was filtering out to either side. Karina led the way off to the left, followed by Maxwell and Emma.

"That sounds fine," Emma conceded.

Karina grinned. "Well then, this way." She hurried down the lane and to the little food stall she knew would still be open, even now. She had to admit, although she did eat a decent amount, she was still hungry as well.

Considering most of their meal was focused on Madeline just trying to speak a coherent sentence to Maxwell, she wasn't surprised.

~ * ~

It didn't take much time before they reached the stall and ordered food. The food sat heavily in Maxwell's stomach as he finished off the last of it. He definitely ate too much, but it was good, so he wasn't too upset. The night was growing on them and the streets were dark and damp. A rainstorm blew through when they were at the stall. He could see Emma and Karina chatting behind him. He glanced forward, hands in his pockets with a small smile.

The stall was a bit out of the way from their home, but it wasn't too far.

Unfortunately, it crept too close to the hostel for his taste.

"Hey, Maxwell, why don't you slow down a bit?" Emma called, hesitant.

Maxwell looked back as Karina glanced up, seemingly not noticing the distance. She rolled her eyes, probably at the irony.

Maxwell slowed down, waiting for the girls to catch up. "I wasn't that far ahead of you."

"I know, but it's dark and it's always better to walk in a group at this time of night." Emma looked around, a little fearfully, not that Maxwell could blame her. "After all, this is the time spirits walk, especially after the epidemic strikes."

That caught him and Karina off guard, who stumbled to a halt, staring at the girl. She must have noticed because she stopped a little ahead and peered back. Maxwell could just see the embarrassed horror on her face. "I said that out loud, didn't I?"

Maxwell nodded, spotting Karina doing the same with an incredulous expression.

Emma groaned and slapped her face, letting her hand trail down. "Oh, that's embarrassing," she mumbled weakly. Maxwell stepped forward, with Kari only a step behind.

"It just startled us."

"Yeah, I didn't know you believed in spirits of the dead and all that." Karina shrugged, placing her hands behind her head with a sharp-toothed grin. "I'll have to remember that one though."

"Karina," Maxwell admonished, garnering a shrug from Karina. He heard hurried footsteps and looked over. They were just passing an alley, barely lit by streetlamps. He frowned.

Squealing tires reached his ears and he jumped, glancing over in time to see a van zip around the corner. It slid to a stop in front of them.

Maxwell stiffened alongside Karina. Emma reached toward her waist and cursed, staring at the car with narrowed eyes, normally not seen on the cheerful and pleasant girl.

The door slammed open just as footsteps rang out behind them. Maxwell whipped around, just in time to get a gun in his face. He froze, eyes wide. He could see the grooves and rivets in the guns barreling.

He heard a slew of curses he didn't even know existed from Emma and glanced sidelong toward his friend. The men from the van were on them in no time and Maxwell felt terror shoot through him.

It wasn't hard to guess what was happening. Karina was only frozen for a second. She glanced over, saw the gun, and darted forward, catching the man off guard. She slammed into his waist before slipping low and kicking out his feet.

Maxwell jerked his head, just as he heard a shout and a bang. He could see smoke drifting up from the muzzle of the gun and heard a pained shout. He didn't look over to see what happened. He pulled Karina to her feet and glanced over to Emma. To his surprise, she was holding her own. Her hands slid to the ground as she kicked outwards before flipping back.

Where the hell did she learn those moves?

She spotted them looking and shouted," Run!"

Maxwell went to argue, only to spot another man sneaking up behind Karina. He tugged her away, hearing her shout in surprise before darting back down the street, the way they came. He heard pounding footsteps behind them and words he could barely decipher. There was a cry. Maxwell looked back in time to see one of the men grab Emma around her neck, lifting her off the ground. She scrabbled at her neck yet was unable to do anything as she was thrown into the van.

Yet, the thing that shot fear through Maxwell was the other man on their tail, eyes squarely on them and radio crackling. Maxwell slid to a halt, almost against his will, only to have Karina tug at his arm. "Come on."

Maxwell looked back to see a pained expression on her face. He nodded, and they raced down the road. The man following cursed. "Come back here, brats!"

Karina turned, running into an alley. Maxwell could hear squealing tires and guessed the van was moving again.

Why was that vehicle after them? What did they do? Their footsteps rang out down the road, along with those of their pursuers. He could hear screeching tires up ahead and felt his throat close up in worry and fear. His heart pounded, louder than his footsteps. Karina's grip was tight enough to almost cut circulation.

They zipped around another corner, sliding out on the soaked ground. Their pursuer cursed.

Maxwell glanced ahead and almost sagged in relief. He picked up his steps, even with Karina. He didn't see the van anywhere and they were outrunning the pursuer, who was already heaving from exertion and fatigue from the epidemic. Without much pretense, they slid to a halt and started banging on the doorway.

Please, by gosh, he hoped dearly that Arik and his father were home, or both, he could deal with both. He heard loud footsteps and, jerked around, pressing against the door as the man, panting, glared at them from the end of the driveway. "You two, you are coming with me." His voice cut through the silence, heard even from so far away. Maxwell heard tires and looked over to see the van slam to a halt right behind.

"Hell no," Karina shouted before turning to the door. "ARIK, OPEN THE DAMN DOOR!" Her shout rang clear through the humming night air.

The radio crackled, too soft for Maxwell to hear from a distance.

He felt the door shift behind him, and almost cried out as it swung open.

Without really thinking about it, he pushed inside, tugging Karina with him and turned, slamming the door shut. Arik stared at them in shock. Only about a moment later, he heard a loud thump as both of them leaned against the door. After a moment, it stopped. Arik seemed to realize. "Cover your ears." He darted down the hallway.

Maxwell and Karina followed his instructions just in time. A loud siren screeched through the house, erupting into the night air. The pounding against the door stopped as dogs barked from the neighboring houses. Maxwell would have jumped out of his skin as the screeching "intruder alert" sounded through the house and broke in waves out the door.

Maxwell heard loud cursing before the footsteps faded, followed by the squeal of tires disappearing down the street, even through the racket. He let out a breath before exchanging looks with Karina, worry suddenly slamming through him as the sirens cut off and Arik returned, a strange expression on his face that looked anything but welcoming.

"Arik, where's your father?" Karina demanded, hurrying away from the door, causing the boy to jerk and shake his head. His narrowed gaze turned to them.

"He's coming, but I'll call him as well. Now what exactly happened?" he asked as he pulled out a thin phone.

He clicked a few buttons and put it to his ear even as he continued to gaze at them, gesturing for them to follow. He locked and bolted the door. He checked the windows before leading them into a kitchenette area. The blinds were closed, and the room was dark except for a single light above the sink.

"Emma," Maxwell spoke, seeing Karina's gaze darting to the door. "She was kidnapped."

"The disappearances." Arik grimaced as the phone clicked on. "Father, I have a kidnapping to report." He looked at them and Maxwell realized he was wondering about the description.

Quickly thinking it over, he spoke. "There were about five guys,

I think, all well-built. One guy ambushed us from behind with a gun. It had a long barrel, I know that."

"The van was white, large with scraped-off lettering on the side. I couldn't read it in the light." Karina slipped in, voice soft and uneasy.

Maxwell didn't need to guess why. Emma saved them by distracting the group, even though it was clear the group had been after the two of them for some reason. He gritted his teeth, fists clenched as he listened to Arik report the information to his father, saying they didn't get a vehicle license plate.

He was unable to do anything, again. It was frustrating.

"I think they were after two of my friends, they even tried to get in the house before I set the alarm off," Arik finished, garnering Maxwell's attention.

Oh, so Arik noticed.

Karina had her hands clenched to the point Maxwell worried she would cut herself. That was the other thing. Kari was close to Emma after the last few months of spending time together. It must have hurt her deeply to watch Emma get taken like that.

After some time, Arik hung up. He gestured to both of them. Maxwell and Karina took a seat around the kitchen table. He stepped over to the fridge and pulled out two water bottles. He dropped them in front of Maxwell and Karina. He leaned back, head in his hands and worry clear in his posture.

"Dad said he would look into it, but…"

Maxwell could see the slight tremor as the boy let out a breath and looked up, eyes narrowed. "They were after you two, right?"

"I think so." Maxwell agreed, glancing to Karina who was nursing the bottle quietly, staring at the water as it swished back and forth. "Even when they grabbed Emma, they still chased after us both on foot and with the van."

"We'll use that."

Huh?

Arik must have seen his confusion because he explained, "We'll use you two as bait to find those people, get to them and rescue Emma."

"No," Karina shook her head. "I know we caused it, but we're not just going to throw ourselves out there to be kidnapped," she snapped.

Maxwell found himself agreeing, though at the same time, he could see the frustration and anger on Arik's face, as well as the deep-set worry.

"We have to. We have to get to her and quickly." He looked uncomfortable even as he said that, staring right at Karina's annoyed eyes.

Maxwell peered sidelong toward his sister, who appeared conflicted, yet still against it. "Just give us some time," Maxwell muttered.

"We don't—"

"We have some time," Karina snapped, cutting Arik off. "They didn't come right back, correct? They are still probably out there. If they are after us, they will hold off doing anything to Emma, right?"

Arik shut his mouth and nodded, letting out a sigh. "I'm sorry."

"It's fine." Maxwell shook his head, placing a hand on Kari's arm to calm her a little. From the looks of things, it was their fault Emma was in this situation. Karina seemed to realize because she looked away, tightening her grip even more. Maxwell swore he saw thin streams of blood trail down her fingers, but she quickly loosened her hands anyway, so he stayed silent.

Maxwell let out a breath, pulling away and glancing toward Arik. "So, what now? Can we trust your father…?"

"Are you another one who doesn't trust the police?" Arik furrowed his brow, anger spiking. "I didn't want to think that's the case, but…"

"Police? You mean the black-clothed ones, correct?" Maxwell verified. He never met Arik's father, only Lex had for a brief time when they were first introduced. Since then, Arik's father was busy more often than not. Yes, Lex spoke of them differently, but Maxwell wasn't sure what to believe.

"Black-clothed…" Arik trailed off, pushing himself back, arms crossed and lost in thought. "You're talking about the Enthrope police, aren't you?"

Enthrope police? Maxwell recalled hearing that from Lex but didn't expect Arik to know.

Probably noting the twins 'confusion, Arik looked away. "My apologies, it seems you don't know." Arik shook his head and turned to them. "My father is chief of the police brigade. They are the organization that protects this side of the town. The Enthrope police you are speaking of kind of go-between the two sides yet are controlled by the gated community. From what I've heard, sometimes they have special guards specifically for inside the community, but I think that's more for the individual families than an overall group." Arik shrugged, giving a weak smile. "Don't worry, a lot of people say they don't trust the police brigade. You can trust my father. He is a good man. Still, how do you know the Enthrope police, but not the police brigade?"

"We've seen them around. They were a lot more common where we're from," Karina admitted.

Arik looked them over before a flicker of a smile appeared. "That makes sense. All right, I'm going to contact Emma's friends. We'll need all the help we can get, and soon." Arik turned and hurried away.

Maxwell dug into his pocket and slipped out his phone, which was still dead. "Arik?"

Arik's head popped back into the room, phone at his ear. "Hm?"

"Do you have a charger? My phone's dead."

Arik gestured toward the kitchen table. "The far one on the left." With that, he disappeared around the corner. Maxwell stood and walked over, plugging it in. He saw the insignia turn on and slumped over in relief when he noticed the charging signal. He went to turn and sit down when a shrill sound cut through the silence. He jumped and turned back around to see his phone ringing. He quickly opened it and put it on speaker, unable to put it to his ear due to the cord.

"Finally connected, are you okay?" Lex's voice rang through, sounding gruff and worried.

Maxwell grimaced as he noticed Karina stand and hurry over.

"Considering your lack of response, confused or otherwise, I would say probably not." Lex let out a sound of annoyance and Maxwell could almost imagine him swiping his hand through his hair. "All right, what happened?"

"That's way too accurate," Karina muttered, and Maxwell sent her a quick look before turning to the phone.

"We were attacked on our way home. Emma was kidnapped and…"

"You believe the kidnappers are after you, correct?" Lex must have heard Maxwell's quiet yip. Lex let out a groan, seeming frustrated. "I got a call from my contact earlier. I tried to contact you, but your phone was off, and I didn't have another number."

"My phone died."

"That would explain it." Lex seemed to shift, the rustling of clothes and the soft pat of footsteps indicated he was moving around. "He told me the black market is active in this city. His contact told him they found a rare case of clean siblings. I believe I don't have to remind you what that means."

Maxwell heard Karina gulp, face pale as Maxwell's fingers dug into the plastic of the counter. "Our friend got involved because of us, what can we do?"

"I wish I could say, but I'm unable to join and help." The aggravation in Lex's voice spoke volumes as he cursed soft enough that Maxwell couldn't quite make it out. "More to the point, what are you two planning to do? Where are you now?"

"We're at Arik's." Karina spoke up, voice soft.

"Good, at least you have that protection for you." There was a ruffling sound through the phone as Lex spoke. Maxwell could almost picture Lex pushing a hand through his hair like usual.

"We're going to stay here. Arik is getting Emma's friends. I'm not sure why he's getting them though. However, he is determined to rescue her," Maxwell trailed off, hesitant to continue before letting himself slump down, gaze on the floor. "They were after us, so I have a feeling that we might end up as bait."

"What? I said no," Karina said, glaring at Maxwell.

Maxwell quickly threw his free hand up, wincing as Lex said, "Idiot," at the same time.

"I'm just saying, looking at things the way they are now, that might be the case. We have no idea where she was taken, who they are or anything. I also know we're on a time limit. Those people know we're here and they won't just sit around all day. We also can't stay here. You both know that."

Karina looked like she wanted to argue, but instead pursed her lips into a thin line.

Maxwell heard Lex hum quietly. "You've thought it through. I won't be able to say contrary to how stupid it is."

"I know it's stupid, I don't like it, but what else is there?" Considering Lex didn't have a response, Maxwell knew he hit the nail on the head. "Still, we'll see. If there is any other way, we'll go for it, all right?"

"All right, just be careful." Lex's tone was despondent and almost monotone. "Let me know when it's all over. I'll keep in contact with Antonio and make sure no one here suspects there's anything wrong so you can work in peace. Good luck, that's all I can say." Lex's voice sounded annoyed and resigned.

Maxwell couldn't blame Lex. He was frustrated even though he technically was able to do something.

He noted Kari was awfully quiet. His gaze skipped to her. She seemed to be lost in thought. He reached a hand over to place his fingers to her head to check on her when she jerked and sent him a glare. Maxwell backed away, hands up before turning back to the phone. "All right. We'll be careful. I'll call you when anything changes."

"See that you do. Stay safe out there." Lex hesitated a moment before, with a quiet voice he spoke up once more. "We're going to find and save your mother, remember that. If things get out of hand, just keep that in mind, all right? I promise." With that, there was a click and the phone turned off.

Maxwell heard the faint beeping before he closed it, thinking over Lex's words. That's true. Their mother was more important, even though right now, everything screamed to save Emma, they couldn't just charge blindly in.

He turned to Karina and, noticing her tense posture, walked over to her. He hadn't realized how much he grew during this time. "Hey, Kari, come on. Don't worry, we'll figure something out, we always do."

Karina pursed her lips before tilting her head to look toward him, face pale and tired. "Yeah, I know." Yet, her voice indicated she was resigned.

Maxwell winced, but before he could say anything, footsteps sounded from down the hall.

He looked over as Arik returned, phone closed and stuffed into his pocket. "All right, I contacted everyone. Leon's already researching any locations. I wouldn't be surprised if he's hacking into the camera systems or something." Arik rolled his eyes and shook his head.

Hacking? Damn, there was a lot he didn't know about those people.

"What about everyone else?"

Arik's gaze shifted over to Karina before he leaned heavily on one foot, waving a hand. "Madeline says she's already on it, having suspected something was wrong when an epidemic victim died right nearby. Yes, the epidemic does hit randomly, but that couldn't have been just a coincidence. Mitchell is speaking with my father to help in the search and Andrew is, well, I'm not sure where he is, really." Arik shook his head and centered his balance. "Madeline will call if she needs us. For now, you two need to rest, even just for a few minutes. We need to make sure you won't drop from exhaustion when we need you."

Maxwell bit his lip but found he couldn't argue. There wasn't much else they could do, and there was no point going back to the apartment. After all, stepping one foot out the door was stupid at the moment. They were safe because of their location, but the apartment was still a ways down the street and while they could run fast, they wouldn't be able to protect themselves there. Locking the door wouldn't help if the enemy had guns and could just bash in. At least here, they had the surroundings to their advantage, case in point, Arik scaring them away with the alarm and neighbors.

"I'm worried about Emma. Is there really nothing we can do right now?" Karina's voice sounded uncertain, even a little shaky.

Pain shown clear on Arik's face as he shook his head. "Believe me, I understand."

"Do you?" Karina's voice went up a notch. "We were there, we could have done something. We should have been able to do something, unlike with Mom."

Maxwell's eyes widened, and he reached over, grabbing Karina and tugging her around to face him, causing her to yelp. "Kari, calm down," he hissed.

She struggled for a moment before biting her lip hard. Maxwell looked at her for a little longer before glancing toward Arik. "Do you mind if we borrow a room? I think we do need some rest."

Arik nodded, watching in silence before gesturing for them to follow. Karina pushed herself away from Maxwell and hurried after Arik. Maxwell watched her go, feeling a mix of uncertainty and hurt.

He could not figure out what was going through her head right now and part of him wasn't sure he wanted to know.

~ * ~

Karina wanted to scream and cry, aggravation and worry shooting through her. She could see Maxwell's worried and pale expression, the fatigue he was barely hiding, or probably didn't even know he had with all the adrenaline pumping through their veins. Arik seemed to be looking at her in a mix of uncertainty and anger. She could understand that.

After some time, she found herself in a small room. It seemed to be a bedroom with a small chaise couch off to one side. A few wooden dressers lined the walls and a door sat off to one side, open enough for her to see clothes hanging loosely inside. She sat on the couch, pulling her legs in and stared at the ceiling, lost in thought. She heard the door close, followed by footsteps. She looked over when she felt a gentle weight on her back and a shadow fall over her face.

She tilted her head back to see Maxwell leaning against the arm she was against, his back toward her and arms crossed. He must have noticed her look because he stood and stepped around, taking a seat on what was left of the chaise. Karina debated on moving her legs, but decided against it, not wanting to uncurl from her position.

Maxwell's worried expression shifted to one of deep concern. "Kari, are you relating this to what happened with Ma?"

So, he did notice her slip. She shifted, dropping her legs over the side. She glanced sidelong as anger and hatred at herself shifted through her, burning in her. She reached over, grabbing him around the neck and ruffling his hair, causing him to yelp and wave his arms in surprise. She chuckled and let him go. She was surprised to find that, instead of pulling away, he let his body flop onto hers.

"Maxwell?" She looked down to see Maxwell's eyes closed, weary.

"Sorry, Sis. I guess we both couldn't do anything again. I'm sorry."

"You dolt." Karina shifted, making sure she was more comfortable, jostling Maxwell enough, so that he would accommodate her movements.

He looked up to her with a worried grin. "There you are. I was wondering what was going on through your head earlier. Do you know how worrying it is to have my usually reckless sis thinking?"

"I think," Karina retorted, annoyed, causing Maxwell to laugh and sit up. He leaned back into the seat, glancing sidelong at her. She couldn't keep eye contact, her gaze flicking to the floor as she said, "Still, thanks, little bro." After all, she didn't need him worrying about her. She was strong.

The hate she was feeling. The loathing. She would deal with it later. Maxwell was, no doubt, probably feeling it too. She couldn't think about it, so she grinned. "So, we're going to rest up, then what?"

Maxwell ruffled his hair, closing his eyes in annoyance. "Not sure. I think we'll just nap first and figure it out from there. Though I doubt either of us could figure out what to do next anyway." the last bit was said so soft, Karina almost thought she mistook it. Maxwell's slumped shoulders and expression told her enough he really did say that.

She couldn't argue though. She doubted either of them would get much sleep right now, even if their wired bodies were drained of adrenaline.

"Come on, close your eyes." She reached forward, placing her hand over Maxwell's eyes.

He yelped, cursing quietly under his breath. "What are you even doing?"

"Making sure you get some sleep." Karina kept her voice quiet as she stood and had him lay down. She kept her hands over his eyes and he muttered incoherent sounds of annoyance under his breath.

Yet he didn't resist and she was grateful for that. She peered up toward the lights. "Get some sleep, little bro." She pulled away and hurried over to flick the lights off. She stepped back, grabbed a pillow and the quilt from the bed then returned, draping it over Maxwell, who seemed to, surprisingly enough, be struggling with sleep.

He didn't realize how fatigued he was. After all, he had been working all day, only for this to happen. She decided not to think about it anymore as she knelt down, slipping her hand through his hair.

"Kari, get some sleep yourself, okay?" Maxwell murmured.

Karina only smiled as his eyelids fluttered. She gently maneuvered the pillow under his head, keeping her hand moving through his hair.

Finally, after some time and with the moonlight shining gently through the window, he slipped off to sleep. She pulled her hand away before pushing herself to her feet. "You're too observant, little bro."

She walked away and sat on the bed, staring up at the ceiling, feeling aggravation thrum through her. Honestly, part of her hated how she hadn't been able to do anything to help Emma. She managed to save Maxwell, but… She draped her legs outward as her hands gripped the edge of the bed.

It was their fault again, yet they couldn't do anything except to sit and wait, just like they were doing for the past couple months with

Mom, like they were doing for the past few years with Dad.

They always seemed to be waiting, and she hated it. Hated herself for letting herself get to the point where it was all she could do. She let out a world-weary sigh, thoughts flying too fast for her to sleep and body too wired even now to really even lie down. Yet, she knew she couldn't keep thinking this way, she couldn't let herself get down. She needed to save Emma, and if all she could do now was wait? Then she would wait. As much as it killed her to say it, she knew there wasn't much else she could do.

Chapter Fifteen

Maxwell awoke with a start. He sat up, feeling the quilt drop around his waist as he looked around the unfamiliar room. Off to one side, he spotted Karina, dozing against the headboard of the bed, eyes closed in sleep and mouth slightly open. He shook his head, feeling a hint of annoyance well up as he spotted the dark circles under her eyes. He heard footsteps and a knock on the door. He looked over. "We're up."

The door opened, showing Mitchell, to Maxwell's surprise, standing in the doorway with an even expression and worried smile. "Hey, guys." He entered. "Arik told me that you two were upstairs."

"What time is it? When did you get here?" Maxwell murmured as he slid his legs sideways off the couch, stretching the kinks in his neck.

"It's around eleven. We all snuck in about an hour ago. Are you two okay?" He glanced between Maxwell and Karina.

Maxwell shuffled to his feet and reached over to shake Karina's shoulder. She awoke with a start before rubbing her eyes.

"I'm up, I'm up," she mumbled as she shook her head and swung her legs out of bed. "Did you sleep all right?"

Maxwell just sent his sister a look, receiving a sheepish smile in return. He rolled his eyes and turned to Mitchell. "So, what's going on? What's everyone up to?"

"They're downstairs, I came up to get you two, so we can get started and tell you what we've come up with."

Karina perked up, eyes narrowed. "All right, we're coming." She stood and walked to the door. "Hurry up, sleepyhead."

Maxwell blinked and opened and closed his mouth, unable to find a response. Mitchell smiled before he hurried after Karina and down the stairs. Maxwell reached a hand to his face with a tired groan. He hoped

Karina wouldn't do anything reckless.

He followed after the two and headed into the front entrance. Off to one side, in the living room, chatter could be heard, loud and clear. He slipped inside, staying off to the back. He spotted Karina and shifted over to her. She sent him a look, arms crossed over her chest, before she turned back to the group.

Everyone was there, to Maxwell's surprise. Madeline looked over to him, a sad look in her eyes before she straightened. "It seems like we're all here." Her voice was curt, to the point and almost a little cold. "We've finally discovered the reason behind the local disappearances at the cost of one of our members, as you all well know."

That terminology... Maxwell exchanged looks with Karina. He didn't recognize this. Everyone here seemed like a different person. Then again, the way Emma reacted to the kidnapping attempt, the way she fought, it was like she was trained.

"Arik's father has been gracious enough to let us work freely to discover their whereabouts. After, the Police Brigade will deal with clean-up. Is that good?"

Madeline surveyed the room, receiving affirmative nods from Mitchell, Andrew and Leon, the last of whom was typing away at a computer reminiscent of the one Maxwell had back home. How Leon got that, he wasn't sure, but he was impressed.

"Leave that part to us." Arik waved. "Now what is the plan to find them? You don't honestly expect to use the two of them as bait? I brought it up earlier and they aren't that stupid, considering they ran to a police chief's house."

"From the sounds of it, it's the black market trade. They don't particularly worry about the police brigade. You know that as well as I do. We're lucky they haven't already done anything." Madeline pointed out. "Plus, the police may deal with the minor criminals, but can't do much without the government's complete backing for the larger criminals."

Arik clicked his tongue and looked away in disgust. Madeline sighed before she turned to Maxwell, her eyes flitted over him, pained, before she turned to Karina. "We do have a pseudo plan. It's not great, but speed is of the essence in cases like this." Madeline gestured toward Leon. "Can you fill them in?"

Leon looked up, slipping his glasses back up his nose. "Thanks to Arik's father, we have a means to track you." Leon nodded toward Arik, who waved it off before turning back to them. "We will attach the tracker onto you and have you go onto the streets. Mitchell and I will be in the police car with Arik's father while Arik, Madeline and Andrew will be the invasion team. As soon as we pinpoint a location, we will attack. If the signal gets scrambled, we will capture the car itself. We can't risk losing more people than necessary." Leon's glasses slipped right back down, but he ignored it this time, finishing typing away.

"Wait, so you are using us as bait anyway?" Karina looked downright murderous. "I've already told you, and even Arik told you, we aren't stupid. Why would we do that? Is there nothing else?"

"Not really." Mitchell's voice was quiet. "Even just to get them to come out, we would need someone as bait. We know they are after you two, so, considering the circumstances, you two are our only option."

"So, what if only one of us goes?" Maxwell spoke up, catching everyone's attention. Karina's head snapped in his direction, stunned. He quickly continued while she stood there in shock. "We don't need two people to be bait. If just one of us goes, the other can help with the infiltration."

"That won't work." Madeline spoke up, voice even. "Obviously, they are not stupid. If only one of you goes out, then they will know something is up. They might even decide to flee and come back with more men or something. Yes, it's still going to be suspicious if you both go out, but it'll also be for your protection. You're siblings, twins, if we can set it up, they won't want to separate you, at least not right away. We can use that to our advantage."

Maxwell closed his mouth and Karina seemed mollified by Madeline's words. As horrible as it was, it made sense. He hated the idea of putting Karina in danger like that, but he knew, with how she was, it would be ten times worse for her if he went alone.

Leon handed Mitchell a set of what seemed to be earplugs, wires curved around the ear, pale and see-through. Mitchell handed it over, giving them to Karina. Karina took them, confusion clear on her face. "Just insert one into your ear. You'll be able to listen to what we say, but you won't be able to reply back. It is also a way to track you two."

"So, we're going through with this?"

Karina seemed almost resigned and Maxwell felt the same way. Part of him wondered if he should contact Lex, tell him what was going on. Though, what was the point? He'd already basically figured out this would happen. Maxwell shook his head. No, he didn't want to worry their friend further. Plus, there wasn't any time. Still, like Lex stated, what about their mother? If something happened to them, then... So much could go wrong here, yet their options were getting fewer and fewer. Madeline was right. Now that someone knew, or at least suspected that they were clean, things could only go downhill.

He abandoned that thought as Karina shoved the ear piece into his hand. Her gaze was firmly on his and he realized then that she was leaving it up to him. He gently took the item, examining it. Talk about high tech. It seemed strange. Most of the stuff he found on this side, away from Claremore, was almost dated in its antiquity. To see something so advanced, and by someone around his age was not what he expected. He pursed his lips. Who were these guys? Did they really get this stuff from Arik's father?

His gaze flickered to Arik, who was watching them with half an eye, his expression carefully neutral. There was something outright strange about it. He felt his teeth digging at his lip and forced himself to relax, reaching toward his ear. He slid the earpiece in, adjusting it so it would feel more comfortable.

He noticed Karina doing the same before she dropped her hand to her side. "All right, so somehow, you have high-tech gear for tracking, okay, I'll ignore that, but how do you expect to go after grown criminals? Just this small group isn't going to be able to take them down, plus they had guns."

Karina gestured. A frown was clear on her face. Mitchell pulled back, almost looking like he was trying to sink into himself. Arik let out a breath as Andrew gave an annoyed sound, looking away.

Madeline turned toward them and smiled weakly. "I know you are uncertain about all this. What else can we do? Emma is our friend too."

Karina's face twisted in that way Maxwell recognized. That stubborn refusal she so usually harbored. Just as quickly as it came, however, it left. Her shoulders slumped and, bringing one hand to grip her other elbow she spoke, voice soft. "Okay, fine, I'm just saying."

Maxwell sent her a sad smile, she was antsy, and so was he, it was understandable, however... He turned to Madeline. "Before we do this. I do have to ask…" He examined them with a discerning gaze. "Who are you? Emma was able to fight like she was trained, the way you have this set up is like some underground meeting and Mitchell mentioned you snuck in, past the kidnappers, I'm going to suppose, since they haven't rammed down the door yet." Maxwell waved a hand, as nervous expressions flashed across everyone except Arik's face, who was watching with an amused smile. "Mind explaining at least something? We're about to literally jump into the deep end, so, can we trust you?" He finally finished, not realizing till the end that he literally sped through that in one breath.

Madeline opened and closed her mouth, however, to Maxwell's surprise, it was Andrew who spoke up. "Emma grew up knowing how to fight, we all did. Living in the south, why do you think we were hit so hard by the epidemic? It was already tough down there. We had to learn." Andrew's gaze was cold as Mitchell looked away and even Leon stopped typing. "Emma and Madeline both like you two as friends and..." he clicked his tongue, glaring at Maxwell before he continued, "We won't let anything happen." Andrew pushed away from the wall. "Now, are we going to get started or not?"

Maxwell couldn't stop the guilt and looked away. "Sure."

"Hold on, let me check to make sure those things work," Leon muttered, seemingly lost in work once again, though his typing was just a bit out of sync, as if he was trying to get himself back on track. "Yep, seems like they work." He slid a headset, held together by tape, onto his head and adjusted the mouthpiece. "Can you hear me?"

Karina cringed, and Maxwell reached a hand up to his ear. *Yikes, that was loud.* Leon nodded, and turned down a couple controls before repeating himself. This time, it was faint enough where Maxwell didn't feel as if his eardrum would burst. He nodded.

"All right, so can we get going?" Andrew gestured, annoyed. "It's already been a couple hours, which is never good."

"I know," Madeline cut in before turning to Maxwell and Karina. "Are you two ready?"

Maxwell and Karina exchanged looks before Maxwell let out a groan. "As ready as we'll ever be."

"Don't worry, we'll be right there if anything goes wrong." Mitchell spoke, voice gentle. "We're not going to leave you two behind. If you have Andrew promising that, then it's as good as certain." Andrew sent Mitchell a glare, only to pause.

Maxwell blinked as Mitchell's expression shifted, panic forming on his face before his hand darted to his mouth and he let out a choking cough. Everyone stilled, eyes glued to their friend. Karina shifted close to Maxwell, hands trembling. Maxwell found himself shocked as rough gasps and coughs erupted from Mitchell's throat. Madeline rushed over as Leon almost tossed his computer to scramble up to their friend.

"Mitchell, breathe." Andrew spoke sternly, being the closest. "It's not the fourth stage, you're fine."

The wavering in his voice spoke otherwise. After a few more coughs, it died down and Mitchell slumped, shaking. It was only then when Maxwell realized how tightly he was gripping Karina's arm and how he'd lost circulation in his hand from her grip.

Arik walked over, handing Mitchell a glass of water, which he downed. "Sorry," his words were raspy as Madeline and almost everyone let out a relieved breath.

"Why can't you be more like Andrew and just faint? At least fainting doesn't look like you're hitting the fourth stage," Madeline muttered as she looked him over, eyes roving to check for any other damage.

It seemed it was just a bad coughing fit, no wounds reopened, from what Maxwell could see, and he was still alive.

"Not everyone faints, you know." Arik spoke up quietly. "Mom keeps throwing up and Grandma randomly comes down with damaged blood vessels."

Madeline pursed her lips and Mitchell waved them away. "I'm fine. We need to get moving."

"Right," Leon said and the sound, heard through the twins' earphones as well, jerked them out of their shock.

Maxwell pulled in a breath as Karina finally let go, visibly shaken.

"I guess you two have lucked out so far, huh?" Arik spoke up, voice quiet, but still heard in the silence of the room. "I overheard you talking. This all happened because you two are clean, right?"

Maxwell nodded, deciding not to deny the fact. No one seemed particularly surprised and Madeline shifted, turning away from them. "I think we all guessed that. After all, you never really showed any symptoms and even your bandages didn't look like they were changed out every day, like some of ours."

So, they noticed. Maxwell bit his lip. He was hoping that wasn't the case, but admittedly, they had been close to them for months now. Neither Karina nor himself knew how to pretend to be sick, he didn't think it was something they would ever have to deal with.

"When can we go?" Karina spoke up, her gaze firmly on the wall beside them. Maxwell found himself weakly smiling. Yeah, they did still have work to do, they couldn't think of the epidemic right now. First Emma, then Mother, then the epidemic.

Hopefully, they wouldn't lose anyone they knew. His gaze flickered to Mitchell, who seemed to be pacifying Madeline. What if one of them were to keel over? What if one of them were to hit the fourth stage, what would he do?

Could he do anything?

This was so stupid and reckless, but honestly, in the short time they had, what were their options?

~ * ~

Karina wanted so badly to stop Maxwell from going as well. After all, they should only need one of them, but Madeline's points were valid, and she couldn't come up with a better argument. Though, the fact that Maxwell brought it up surprised her. Had he been thinking of going himself and have Karina stay back? He'd grown stubborn as of late. They walked down the street, hurrying to one side and heading for the apartment.

"We don't know where they will come from, so stay on the lookout, got it?" Leon's voice sounded in her ear, almost professional in the delivery.

She felt uncomfortable, the way everyone talked earlier, the way the epidemic struck, even Andrew's words about their past. She knew Maxwell was still questioning it, with his furrowed brow and pursed lips, but she wasn't sure what to think. She looked around, wary, then gestured for him, continuing down the street. They weren't far from the apartment. She almost wished she could make it there and not deal with this ever again. Maybe they could sneak into Lex's place? Inside the gated community? What about Emma?

After a moment of thought, she grasped Maxwell's wrist, noting that he didn't jerk away at her touch. Though, he did wince.

Maxwell stepped even with her, sending her a comforting smile, or at least, he probably thought it was, but she could see the uncertainty in his eyes, the way he held himself was tremulous at best. She sent him an encouraging grin.

The sound of tires, faintly trundling down the road behind them, shattered that grin, causing it to crumble into a grimace. She exchanged a worried look, hand tightening on his wrist. He winced once more, eyes darting behind them before he gulped.

"If you think they are there, run. We need to make this believable."

"Believable, sure," she muttered, knowing full well the stupidity of them going outside again after the initial incident.

"Better than nothing," Maxwell concurred before suddenly racing ahead, pulling Karina with him.

Karina only stumbled for a second before drawing even. She looked around as the squeal of tires sounded behind them. Before they could even turn, the car sped past them and did a spin, stopping perpendicular to the road. Maxwell slid to a stop, alongside Karina.

"There they are."

Karina jumped, glancing behind her to see a man step out of an alley, the one with the gun from earlier. Was he their man on the ground? Unlucky bastard.

She really hoped she could trust those guys, but they were Emma's friends, and Maxwell seemed to trust them.

Before she could think anymore, she felt hands on her arms. She let out a cry as she was tugged backward, toward the van. Maxwell struggled for a moment, only to stop as one of the men attempted to smack him with the gun. The gun stopped just short, much to Karina's relief, but it still threatened him if he continued to resist.

Within moments, she found herself loaded into the van, lying on her side with her arms tied. When did they do that? Didn't they usually blindfold people or something? Guess they were in a hurry. Joy. She didn't have time to think as Maxwell was shoved on top of her and the van closed up, speeding away.

"Wow, to think we actually caught them."

Karina could hear a nasally voice as Maxwell shifted, trying to sit up and off her. She shook her head and sat up as well, taking in the back of the van. She couldn't see much in the dark except for the men sitting on either side. She felt something touch her face and trail down her neck. The hand never touched her ear, so thankfully they didn't notice the little earbud. Still, the fingers sent a chill up her spine and she growled.

"It seems to be true, that wench was right. They're both clean."

"Damn, lucky." Another voice spoke up, whistling. "We'll get a pretty penny out of this."

Karina stayed silent, though she could feel Maxwell tense beside her, probably worried. The touch traced down her face once more before pulling away.

She could feel her heart pounding, everything caught in her throat. Her fingers flexed as she shifted, trying to pull at the ropes binding her wrists. She could feel the roar of the engine and winced as they passed over the occasional bump and pothole in the road.

"We're tracking you, just be patient," a quiet voice slipped through the side speaker into her ear.

She almost wanted to slump with relief, but she decided keeping up the act might work out better.

"So, what do we do with the boy? He seems to be getting close to the age where we can't sell him like the girl, and no one is looking for manual labor except in the gated communities."

"People are still looking for organs. Don't worry. If we can't sell him as a prostitute, or the two of them as a dual set, the human body has plenty of other resources."

Karina could almost taste the fear rolling off Maxwell as he pressed into her. Anger pierced through her and she glared toward the man who made such a suggestion. She was going to enjoy pummeling them later.

Still, they said someone told these people that Karina and Maxwell were clean. It couldn't have been Emma or the others, after all, the group was helping them, so then who?

Karina made sure to stick close to Maxwell the rest of the ride, her back pushing into his and against the back wall. The kidnappers didn't seem to care, letting them do what they wanted.

The kidnappers probably thought neither of them would be able to escape, especially in a moving vehicle. It was only now that she was glad, she wasn't in this alone.

It didn't take long before they drew to a stop and Karina heard the faint sound of grinding. A few moments later, the grinding stopped, and the vehicle moved forward once more. Karina felt Maxwell tremble and quickly squeezed his arm, trying to calm him, even as panic slid through her own system.

Finally, they drew to a complete stop. She heard movement and looked up just in time to see a hand reaching down for her. She jerked back, banging her head against the metal of the door. She winced as a dull throb hung against the back of her skull. Fingers clasped her upper arm and she stumbled as she was wrenched to her feet. She felt herself be patted down and almost snapped as he got too close to some areas. The same thing happened to Maxwell at her side, who looked completely perturbed. What, were they looking for weapons or something? Why not just do that earlier, when they were first taken?

"Almost forgot, almost forgot," a voice muttered next to her ear and she gulped. Oh, that was why. The doors opened and everything in Karina told her to move. Yet, before she could, she felt the man tug her down and out the door. The crack of her footsteps against the cement sounded loud in her ears as she struggled, Maxwell kicking and tugging at the person holding him. She would have screamed if it would have done any good, but she doubted it would help.

The large warehouse building that hovered over them was dark. Smoke could be faintly seen coming from the other end and Karina just barely caught a name off to one side. She could tell, with one look, that this wasn't some abandoned warehouse. She could see people working through the thin barred gates, barely giving them a glance. The gates did create two distinctly different buildings, separating the two sides. Karina didn't have much time to think of it, more pissed off then anything.

How could they stand not doing anything when they could obviously see two people being dragged against their will into a place so close to where they work?

"A warehouse that's connected to one in use. Genius." She heard the voice sound annoyed and amused. "Madeline, Arik and Andrew are on their way. Just stay calm."

"Easier said than done," Maxwell said under his breath so that only Karina could hear, though just barely with the pounding of her heart and the voices of the kidnappers that pulled them through a side door.

The inside was dimly lit with fluorescent lights hanging from the ceiling. The surrounding area was dark. She could hear the sound of their breathing and footsteps echoing around the cavernous room. She could faintly hear talking in the distance, along with machinery. Before long, they found themselves moving down a long hallway toward a back-storage area. The route was winding with a few different paths.

She could hear the faint sounds of screams in the distance and shuddered. Finally, they reached the end of a hall. The man reached forward and opened the door. Karina tried to wrench herself away when a fist slammed into the back of her skull. She winced and, before she could recuperate, was sent sprawling with a forceful shove.

She heard Maxwell let out a pained grunt before the grinding sound of the door caught her ears. She heard running footsteps and looked up just as a person flew by, the door closed, and the person skidded to a halt, barely managing to avoid smashing their face into the wall.

They cursed before turning to Maxwell and Karina.

In the dim light, it was hard to tell, but she could have sworn the figure was familiar. Karina shook it off and sat up, wincing. "Maxwell? You okay?"

"Been better, you?"

"Peachy."

She peered around, her eyes growing accustomed to the darkness of the room to the point where she could make out vague shadows.

"They caught you two as well?"

The pained voice was familiar and choked. Karina glanced toward the figure that flew past them. The figure squatted down before them, arms behind her back.

"Emma?" Maxwell's voice pitched up slightly as he sat up. "Is that you?"

The figure slumped and placed herself down fully in front of the twins. Karina sat up, carefully checking herself over before looking toward Emma in the dim light. "It's good to know you are all right."

"All right? Ha." Emma's voice was filled with sarcasm as she let out a grunt. "I'd hoped you two got away. Do you know what they are thinking of doing to you two?"

"I have a fairly good idea." Maxwell's voice was strained, to put it mildly, the uneasy sound ringing in her ears.

Karina shifted to nudge him in comfort before returning her attention back toward Emma. Karina quickly scanned the room, then leaned forward, voice low. "Emma, don't worry."

Karina felt Maxwell's gaze shift to her, even in the darkness. "We didn't just let ourselves be taken." He spoke, keeping his voice down. "Anyway, who else is here?"

Emma shifted and, from what Karina could see, shrugged. "Don't know, I think we're probably part of the last batch, from what I heard. I'm not sure where the others were taken."

So, there were others. This must be where all the people who disappeared were kept. Karina frowned, thinking through it. In the corner of the room, she could hear shuffling and quiet whimpers, indicating there were other people. She couldn't tell if they were girls or not.

She felt Maxwell bump into her. "Well, we got inside at least. We're part of the way there."

Karina snorted. "Yeah, I guess that's better luck than we've had with Mom."

"Never mentioned that..." Maxwell shrugged. "Still, it's worrying whether they will be able to act in time or not."

Karina sent him a look, noticing the nervousness in his posture, even in the dim light.

"After all, it's not hard to guess what's going to happen next."

Karina bit her lip. She was trying hard not to think about it, but the thoughts, along with the worries, were finally catching up with her. After all, they couldn't just avoid the possibility.

"You know, it would be a miracle if they kept you two together. Even though you are siblings, that doesn't mean much of anything. I mean, change hair and eye color and you two look a lot alike, but you aren't identical."

Karina looked away. She could feel Maxwell's gaze on her before he slumped, the movement heard through the oppressing darkness.

"There is no point thinking about that. The only thing we can do now is wait."

"I very much hate that word," Karina found herself voicing out loud, even as she moved off to one side, away from the doorway.

The darkness was oppressing and cold. The silence almost as painful. Yet she felt uncomfortable with quiet chatter, after all, what could they talk about?

After some time, Maxwell leaned forward, having sat down beside her. He stretched his arms back, trying to loosen his shoulders before turning toward her. "So, do you think eventually we'll manage not to get kidnapped?"

Karina rolled her eyes, knowing full well her brother couldn't see the movement in the darkness. "With our luck? You're dreaming."

"I was afraid you would say that." Maxwell groaned. "Well, I guess it does come with the territory," he muttered the last part, so soft, Karina struggled to hear.

Well, yeah. That made sense. After all, they were supposedly some cure to some great disease. Though she already saw it work, so it wasn't so much a supposed thing, but still. That meant, no matter what, they would have people after them.

And yet, every time, she wasn't able to do much of anything. Comforting Maxwell and making sure he kept his sanity was a plus, but that didn't mean much in the long run.

She shook those horrible thoughts from her mind and nudged Maxwell. "Stop getting me all depressed."

"I don't know why you never worry about yourself." Maxwell joked weakly.

"That's the pot calling the kettle black," Karina responded right back.

Maxwell let out a laugh and Karina chuckled, feeling glad. The mood, however dreary, lightened a bit.

She heard a loud bang and jumped, looking up to see the door open and one of the men from before step in. "Keep your traps shut," he said, closing the door behind him after giving a nod to the person outside.

He stomped over to them, gun in hand. He placed it under Karina's chin and she grimaced, feeling the cold hard metal push her chin up.

"Unless you want this placed someplace else, I would be very careful, wench. We're just doing last-minute finalization, then all of you will be out of our hair. After, we'll be that much richer."

She felt Maxwell shift beside her. He slipped forward, as if to swipe a foot out. The man moved back. Before she really realized, she heard a thud and a sharp gagging cough. She felt Maxwell lean heavily against her, squirming as he struggled to breathe.

Wait, did that guy realize what Maxwell was doing? Did he just kick her brother in the gut?

She heard a snort as the man backed away. "As much as I hate damaging the merchandise, sometimes it has to be done. Too bad we didn't have time to strip you all down and do the proper search." The man shook his head and hurried out the door.

"Maxwell?" Karina leaned forward enough to look up at his face as he grimaced.

"Fine," he coughed out, catching his breath. "Wasn't expecting it."

"Who would?" Karina muttered.

"He is right though." Emma spoke up, catching their attention.

What did she mean? Karina glanced toward Emma, who was sitting in silence up till this point.

"There was someone I knew who escaped from the black market. When they were initially brought into the holding location, they were completely stripped and searched, left with nothing even as they waited in a place just like this, slowly being broken down piece by piece. They must be in a bit of a quandary not to do the same now…" Emma trailed off.

The cold chill that settled into her bones was the only thing Karina could feel as she thought over what Emma said. Maxwell leaned into her side, shaking violently, or was that her?

She couldn't tell anymore.

"Karina? Maxwell? This is Mitchell."

Karina jolted, barely avoiding knocking heads with Maxwell, who jerked at the same time.

"Leon is busy getting into the security system and cameras. I'll be the one talking with you."

His voice sounded worried and anxious, yet steady. Karina knew they both appreciated it, hearing another voice besides their own echoing within the dim cell.

"Right now, Arik and the others are waiting for news on Arik's father. Leon's connected to the kidnappers' radios and is sending false reports. We should be moving in soon, just hang tight."

"Won't be long now." Karina smiled in relief as she turned back toward Emma.

"What do you mean?"

Karina didn't feel the need to answer as she turned back to Maxwell to check on him. His breathing was starting to even out. He pressed close to her for a moment, reassuring her before moving away to give them some space.

She was tired of straining to see in the dark room. The adrenaline was still pumping, but she could tell it was doing more harm than good, draining her. Emma stayed quiet, probably lost in thought.

A while later, loud sirens cut through the silence like a thunderclap ringing throughout the place. In the distance, she could hear the faint sounds of sharp wailing and shouts. Emma jumped and whipped around to face the door.

Within no time, they heard a click and the door swung open. Andrew stood there, holding the door open and wearing clothes black as night. Emma grunted as Andrew flicked on a flashlight. He scoured the interior and Andrew quietly cursed. "Seems this isn't all of them."

"Well, that answers that." Emma's voice was soft and relieved as she hurried forward. She spun and waited for Andrew to slice through the ropes before shaking her wrists and taking the proffered knife.

Karina watched Emma hurry up to her, slicing carefully through the ropes as Andrew did the same for Maxwell.

Within short order, they cut through the bonds on the other woman and children and helped them to their feet. The captives raced out, realizing they were free with Maxwell, Karina, Emma and Andrew close behind.

The warehouse was in chaos, the sound ringing down the long halls and a few employees fleeing past, barely dodging around the large group of escapees. Andrew held a hand to his ear, listening before looking around. "Madeline has found some of the captives. She believes the rest should be in another hall. I'm going to need someone to help me search for them."

Maxwell and Karina exchanged looks, before glancing toward Emma. Emma's clothes were torn, and her hair mussed, semi pulled out of her twin braids, but she seemed all right. She caught their gaze. "I'll lead these girls out. I can probably guess where Madeline will want them to go. You three take care of the others."

With that, she turned and hurried up to the nervous girls, gently leading them through the winding hallways. How did she know the way out? Karina never got a chance to ask, though she figured it was along the same line as the two of them. They never were blindfolded after all.

Which had been stupid on the kidnappers' part, but then, as they mentioned, their kidnappers did seem forgetful near the end.

"Good job." Andrew's voice was soft, reluctant as he turned to them. "Now let's go, we don't have a lot of time, we need to get everybody out and soon."

Karina knew that receiving a good job was quite an achievement to hear from the stoic boy.

Karina looked around and tried to suppress a shiver as they slipped into another hallway. Andrew's gaze flickered back and forth over the doorways before he stopped at the end of the hall. He glanced toward Karina and Maxwell and gestured for the two doors on either side. Maxwell nodded as Karina pursed her lips. She turned and, with a quick flick, opened the door.

The door slid open with a loud squeal and she cringed, looking inside. The light from the hallway was bright enough to display the line of girls. They were all stripped down and wounds crisscrossed their bodies. Karina tilted her gaze up and froze.

Familiar eyes stared back at her in a mix of shock and utmost hatred.

"There's no one in here, Kar—" Maxwell's voice cut off as he looked over.

Karina quickly shoved the door shut enough, so he didn't see, but he could still hear her. "Maxwell, Andrew, get some clothes now."

There would be enough time, right? Considering she didn't hear any argument, she figured it was the case as she turned back to the line of girls.

She felt herself tremble as she stepped up to the first two, keeping her gaze carefully away from any areas she shouldn't be looking at. With careful movements, she began to unclip them, helping them drop to the floor. There were four girls in total, two older girls, one little girl and an older woman who was probably around her thirties. The woman, once down, sighed in relief and quickly helped Karina bring down the little girl. The woman scooped up the little girl, who was bawling, into her chest. Karina hesitated before turning to the other two girls.

"Why are you here?" Abby spat, glaring down at her as Karina found herself stopping before the hung girl. "I told them what they wanted to know. You and that sissy brother of yours should be sold and gone. They said they would let us go for that information, so why are you the one here?"

Karina clenched her fists as her brain made the final connection. "You told them? Told them that you believed we were clean? Do you know what they threatened Maxwell with?"

"Did you know what they were going to do to you, you prissy little princess? You should have realized with all those guys making passes at you, they would be glad to sell you. Just like—"

Abby cut off as the other girl—wasn't that the girl that collapsed when Karina first got to the hostel? Gab?—Karina pushed the thought away as Gab made a soft sound.

"Karina? Can I come in?" Maxwell's voice was hesitant.

"Fine." She glanced at the older woman, who nodded before stepping to the side, child close to her chest.

Maxwell stepped inside with Andrew, sweatshirt and jacket draped over his arms. Karina took the jacket and threw it to the older woman, who caught it and slipped it around herself and a little around her child before hurrying toward the door. Karina stared down at the sweatshirt, then toward the two girls. A glare sat over Abby's face while the second girl, who looked like the guard involved in Maxwell's ambush, now that she also thought about it, hung there with fear and anxiety clear in her features.

Karina gritted her teeth, hands shaking for a moment. She hated these girls, hated them so much, but she pushed thoughts of anger to the side. Karina pulled off her own sweatshirt and hurried up to them. With precise movements, she released the ropes holding the two girls, causing them to drop. Maxwell let out a yelp, probably surprised by the noise. He must have kept his eyes shut. Karina threw her and Maxwell's sweatshirt to the two girls. "Put those on already and let's get out of here."

Gab smiled in relief, slipping the sweatshirt over her shivering frame. Abby stared up at her, expression dull, she opened and closed her mouth. Karina turned and hurried over to Maxwell, gripping his wrist. "Come on, that should be everyone."

She didn't realize how much she was shaking until she gripped his hand and pulled him down the hallway. She passed Andrew, who watched curiously before helping the two along, following behind Karina and Maxwell. The older woman was waiting for them. Upon seeing them, she hurried down the hall. Karina didn't look back again, just continued after her.

Maxwell glanced sidelong at her. "Karina, that girl…"

"I know. I couldn't just leave her there."

A bright, proud smile flitted on his face and she looked away, feeling distraught.

After all, she'd been all too ready to leave the girl hanging, literally. That girl was the reason Maxwell was hurt all those months ago, why both of them were struggling to make ends meet and now, that girl was the reason behind why she and Max were targeted by these monsters. Why Emma was kidnapped in the first place.

A small part of her, a part that she found disgusting and sort of admired, wanted to just jeer at those girls like they did to Maxwell. To let them be hurt. To let them hang. After all, they would have only been hanging for a little while longer. The police would have come by later to save them. She had no reason to let them go.

Yet the larger part of her, the part that knew Maxwell would never condone it, the part that was still left from home, vehemently denied that desire, reminding her to avoid that cruelty.

"I've got everyone." Andrew reached for the radio at his waist, something she didn't even notice.

"You guys all right?" the voice in her ear called and she nodded, even knowing that Mitchell wouldn't be able to see or hear.

"How is the capture of the black-market employees coming along?" Andrew called over the radio.

"They're slippery. We caught a large number of them, but a few have escaped. That includes one or two people involved in their kidnapping." The voice that crackled through the radio sounded like Arik, though his tone was anything but happy.

Andrew clicked his tongue, annoyance shining through. Karina bit her lip. So, some of the people that captured them escaped.

"That's not good," Maxwell murmured, and she nodded.

They were in this mess because someone realized they were still clean. If those same people noticed them later down the road, they could be in trouble.

What was the likelihood of someone staying clean for so long? Who would know with the bandages wrapped around their neck and arms?

She shivered, remembering as the fingers that touched her bandages earlier from that creep. He would have noticed there were no bumps or contusions under the bandaging, and Karina didn't really think of reacting to the touch, besides moving away from it.

Maxwell was the same, he struggled, but the bandages never got damaged or bloody or anything, which was highly indicative of the disease.

They realized just from that, same with Madeline and the others.

Karina clenched her fist, only to hear a short squawk of protest. She glanced over in time to see Maxwell's gaze flit to hers, grimace on his face. She quickly loosened her grip but couldn't find it in herself to let go. "Sorry."

He shook his head as they slipped out of the hall into the main area of the warehouse. Lights flashed off in the distance as figures shouted. The girls were bundled forward, past the boxes and out a side door. Emma and Madeline stood nearby, directing the scared girls. Arik was standing off to one side, radio on his hip and talking with an older man who looked like him, just scruffier, taller and in a blue police uniform.

Karina cringed, even despite knowing to expect it. Andrew's gaze darted to her before he walked up to Madeline. "Any changes?"

Madeline shook her head. "We're just focusing on getting everyone out. The police, the ones who were willing to do it, are rounding everyone up."

"So, our best choice is probably to leave now," Emma said uncertainly.

Yes, let's get out of here. Karina almost said the words out loud but stopped herself. She couldn't deny she wanted so badly to leave this place. She wanted to go home, but there was no reason to outright point it out, Emma was probably feeling the same way after all.

Madeline sent her a look before turning to Maxwell. Complex emotions flew across her face, ending in uncertainty. "You're all right, right?"

Maxwell blinked, before he nodded, and she smiled with relief. "All right, Emma, can you bring them home? Leon and Mitchell are outside finishing up the last of the arrangements. Though they might be a while."

Emma nodded. "It's no problem, I'll get them home safely. Thanks, Madeline."

She reached forward, taking Karina's and Maxwell's hands. Karina let her, as her gaze flitted to Madeline's relieved smile and soft expression. A moment later, the girl turned, her posture rigid and commanding. Karina pulled away from that, following after Emma's constant footsteps. She wanted to be done with all of this.

~ * ~

Maxwell curled into the couch, phone to his ear, grateful that Andrew passed it to him after everything was said and done. He figured it was better not to keep it on him, so he was glad Andrew was willing to hold it for him.

He closed his eyes as he listened to the quiet ringing. Karina was taking a shower in the other room, probably trying to scrub the stench and dirt of that cell off. He wanted to as well, but first, he needed to make sure—

His thoughts were cut off when he heard the phone connect. "Hey, Lex."

"Maxwell, you're all right." The relief in Lex's voice would have startled Maxwell, if he hadn't partially expected it.

Maxwell felt a weak smile flash on his face as he let his eyes open to stare at the room, flooded with moonlight. "We both are. We're back at the apartment, actually."

"Well, it only took till about three in the morning." The quiet chuckle from the other end sounded tired, but happy. "I take it everyone is safe?"

"Yeah," Maxwell breathed out.

"I'm sorry I couldn't help. It is good to hear that you and your sister are back." A slight note fluttered in Lex's voice that Maxwell couldn't quite pinpoint, but he could guess.

"Thanks, Lex. That means a lot." It really did, to know their friend truly did care for their wellbeing helped him calm down. "I'm guessing you were waiting for us?"

"Why would you think that, idiot?" The sarcasm and fondness in his voice caused Maxwell to chuckle.

He heard the sound of the door opening and looked over to see Karina step out of the bedroom, clean and in her pajamas. She nodded to Maxwell. He passed the phone over and stood.

"Hey, Lex, good to hear from you. I hope Maxwell didn't annoy you too much."

"Kari," Maxwell huffed, earning a sheepish salute from her before she turned back to the phone. Maxwell shook his head and slipped away.

The water felt great on his skin, washing away the dirt and fatigue. He stared up at the ceiling, letting the water run through his hair. What if Madeline and the others hadn't come? What if they had never made friends with them in the first place?

What if it had been just the two of them?

He shivered at the thought. If he and Kari were alone, like when they first left Claremore, they would have been no better off. It was a scary thought, to realize not much changed in that regard.

He would need to talk to Karina. They needed to find a better way to defend themselves. He couldn't keep relying on her, or Lex. It had been hard enough for Lex to leave the gated community at home. Here, he had even less knowledge of the location, so it would have been harder to leave. Maxwell clenched his fists, his hair sticking to his face as the water trickled down. He also needed to find out what was going on with those…with Madeline, Emma and the others. Who were they? To make such a concentrated effort in such a short time was not easy. He knew Andrew mentioned it not being easy even before the epidemic, but that didn't necessarily explain how they coordinated something so detailed so quickly.

Not only that, but could he ask them for help? They knew what they were doing and knew how to maneuver through the situation with such ease, it was almost mind-boggling. Yes, Andrew said they grew up that way, but as he was watching, as they escaped, he noticed there was more to it. So, would it be so far-fetched to think they might be able to help him and Kari get their mother out?

If so, what price would they have to pay? After all, he already saw, time and time again, there was always a price for these things.

He just hoped it wasn't too expensive.

He pulled from that thought and turned off the water before quickly getting changed and slipping into the main room. Karina held the phone in her lap, closed. She gazed at the ceiling, lost in thought.

She looked over upon hearing him come in and grinned. "All done?"

Maxwell sent her a deadpan look and she laughed, before pushing herself to her feet. Her stance was firm, eyes sparkling in relief. Hadn't she been scared, nervous? He thought so, in the darkness, but looking at her now, he wasn't sure.

"Sis?" He wanted to ask where she got all that strength from and wondered if he could borrow a little.

Karina shifted in her stance and walked forward, ruffling his hair. "Hey!" He batted her arm away, earning a raised eyebrow from her. "I think we should get some rest. It's late and we didn't sleep much earlier." He made sure to give her the stink-eye when he said that, knowing full well he got much more sleep than she did.

She waved it off, a sheepish expression on her face. "I do agree, though." She stretched, reaching her arms toward the ceiling before heading toward her room. She paused, her fingers hovering over the doorknob before she glanced over her shoulder, a strange expression on her face that Maxwell couldn't decipher. "Do you…" she trailed off and shook her head. "Never mind." She slipped into the room and closed the door.

Maxwell stared after her, brow furrowed. He pulled at his lip for a moment, almost biting it before he glanced toward his room, back and forth, indecisive. He could guess what she was asking, yet at the same time, he wasn't sure whether he wanted the comfort or not. He returned to his room and sat on the bed, staring through the window. He sat there for a long time, not much going through his mind, but unable to sleep. He lay down, hoping that would help, but the moonlight felt piercing, even though he knew it should be tranquil.

He frowned, staring at the sheets, lost in thoughts that had nothing to do with each other. He threw the sheets off in annoyance and stood, stepping back into the living room, just as the door creaked open from Kari's room. She almost stomped into the living room, annoyance and tiredness clear on her face. He took one look and sighed.

So, neither of them was going to be able to sleep tonight.

Karina must have noticed because her entire being seemed to collapse. "I'm guessing I didn't wake you."

Maxwell shook his head. Karina took a seat on the couch. Maxwell sat across from her and she frowned.

She shook her head and spoke. "Lex said he would make sure you don't get blamed for not being in work tomo—later." She glanced at the clock and grimaced, adjusting her last word. "He also said he managed to get a little extra in the shared account this week. I guess I should probably get myself a phone."

"That would be nice," Maxwell agreed. "It would have saved us both some grief if my phone hadn't died, or if we had two ways of being in contact with the only one whom we trust."

Maxwell gave her a sharp look, admittedly a bit annoyed that she'd been so stubborn about this until now. Though he shouldn't really blame her, it felt good to right now, in his tired state.

"Well, I'm sorry if I didn't think we needed to waste money on picking me up a phone since we are just trying to make ends meet."

"We've had enough for a few weeks now, ever since Lex's upgrade. So no, I don't understand." He could feel a hint of anger run through him. Whether that was from being overly exhausted and at his limit, or whether it was because of Kari, he wasn't sure.

"I was thinking of you," Karina snapped, standing up, seeming just as tired and frustrated. "You're still growing, you need to eat, and we need clothes since it's been so frigid. We have your phone. We have Lex's phone. I figured we would be fine."

Maxwell shot to his feet. "Will you stop thinking about me already? Can't I worry about you for once?" His voice pitched up along with his anger and annoyance. "I swear, it's almost like you care more for me than for yourself. Come on, Kari, that's enough. I can take care of myself."

"I know you can," Karina said, fists clenched and shaking in frustration. "I never said you couldn't. I'm just saying I didn't think it was necessary and I'm your older sister, I'm going to try to take care of you, that's just the way things are."

"Why won't you ever let me take care of you?" Maxwell slashed his arm sideways. "You never seem to let me, always keeping that smile on your face."

Karina seemed like she was slapped. She took a step back, teary. "I'm just trying…" Her voice faltered before she stepped forward. "I'm just trying to get us through, so we can see Mom." Karina shook her head. "So, what if I have to smile to do it? You do the same thing," she growled. "So, stop saying I'm the only one who's forcing themselves."

Maxwell blinked, mouth opening and closing. "I never said anything about forcing yourself," he whispered.

Karina, his strong older sister, turned away, suddenly seeming almost fragile in that one moment. "I think we're tired. We're just getting upset at each other for no reason. I'm going to bed." With that, she hurried back into her room and slammed the door shut.

Maxwell felt himself drop back onto the couch, unsure what just happened. After a moment, he let his head drop forward, face in his hands.

He definitely wasn't going to get any sleep now.

Chapter Sixteen

Caym paced back and forth over the posh rug of his rented home. The room wasn't large, by any stretch of the imagination, but it wasn't as small as Leo's room. He tapped his lip, feeling a hint of frustration. He kept tracking down leads, which ended up at dead ends. He kept having to deal with Father's incessant calling and tracking, Leo's silence and his uncle's unwavering distance. He figured it would be simple: in, out, done. That didn't seem the case and he had no clue why.

It was frustrating, to say the least. He stopped his pacing, lost in thought.

He turned to his closet and parsed through the clothing. After some time, he came across some clothes he saw Leo wear. The faded jeans and vest were warm for the frigid temperatures. He stared over the clothing before slipping them on. They were a snug fit, having been quite loose on little Leo, but they worked. He looked himself over, nodded and walked down the hall.

He didn't have to worry about anyone seeing him. After all, he had rented out the whole place. It was just easier to stay in one room.

He stepped out the back door and toward the edge of the gated community. It didn't take long for him to meet up with the guard at the gate. He flashed his pass and the guard quickly unlocked the doors, lips shut.

Good, they knew what to do.

He slipped his hands in his pockets and hunched his shoulders to appear more like Leo did upon first reuniting with him. After all, he was going into the vermin-infested outside; he didn't have much choice. He walked over the bridge and made his way through the winding streets. He managed to collect some intel in regard to where little Leo liked to stay.

It didn't take him long to come across an old abandoned parking garage. It looked even more dismal than he thought, disgusting and overridden with all types of vermin, two, four, multi-legged, it didn't seem to matter. He curled up his nose, scrunching up his face at the smell and decay. He doubted there would be anything left here. He looked around before turning and heading down the street, passing by the cretins that lined the side. They only gave him a quick glance before looking away. He made sure to look the part, as disturbing as it was. A little dirt for this god-forsaken place did a lot of good.

Within no time, he reached a residential area. The brick and mortar stank of filth. He pushed through, stepping up to a doorway with splintered wood and peeling paint. He brought up his gloved fingers, grateful he thought to wear them, and knocked.

"I'll be there in a minute," the voice called from inside. A woman's voice.

A moment later, the door opened to reveal a middle-aged woman, just past her prime with limp and frazzled locks that made her look deranged. Though, Caym had to admit, her brief smile was pleasant. Her left eye was swollen, and she was wearing a tattered green dress that somehow fit her well.

He tried to withhold his grimace as he bowed. The woman gave him an uncertain look. "Who are you?"

"My name is Caym," he spoke, voice even and maintaining politeness. "Would you be Martha, by any chance?"

The woman stiffened, nails digging into the door. "I am." Her voice was tense. Good.

Caym smiled. "I'm Leo—Lex's brother." Caym straightened up. "I heard he used to stay with you and your daughter for a short time before heading back south. I just have a few questions."

"Caym, Lex never said anything about you. He never even mentioned he had a brother." Martha held the door tightly, her posture indicating she was ready to slam it shut.

"Mommy, who is that?"

Caym looked down as Martha jumped. A little girl, probably around the age of eight, stood in the doorway, rubbing one eye. A worn blue ribbon sat in her dirty locks which matched the ragged blue dress. Her hair was up in pigtails and it looked like there was a little flower clip to keep her bangs back.

"Agatha, get back inside." Martha gestured, pushing her daughter behind her.

Agatha took a look at Caym and shrunk back. "Mommy, why does this scary person look like Uncle Lex?"

Caym narrowed his gaze, a smile crossed his face without a hint of warmth and it was all he could do to keep it from looking cruel or disgusted. "That's because I'm his brother and I want a few words with your mother."

"Agatha, get inside, now." Martha's voice was stern.

Agatha nodded and raced back inside, her little feet sounding against the wood of the flooring. Caym watched her go before turning to Martha, who seemed to want to be anywhere but there. "I don't know what you want, but…"

"I only wish for some information."

Martha pursed her lips. "Come inside." She pushed the door open and stepped to one side.

Excellent. Caym nodded and slipped past Martha. The inside was as dismal as he expected. A dining room led into a kitchen area with some sewing implements off to one side, placed lightly on the couch. Part of him wanted to keep standing, but he knew it would be better to take a seat. So, much to his disgust, he sat down on the lumpy couch, back straight as he stared across at Martha's semi-hunched form.

"What do you want to know?" Her gaze was cold, but that wasn't anything new.

"You don't have to worry, it's nothing harmful. I just wish to ask about my little brother, what his relationship is with those twins, how did he find them?" He stopped as the woman clenched her fist and he grinned. "I also heard your daughter got a chance to meet with Hugh, isn't that right?" His gaze flitted to the little girl, somewhat trying to hide behind the doorframe. She shrunk back, and he turned back to Martha, who looked like she wanted him gone, now.

"Yes, she met him. I don't know much about Lex, he only stayed here after meeting the twins and he never explained how he met them, so I can't tell you that either."

Caym narrowed his gaze at her vague answer. He could see her nervousness in the way she stiffened, her fingers clasping and unclasping in an attempt to look natural, comfortable. She did know, but how could he convince her to tell him?

~ * ~

Caym left the home, amused. Martha was a rather lovely woman to talk to, actually. She knew a lot about little Leo, a lot more then she originally let on, and even regarding the twins. He made sure to compensate her for all the information, of course. It wasn't easy dealing with the lower class, but he got the information he was looking for.

He frowned as he continued down the street, taking turn after turn. While the information was helpful, it wasn't encouraging, nor did some of it make sense. Her shock when he asked how Leo remained healthy spoke volumes, yet she covered it so quickly he would have never noticed if he wasn't paying attention. So, the twins must have done something to little Leo after they left here. What could have caused that? Why would the cu—he stopped, realizing where his thought process was going and scowled. He was starting to think like father. He pulled from that thought as he glanced over to the brick and glass building, he was walking up to.

Antonio. That was the name of the man Martha spoke of. He sounded like the type for information gathering and, while he got everything, he needed from Martha to meet with Hugh without the man turning him away, he figured one more stop couldn't hurt. After all, maybe Hugh would know just what little Leo was up to. He looked up and down the dreadfully quiet street, noting the inside seemed to be deserted. He walked up to the door and knocked, not even caring to do a quick perusal.

He stood there, waiting, yet there was nothing, no signs of movement, no people. He turned and kicked the door in, hearing the crack and clatter of rotting wood. The inside would almost be qualified as nice. He walked around the area, taking in the recently used furniture and desk. He stepped into the kitchen, spotting a pot, left on the counter, as if the cook was pulled away in the middle of cooking. He dipped his finger in and shook it. It was still somewhat warm, so they only left recently.

That Antonio that Martha spoke of. He was slippery, that was for sure. He must have known that Caym was coming. Caym found himself annoyed and amused. Though, he supposed, he wasn't exactly subtle when he came in.

He turned and stepped out the door, walking down the walkway. Ah well, it was worth a shot. So, next he needed to meet with Hugh, shouldn't be too difficult now. Afterward, well, he did still have a few months left. He could wait and prepare. Make sure everything was ready for Lex's return. He slipped his hand into his pocket and pulled out his phone. "I got everything, open the gates."

Before he even heard the affirmative reply, he clicked it off and headed back to his rented place. After all, he now had the information he needed to meet with his uncle. Just use a few key words here and there and he should have no problem.

Now if only little Leo was that easy to deal with.

Chapter Seventeen

Lex heard a loud ringing and jumped, looking over to the phone with a tired gaze. The day was rough, after staying up a good portion of the night, waiting for the twins 'call. He turned away from his computer desk to take the call. "Who is it?" He didn't even pretend to be awake, if it was the twins, they wouldn't particularly—

"You bastard."

Lex sat upright, stunned. "Antonio? Well, that is a rude introduction." He placed himself back into his seat, leaning on one arm. "May I ask why?"

Antonio let out a grunt of annoyance, and it was only then Lex heard the distant sound of cars, something he never heard when contacting the information specialist. "Thanks to that little search, your brother found us. Roxanne and I barely got out in time."

"Barely…" Lex trailed off, uncomfortable feelings rising in the pit of his stomach. "He went into the outer districts?"

"Exactly. I don't know why, and I don't want to know. I'm assuming he made contact with that friend of yours, but…"

Lex was unable to hide the annoyance and downright worry. "I'm guessing you are on the move?"

"Yes, Roxanne and I decided we cannot stay here any longer. Your uncle is about to break, and I have no doubt your brother has found everything he needs."

Lex grimaced. There wasn't anything he could do now, yet… "Do you know what happened?"

"To your friends? From what I know, they are fine."

Lex let out a heavy sigh. Caym was unpredictable lately. He used to be so good at games and drugs; it seemed like he'd changed his sights after Lex left." Thank you, Antonio."

"Let me know when their mother is safe."

Lex smiled, sitting back and letting his head rest against the back rest, neck craning gaze toward the ceiling. "Of course. Be careful out there."

Antonio let out a snort but didn't respond. Lex heard shuffling. Roxanne's soft voice filtered through the phone, almost sad. "Hey, Lex? It might be a while before I speak with you again. Stay safe, okay? Please?"

"I'll try. Take care of that brother of yours."

"I always do. Say, Lex. When I see you next, I'm going to make sure…" Roxanne's voice faltered for a moment before becoming firm. "I'm going to make sure you see me for me, not just for the sick girl you once helped. You got that?"

Lex blinked, surprised. That still bothered her? Well, then again, it was about two years ago.

"Roxanne, what are you saying?" Antonio's angry words were faint, filtering through the phone, as if from a distance.

"Antonio, leave it. Well, I'll talk to you later. Bye." Roxanne hurriedly hung up, her voice pitched up and almost embarrassed.

Lex pulled the phone away as he heard the steady beep indicating they hung up. Well, that girl definitely grew since he first met her. He could still remember when she collapsed, handing out little charm pendants and looking on the verge of death. Well, a different death from the epidemic, but still.

He shook his head and placed the phone back into his pocket. So those two were moving. His uncle was probably next, but what about Martha and Agatha? He hoped they were all right. Antonio said they were, but he still worried. Yet he knew there was nothing he could do. He hated this, honestly, being stuck in the gated community like this, unable to move about without being stared at like some trophy or something. His fingers slid through his hair.

Though, the twins seemed to have it worse. Those two didn't have any luck, did they?

He hoped that, at least, the rescue of their mother would go a little bit easier.

~ * ~

Karina rubbed her eyes tiredly, feeling weary to the bone. She didn't get a wink of sleep last night. The argument with Maxwell just kept running round and round through her head. She stumbled out of bed, barely managing to avoid slamming her face into the door. She turned the handle and slipped out, aiming for the kitchen. The blurriness making it difficult to spot the dozing form of her little brother, sitting on the couch.

Or maybe he wasn't dozing, because he tilted his head enough to face her upon her entrance, dark circles under his blurry gaze and skin pale. She could almost feel his exhaustion and, with the way he was looking her over, he could probably feel hers. She looked away, toward the kitchen. She needed some water, and maybe a couple energy bars. Something to wake herself up for the day. Too bad they didn't have coffee. She didn't drink it much, not too fond of the bitter flavor, but she would get one sometimes, especially at work.

Speaking of work...

Did she have to work today? She didn't think so, after all, they did just have an epidemic strike yesterday, it would probably be slow today, so it was fine.

"Hey, Kari?" Maxwell's words were weak, at best, almost grunting.

She hummed a soft sound, turning on the tap. "What?"

"About yesterday."

"What about it?" She turned off the tap and drank down the water, throat dry and scratchy.

"I..."

Karina stared at the metal of the sink, watching as the sun

sparkled over it. She turned. "I'm sorry, okay? We're both tired, let's just—let's not think about it for now. Lex said he sent some money, right? I'll pick up a phone tomorrow. Let's get some breakfast and make sure Emma is okay, sound good?"

Maxwell looked at her, lips pursed before he nodded, looking away. "Yeah, I'm worried about her." He stepped around her, shifting through the fridge.

Karina grabbed an energy bar and headed out of the kitchen. She got changed and waited by the door, chewing at the bar slowly.

It tasted nothing like what they used to have. While she thought the ones she brought with her from home tasted dry and sand-like, it was nothing compared to the ones she found around the city. Every one she tried had the consistency of cardboard and the flavor of toenail clippings. Not that she ever tried something like that, but the taste just kind of reminded her of the smell of feet.

Disgusting, but it did its job. She swallowed the last of it, grimacing before stuffing the wrapper in her pocket. She heard footsteps and turned to see Maxwell step up to her. He cleaned up a bit, but his posture was completely slumped over and every part of him seemed to be on the verge of collapsing.

She felt the same way. A pounding headache was starting to form in the back of her skull. Maybe she might be able to get some sleep later. A nap sounded good.

She shook her head and walked out the door, locking it behind her, making sure Maxwell slipped out first. She turned just as Arik walked down the hall.

He spotted them and waved. "Are you two feeling better?" he asked, stepping up to them.

Karina shot him a look, not particularly in the mood. "What do you think?"

"That I wouldn't be surprised if you two were still out of it, and that seems to be the case. Though, most of us are in a similar state. After all, we just got back too." His gaze drifted toward the doorway at the end of the hall, sour expression clear in his posture.

Karina grimaced. "Anyway, are you checking on Emma?"

Arik glanced away, shrugging. Karina couldn't help but smirk as she spotted the relief and slight blush visible on Arik's face. "Well, we're heading over to Emma's now to check on her. Want to come?"

"Of course." Arik gave a sharp nod, wide grin flitting on his lips.

He trailed after the twins as they headed toward Madeline's room. Voices could be heard from the other side. Maxwell and Karina exchanged looks before knocking on the door, so that meant everyone was already back.

The door opened, and Madeline spotted them. She took one look and her smile faltered as she glanced worriedly between them. "Oh, come in." she hurried to one side, gesturing for them to enter.

We must look like crap. Karina trudged inside with Maxwell and Arik as Madeline closed the door, hurrying away. Leon, Mitchell and Andrew glanced up, before looking back down, talking quietly amongst themselves. Arik looked around before heading off to another doorway that probably lead to Emma's room.

Karina shook her head as Madeline returned with two cups, handing them over. Karina looked at it, confused.

"It's tea. It's not much, but it should help a little."

Karina nodded and took a sip along with Maxwell. Silence descended on the group as Karina focused on her drink, the warm liquid sitting on her tongue with the gentle flavor of ginger and peppermint. She closed her eyes, taking quiet sips.

Karina turned to Madeline. "So, everyone's all right?"

Madeline nodded. "What about you two?" She turned to Maxwell and, must have seen something on his face, because she looked down, her posture slumping. "I didn't want to get you two into that mess. Especially…"

Karina stared down at the tea that simmered in the faint light from the room. She swished it back and forth. It was easy to ignore the three in the corner, who seemed to be trying to make themselves scarce. "We'll be fine. It could have been worse, from the sounds of things, and honestly, I feel like we both expected it to happen one of these days."

"You shouldn't expect something like that." Madeline jerked up, staring at them in disbelief before she shook her head. She went to open her mouth when Maxwell interrupted her.

"You five, who are you?" His gaze bored into Madeline, almost cold. "The way you were able to set up that meeting and receive the right equipment so quickly, the way you infiltrated a place that was obviously a criminal hangout with ease. I know Andrew said you grew up like that, but there seems to be more to it." Maxwell narrowed his lips into a thin pale line. "Want to explain that?"

"She has no reason to tell you."

Karina almost jumped as Andrew spoke up from where he sat.

"Andrew, that's enough." Madeline's voice was harsh and demanding.

Andrew only huffed but sat back down. Mitchell spoke to him quietly while Leon just watched behind his thin rimmed glasses, silent.

There was the faint sound of a door opening, causing Karina and Maxwell to glance back. Arik stepped out, closing the door softly behind him before looking at the group, expression solemn. "I talked with my dad before coming here. He's taken everyone into custody and is the one taking credit for finding all those who disappeared. This is good, considering I highly doubt anyone here wants attention?" At this, he gave a sharp look to everyone but the twins.

Karina pursed her lips, unsure how to read that. Did he know something? Considering how close he was with Emma, it would be possible but...

Madeline nodded. Her expression neutral. "Thank you, and also thank you for keeping that under wraps."

She turned to Maxwell and Karina. "It seems everyone has returned home safely, and the factory is being shut down since it was found to be working in conjunction with the kidnappers."

Well, that was a relief. Karina couldn't help the faint smile from forming on her lips, even as Maxwell leaned forward. "So, what now?"

Madeline shrugged, shifting back and forth. "Not sure. However, I think we need some time to get back into the swing of things." She bit her lip, looking uncertain, before nodding and gazing straight at Maxwell. "I'll tell you what you were wondering about, but not yet. It's a huge issue and one I need to discuss with the others." Her gaze flitted from person to person. The other four looked down or away, seeming uncomfortable. "I'll tell you later, give me a couple weeks, all right? That should give us enough time to get everything situated, okay?"

"A couple weeks?" Maxwell's words were incredulous at best.

Karina felt annoyance creep up her spine and glared.

"What's wrong with that?" Andrew spoke up, sounding irritated.

"What's wrong with it?" Karina huffed, arms crossing over her chest. "I'm sorry, but who helped to get one of you five out of a bad situation? Who put themselves on the line to do it? I believe we deserve the right to know what's going on now." Karina couldn't help but say.

The way Madeline just scoffed off what Maxwell said, how she avoided the topic all together, it pissed Karina off. Karina knew she wasn't being necessarily rational, but she was incredibly tired, and she didn't particularly care.

Madeline winced, glancing between the two of them, gaze lingering on Maxwell, an excruciating expression crossing her face. It was almost as if she both wanted and didn't want to say something. "I can't. It's not my business to say. I need to talk with the others, I can't just tell you on a whim."

"Yeah, come on, you two. Just get some rest and…" Mitchell spoke up, only to stop as Leon sent him a glare.

"It's classified information; they shouldn't act like this in front of Madeline anyway."

"Yes, but…" Mitchell shook his head. "They do have a right to know, I agree with Madeline on that thought."

"Then, why can't we know now?" Maxwell pressed, his voice soft. "What's the harm in finding out now?"

"I can't. We can't." Madeline shook her head.

"Really?" Karina found herself feeling downright annoyed. "You can't tell us anything? At least Andrew mentioned that's how you grew up." Karina ignored the way Andrew seemed to stiffen and growl where he sat. "Still, that's all you are going to tell us? After we risked our lives to save Emma? We risked a hell of a lot for you to keep silent."

Madeline straightened, expression turning stern. "I already told you, I can't. This is more than just about me and even about the other four. It could jeopardize a ton of people and I won't just go spilling things because—"

"You can't trust us? Is that it?" Karina hissed, causing Madeline to jerk back, shrinking back a little. The others scrambled to their feet, but Madeline quickly shot them a strange expression that caused them to freeze. Karina only partially made note of the movements as she growled, "We trusted you, we allowed ourselves to even be used by you, and yet you can't even..." Karina shook her head, hair whipping at her face as her fingernails dug into the skin of her palm. "That's so stupid."

She didn't realize she was on her feet until she found herself glaring down at Madeline, teacup almost shattering as she slammed it on the table. The hot liquid that remained splattered over her fingers, but she ignored it.

"I can't believe I allowed myself to even think you would trust us, that we could trust you."

She stomped toward the doorway, partly hoping someone would stop her. Instead, all she heard were her little brother's soft footsteps, padding after her as she slammed the door shut. Maxwell's gaze met hers and she realized she'd been speaking for both of them. She huffed and walked down the hallway, Maxwell at her side, lost in thought.

So, it startled both of them when the far door opened and running footsteps caught up to them. Karina jerked and looked back to see Emma standing before them, hands on her knees and dressed in a nightgown. Arik stood a little behind her, appearing hesitant as he glanced between her and the twins.

"Emma? Are you okay?" Maxwell asked, examining her quietly.

"Yeah." She stood up. "I'm sorry about Madeline and the others. I happened to overhear the conversation."

Maxwell pursed his lips, frown on his face. Karina looked askance, away from her earnest gaze. "So, you know how we feel about that silence."

Karina glanced back in time to see Emma flinch and went to turn to head into the apartment when Emma spoke. "We do trust you. A lot, actually. We never usually expose ourselves this much." Emma's voice pulled her back around and even Maxwell seemed to be listening with interest. "I'm not sure you realized, but this is tearing Madeline apart as much as it is you two. She wants to tell you, but she can't, not yet. Neither of us can." Emma let out a sigh, shoulders slumping. "I know that doesn't help, after all, your anger is, well…"

"Explainable? Justified? Accurate?" Maxwell put in, voice quiet.

"Yeah," Emma nodded and glanced toward Karina. "I'll see what I can do. I'll talk to Madeline, see if she can speed up the process, but I can't make any promises. Still, I want to thank you, both of you. I might have sounded curt when I realized you were both captured, but…"

Karina couldn't help the small smile from crossing her face and Maxwell just gave a nod, his own expression lifting. "We figured," he chuckled. Soon, however, the chuckling died down. "All right, we'll give it some time, but I think we need to talk." He sent a look Karina's way before saying goodnight to Emma and slipping into their apartment. Karina watched him go, before turning back toward Emma.

"I'm glad I caught you two. I couldn't let you leave on such a note, not after everything you did for us." Emma shook her head, slow and meticulous. "Still, why don't we both head back and rest?" Emma examined her with a worried gaze and Karina found herself agreeing, surprised to also see the dark circles under Emma's eyes.

"Rest, then we can throw a party to lift everyone's spirits," Arik pointed out, startling the two girls. He gave a warm, but faint smile. "I think we're all stressed. A party should liven things up and let us all relax a bit. What do you say?"

Karina stared at him before she turned away. "I would have to ask Maxwell."

"That's fair, and you, Emma?"

Karina waited, wondering about Emma's response, even as her hand hovered near the door handle. Emma's voice was soft, yet warm.

"Yeah, that sounds good. We can plan it for tomorrow afternoon. I'll let the others know." Karina heard footsteps fade away and couldn't help but to let out a weak chuckle.

She jumped when Arik stepped perpendicular to her, catching her attention. "I forgot to mention..." he trailed off, biting his lip as he glanced askance to the far wall of the hallway. "I wanted to thank you. You and Maxwell. You could have just given up on her, you didn't have to put yourselves in danger like that to save Emma but you did so, thanks." He turned and continued down the hallway. "I hope everyone can get some rest even though it's now quite late into the morning. It's no good to see everyone at everyone else's throat." Karina watched him go, unable to respond. She gripped the handle tightly for a moment before she headed inside.

She closed the door and found the living room empty. Same with the kitchen and even Maxwell's room. She hesitated before she stepped into her room to see Maxwell holding their mother's Bible, unopened. He looked over to her from his seat on the floor, curled into the corner on the soft rug. Karina stood in the doorway, unsure what to do. Maxwell pushed himself to his feet, Bible still in a tight grasp. "Karina." His tone of voice was soft, yet stern, and Karina couldn't help but grimace at the worry filling it. "We need to talk."

Karina looked at him. "One, you've already said that and two, we need to sleep too. I highly doubt either of us really slept last night, and it shows."

Maxwell grimaced and gave a sheepish expression, disrupting his calm mood. He shook his head and sat down on the bed. Karina hesitantly stepped up and took a seat, curling her legs up cross-legged so she could face him. "All right, what is it?"

"I want you to tell me, honestly," Maxwell hesitated, catching his breath before continuing, "were you scared?"

Karina stared at Maxwell, scrutinizing him as much as he was her. "What do you mean?"

Maxwell seemed hesitant, unsure how to continue before he nodded, as if thinking over something before catching her attention once more. "You mentioned yesterday, or earlier today actually, that you were forcing—"

"Why did you only hear that part?" Frustration welled up in Karina as she frowned. "All I was saying was I was trying to make sure we both got to Mom, everything intact."

Maxwell seemed confused for a moment, muttering a soft, "I never mentioned Ma." Before he shook his head and pursed his lips. "Which gets me back to my point. I want to know if you were scared." His grip tightened on the Bible as his gaze met hers for a brief moment before he turned away, shrinking inward. "I'll admit it. I was terrified when we were being dragged off to who knows where. Being stuck, unable to do anything, yet also knowing, if it didn't work, what was going to happen to us, to you…" He shook his head, hair falling in his face as his voice wavered. "I was scared."

Karina bit her lip, surprised at his upfront declaration. She looked away. "Fine, I was a little…I was scared too, happy now?" Little was such a lie. She was as terrified as Maxwell made it sound, for both of them. Not just with the black-market deal, but also this whole situation. She knew that wasn't originally what Maxwell was asking, but she couldn't help thinking about it. She hated it, being unable to do anything, just sitting there and waiting. Hoping and doing the same things they were doing for weeks, if not months now. She was angry that she almost did something cruel to two people, simply because one of them was trying to save their own skin. She was upset that she argued with Maxwell over something as stupid as getting a cell phone, which led to that disruptive argument and this conversation. She found herself annoyed that she would be having to wait even longer just to find out what Madeline and the others were up to.

"I'm just glad we're both all right." *That was also the truth.* Karina was utterly glad that they came out of that unscathed. Now, though, she was curious. About their friends, about what was going to happen now and about Maxwell.

Karina looked up, seeing a sad expression on Maxwell's face as he whispered a faint, "Oh, Right." He smiled. "Well, I just wanted to make sure that you were all right. It wasn't easy for either of us, so I figured we might as well just talk about it and get it out of the way."

"Thanks, little bro, but I'm fine, and from the looks of things, it seems you are all right yourself, if still a little shaken."

"Of course, I am." Maxwell gave her a deadpan look and she found herself smiling. He shook his head. "Anyway, tomorrow I'm going to pick up a phone for you, got it?"

Karina went to open her mouth to argue, only to get a sharp look in her direction. "Fine, whatever."

"Thanks." Maxwell stood, placing the Bible back down.

Karina peered up at him before standing. "Arik came up with the idea of having a party tomorrow afternoon. I figured, well…"

"You wanted to get something to apologize?" Maxwell spoke, faint smile on his lips.

Karina looked away with a huff but couldn't argue. She knew she shouldn't have snapped at Madeline like that, not when it was obvious what Emma said was true and how Madeline was going to tell them, at least eventually. Yet, she'd felt it was necessary, that if she didn't, she would burst or something from all the fear, worry and anger that had been building in her lately.

She shook her head and turned to Maxwell who already had a knowing look on his face. "We're tired." She hesitated, dropping her arms to her side. She wanted to ask Maxwell to stay with her, for tonight.

Maxwell waited in silence, seeming uncertain even as he continued to gaze at her.

"Stay." She finally put the word out there, finding her fingers slowly digging into the fabric of her shirt, the ends wispy in her grasp.

Maxwell didn't look at her, just sat there, debating. After some time, his head dropped, and he chuckled weakly. "All right."

Karina found herself surprised. She didn't think he would want to.

In truth, she honestly was comforted by his presence and while she was grateful that they now had separate rooms, this particular time, and last night, she couldn't sleep, unsure if he was safe or not.

She watched as he slipped out the door and returned with most of his pillows and a quilt from the other room. He plopped down on one side of the bed.

Karina snorted, but felt a smile cross her face as she took the other side.

Almost instantly, she relaxed, and her breath evened out, the quiet rise and fall of his chest and the warmth near her back was enough to finally let her mind drift off into sleep.

~ * ~

Maxwell wasn't sure how long he slept, but he must have needed it, for it was really bright out. He could feel a steady pressure around him and a soft breath. He shifted just enough to see Karina curled up beside him, pushing against the blankets that cocooned him.

He watched her sleep for a moment. She was peaceful, the sleep pushing away the worry lines and deep furrowed brow that she seemed to have as of late. She was always in thought lately, and it worried him. He closed his eyes, relishing the warmth and comfort.

Guess they were just so used to sleeping together or at least in the same room, whenever something awful happened. It was almost natural now.

"Morning."

Maxwell jerked upright to see Karina rubbing her eyes tiredly, mumbling words.

Maxwell chuckled and swung his legs out of bed, just managing to untangle the cloth. Karina slipped out as well and stretched. "We both needed the sleep, and I think we were both so tired yesterday."

Maxwell had to agree if the way he felt was any indication. Did they sleep the whole day away? He winced remembering her plaintive tone of voice from what felt like many hours ago. She was more scared than she let on. Part of him was glad she asked him to stay, simply to show it was still his sister there and that she was in the same boat as him. "Well, I did promise I would pick up that phone for you, and maybe I'll look for something to bring to the party."

Karina snorted. "Yeah, sounds good."

They quickly went their separate ways, Maxwell slipped out of her room, dragging his quilt and pillows with him and to his room. He threw them back on the bed and got changed before heading into the living room. Karina was just finishing up. She walked into the living room, hairband on her wrist and arms up to pull her hair back into its signature ponytail. He headed into the kitchen and pulled out two waters, tossing one to Karina, who caught it. She took a sip. Maxwell glanced toward the doorway, but decided against it, spotting the clock that practically verified his earlier thoughts. He cringed, not having thought it possible to sleep that long before he took a seat on the couch, startling Karina.

Karina looked at him before hesitantly following his lead, arms flopping onto her lap. "Maxwell?"

"I figured, since we're more rested, we can talk through what happened yesterday."

"Like what?" Karina turned her head, gaze on the far wall. "Didn't we talk enough..."

"I meant about the couple weeks thing."

Karina seemed to jerk. She turned back to him, startled before quickly schooling her features, the fakeness hurt but he ignored it as she grinned. "Oh, that's what you meant. So, what do you want to talk about?"

"I was thinking, maybe having a month break wouldn't be so bad. We just dealt with... that." He waved his arm vaguely, trying not to think of the past few days before continuing, "and we still don't have any information on Ma whatsoever."

"So then, we just wait? Some more?" Karina seemed outright annoyed at the idea, but she didn't argue.

"Basically. After all, what's a couple more weeks waiting?"

"Fine." Karina stretched, letting out a yawn. "If we're going to do it that way, then I'll just not think about it. Plus, I do want to apologize. I was a bit..." Karina waved, glancing away.

Right, they were a bit snappish earlier, though that was more due to how tired, cranky and annoyed they were more than anything. He winced at the memory. "Well yeah, Anyway, I'm heading out to grab something for the party. Want anything?"

"Nah, I'm good. Just be careful."

"I'll be fine, see you soon." Maxwell hummed, waving good-bye as he slipped out the door.

He walked down the chilly street, noticing the relief in the air from the loved ones of those kidnapped. Quiet chatter and laughter filled the streets as he entered the shopping district. Off to one side, he managed to spot a crowded store. People were shouting and yelling, reaching toward the entrance. He looked at it to see it was a general store, nothing particularly special.

He looked over just as a person slipped out, mask gripped tightly in her clutches, a broad smile on her face.

Oh, they must have gotten some masks in. He examined the place, debating, before he reached to his wrist, where he had the bandages peeking out and around his thumb. He touched it lightly before he shook his head and walked down the street. He wasn't going to try to rush into chaos like that to pick up some masks, just so he and Karina didn't stand out as much. To think people would get so savage over a flimsy piece of cloth. Then again…he looked over his shoulder at the crowd. He could see young and old mixed in, reaching, almost begging, money sparkling and rippling. It made sense. To them, it was the only means of feeling secure and safe. He found himself touching the little clip and quickly dropped his hand. It's interesting, what people held onto when they lived in fear.

He turned and hurried down the street to pick up what he was there to grab. He found some chips, dip and a cheap phone, which he set up right then and there. He also grabbed himself something to eat, starved.

As he walked down the street with his old phone and his sister's new phone, he looked between them. He carefully placed in his and Lex's numbers before using her phone to call his own. As soon as he heard it ringing, he felt a surge of relief and quickly cut it off. He slipped his phone into his pocket and gripped hers tightly. Now he felt better, to know she had some means to contact them.

When he got back, the party was just starting. He slipped her phone into his pocket, deciding it would be best to give it to her later. Though, he was a bit surprised to realize he'd been out most of the day. He could see people chatting and playing games, music played in the background. Mitchell sang out of tune to a song with a cheery voice while Andrew demanded him to stop, annoyed and amused. Madeline was laughing while Emma chuckled. Karina spotted him and waved him over, already seeming more cheerful. He figured going to the party would help them feel better, and it seemed to be the case with the others as well. Tensions were not nearly like before. If anything, everyone was surprisingly relaxed. He knew it had taken a while in the phone store, but maybe he was more distracted in his thoughts than he, well, thought.

The room was nice, the warm glow permeated the area, lit by soft lights and the setting sun. He could appreciate this. He hesitated for a moment before walking up to Arik, around the same time as Karina. They exchanged looks as Arik raised his eyebrow.

"Would you be willing to show us how to defend ourselves, so this doesn't happen again?" Karina asked.

"Why me? Why not someone else here?"

"Because…" Maxwell didn't want to say it was because he didn't really trust the others right now, and it seemed Karina was being surprisingly silent.

Arik let out a quiet groan. "I can do it. It won't be much, but I can teach you two basic defense moves. I'll ask my father about other ways to help you two, is that all right?"

"That's fine. Thank you." Karina's expression was filled with gratitude. "Anything will help."

Maxwell hoped that would be the case.

The party ended without much worry and Maxwell found himself passing the phone over to his reluctant sister. Still, she took it, soft smile and all.

Now they just needed to get back into the normal, like Madeline said. Why did it always sound so easy? He wondered as he returned to his room, is there any way to ever turn things back to the way things used to be?

After all, how could they return to normal if there was no normal? He let out a heavy breath. He would have to go back to work tomorrow. Yet, he found he was in no hurry to do so, even with the prospect of looking for Mom.

After all, once they found her, how would they get her out?

Why were things never easy?

Chapter Eighteen

It took a month. Caym clicked his tongue. At least a month to use the information enough to break down his stubborn uncle.

He listened to the rattling as the elevator trundled up to the top floor. It opened slowly to reveal a decent-sized room with large windows and normal furniture. Nothing grand.

Caym stepped into the room, spotting his uncle sitting behind a mahogany desk. The man's hands were clasped in front of him, mask in his pocket and expression stiff. "Caym." His voice was booming, yet curt.

"Hello, Uncle, thank you for seeing me."

The man narrowed his eyes. A face that probably often held a smile, was in a deep frown. His slicked-back hair stood awkwardly as if he ran his fingers through it a bunch of times in frustration. "What do you want? You've been badgering to see me for months. Why?"

"I thought I told you in the initial letter." Caym stepped forward, taking a seat on one of the couches, legs crossed. "I wish to talk to you in regard to Leo, as well as my father."

"I can't believe you still call that man your father." Uncle shook his head, disgusted. "He's nothing but a vile corrupted corpse that died long ago."

Caym narrowed his eyes. "I won't argue that Father is a devil-like man, but that seems like a strong way of putting it. I know you were estrang—"

"I was thrown out almost five years ago," Uncle Hugh said curtly, expression cold. "You know your father's position in the community.

Being head of that governmental department of his, he is almost on level with the president and his cabinet. To think one thing I said pissed him off enough to throw me out. Not only that, but the one person who remained in contact with me…" Hugh clenched his fist so tightly they were turning white. "Now, enough of that. Why do you wish to know about Lex?"

"He's coming home, and I want to make sure he stays home this time," Caym said, keeping it short and to the point. It wasn't wrong. He honestly had no one else to ask, Mother and Father were useless in that regard and never valued Leo anyway. Antonio and Martha had been dead ends, at least in that regard.

"He is, is he?" Hugh hummed, sounding unconcerned. "That stubborn brat actually agreed to go home?"

"He's not a brat."

"No, I suppose not." Hugh pushed away from his desk. "Do you have no one else to ask? I'm surprised you've been trying to speak with me for so many months on such a simple topic."

"How is the wellbeing and protection of little Leo a simple topic?" Caym leaned forward, hands in front of his mouth to hide his expression, even as his gaze bored into his uncle.

Hugh nervously ran his fingers through his hair, much like Leo did. "I see, you do still care for him."

"Why would you think otherwise?"

Hugh peered toward him, confused, before he frowned. "So, you didn't throw Ariel and your daughter out."

"What?" Caym sat up, stunned. "Why are you saying I threw Ariel and little Kiera out? I was told they left with another man." Caym felt something come unsettled, his heart clenched.

"You didn't know?" Surprise and heartfelt sadness fell across Hugh's face. "You honestly didn't know."

"Didn't know what?" Caym found himself on his feet without even realizing it. He could feel his calm exterior breaking. "I loved them, and they left me!"

"No. They didn't."

Caym stilled, feeling like he was punched in the gut, or as if Leo just slapped him. "Then…"

Hugh put his head in his hands, letting out a steadying breath.

Caym found himself slamming his palms on his uncle's desk, hearing the loud thud and feeling the stinging pain that surged up his wrist. "Uncle. What happened? What do you mean, they didn't leave? Why did you say I was the one who threw them out?"

"You truly do love them. You truly did…"

Did?

Something in Caym cracked. "What happened to them? Are they all right? Are the—"

"So, it must have been your father." Hugh looked him straight in the eyes, pain sketched into his face. "My niece…" he paused before putting a hand to his face with a deep sigh. "To think we weren't even blood-related. After all, her whole family was still in the gated community. She would have had no one else to turn to."

He shook his head and turned, standing up and stepping to one side, where a little safe was embedded into the wall. He turned the combination, even as he continued to speak, words distant. "She sent me a letter, saying that she was being forced out of her home, along with your child. She couldn't speak with you, because you were away at a meeting in another community. She said not to blame you. I couldn't understand why when it made it sound like you let her go." Hugh shook his head, his voice distant to Caym's ears. "She and your daughter were thrown out of the gated community with barely the clothes on their backs and left to die. They were found dead in the river three years ago."

Caym would have collapsed, if his grip on the edge of the table hadn't steadied him, the faint sound of cracking wood reaching his ears. He vaguely noted as Hugh returned to his seat, gently placing something on the table. "Father… Father banished them and told me a lie. Father lied to me. He said my wife left me and…" Caym found himself mouthing the words, but not going anywhere.

His father lied and said the love of his life left him for another man, taking their child with her. He hated it, but he thought at least one day, he might be able to see Kiera's shining smile, maybe even perhaps hear her mother's radiant laugh or her out of tune, yet cheerful singing. To think…he thought they were happy, as much as it pained him. "Let me see the letter."

He didn't even really see his uncle's movements or hear it. He just found a piece of paper in his hands as he read it with shaking limbs.

Uncle Hugh,

It seems that my father-in-law has finally had enough of me trying to help Caym. My husband has been trying to find some time to get away with me and Kiera for a few weeks now, just for a vacation, and his father is absolutely refusing.

I guess it got to be too much. He's going to throw us out tomorrow and there's nothing I can do. I've tried everything. My parents, they're too scared to contradict him and don't have any say in the matter. I don't know what to do.

Caym is away, I'm not sure if he knows, but please, don't blame him. I loved him deeply and I really wanted to live with him and our child. You're in Reinmark, right? I'm going to try to travel there as soon as they let me out. Once there I'll see if I can get a letter to Caym. It hurts, not to be able to see him one more time. Not to be able to contact him like this. He was always so gentle to us, protecting us from his father and speaking of his brother with such a reverent and warm tone.

I miss him. I want to see him again. Oh, Kiera is crying, I guess she misses him too.

Well, I'll hopefully see you soon, but I figured I would send one more letter out just in case. After all, we both know how dangerous it is out there and…

No, I'll make my way to you, no matter what.

Love you,

Ariel

P.S. If you see Caym, tell him that I don't blame him. He tried to protect us from his father. I wish I could tell him that myself, but… Caym, if you do end up reading this, and I haven't seen you. I'm sorry, I guess I didn't make it. But I know you're strong, you adore your brother, so make sure to protect him, even if you don't see him. Be proud that he was able to live outside this place.

I miss you...

Wet tears dripped onto the already stained page. The letter was tattered, but intact. That was definitely his love's handwriting.

He could feel something inside shatter and he wanted to cry out. His attention slowly drifted back to his uncle, who seemed to be staring at him in a mix of shock and sadness. "I'm keeping this letter."

"I figured." Hugh looked away. "Thank you. I know she was happy with you, just from that letter. I should have trusted her when she said not to blame you."

Caym found himself gripping the paper tightly. "So, you say they found her floating in the river?"

"Yes, she was raped and stabbed to death. Your daughter must have been killed in the struggle, they found her a few days later, mutilated."

What hadn't shattered earlier *snapped.*

Someone raped and killed his wife and child. His father let it happen. His father pushed them out of the gated community just for simply being with Caym, for loving him and trying to get him away from that place.

His father—No. That THING was now after his dear Leo. His mother, she must have known. She knew everything that happened.

His parents...no, they meant nothing to him now. Only Leo mattered.

His little brother was the only thing he had left.

He carefully pulled his mind back together, gaze drifting toward his uncle as his tears stopped. "Thank you, Uncle. I'm sorry for your loss. I best be going."

Hugh's eyes widened. He appeared uncertain and nervous. "Dear boy, you can't already be all right."

"Uncle, it is not an opportune time to speak of this. I need to make sure things are sorted out. Thank you for telling me the circumstances behind my wife's disappearance." He nodded and turned, footsteps sounding sharp and metallic as he left for the elevator.

"Wait."

Caym stopped but didn't turn around.

"Lex has already survived this long, he can take care of himself, remember that. He isn't… he isn't Ariel and Kiera."

"I know." Caym stepped into the elevator and, reached out to hit the button to descend.

No, he knew full well Leo was alive and well, even going so far as managing to stay clean. Maybe it was the twins, maybe he was simply pretending, but he was clean when he came home. Yet, what if something happened? What if Father became tired of him, of both of them? It wouldn't be hard to have them killed or worse. Caym knew he came here for information about Lex and how to help him, but…no, this was enough information, he didn't need to, nor want to, know anything else.

He couldn't let what happened to Ariel and Kiera happen to Leo. He couldn't let another loved one perish.

He had some work to do.

Chapter Nineteen

Lex looked up from his paperwork, surprised as someone knocked on his door. "Come in," he called.

After a moment, the door opened to reveal Finnien Gladius, his employer, grin on his face. Finnien walked forward, taking a seat on one of the chairs across from his desk, eyes gleaming. Lex turned his chair and watched him with a wary gaze. "Sir, what brings you here?"

"Oh, I just wanted to inform you that it turns out that my information was false. Seems like nothing has been happening. No suspicious activity has occurred in the last month, so it seems there are no problems, just a clerical error."

"Oh?" Lex tilted his head, eyes scrutinizing. "So, there are no problems? What about our deal?"

Finnien shrugged and stood, stepping around the desk. Lex shifted, watching in uncertainty as the man leaned against the desk, uncomfortably close. "I'll say our deal is null. However, I have watched you for the last few months. I don't see any problem letting you have a bit more information. After all, this is important for you as much as the rest of the gated community."

Lex narrowed his eyes, leaning one elbow against the desk. He didn't say anything though, waiting. Finnien pulled back enough to let Lex breathe. "So, as you might know, we are the main manufacturers of fertilizer. However, much of our business is actually within the gated community."

"But the website..."

The man placed a finger forward, stopping him before continuing,

"Isn't it easier to show the outside vermin that some people within the community are actually looking out for them?" His employer stood and stepped back to the other side of the desk, placing his elbows on it and leaning his chin into his hand. "After all, it's easier to maintain them if they think they are somewhat important, which is also why we hire some people from the other side. Don't worry though, anyone who works here is sworn to silence. We also use this as a recruiting center for those within the gated community. After all, we do need more servants. I figured this would be a good chance for you to find one as well. Are there any you're interested in?"

Lex stiffened and Finnien's grin widened before he pulled back, letting out a short laugh. "Seems like I got you there. Don't worry, the last bit was to get a response out of you."

Lex glared, and the man's eyes seemed to gleam in a way that made Lex feel even more uncomfortable. "Now, why don't I give you a little tour?"

"That would be helpful, thank you," Lex spoke, feeling perturbed.

After all, was that last bit only to get a reaction out of Lex? His thoughts flickered to Maxwell and he quickly pulled away, standing. "It is a little cramped here."

"Of course, now come this way."

They walked back into the gated community, through the glass tunnel. "This and the sewage system are the only things that connect the two sides. I don't think I ever got a time to mention that."

He shook his head.

"Most of the outer side is watched by servants from the gated community. There isn't much to see on that." His employer's eyes flashed. "However, we do have some things on the gated community's side that are incredibly important for the vitality of the gated community."

"Vitality?"

"You caught on."

His employer led them through the far door and into a dual hallway, the same one Lex came down almost every day. The man turned left, continuing down the hall, past the guards, to the other end of the hall. Windows lined the left side, showcasing the rigid gates and beginning signs of spring. Two doorways stood at the end, one leading out and one turning right.

His boss turned to the right door and swiped his card before entering with Lex on his heels. After a few twists and turns, they reached one more doorway that stood out from the rest. Its thick metal shone against the white of the walls. The man gestured to a panel on the right that seemed to be a scanner. Lex hesitated before he reached a hand up and pressed against it. Red scanned over his palm and he winced as a pricking sensation caught his attention.

"Blood sample, to prove it's you. Don't worry, I've already set it up to accept you."

Lex pulled away, holding his fingers as a thin stream of blood trailed down. How did he already set it up if it needed a blood sample? He decided not to think about it as he looked over, disconcerted. He noticed the man leaning toward him to take a look at the machine. "Looks like it worked, go ahead."

Lex didn't need to be told twice. He reached forward and turned the handle, hearing a faint click. The door swung open, exposing a set of stairs that led down. He stepped down, followed by his employer.

"This is the research section. This is where we do the intensive research on both fertilizer and other things."

Lex felt like he didn't want to know what other things he meant.

They walked down the hall, passing door after door with windows just past them. Each room seemed to be a lab. Men and women in the familiar white of doctor uniforms with skin that was equivalent of the color of the walls worked in each.

"These are our scientists. Most of them stay down here in the sleeping quarters. We provide all their necessities, food, water, other things. They work day and night to study for us. Most of the scientists here are from the outer community, so this is a reprieve for them."

Lex made sure to not make eye contact with Finnien as they continued down. "Where are the sleeping quarters?"

"To the left at the end of the hall. If you take a right, it leads to the more sensitive material and the sewage system is straight ahead, through that doorway. We have someone maintaining it for the whole building there."

Lex looked where Finnien was gesturing to see a doorway different from the rest in its plainness.

"Cameras are kept on it so none of the workers decide to take a little vacation. Now, this is about as much as I can show you. However, you do have the authority to come down here, and I might ask you to send some things down that are more sensitive."

Lex looked around. "That's fine." Not really, everything about this place made him feel anxious. However, this was also an opportunity. "By the way, what is in the area to the right?"

"Things that your father has control over as well as higher-ups." The man shrugged. "Unfortunately, without express permission from your father, I was unable to show you the area. However, you've been here for a while and many within this community appreciate your presence, so I find myself letting that slide."

"Joy," Lex muttered under his breath before speaking up a little louder. "Thank you, that is much appreciated."

His employer didn't respond as he turned away. Lex stared at the doors once more with a worried frown. So, that was their destination. Wasn't it? Plus, the sewage system…

Maybe that might work. He would have to notify the twins, and quickly. He felt that something bad was coming, but he wasn't sure exactly who was in danger.

~ * ~

Karina couldn't believe a month flew by without her noticing. With their new self-defense classes and the recovery from the kidnapping, it had been a little hectic. Now that things finally quieted down, she was stunned and unsure.

She found herself staring at the thing sitting in Arik's grasp with an unsettled feeling. Emma stood beside him, looking uncomfortable, but sure. The black gleam of the gun stood out against his pale skin. There was the thick piece of what almost looked like a storage cartridge or something strewn over his hand, gold glinting on the inside. The main part of the gun was pulled back to reveal the innards of the gun, showing there was nothing there.

"Why are you giving me this?" Karina carefully took the gun, pointing away from the other two. Even with her limited knowledge on guns, considering the lack of them back in Claremore, it wasn't hard to guess which part the bullets came out from. It felt heavy in her sweaty palm and it made her feel queasy.

"Arik mentioned it, that you two have been learning to protect yourselves, right?" Emma leaned forward, arms behind her back and nervous smile on her face.

Karina tilted the gun toward the floor. "Yes, but why a gun? Wouldn't it be really hard to get one? I don't even know how to use it. Isn't that pointless?"

"Not necessarily." Arik broke in, showing her how to put that storage unit into the gun. She noted, with trepidation, it already seemed loaded. "That's why I called you here. My dad sometimes comes here to practice. He's actually the one who gave it to me. He was impressed when I told him what you two did for us."

Karina scrutinized the small park area. It was separated by trees that seemed stunted in their growth. The dark clouds above threatened rain, but the air was cool and refreshing. Emma called her out earlier when she noticed Maxwell was still at work. She led Karina here, to this place. At the far side of the little clearing, Karina could see a rough wooden outline, similar to a bullseye target.

"A lot of people come here for shooting practice, since there aren't many places around that allow it. Well, those that still have guns at least, like the police. People who have them unregistered usually avoid practicing here."

"So, people do still have them." Karina stared down at the metallic sheen of the gun and looked toward Arik, who nodded. "Still,

thanks, I guess. I didn't think your father would just give one out though."
She raised her eyebrow with bemusement while Arik shrugged
sheepishly.

"What can I say? He was impressed, though I might have
embellished a bit, but hey, I would say it's for a good cause." He pointed
a finger at Karina, amusement clear on his smiling features.

Karina found she couldn't argue with that. She shook her head as
Emma watched, amused. "To answer your question. Yes and no. The
police have them, but most people don't." Emma frowned. "Yet you can
still find some for sale and people will often get them illegally, so it
doesn't make much difference. It's for protection anyway, right?"

Karina looked down at it and nodded slowly.

"All right, then let's get started. You've already put the magazine
in, now pull back on the slide and release, putting it back in place. Be
careful now, don't put your finger on the trigger. As soon as it went
forward, it brought the bullet up, so you have a loaded chamber." Arik
spoke firmly, yet kindly. The gun felt heavy in her grip, but not
overbearing. "Now, make sure your hands are holding it firmly, yet don't
grip it from the back. It's a semi and if you're not careful, you can rip the
skin off your hand when it shucks."

Karina blinked and glanced over to Arik, who seemed to note her
confusion. He chuckled a little self-consciously. "Ah, sorry, forgot you
probably don't know that word." Karina was unable to hide the affronted
look from crossing her face, but before she could get a word in, Arik
continued. "Shuck, in this case, means when the gun fires, the top part
will shoot back as recoil before returning to its proper place. As such, it
extends past where you would usually grip, which means if you hold your
hand there, well…" he grimaced. "Don't expect to have any skin left, or
a thumb." Karina winced at the image as Emma hissed a warning toward
Arik, who waved it away. "Better to know, right? Now, you see that area
where it looks like there's a dip? See if you can line that area up with the
piece at the end of the muzzle. There we go. As soon as you feel like
you're ready, put your finger on the trigger. Make sure you don't
anticipate the gun going off, just lightly pull the trigger—"

A loud bang shattered the quiet silence and Karina blinked, surprised. Residual smoke curled up from the barrel. The recoil hurt a little, snapping her wrist back just a bit. She quickly removed her finger from the trigger and looked over at Arik who whistled, staring toward the target. "Not bad. This is your first time holding a gun and you actually managed to hit."

Karina looked over and frowned. Where did she hit? She saw a nick at the edge of the circle and glared. "That's not hitting."

"No, I would say it is. After all, most people can't even get a piece of the circle, or will hit the floor or, gosh forbid, sky." Emma chuckled, waving. "When I first did it, I think I hit a tree."

"I think the bullet's still there actually." Arik hummed. Emma blushed and glared, causing Karina to chuckle before she found herself looking at the gun, careful to keep the barrel away from anyone. The recoil was tough, but not terrible. It was both extraordinary and scary, the power this little thing had.

She gripped it tightly. This would help her protect Maxwell. Yet…

"Why did you only want to show me?" She turned to face Emma and Arik, gun at her side. "What about Maxwell? Something like this would be able to help protect him too."

Emma and Arik exchanged looks before Emma sheepishly put her fingers together. Arik glanced toward Emma before facing Karina. "He's a bit too kind-hearted. Between the two of you, he seems the type to avoid confrontation at all cost. Not saying that you dive into it…" He quickly threw his arms up, waving them in defense.

Emma rolled her eyes. "I'm just saying you seem more the type who could and would be able to use a weapon against another person. Maybe eventually, you can convince your brother to do the same, but neither of us would probably be able to. After all, as much as you two might trust us, well, that's a whole bag of moral issues that I don't want to go into. After all, those things are deadly for a reason."

Arik's gaze hardened, and Karina found herself looking down at the gun once more in an uneasy light.

Karina thought through his words quietly. In a weird way, it was true. Maxwell could be quite stubborn, and she could barely keep count of the number of times he'd avoided hurting anyone. For instance, during the riot all those months ago when they arrived in New London City or, case in point, during the kidnapping, Maxwell did not react physically. She knew Maxwell wasn't weak, but he also wasn't one to fight.

She pulled herself from that thought. She might be able to talk with Maxwell later, see what he had to say.

"You know, it was difficult to find that."

Karina looked away from the gun toward Arik as he reached a hand to his chin.

"I mean, weapons aren't easy to get, even for my father." His eyes shifted to Emma, a strange expression on his face before he shrugged. "Yet Emma and her group have a few as well, isn't that interesting?"

"Arik? What are you implying?" Emma's voice came out soft as she scrutinized him.

He waved it off, turning to Karina. "They were supposed to tell you later today, right? Why don't we work on practice before then? Sound good to you, Emma?"

Emma stiffened and looked between Karina and Arik, blush forming on her cheeks. "Of course. Don't forget though, I still have to go to work, you know. The hostel isn't going to clean itself."

"We both have to," Arik pointed out.

Karina glowered. "I'm still not happy with the fact you two decided to work there even after everything that happened."

"It's not that bad. With those girls you warned us about gone, there haven't been any problems." Arik shrugged.

Karina shook her head before turning to the target. She hesitated before bringing the gun up, listening as Arik and even Emma, pointed out something in her stance or hold. She wasn't sure how many rounds she fired as the sun sank into the distance. Finally, they decided to stop and Arik grinned, passing her a holster, as he called it. "It's all yours, good job there."

Karina took it, staring at the leather before slipping the gun in and closing it appropriately. After making sure the safety was on, having gotten a quick explanation from Emma when she nearly shot herself in the foot. Karina put it onto her belt, glad to be back in her normal clothes. The loose-fitting top lay over the gun, hiding it accordingly.

Though she would have to find another place to put it and soon. She didn't want Maxwell finding it until she talked with him.

She looked at Arik and Emma, hands on her hips. "So, you two are heading to work. Will you be back in time for our talk?"

Emma pursed her lips as Arik's expression grew neutral. "They won't want me there. What about you, Emma?"

Emma looked at the ground, the way her fingers curled and uncurled showed her uncertainty. "I won't be there, but I think it should be fine." She looked toward Karina. "I heard she managed to convince her mom not to come and meet them."

"Mom? Why do we not want to meet Madeline's mom?" Karina frowned.

She couldn't really understand that notion, but from the wince Emma gave, it was probably quite serious.

"Honestly," Emma glanced toward Arik, who conveniently walked away to appraise the damage Karina did to the target and surrounding area. "She didn't want to get you two involved. With her crush on Maxwell. Well, she's usually the first one to bring someone to her mom's attention, so it goes to show just how much she likes him that she doesn't want the two to meet."

So, Madeline didn't want them involved. Is that why it took so long before she was willing to explain anything?

"Of course, the other reason was she was trying to get up the courage to talk to Maxwell alone," Emma joked, and Karina rolled her eyes.

"I'm going to guess she's not normally like that."

"Yeah." Emma sighed and turned toward Arik. "I wish I could do the same, keeping the person I like away from all this, but I guess just like Madeline, it's not really an option."

As if he heard her, Arik turned toward them, a confused

expression his face. "Are you two done? Because we do need to get going."

Emma smiled, eyes sad. "Yeah, we're ready."

Karina glanced toward Emma. So, what exactly was she unable to keep Arik out of?

Did Karina want to know who they were? She almost wanted to say forget it and focus entirely on getting to Mom. She mentally groaned at the notion. She couldn't do that, even if she could convince herself not to go, she couldn't convince her brother. Ironic as that was. Wasn't she the explorer of the group? She felt like she was starting to lose that title.

She followed after Arik and Emma as they returned to the main street where they split off, Emma and Arik heading toward the hostel and Karina returning home, her thoughts a whirl of confusion and worry. Why couldn't anything be easy?

~ * ~

Maxwell perked up as Karina slipped into the room. She spotted him and stiffened before a quick smile flew onto her face. "Hey, bro, home already?"

Maxwell blinked and sighed. "I asked to be let out early, remember?" She wasn't one to forget something like that. He shook his head and stood. "Anyway, we were supposed to meet with Madeline."

"First, we get something to eat." Karina walked into the kitchen. "I'm starving, and we don't know how long it will be."

"I guess we can do that," Maxwell muttered, walking into the kitchen.

As Karina worked, pulling some leftovers out of the fridge, he leaned against the doorway with a frown. "Hey, Kari, are you okay?"

"Little bro, why are you asking?"

She didn't even turn, just kept working on the food. Admittedly, her time at that cafe helped with her cooking skills a lot. She wasn't quite up to his level, but at least she no longer burned water. He hadn't even thought that was possible until his sis did it.

He chuckled at the thought before focusing back onto Karina. "You just seem much quieter lately, like…" He furrowed his brow, hesitant. "Remember when we first left? You were so excited to see everything that was out here."

Karina stilled, staring at the microwave as the thing moved back and forth inside as if it was the most interesting thing in the world before she shrugged and turned to him. "I'm still fascinated by it all, but I mean, this city looks just like any other we've been through. I wanted to see more of the nature Mom talked about, you know, like the ocean and stuff?" She gave him a weak smile. "I guess everything is catching up to me. After all, we're not much different than when we left, right?"

Maxwell opened his mouth and then frowned. "What do you mean?"

Seriously, what did Karina mean? They'd changed, right? He examined himself, frown deepening. He wasn't that much taller than his sister and still appeared as scrawny as usual, even with the new job. However, they were still the same people. His sister was overprotective as ever and he was still a bit of a coward. He felt himself flash back to the faux kidnapping and cringed. Honestly, what was the point of having him there? Karina was the one to actually do something. He was just kind of following. Maybe hearing that they were the only cure to a stupid epidemic was something, but… "Come on, sis, this isn't like you. To be thinking so much ab—"

"To be thinking? True, I'm more the reckless type, right?" She grinned, waving it away as if she never brought up such a controversial comment. "Anyway, we need to meet up with the others. Here you go, food's ready." She turned back to the microwave and clicked it off before pulling it out. She split it, giving him some. He took it. Though he wasn't really happy with her silence, he didn't argue. Karina downed hers with barely a slurp and headed toward the door. "Now hurry up, slowpoke. Don't want to be late because you were dilly-dallying."

"Oh, come on, Karina," he groused, scrambling to down his food, which he barely noted was just the ramen from last night—it was still a little lukewarm, but it would do—before hurrying after her. Wait, when did she go to her room? He blinked, startled, as she stepped out of her room instead of being in front of the doorway. "What…"

"You took too long." She shrugged.

"That's not fair. You were the one who was taking her sweet time to cook ramen of all things!" Maxwell snapped, deciding to ignore the fact Karina went to her room instead of outside. She would tell him if it was important.

"Hey, we needed it," she pointed out with a cheeky grin. She slipped into the hallway. Maxwell didn't get a chance to retort, hurrying after her as she reached Madeline's room. She barely knocked once before the door opened to reveal Madeline on the other side.

Maxwell stared, mouth dry. Madeline was dressed in a short dress that fluttered around her legs and a beautiful jade-like necklace that sat daintily against her throat. He heard Karina chuckle and he glared at her as she gave a Cheshire cat grin back.

"Oh. You made it," Madeline stammered, fingers gripping the front of her dress. She appeared flushed and was giving Maxwell a small smile that Maxwell found himself unable to quite figure out.

What the hell?

Maxwell gulped and waved weakly. "Hi, Madeline." How the hell was he supposed to respond to this? He knew the girl liked him when she almost called him cute all that time ago, but this felt different. "Nice dress?"

She lit up and his sister snorted. "So, you did notice. I knew my brother wasn't clueless."

"Hey." Maxwell's glare sharpened, feeling the heat on his face. "Uh, that's not important." He quickly brought up his hands, waving them about before turning away slightly. "We were here to talk." This didn't sound right for some reason.

Madeline's expression fell. Karina patted her on the shoulder and slipped past. Madeline gazed up and down the hallway before turning to face him. "Uh, right, so…come in."

Did he do something wrong? Oh gosh, why were girls so confusing? He quickly shook his head and hurried inside. Karina and

Madeline were already seated. There was plenty of room near Madeline, but Karina had chosen a chair. Maxwell quickly took a seat beside Karina, almost pushing her over. She rolled her eyes but didn't comment as she scooted over to fit them both. Madeline seemed a little upset, but quickly hid it behind a smile as she shifted in her seat. Did he screw up something? Never mind, he wasn't going to bother with this anymore. He noticed how quiet the room was. It was clean and light. For a moment he wondered where everyone else was but shrugged it off. "So, about what you were going to tell us. You said that it was a major thing for your group. So where are the others? Why did you want to wait for so long?"

Her cheeks reddened so much he grew a little worried. "Uh, I figured the two of us could talk and…" She shook her head quickly, her hair falling around her shoulders in combed ringlets. They were pretty, he noted, before his brain caught up with her words.

"Wait—what?"

Madeline's expression grew stern and she sat upright, similar to the way he saw her when they first devised a plan to save Emma. "As for the second question. I needed a month to prepare. After all, I can't just tell anyone. Mother would kill me." The way she said that made Maxwell shiver. The truth in her eyes scared him. He almost wanted to go back to the previous question, but it didn't seem like that was happening now.

He supposed Karina didn't notice as she tilted her head, confused. "What does your mother have to do with this? Emma mentioned something along those same lines."

Madeline stared at her in silence before she closed her eyes. "Have you ever heard of the Resistance, or as some might call it, The America Liberation?"

Maxwell furrowed his brow. The America Liberation? He never heard of it. He peered sidelong toward Karina, catching her eyes. She shook her head.

Madeline's eyes widened. "You don't know?" she muttered, lost. "Most people have at least heard something about them. How do I go from here?" She sighed and returned her attention toward them. "The AL is an underground organization that focuses on recruiting teens , adults and even kids to fight against the government as well as the gated communities. After all, those walls are impenetrable."

Maxwell quickly averted his eyes, trying not to think of the time he and Karina were dragged into one of them because of their association with Lex. "I see."

Madeline gave a sharp nod. "The reason I didn't want to mention the organization is because I didn't want you two involved. After all, I'm one of the recruitment officers for our teen section. Mother is mobilizing the adult recruits outside the city as we speak."

The truth in her words pierced him and he frowned. How come? Weren't they involved anyway? Though, he supposed, she didn't really know that. After all, they probably seemed like just two lost teenagers, which wasn't that far off.

"So, what now?" Karina brought up, gesturing in a brushing off motion. "You told us, so what are you going to do now?"

"Usually, I would have you meet Mother and have you join us. That was what the proper protocol was supposed to be." Madeline stood and patted down her dress before peering right at Maxwell, gaze determined. "But I can't do that. You've already seen too much, and I don't want you caught up in that mess. Mother didn't know until now that I was telling you and she's pissed. I explained the situation to her. She's agreed for now, but…" Madeline shook her head before seeming to switch her train of thought. "There is no reason you should be involved in our fight unless you want to be." She bit her lip.

Karina crossed one leg over the other, leaning back as if to scrutinize the ceiling, picking out patterns in the smooth pane above. "What if we were involved?"

"Karina?" What was she getting at?

Madeline's eyes sharpened as she turned to Karina, who responded evenly, "You're an organization with means and tools. Maybe even weapons, correct?" Karina inquired, giving Madeline a surprisingly calculated look.

"Yes."

Karina seemed to debate for a while before turning toward

Maxwell. "Maybe they can help us."

Maxwell scrutinized Karina, only to realize what she was saying a moment later. Wait, she actually wanted to let them know about Ma? That might actually work. They did trust Madeline and the others to rescue them after their pseudo kidnapping, so... "Geez, Kari." He let out a sigh, seeing his sister's relieved grin out of the corner of his eyes. "Still, I think we should ask him first." Maxwell made sure to give her a piercing look and she seemed to realize who he was talking about because she grimaced.

However, before Maxwell could berate her any farther, he heard Madeline pipe up in confusion and a hint of anger. "You're hiding something as well."

She tilted her head, watching him with a narrowed and somewhat cold gaze. He winced and would have argued if Madeline hadn't interrupted by standing. "I think our discussion is over. You have someone to talk with, right? Don't let me intrude. After all, I won't be so hypocritical to stop you from speaking behind our backs."

The sarcasm in her voice was thicker then what Maxwell could only imagine a fourth stage person would have.

He gulped and exchanged a glance with Karina who sighed and waved her hands. "You know, it won't hurt us, we're only talking with Madeline. She'll keep silent until we make any final decisions, right?"

Karina glared, and Madeline sat back down, expression neutral as she nodded.

Maxwell turned, catching Madeline's blue eyes. He felt that same feeling he held with Lex all that time ago, that sincerity. He felt a warm smile cross his face and, for a split second he saw the strong girl persona she held crack as she fidgeted, her own smile flitting on her face. It was gone as fast as it came, but it was enough. "Do you know Enthrope?"

Madeline nodded, eyes widened only slightly, but expression still even. "Go on."

"Our mom was taken by them almost half a year ago," Karina spoke up, leaning forward.

"We want her back," Maxwell said with ease. "We found out that she is held in L. J. Fox Incorporated. We were trying to find a way in."

"Maxwell hasn't had much luck, and neither has our other friend." Karina couldn't have been any more annoyed even if she tried. "With only the three of us, there isn't much we can do, so…"

"Can you help us rescue Mother?" Maxwell was only slightly startled when Karina's voice joined his, but Madeline jumped, utterly surprised, stiffening and posture straight as a wall.

She opened and closed her mouth, uncertain, or, well, more upset, Maxwell guessed. "Your mother? That's why you're here." She let out a weak little laugh. "Right," she sighed, eyes closed as she thought over her answer.

Silence filled the room, and Maxwell stopped himself from fidgeting, Karina doing surprisingly well herself as she kept her gaze fixed on Madeline.

Finally, Madeline opened her eyes and gave a sharp nod. "We'll help you, but that means you'll have to join us after. After all, Mother will find out one way or another."

Join the Resistance? He exchanged glances with Karina who appeared uncertain. A group to back them up sounded nice, but something was bothering him. He wasn't sure what.

"What might happen if we join? What would have happened if someone found out about you or the others?" Karina asked.

Madeline gave a weak smile. "I wasn't joking when I said Mother would kill me."

Maxwell stiffened alongside Karina.

Madeline looked away. "Mother is the head of the branch in this area. She has a lot of people to protect and watch out for. We can't rely on the police because, as much as we want to, and they might want to, there are only so many things the police can do. As you saw, only those who volunteered were able to take down the black market people, and did you see what it got them?"

Maxwell tilted his head down, fingers to his lips as Karina frowned. "I don't recall anything, actually."

"That's exactly it. Those that go against the scheme of things are pushed to the back. If anything, many of those officers probably got demoted, even though they couldn't cover everything. So, the people were sent to jail, but…" Madeline shook her head. "The police follow a delicate line between this community and the gated community. There isn't much they can do. The Resistance, however, doesn't follow those same rules. We will do whatever is necessary. Whatever is necessary." she repeated the word as if it was a mantra, her voice hollow and eyes haunted.

Karina shivered, and Maxwell found himself holding his arm close to his side, worried. So that's what worried him. It was a no-win situation. "So, basically, we either try to get our ma out with the three of us, probably dying or join you, get Ma out, only to become pawns to eventually be led to our deaths." Maxwell ended up summing it up weakly.

"I would say they're both awful situations," Karina deadpanned.

Madeline quickly shook her head. "No. We're good. We're helping liberate the people. We just have to do whatever is necessary. I'm proud Mother is the leader of such a group. She's fighting for something she believes in."

Fighting for something they believe in? Something about that line felt familiar to Maxwell.

"Martha," Karina's voice startled Maxwell, causing his gaze to flicker to Karina, who was staring at Madeline in shock. "Did…was there a man that used to be part of the Resistance? Someone with a wife and child named Martha and Agatha?"

Madeline's eyes narrowed, and she frowned, uncertain. "I, uh, I can look it up, but…" She furrowed her brow. "I mean, do you have a last name?"

Did they ever get Martha's last name? Maxwell slipped his phone out and stared at the screen in silence. He almost wanted to call Lex, but he wasn't sure if his friend would know either.

Madeline's brow creased as she muttered under her breath before she snapped her fingers. "The suicide arsonist."

Maxwell stiffened alongside Karina as Madeline nodded. "I

remember now. Mother mentions it with pride and sadness occasionally. Five years ago, before the epidemic hit, things were always on edge. Mother mentioned a very passionate man who kept saying he was fighting for his wife and child. He ended up going into a gated community, no one knows how, and…" At this, Madeline's eyes lit up and she smiled. "He screwed them all over. He actually managed to kill off those accursed nobles hidden behind their walls. Supposedly, the entire gated community went up in flames before they finally caught him. He killed himself, taking the lives of most in the community with him. He's considered a hero by many within the Resistance. I can't believe you know his wife and child. Where did you meet them? They left after that."

Maxwell felt a cold shiver trail down his spine at the admiration in Madeline's voice. How could she be so happy about the death of so many people? He knew full well how many lived within those communities, not everyone was evil. His thoughts instantly jumped to Lex, and the servants. He cringed. He was glad neither of them mentioned Lex being from the gated community now.

"Why?" Karina's voice was a little shaky and her expression was guarded and uncertain. "Why can you be happy about someone killing other people? I mean, I get you don't like the gated community, but…"

Madeline blinked and glanced between them in confusion. "He killed all the people oppressing us. No, not people, monsters. In one fell swoop, he destroyed an entire community to help free the people. Why wouldn't I be happy? He was a hero."

So, did that mean Martha was…he turned toward Karina, who was staring at the floor with wide eyes. He quickly stood up and forced a smile on his face as he turned to Madeline, who stared at him, startled. A strange sadness crossed her face as her eyes focused on his lips as he spoke. "Sorry, thanks for telling us this. We have a lot to think about." He glanced toward Karina before continuing, "Give us some time, all right?"

"Uh, yeah, sure." Madeline appeared flustered and even a little upset. "I'll talk to you later."

Karina stood and walked stiffly toward the door, Maxwell hurrying after her.

He wanted to get out of there. Now.

~ * ~

Karina's mind was in a tizzy. She was shaken by Madeline's words. Martha, Agatha, the people who helped take care of them, who helped take care of Lex, had been the wife of a suicide bomber.

"Kari?"

Karina glanced sidelong toward Maxwell, who was gazing at her with uncertainty. "That was a lot of information at once, wasn't it?"

Karina chuckled weakly. "Can't deny you there, Maxwell..." she trailed off. "What do you think of what Madeline told us?"

"I'm going out on a limb here and guessing you mean regarding Martha's husband? Because there were a lot of things." Maxwell's tone was light, if a little shaky.

Karina lightly smacked her brother.

He yelped and glared. "What was that for?"

"Sorry, bro, but that was just kind of stupid." She grinned, and he huffed, looking unhurt as he dropped his hands to his sides.

The room was quiet, the door having closed behind them a while ago and the couches as comfortable as they left them. Sunlight slipped through the far window, shining and dancing over the wood of the table set between them. Karina tilted her head up to meet Maxwell's eyes. "Martha was proud of her husband. I remember how fond she was when she talked about him. Did that mean...?"

"No." Maxwell shook his head, certainty in his gaze. "Martha truly cared for Lex and I know she probably guessed where he was from, same with us. Kari, it was five years ago, people change. You know that."

"I know," Karina chuckled. "I know as well as you do, but it still raises a lot of questions, doesn't it? What if Lex met with her years earlier? If he hadn't saved Agatha? What about Allen? His friend?" Karina found herself spouting, remembering Lex's words, so long ago.

"Allen," Maxwell murmured. "He mentioned how he hated the gated community. How he was surprised by how different Lex was. Same with that boy who…"

Karina frowned, wondering who he meant before she leaned back and examined the ceiling. After some time, she snapped her fingers and leaned forward. "That boy we met at Doctor Gershwin's! What was his name again?"

"I think it was Oliver?" Maxwell nodded, as if verifying with himself. "He absolutely despised Richies, so would it be so far-fetched to think others might as well? Heck, I can't blame them."

"Maxwell…"

"I said I can't blame them. Not that I agree with what they're doing," Maxwell quickly spoke up, uncomfortable. "After all, they're condoning death. So…"

Karina sighed as her eyes flickered toward the window, seeing the sunlight gleam off the glass and a hint of the building beside them. "Still, Martha was so kind. I…"

"Can't believe she's related to someone who would go on a killing spree?" Maxwell put in and winced. "I can understand that and the fact Madeline called him a hero…" Maxwell shivered, and Karina grimaced. This just proved her earlier point. Her brother wasn't a killer.

After all, his blood was a literal cure. It was almost ironic to think he might have to kill someone if they joined the Resistance.

"So, what should we do?" Karina waved. "Madeline already knows our situation. Even if we say no, she'll probably still help us somehow, then we'll end up having to join them. Well, sort of… I think?"

"Hypothetically speaking, yeah, that sounds about right," Maxwell murmured.

Karina rolled her eyes before looking away. "Can you see a way around it? I can't. After all, right now, it's just the two of us. Lex can't help us, at least not much." Maxwell gulped, fingers twitching in uncertainty. Karina felt her shoulders slump. "Why can't we ever get an easy decision?"

"Because we're just not that lucky?" Maxwell joked weakly and

Karina snorted. She couldn't deny that. Their luck was absolutely crap. Maxwell stood and stepped around the table, sitting beside her. She glanced sidelong as he shrugged. "However, we have a better chance of success by joining them than trying to do this ourselves. I mean, if we fail with them, we die. If we fail with just the two of us…" He grimaced and rubbed his arm, fingers gripping tightly.

"We become experiments," Karina said, realizing where Maxwell was going with his statement. She would rather die than be used as some object or tool." So, I guess that means we have our decision?"

"We should probably let Lex know." Maxwell dug into his pocket.

Karina didn't stop him as he typed in the number and put it to his ear. She trusted Maxwell enough to know why he told Madeline, yet it still bothered her a little. She could hear the faint beeping, followed by a click. "Lex?"

Silence followed for a moment before Maxwell brought the phone down and put it on speaker.

"Oh, it's you two." Lex seemed quiet, as if a little uncertain, causing Maxwell and Karina to exchange looks.

"Lex? Everything all right?" Maxwell asked.

Lex chuckled weakly. "Yeah, it's fine. Just found out some interesting things…" he trailed off. Karina could hear the rustling of clothing, as if Lex shifted and then he spoke again. "I found a way in."

"Really?" Karina leaned forward, startling Maxwell. "Where? Did you find Mom?"

"Not exactly, but I know roughly where she is," Lex said, voice stern. "My employer…" Karina could almost hear the disdain in Lex's voice, "…showed me around earlier. It turns out that little situation he gave me months ago? He called it a clerical error."

"Not that you're surprised." Maxwell spoke quietly.

"You're right, I'm not, just annoyed. Needless to say, he gave me the little grand tour. There's another level under the gated side building, and there is a sewage system that connects the two."

Karina couldn't help but flinch at the implication. Maxwell just seemed sick at the idea. "You don't mean…"

"Sorry, kid, that's exactly what I mean. That's the only way I know for you two to get into the right area, though it is dangerous. There are cameras everywhere and it's designed so it's difficult for those working down there to leave."

"What do you mean?" Karina spoke up, confused. "Stopping them from leaving, are there others like Mom down there?"

Lex let out a huff. "To sum it up, they have scientists from your side of the gate down there, and they have the same freedom as I did when Caym brought me home."

Both of them couldn't help but flinch. "So, none," Karina murmured. "So, they're stuck down there. How is that any better?"

"They're given everything, or so my employer said." Lex shifted before continuing, "Food, drink, probably even women or men, depending on the situation. Everything anyone could want, they just can't leave. Compare that to your side where you have quite a bit of lawlessness and uncertainty, it seems logical to take what you can get."

The delight on Madeline's face, the fear Martha showed at almost having lost Agatha, the girls caught by the black market. "Right, that makes sense." Karina wasn't sure where she was going with her statement. Maxwell just nodded, probably having thought along the same lines as she did.

"Oh." Maxwell perked up. "There was a reason why we called. We ended up talking to Madeline."

"Hm?"

"Madeline is part of the Resistance," Karina put in bluntly. She was sure that Lex knew of the group.

His scoffing response and unamused voice confirmed her thought. "You're not kidding." He sighed. "You two. Why is it that you two always get caught up in everything? I swear…"

"Not our fault," Karina defended indignantly.

"No, I suppose not," Lex put in, his voice becoming distant for a second as he shifted, probably changing sides for where the phone was to get more comfortable. "I will take some responsibility for that one. So, what did she have to say?"

"We ended up telling her about Ma, and asking for her help."

Silence filled the other end of the line for a moment, to the point where Karina couldn't tell whether Lex was even going to respond.

"Idiots."

Karina cringed along with Maxwell.

Lex let out a heavy sigh. "Why, after she told you she was part of the Resistance, would you think of spewing everything to her?" Lex groaned. "Never mind, let's just focus on what you'll do now. Do you know what happens regarding the Resistance? Who they are? What they do?"

"They go against the government." Maxwell's voice was soft, and his hand was clenched. "Madeline mentioned they would do anything to get what they want and when she mentioned she would be killed if anyone found out, she wasn't lying. She truly believed she would die and didn't particularly seem to care. I mean, with the epidemic, that's understandable, but it sounds like it's been happening like that for a while."

"Lex? Did you know anything about Martha's husband?" Karina asked as Maxwell's voice failed.

"Martha's?" Lex stayed silent for a while, probably lost in thought. "That's… Why do you ask?"

"Did you know he was a member of the Resistance?"

Lex let out another heaving breath. "Antonio mentioned it once before. That's why he wanted to go after Agatha, all that time ago. After all, capture the daughter of the hero of the Resistance and you can get quite a bit of money." Lex's voice was filled with anger and disdain and a hint of sadness. "Needless to say, it wasn't hard to figure out, plus I heard the rumors when I returned home for that short time. It happened to a gated community in the south, only a few survived the massacre. Father worked day and night to cover it up from the other communities and move the survivors."

"How did you deal with finding out Martha's husband killed so many?" Karina's voice shifted without her meaning to, catching

Maxwell's attention.

"Martha is Martha. I only found out after I helped her daughter and stayed with her for a while, yet she probably guessed who I was long before that. After all, a year does a lot to a person."

Karina winced.

"Yet, she never did anything, and she never seemed to want to. You should know that. I know Karina talked with her right before we left."

"She told you?"

"She let me know that she gave you some money. I inferred the rest. After all, she stayed up late a lot. I wouldn't doubt she was still sad about her husband's death. Still, I wouldn't worry, she honestly liked you two and she wasn't lying when she said she would support you. Your brother knows that as well as I do."

Karina's attention shifted over toward Maxwell, who, after a moment, gave a short nod. She sighed, he always could trust people more easily, after all, he always seemed to be able to see something in them that she couldn't. Either that or he could read them a lot easier. Considering he was usually pretty quiet, that made sense. She would have to believe them, after all, what could she say otherwise?

"So, what now?" Maxwell turned the conversation back. "Should we just go for it or…"

"In other words, should we work with them or try to avoid them?" Karina pointed out, clicking her tongue. "Not really much of an option. We may trust Madeline, but the others would find out eventually, just from the situation. Plus, Madeline's too worried about you, my dear brother, so she's going to try to make sure you don't get hurt." Karina shrugged.

"I concur, for the most part." Lex seemed to resist the urge to let out another heavy breath, though a hint of amusement shown at the end. "However, you might as well get their help. The more help we get, the better off we are, and it's not like we haven't done stupid things in the past. Anyway, I'll keep looking into how to get to your mother. Talk with them and see if you can devise a plan, I'll see if I can find the schematics."

"Just be careful." Maxwell pursed his lips. "It sounds like you're going in deep."

"Idiot," Lex said with no animosity and a hint of fondness. "I wouldn't worry. I'll speak with you two soon, but I'll call you. Try to avoid calling me unless absolutely necessary."

"Yeah, makes sense, you probably don't want your phone going off in the middle of sneaking around a place," Maxwell joked.

"Right… I'll talk to you later." With that, there was a click, followed by the beeping of the end call. Maxwell stared down at his phone before turning to Karina. "Did he seem…"

"Kind of out of it?" Karina asked, arms crossed over her chest. "So, I wasn't delusional. I wonder what happened."

Maxwell examined his phone quietly before slipping it into his pocket and turning to her. "Well, we won't find out here. Let's talk with Madeline, she'll probably want to know that we want to work with her."

Karina watched as he headed toward the doorway and groaned. She was not going to enjoy this conversation. That was for sure.

After letting Madeline know their decision, she called the others. In almost no time at all, Karina found herself seated beside Maxwell with Madeline across from them. Mitchell sat on one side with Leon on the other. Andrew stood behind them, arms crossed and watching quietly. The only one not there was Emma, and Karina dearly wished her friend actually was, even if she was part of the Resistance, or America Liberation, as Andrew kept calling it.

Mitchell had a soft, nervous smile on his face, yet his posture screamed stoic and cold, something she wasn't used to from the normally warm boy. "So, Madeline told you who we are. You still want our help?"

Karina exchanged a look with Maxwell before she nodded. "Our friend agrees, the more help, the better. After all…" she found herself halting in her thoughts. Should she mention what Lex told them? Yeah, it was information they needed, and they hadn't told Madeline yet either, so might as well. "After all, Ma is being held under L. J. Fox Inc. on the gated community side."

She didn't miss how everyone stiffened and a strange gleam appeared in Madeline's eyes. "Within the gated community? Why? Was she taken like the others?"

"Others?" Maxwell asked, confusion clear in his voice.

Madeline spat, surprising both of them. Andrew clicked his tongue as Mitchell turned away. Leon seemed the only one unaffected, as he pushed his glasses up and then kept his hand there for a moment before turning to them. "I guess that would be a no." His voice was quiet and level. "That black market incident? It wasn't the first time we've had to deal with people being kidnapped. Every so often, someone near the community, or well known on this side, mysteriously vanishes or is killed. The few times the police investigate these incidents, they immediately are stopped. The Resistance did a little research when one of their own was killed."

"The people from the gated community." Madeline spat again, appearing beyond pissed as she clenched her fists hard enough to bleed. "I heard they have means of watching us, out here, and they'll kill or capture anyone they want. Father—" She stopped, and Mitchell put a hand on her shoulder when she started shaking.

Karina felt uncomfortable, like they stepped on something they weren't supposed to. From Maxwell's wary appearance, he realized too.

"Enough about that," Andrew cut in. "This isn't time for a life story. To put it bluntly. People are taken or killed by the gated community. The Richies have already found a way to avoid this epidemic and you can see that with them walking around without a care on the other side of those gates if you get close enough. I doubt they even know how hard it is to live on this side."

Karina didn't miss the air quotes or the venom in the boy's voice. She also didn't miss that it was the most Andrew ever said before either. Still, what he said sent a chill down her spine. After all, it wasn't that hard to believe. That's exactly what happened to them, though it was mostly because of Lex's situation, but still.

She turned toward Maxwell, who seemed to be deep in thought. His fingers sat on his lips as he furrowed his brow before nodding. "I know none of you are very happy with the gated community." Karina winced as the others scoffed. Where was he going with this? Maxwell's fingers scrunched, curling into his palm as he continued. "What if you could get someone in there to help?"

"What do you mean?" Andrew lifted his head, so much so that Karina wondered if he could even still see Maxwell. "Why would we do that? Why would someone try to blend in? It doesn't work, we've tried, a long time ago."

Karina pursed her lips. I see... She glanced sidelong at Maxwell, who was staring at them all carefully. He's trying to bring up Lex without putting him in danger. What could she say?

"What if...?" she began, startling Maxwell. "What if there was someone who didn't WANT to be from the gated community?"

Andrew snorted.

"That's not likely." Mitchell shrugged. "I mean, they have everything they could ever want, why would any of them want to leave that safe area?" Mitchell shook his head. "That just seems crazy to me."

"Very." Leon leaned forward.

"My sister was speaking hypothetically," Maxwell said, quickly sending her a look to stay quiet.

She huffed. She was just trying to help, but she could see her words had the opposite impact than was expected. She decided to bite her tongue, though it took a lot of her willpower to do so as Maxwell continued, facing the group once more. "We once met someone who could impersonate someone from the gated communities who lived outside it, in Reinmark. Would it be so far-fetched to see if they could help?"

Madeline opened her mouth before she frowned. "That could work. So, do you know how to contact this person?"

Karina felt herself slump slightly as Maxwell let out the softest of sighs and grinned. "You know Lex? He actually is from Reinmark, we met him while trying to find Ma. He used to watch the Richies before we met him, so he knows their mannerisms. He actually snuck in a few months ago and is the one who told us about where Ma is."

"Lex?" Mitchell perked up and grinned. "I see, so that's where he went."

"He was a smart one, that's for sure." Leon spoke up, amused. "So, he's our insider? He didn't seem like a Richie when we met, so I guess he was his normal self?"

Karina would have whooped in relief but kept her expression steady as she nodded. After all, it wasn't completely a lie, just a half-truth. After all, he did used to watch his parents and he did live in Reinmark.

The only one staying silent was Madeline, who appraised them quietly before nodding. "All right, we can work with that. So, he's going to send us more information?"

"Probably." Maxwell shrugged. "I'm not sure when or how, but that's what he said when we talked to him."

"If that's the case, then we better get everything we might need to infiltrate a high security base." Leon spoke, shifting in his seat and glasses slipping down his nose, which he ignored. "After all, L. J. Fox Inc. has some of the best security around due to it being viably the weakest link into the gated community."

"Lex mentioned that a sewage system connected this side to the gated side, close to where our mom might be kept," Karina threw in, causing the group to glance at her. She waved it off. "I'm not keen on the idea, but it might work."

"All right, so we have a route, now we just need the schematics and a means to hack into the system," Leon muttered.

Mitchell sighed before turning to Maxwell and Karina. "Well, I would say we're already working on it, so I wouldn't worry too much about it. Let us know if you hear anything else. For now, we'll all just sit tight and wait."

Karina glanced at Maxwell, who nodded and spoke up. "That sounds good. We'll talk to you another time." With that, he stood. Karina joined him, finding she didn't mind the idea of leaving.

At least now, their path was set. They were going to be working with the Resistance. It should be interesting, at least.

Chapter Twenty

Caym heard the creak of the gates and found his gaze drifting up. The familiar two-layered fountain and white balustrades shone in the afternoon light. The car pulled to a halt and he stepped out, walking up the stairs. The doors opened with a flourish and he saw the hall empty, not a single person, but the maids and Machael to greet him. Machael, Leo's butler.

"Sir Caym, it is a pleasure to see you home. Is everything well?"

"Fine," Caym spoke, voice clipped as he passed his coat over to him. "Where is Father?"

"He is in his office. He's been in a rage for quite a few weeks now because of lack of information." A smug gleam appeared in the butler's eyes, filled with pride. "It seems Sir Leonard has yet to be captured, and his two servants are just as difficult to pursue. I heard they were last seen heading south into the quarantined zones."

Caym smirked. "Is that so? That's too bad. Father would have quite a struggle pursuing them in there, but alas, that is not my worry." He nodded toward Machael. "I wish to speak with you later. There are some things I need to take care of and verify."

"Of course, my lord." Machael bowed and walked away.

Caym watched him go. "So, Father is still following that lead." He shook his head as he walked up the steps. It was sadly much easier to waylay his father than he expected. He wasn't sure why he had such a difficult time of it to begin with, but it seemed so easy now.

Not many people actually liked his father. The cruel man was powerful, but not invincible. Plus, he was so narrow-minded that a slipped word here and there could lead him on a wild goose chase. Little Leo was right: it was more of a challenge to keep him going on those tangents for a much longer period of time.

Either that or find another way so he and Little Leo would never have to worry about it again. He heard his feet clack against the floor. The house was quiet, but far from serene. He ignored Mother's room, hearing her saying her psalms in quiet contentment, and headed to his father's room.

He knocked on the door and waited. After some time and the ruffling of papers, he finally decided to open the door. He pushed it open and walked in, seeing his father spot him, unamused and angered. "Did I ever say you could come in? What have I taught you, boy?"

Caym felt one hand drift up to his arm before he mentally pushed it down. He was older now, no need to be afraid of the man. "To only come in when I am told to. However, I might have news of interest and a question."

"Of interest?" His father perked, placing his papers down. "Have you found those gems? The cures?"

Caym's gaze flickered around the room before he turned to his father and tilted his head up. How usual of his father, not to even see them as humans. "Alas, I have not."

"Why are you taking up my time? Get out."

"I do wish to ask why you lied to me about the truth of my wife and child's disappearance." He couldn't stop the words from coming out, but he kept his tone and expression neutral.

His father stiffened. "What are you talking about?" His voice was low. "You dare insinuate I did something?" He stood up and stepped around the desk, looming. "Age has made you a reckless and rebellious child. Rebellious children need to be corrected."

"Like you did to Little Leo and me when we were children? Like you did to my wife?" The words came out, biting and harsh against his will. Thoughts he always figured he suppressed were beginning to surface.

The floor met him face first before he felt the pain in his cheek and tasted metal in his mouth. He went to sit up when he felt a foot slam into his gut.

"You stupid child. You are not supposed to speak back to your father. Your mother would be appalled at this disgrace." Father pulled back and returned to his seat behind the desk. "Now, let's speak like civilized folk. Get up, boy, I didn't hit you that hard."

Caym forced himself not to spit out the blood onto the Persian carpet, as much as his mind yelled at him to do so and forced himself up. His side and face hurt. His stomach was throbbing, but he pushed the pain to the back of his mind, much like he was used to doing all those times he tried to keep his father's vile gaze from his little brother. He tilted his head up and took stock of his father. Part of him wanted to run, wanted to just get away from him, just like Leo did. Was he just like that little kid who dreamed of running away?

How much of that dream was actually shattered?

"I apologize for my rudeness. However, I do wish to ask on the circumstances of my wife's disappearance."

Father waved it off. "It's of no importance. Didn't I tell you? She left with another man."

"Who?"

His father narrowed his eyes, staying quiet for just a bit too long before he spoke, voice cold. "I take it you spoke to that fool Hugh? What did he tell you?"

Caym had half a mind to spill everything to his father and call him out on everything he'd done, but he knew that wouldn't work. So, he let out a sigh. "He was delusional, like you said. He kept saying that you forced my wife out of the gated community and onto the streets with nothing but our child." Caym watched his father closely, and as such, caught when his father's eyes widened just a fraction and his lips tightened enough to prove what he said hit the mark.

"How ludicrous of him. A fool will always remain a fool."

"Indeed." Caym bowed his head. "To say you were the reason for their deaths seems preposterous, right, Father?"

His father stiffened just the tiniest bit. If he hadn't been scrutinizing the man, he would have missed it. "To insinuate that they are dead…" Father shook his head. "Fine, believe what you will, boy. I have no more reason to lie to you than I would your mother. Now, if I were to lie in this case, would it not be for your own protection?"

He leaned forward, clasping his fingers as his eyes narrowed to slits and Caym shivered, knowing full well that wasn't the air-conditioning kicking in. "However, say I were to actually tell you that it was me who sent your wife and child outside the gated communities. What would you do? After all, weren't you the one who did that for your dear brother? My own son?"

Caym stiffened and his father leaned back, waving in a nonchalant manner. "That is enough of this talk, I have work to do. You have just returned home. Put your things down and speak with your mother."

Caym examined his father, noticing the harsh dismissal for what it was. He turned and walked out, quickly shutting his thoughts away. He thrust whatever surging emotions came forth into their dark corners as he turned and slipped down the hallway, after Machael.

It didn't take long to find the old servant who was waiting for him. "Sir Caym, are you all right?"

He held out a handkerchief, much to Caym's surprise. He took it and put its soft fabric to his cheek, feeling the coolness of the cloth against his swollen face.

"I will be fine." His voice held a hint of the emotions he was trying hard to not think about. "I have to ask you though. How much did you hear?"

"Enough to know you are asking about the circumstances behind your wife's disappearance…" Machael trailed off before he turned and walked.

For once, Caym felt no qualms about walking behind the servant, listening to his quiet breathing. Before long, they ended up, to Caym's surprise, in Leo's room. He hesitated but found himself following as the butler opened up the balcony doors, as if to air out the room, untouched and serene compared to the rest of the place.

"Why bring me here?"

Michael stepped onto the balcony, glancing over the tree limbs in quiet contemplation. "Did you know that tree was used in those children's escape?"

"I do." Caym furrowed his brow. "I know how well attached you are to Little Leo. How much he tells you."

Machael turned to Caym with the barest hints of a smile, though his expression was sad. "I bet you were unaware of the fact that your wife also tried using this as a means of escape."

Those words drew Caym up short as he was unable to stop his breath from freezing in his throat, chocking him. "What?"

Machael turned back toward the tree and reached over to gently touch the leaves that swayed softly in the breeze. "All those years ago, the day before she was to be shipped out, she'd tried to sneak out of here with your child, to hide just outside the community for your return. Unfortunately, she was caught. The tree branch she used snapped under her and her child's weight." Caym jerked and followed Machael's eyes to see a scar along the tree off to one side, as if it had been ripped away and healed, unnoticed unless one knew it was there. "She ended up twisting her ankles. Yet your father still sent her out the next day. I'm sorry to say, I don't know what happened after that."

Caym stilled, frozen in the spot as his mind raced. *Twisted her ankles? That meant she was probably barely able to move. She wouldn't have been able to escape if anyone attacked her when she left the community. Lex and his uncle barely survived with being healthy which meant...*

Something cracked, and he knew it wasn't the branch he found suddenly being throttled in his hand. No, it was something else. His mind whirled. His wife tried to escape and, as a result, was brutally...and yet those kids, his brother's wards... He could feel the bark digging into his palm until it almost bled, but he didn't let go, knowing he would probably do something incredibly stupid if he did. How dare they be able to flee without hindrance.

How could he have let them go so easily? When they were able to escape using a path that got his wife killed?

"You and Sir Leonard are alike in many ways. You care deeply, something I've been very happy to see and nurture as you two have grown in this place, but there are some things, as a servant, I have no say in."

Machael's expression was uncertain as he spoke, tone even, causing Caym to jerk out of his thoughts. "I only learned from hearsay, but your father did have your wife and child banished, probably to keep a tighter hold on you after Sir Leonard left officially. I know the lady knew of it and let him do as he pleased. I do not know past that."

Caym wasn't sure what he was feeling anymore. Rage was definitely one of the emotions, but it wasn't alone. So, his father was the one behind it, and what if he did the same to Leo? Leo would be in danger, no matter what. Out there, in here. There was no place safe for his little Leo. He needed to make a safe place, for the two of them.

After all, wasn't that the only way they would be free?

He turned to Machael, placing a serene smile on his face. Machael's saddened gaze indicated he could tell something was off anyway. "Thank you for telling me. I'm going to need your help with something, do you mind?"

Machael stayed silent before he shook his head. "I only wish to see you and your brother happy."

"Good. Now come, I have some things to do and I need to speak with Father once more. He has some things he needs to tell me."

Caym felt something slip into his voice he'd never heard before. An almost giddy feeling ran through him as his mind raced with worries of little Leo, a slowly growing fear and hatred that filled him at the thought of his father and a strange sadness that he was doing his best to push away. He threw all those emotions into the trash and focused, back to the main problem. He needed information from his father. His father wasn't a man to relinquish information easily.

His mind darted between different ideas. What exactly could he do?

Chapter Twenty-one

Lex shivered as he stepped into the lower areas, hand aching from the absolutely idiotic security system. He waved it out as he descended the stairs, seeing the labs his employer showed him not that long ago. The hallway was empty, but he could see scientists in some of the rooms, working earnestly. Mostly men, but a few women decorated the interior, hurrying about, pasty, but well fed. He shook his head as he headed toward the right-side door. After all, he didn't see even a glimpse of the children's mother in there, though he doubted she would be one of the scientists at this point, if the children were the cure and his father knew that then, well... He passed the sewage door and down the hall, finding himself standing before a thick metal door. He could not hear anything from the other side. He shifted the papers in his arms, so he could use one hand to tap a button off to one side.

Why was he doing this again? Oh right, because he was basically a glorified paper pusher as some called it, or a secretary as was the proper term. He didn't mind since it got him around the place, but it also put him in direct contact with his employer and, in all honesty? He didn't like it in the slightest. Pushing the shivering thought to the back of his mind, he waited, listening to the other side for any sounds or indication that they heard him. He didn't hear anything for quite a while. When he finally did, it was a faint hissing sound, followed by a wash of spray landing over his head and shoulders. He winced but held still as the door finally opened to reveal a well-dressed scientist, obviously one from the gated community, considering he had a healthy glow to his skin. Lex did a doubletake. It was the same man he met at the Christmas party.

The man recognized him, eyes widening as glee shone on his face. "Ah, it's you. I didn't expect to see you again so soon, come in."

Lex followed him in, hearing the hydraulics of the door as it slid shut. Did that mean there was a second exit out of this part of the building? Considering he never passed the man before in his walks that must have been the case. It did bring up an interesting question of why that was, but Lex decided not to ask.

Lex let himself be guided through the winding hall. The other side of the door was pristine white with a soft gentle music playing in the background, faintly coming through speakers set into the walls. The sounds were those which one would associate with nature.

He wondered how much it would annoy the twins.

He pulled from that thought when he spotted the multitude of cameras along their walk. There weren't that many doors until they reached another doorway, which the man put his hand to. Lex heard a click as it opened, and the man gestured for Lex to follow. Lex stepped in and stopped. The place was large, much larger than he was expecting, with rooms set into the sides and circling the enclosure. Lights shone above a few of the doorways, giving off a strange red glow over the white of the surroundings. There were only three doors without a light overhead, one at the end of the room and two just to the left and right of him.

He almost would have thought it was a hospital, if not for the desks that adorned the middle of the circular room, more like science lab experiment tables than anything. A couple people glanced up and nodded to the scientist before getting back to work. How vast was this place? Taking a quick glance at the papers he carried, it wasn't that hard to fathom what they were researching. Lex felt uneasy but followed after the man with a straight back and neutral expression. As much as he wanted to, he couldn't get close enough to the doors to get a good view through the windows.

They passed through the center to the far door and the man gestured toward the doorway. "The head is inside. I'm guessing the upstairs head sent you?"

"There are two?" He turned to the man who nodded.

"I know, confusing, but it's to make sure nothing gets leaked. You can understand our silence. After all, the research done here affects the rest of the gated communities, the country. We do more than just analyze fertilizer." The man shrugged, eyes gleaming before he bowed. "Oh, excuse me. I know you're probably busy. I'll let you be on your way. If you will excuse me." With that, he walked away, and Lex turned to the door, not even caring to knock.

He wanted to get this over and done with.

He stepped inside to find a room glowing softly from flames and a light that shone dimly overhead, one that seemed to be auto controlled, as it grew brighter upon his entrance.

The woman seated behind the desk spotted him and stood. "Ah, you must be Leonard. Sir Askren's son?"

Lex tried to withhold the wince as he nodded.

"It is a pleasure to meet you. I know you are probably quite sick of the frivolities and attention of your position, so I'll get straight to the point. Where is that information the dolt upstairs sent me?"

Dolt? Lex found a hint of amusement at the word choice as he passed the papers over. The woman gave them a scrutinizing gaze before she sighed. "He's a strange one, that one. Did you enjoy your little tour down here?"

"I didn't realize it was a tour." He spoke formally, words punctual. "I have no reason to believe that to be the case."

"You're not wrong in your assumption. That man just has a nasty habit of being very circular in his actions. I doubt he actually needed YOU to deliver me these papers." The woman waved before dropping the papers on the table. "Anyway, I am the head scientist down here. I bet you're curious what we study."

"Not particularly." He kept his voice neutral. "Unless you wish to tell me?"

"Shrewd one." The woman's expression didn't even change, her eyes cold, glinting in the light from the above lamp. She stepped around the desk. "Well, I don't have much to tell you. So, take this back with you as you return to the surface." The woman riffled through some papers on her desk before pulling up an envelope and handing it over to him. "It's a request for more studies. The last experiments have died out and we need more."

"More?"

"Yes, more diseased subjects. After all, we do need to figure out the truth behind the disease." The woman shrugged. "I heard there were a few new workers in the upper section on the outer side we might be able to use. We're just trying to get more product in."

"To save the worthy?" Lex's voice was deadpan, but he could just barely hide the anger from slipping in as his grip incrementally tightened on that paper.

"Exactly. We have to save the people of the gated community. This research is dependent on that. We can't let them die." She spoke with certainty. "Plus, those outside are just going to die anyway, might as well be put to better use, right?"

Lex just smiled and turned. "I will return these to him. Have a good day."

"Ah, yes, you're probably busy, sorry for taking up your time." The way she said that made Lex doubt she actually particularly cared, it was almost flippant in its delivery, her mind obviously on other things.

Lex pushed his way out the door and walked through the room, taking it all in with a practiced eye. He noticed as one of the lights disappeared and the door opened. A man lay on the moving trolley, withered to a husk, but chest still rising and falling as he stared at the ceiling, pockmarks littered his body and his lungs sounded gargled as if he was on the brink of the fourth stage. The doctor was a young woman who seemed to be humming to herself a cheerful little ditty. The juxtaposition sent a chill up his spine. That man was obviously infected. That begged the question. Why was NO ONE down here actually worried? As he examined the area, he noted how no one wore masks or surgical gloves, nothing that might indicate they were afraid they might get infected. Did they know something?

"Oh, have you finished speaking with the head?"

Lex withheld the need to jump as he peered over to see his guide walk up to him with a kind smile.

"I hope you don't feel too overwhelmed, her views of this research are kind of extreme."

Lex saw him wince as another scream went up, one that suddenly cut off mid-scream. The man sighed. "I really wish we didn't have to do this, but it's true this might be the only course in order to figure out a way to get a cure for this disease. I just wish we didn't have to do it so cruelly. Anyway, are you heading above? I was supposed to leave early and meet up with my wife, but an emergency came up. I know you might not know me, or wish to even speak with someone on my level, but can you give this note to my wife? I'm going to be pulling a few overnighters, so I won't be able to meet with her."

Lex reached over, taking the note from the man. He could tell it was written in a rush, the scrawl a messy scribble at best. "I can do that. Where will she be?"

"She'll be sitting in the lobby, upstairs. Her name is Lanie."

"All right." Lex nodded, and the man grinned before bowing his head and hurrying away. Lex took a peek at the note before heading up the stairs.

Lex dropped his papers off to his employer, avoiding his appraising eye and briskly walked down to the lobby on his way home. Lex stepped into the lobby and looked around. There were a few people sitting around. They all wore nametags, so it wasn't hard to find Lanie. He walked over to her and slightly inclined his head. "Lanie?"

The woman peered up, confused. "Yes?" Her voice was soft and pleasant, and her features were simple, but elegant, a rarity around here. Lex couldn't help the soft smile as he gave her the note. She opened it and then sighed. "Oh, Richard must have given this to you, the silly man." She chuckled and closed the letter before standing up and patting down her dress. "Thanks. He's such a workaholic sometimes. He really should remember the kids more often, but that's just the way he is." She smiled at him. "Thanks for giving this letter to me. It's too bad they have to use those cancelation barriers. He can't even send me a simple text message because of those stupid things. Still, at least I won't be waiting for hours like the last few times. By the way, I've seen you a lot more often lately, who were you again?"

"Lex."

"Lex?" The woman hummed, staring at him for a while before she snapped her fingers. "Is your full name Leonard? Leonard Askren?"

"Yes."

She grinned, eyes wide and shining. "Ah, so you were the one my husband was talking about the other day, the one who supposedly survived the outer community. He was so excited to get your autograph. It's framed, you know." She chuckled, and Lex couldn't help but feel sheepish at the enthusiasm and fondness in her voice. She waved it away. "That's just the way he is, don't worry about it."

"I'll try not to then."

Lanie slipped the letter into her purse and peered back at him. "You're very polite. I'm glad. It seems my husband picked a good choice for someone to look up to."

"I wouldn't so much say that…"

Before Lex could say more, Lanie shook her head and gave him an incredulous expression. "Right there proves it, almost everyone…if not everyone that lives here, wouldn't be so humble, believe me." She fondly smiled at him. "So, everyone thought you were dead, you know? To come back alive from the outer community, that is amazing."

The fact that she said it with warmth and curiosity threw Lex. She didn't seem to be discrediting or degrading the outside. She seemed genuinely curious and concerned. "I've heard the outer community is incredibly dangerous, what with the epidemic, riots, people acting like barbarians in the streets…" she trailed off and glanced at the clock. "I'm sorry. I didn't mean to keep you." She turned and curtsied. "It honestly was a pleasure to meet one such as yourself." She looked up. "My husband must have been ecstatic." Her warm smile widened. "Well, I best be going, thank you for delivering this to me."

"It was no trouble." Lex watched as she waved and swiftly departed out the door. She seemed like a sweet woman. She reminded him of Martha, just a bit. Still, she did bring up something that threw him. She was right. He was popular around the community. He frowned, glancing over his shoulder to where he knew his employer's office was. Why was it that his employer only ever thought to have him as a secretary? He never brought up his father's work because he didn't want to be too suspicious, but wouldn't his employer bring it up as a source of pride? Why didn't he?

What reason did his employer have to not only keep Lex in the dark, but to give him a job many would see as menial labor? He couldn't complain, but at the same time, thinking it over, it was incredibly strange, and maybe even a bit worrisome. He shook his head, deciding to return home, or at least, to where he was living.

After all, he really didn't have a home per se.

Chapter Twenty-two

Caym walked down the hall with a heavy heart. The cameras were slack, their usually persistent red light, dead. Something father would eventually notice, but with the alarm cut, it wasn't anything to worry about. No sound enveloped the place and he knew Mother was gone, pulled away by the servants for a shopping trip. The weight pushing into his back was cold and solid. He wore a set of clothes, reminiscent of the one's he wore on the excursion to the outer community, the same type Leo wore. He stepped up to his father's door. He didn't even knock this time, just stepped on in, face neutral.

"What are you doing, boy?" His father glared over at him. "You don't even knock this time. What are you thinking?"

Caym examined his father, feeling surprisingly calm. "I'm doing something I wanted to do for a while." He walked up to his father and took a seat on the desk, causing his father's face to turn red in anger, almost fuming as he slammed his palms on the desk. Caym didn't react. "What do you plan to do if you find Leo? Bring him home, then what?"

"Why do you care?" His father stood, trying to appear imposing.

Caym was not amused. He let out a sigh and leaned back. "He is my brother. Now, would you mind answering?"

"You've never cared before."

Caym sat up, getting into his father's face. "I may show no emotion, but I've always loved my little brother. After all…" he smirked and pulled back. "He was smart enough to get away from you, even if it was with my help, as you said." Caym's head snapped to the side, his skin stinging from the backhanded slap, but he shrugged it off, seeing his father breathing heavily.

"You impertinent little brat. How dare you speak in such a tone. I have half a mind to pull out the old belt and you've already tested my patience enough with your earlier escapades."

Caym recalled once shivering at such a threat. It didn't particularly bother him now.

He noted, nothing really felt like a threat. His mind was surprisingly serene and calm, almost clear as a lake. He knew what he wanted, and that was information. "Father? About Leo... Mind telling me?"

"Leonard is the second heir to my estate. I can't have my heirs just running around and once I have my hands on the cure, I'll be the leader of the communities. He will sell for a good price for a nice dowry."

Caym drew Father's gun out, slamming the muzzle into the side of his father's head faster than a whip. He was on his feet, finger near the trigger, yet steady.

His father was frozen, eyes wide in shock. It only took a moment before he glared and spat. "You'll be caught, you cretin."

"No, dear Father, I won't." Caym felt the grin crack his face. "The cameras had an unfortunate malfunction if anything does happen, now tell me. Is that what happened to Ariel and Kiera? You threw them out?"

"So, what if I did? Isn't that what I told you earlier? Those two were getting in the way." Father was sweating bullets, but his gaze was firm, filled with anger and fear. "They were corrupting you into thinking you were better than me, into thinking you should leave. I can't have both of my sons make a mockery of this place. Leonard had the saving grace to be able to be presented as someone who practically came back from the dead. That woman of yours was useless. Your mother agreed, you know? My wife always hated your wife for her beauty and pleasant attitude. Her friendliness was annoying. Of course, she then has the audacity of hurting herself, asking that she at least stay long enough to heal. It was her own fault, her own stupidity. I couldn't agree to such a thing."

Caym could feel his whole body trembling with the need to slam that gun into horrible areas and hear his father's screams, just like his wife must have felt. How dare he. How dare he try to get Leo back, only to sell him to some other family. How dare he…how dare he kill his family in such cold blood. How dare he even touch Caym's loved ones!

"I loved them, and you killed them. You would readily do the same to Little Leo, wouldn't you?"

"I'll do the same to you, you miscreant, if you don't put that gun down." His father growled angrily. "After all, I'm the head. What is someone like you going to do if I'm gone? I run this community. I maintain it and the police forces that keep these communities in check. What are you going to do about the cure? Let all our people die?"

"As long as Leo is alive," Caym spoke, the words said in a low monotone that caused Father to stiffen as Caym forced the gun harder into his temple, gloved hand steady. "I don't fucking care." He grinned. "Go to hell."

His father's eyes widened. Blood splattered outward. Slow motion descended on the scene as Caym watched the bullet explode out of the other side, blood and brain matter spilling out as the man slowly slumped back into the seat that was stained with crimson red. Smoke curled up from the muzzle as Caym stared at the lifeless body in front of him, not feeling a single hint of emotions. He placed the gun down and pulled his gloves off before carefully pulling them over his father's cold hands. Once done, he dropped the gun into his father's hand and stepped back, the thin plastic gloves he wore underneath enough to hide his fingerprints from anyone looking briefly over the scene.

He heard footsteps and turned, feeling liquid trail down the side of his face and stain his shirt red.

"Sir?"

Caym spotted Machael standing outside the door, averting his eyes from the scene. "What did you see here?"

Machael looked at him with a firm gaze and a bemused smile. "Your father succumbed to the pressure and stress and couldn't take it anymore. He sent his wife out and killed himself, not realizing that his final moments were never caught on tape like he wanted. Quite sad."

"That is true, it is quite sad." Caym stepped out of the room and wiped at his cheek, smearing blood over his hand. "Too bad. I have other things to take care of. I'm heading to Collern City, but first, I need to make sure that nothing falls apart before I leave. After all, this could be quite the problematic situation to bring little Leo back to, wouldn't you say? In the meantime, set up a ride for me, will you? I should be done within the next day or so."

"Of course, sir." Machael bowed and hurried away.

Caym stared out the window, watching the tree branches lightly thump against the glass pane. Actually, now that he thought about it, to procure all that work, would this place still be safe? Maybe he would have to find another place for him and Leo. No, it was too much to think about at the moment.

"Just know, dear brother, I'm not pulling out of our deal. There's just no deal left. So, I might as well pick you up soon. I'll find someplace safe for us, away from here."

Caym nodded to himself and turned, heading after the servant. After all, he did promise, and Leo didn't know that Father was dead yet, though Caym would be surprised if he didn't know soon. Still, such an unfortunate accident, but what could you do? He would have to make sure that never happened to Leo.

No. It would never happen to Leo. Leo would never be hurt, ever again.

Chapter Twenty-three

Karina stared at the gun in her hand, feeling the polished muzzle with care and let out a sigh before slipping it back on her belt.

"So, you joined them?" Arik's voice caught her, and she glanced over to see him staring at her quietly before his gaze wandered to Emma, who looked away.

"Not much choice." She turned away from the target across the clearing.

"There's always a choice," Emma spoke quietly, still keeping her gaze averted.

Karina sighed and turned to them, hands on her hips. "Are you saying we made the wrong choice? We need all the help we can get."

Arik pursed his lips, hesitant. "I'm not sure I'll be able to help you, at least, not much."

"That's fine. Too many people and it could be a problem, so stay here, okay? I mean, you don't need to be involved. So..." Emma said, turning to Arik.

Arik stared at her for a bit before he sighed. "I can do that. Just be careful whenever you decide to go in."

"We'll be fine. This isn't new for any of us, even those two." Emma gestured toward Karina before facing Arik. "Thanks. We best get going."

Karina watched Emma go and turned to follow when she heard a sound. She looked over her shoulder to see Arik stepping forward as if wanting to stop them. A conflicted expression shone on his face. He noticed her looking and slowly pulled his hand back. "Can I ask for a favor?"

"Favor?" She turned, casting half an eye after Emma, who was already disappearing into the trees.

"Can you watch out for them?" Arik pulled back, straightening his back before bowing his head. "I can't do much from out here, not with my father's position, so, can you watch them in my place?"

Karina stared, surprised, before looking away and giving out a sigh while waving her hand. "I can't make any promises, but sure, I can try." She grinned. "After all, I'm going to be watching out for Maxwell, what are a few extra people?"

Arik stared at her for a moment before a smile slowly bloomed on his face and he let out a short laugh. "That is true. Thanks. Now get going,"

Karina nodded and turned, following after Emma's disappearing form. She could hear quiet muttering but decided to leave him be. After all, she wasn't exactly one to pry, she already stuck around long enough.

She heard a sharp ringing and jumped before digging into her pocket, almost having completely forgotten that she slipped her new phone in there. She flipped it open. "Hello?"

"Ah, good, it is your number." Lex's voice sounded with a fake calmness through the phone, enough so she could just barely sense something was off. "Maxwell is at work, correct?"

"Yeah, why?" Karina frowned as she headed back to the apartment. She wasn't sure where Emma went off to, but she didn't feel like looking for her. "Did something happen?"

"Your brother is fine. I just can't contact him while he's here."

Karina could hear the worry in Lex's voice and it bugged her. Lex wasn't usually one to let his emotions show. "Okay, what's up? You sound completely unlike yourself."

Lex seemed to pause for a moment before a weak chuckle slipped through. "So, you noticed?" Pain filled his voice and he let out a world-weary sigh. "The gated community is in a bit of an uproar."

Uproar? She wanted to ask, but Lex didn't let her, continuing on. "Father, as you well remember, was head of Enthrope." *Was?* "He supposedly committed suicide yesterday. It's already all over the gated communities."

"Your father?" Karina's eyes widened, shocked. She didn't know Lex's father, but it was still surprising to hear something like that. Plus, how do you handle hearing someone you know committed suicide?

"Needless to say, as much as I might hate this, now would be the perfect time to do a raid to save your mother. With the community in turmoil, they will be more focused on—"

"Why are you so calm? You just told me your father committed suicide. How are you okay with that?" she snapped, as silence filled the other end of the line.

After a long delay, in which Karina had time to pass through the entrance doors of the apartment complex, Lex finally responded, voice cold to the point she felt like she was being stabbed by ice. "I never said I was okay with it. I know there's more to the situation and I hate that. Yet this is not an issue that you need to worry about. We need to save your mother and I am just pointing out the obvious. Take this advice or not."

Karina pursed her lips, realizing she probably shouldn't have said what she did. She could hear the hurt in her friend's voice and the hint of anger. She wasn't sure what Lex's relationship was with his father, but even so, she shouldn't have asked. She shook her head. "Thank you, Lex." She found her voice surprisingly quiet. "I'll let them know."

Lex stayed silent for a while, as if calming his breathing before he let out a long-drawn breath. Karina could almost imagine him running a hand through his hair as he spoke. "All right. Call me later tonight and let me know what the plan is. I'll see what I can do from here. Understood?"

"Yeah…" Karina trailed off, unable to say anything else as she slipped into her apartment and closed the door. She slowly pulled the phone away and closed it, staring at the blinking screen for a moment before she pushed her back against the doorway, neck tilted back so that she was staring at the ceiling, her hands pushing into the wood.

So soon… they would be getting to Mom so soon and she wasn't sure if she was ready for it. What if her mom was sick as well? Would her brother be able to help her? Would Mother still be alive? Would they be all right? What if something went wrong and her brother got taken? What would, or could she do? Her hand shifted to her waist, lightly gripping the metal of the gun through her shirt. She hadn't gotten much practice with it. Would she be all right? Would she be able to shoot if any of them were in danger?

Why was she thinking so much lately? She used to just do what she wanted back home, without a thought. She would let her brother do the thinking, but now that wasn't really an option. She closed her eyes, trying to calm her pounding heart and racing thoughts. She heard a click and jumped, moving away from the door just in time for Maxwell to walk in with a yawn. His hand stopped, suspended halfway to his mouth as their eyes met. He blinked, eyelashes fluttering before he dropped his arm, concerned. "Karina? You all right?"

Stupid twin recognition. Stupid brother being way too observant as usual. She grinned. "Nope. No problem. I just got home as well. By the way, Lex called. He said now would be the perfect time to do a raid since the gated community is in an uproar."

"Really?" Maxwell paused, fingers tapping at his lips. "Now that you mention it, I do recall hearing a lot of running and whispers, though I could never actually decipher what they were saying." He shook his head as a wide grin flashed across his face. "Yeah, Lex is right, this would be the perfect time." He paused, glancing toward the doorway, before smiling sheepishly. "I doubt the entire hallway wants to hear our conversation so…" He quickly closed the door.

Karina snorted, unable to hold in the slight chuckle. "Yeah."

Unfortunately, he must have noticed her change of mood, or lack thereof, because his expression dimmed as he glanced toward her uncertainly. "Kari, is something wrong? Why aren't you happy about getting a chance to finally get Ma?"

"I am happy, I guess I'm just overthinking things." She waved it off before putting a hand to her nose in a fake sniff. "Plus, you smell terrible, get changed already."

"Really, Kari? Ugh, fine." Maxwell rolled his eyes and hurried to his room without missing a beat.

Karina chuckled, and she heard him huff and mutter something too soft for her to hear, as if he'd heard her. Karina closed her eyes, wondering what to talk about. Well, it was obvious, regarding Mom, but she couldn't get herself to bring up the conversation. She was excited, there was no denying that. After all, she was impatient at this point to just get in, out and done. Yet something nagged at her, that feeling she always hated, that something was going to go wrong, big time. She couldn't ignore it. Her gut twisted at the thought.

Feeling awkward in the silence she KNEW she caused, Karina crossed her arms over her chest and leaned back against the wall next to the door, trying to pull away from that train of thought. "Hey, Max, you mentioned the other day that you found the entrance to the sewage system, right?"

"I did." Maxwell's semi-annoyed voice sounded muffled through the door. Karina could hear the ruffling of clothes.

She tilted her head, eyes toward the door. "I was going to head over to speak with Madeline, see what she says. Still, I think we'll probably want to go in sometime in the next few days, that entrance, plus Lex's comment, may be our best bet."

The silence from the other side of the door was overwhelming. Karina shifted where she stood as Maxwell slowly opened the door. His face twisted in worry. "Okay, spill, what's on your mind?"

Karina went to open her mouth, ready to plead confusion, but Maxwell glared. She snapped her mouth shut before letting out a long groan. "I was just worried is all. We're diving head first into the gated community, into the very place where they literally want US to experiment on, to rescue Mom, who may or may not be alive."

"Kari…"

"I know, I'm being pessimistic, but it's been months. And you know this disease. What if…"

She was jerked to a stop when she suddenly felt arms wrap around her. She stared at the wall in shock for a moment before glancing down.

Almost as soon as she shifted, Maxwell pulled back just enough to not be hugging her, but close enough where she could just reach out and pull him into her own hug, if she wanted to. Still, the action was enough to cause him to grin sheepishly. "Don't worry. We'll find her and get her out. After all, we've got Lex, Madeline and the others, plus..." His grin seemed to widen as he leaned forward, almost bumping his head against hers. "I'm going to be outright cheesy here, but we have each other, isn't that enough?"

Karina couldn't help but snort even as she found herself leaning forward. "You are such a dolt," she whispered, finding herself feeling a little better. The worried thoughts were still there but pushed away for a later date. Lex's situation clung to the edge of her mind, but she decided not to mention anything. That was up to Lex to tell Maxwell, not her. She would be the only one of the two concerned. After all, they did have more pressing things to worry about. For now, she leaned back, hands on her hips. "Anyway, do you want to join me? I was going to head out."

Maxwell nodded, and Karina turned, heading out the door and over to Madeline's room, her brother's footsteps sounding behind her. She knocked on the door, hearing a "come in."

She stepped inside to see Madeline off to one side, talking with Emma. Mitchell and Andrew were sitting beside them, listening, while Leon worked on a computer, off to the side. Multiple gazes met her own and Karina turned, facing Madeline. "Lex contacted us. It seems the gated community is in uproar. He says now would be the perfect time to go in."

Madeline looked at her, then nodded while Emma smiled. She gestured, and Karina walked over, Maxwell following quietly beside her. Karina took a seat and nodded to the group before facing Madeline once more as the girl spoke up. "That works fine. Leon has found a way to hack into their computers."

"I can only do it for a short time and only a few times. So, it will have to be fast," he called from the other end of the room, glancing briefly up from his computer. His thin eyes were piercing. She never did figure out what descent he was of. She quickly pulled away from that thought, getting back on topic.

"So, what's the plan?" Maxwell leaned forward, curious. "I doubt barging right in will work."

"You're right." Mitchell grinned before letting his grin drop. "You mentioned a sewage system?"

Maxwell nodded. "I checked it out again today. It's a small area past the loading dock. I should be able to get us to there, but I don't know what's past the doorway. It's always locked."

"You can leave that to me." Emma grinned. "I'll take care of the lock."

"So, we have our groups?" Andrew sat up, seemingly itching to leave.

"Seems to be the case." Mitchell shrugged. "Maxwell and Karina will arrive early, Maxwell going in to give Karina a tour, if you will. You, Emma and I will be infiltrating a little bit later through the side gates. Leon and Madeline will be on the outside, waiting for the head and watching the cameras. Your mother has found a way to change those earphones to work both ways, right?" The last sentence, he turned, facing Madeline, who nodded. "All right. So, when do we want to do this?"

"How about tomorrow?" Karina put in, deciding to put in her two cents.

After all, she wanted this over and done with. She couldn't stand just sitting around and waiting. She felt all eyes on her but ignored it as she stared at Madeline.

Madeline's expression was impassive before she finally let out a sigh. "All right. Let's plan for tomorrow night. Sound good, everyone?"

Successive forms of agreement rang around the room and Karina felt relief flood through her. Maybe this would actually work out.

"Thanks, Kari."

Karina glanced sidelong at Maxwell, who gave her a soft smile. "No problem, little bro. I figured you would want to see her sooner rather than later as well."

Maxwell nodded, eyes shining with a mix of worry and determination. Now if only she could get that feeling herself.

She wondered where her own determination ran off to.

~ * ~

Maxwell stared at the building, taking centering breaths to stop his fluttering heart from tearing out of his chest. They made sure everything was all set. Karina called her job, giving her notice of resignation. The woman wasn't too happy to hear about the sudden decision, but she understood. They'd packed their bags and gave them to Arik to take care of, trusting the boy to bring them to someplace where they could pick them up when they left. The moon shone bright and cold over the surroundings. Karina stood beside him, her expression unconcerned and a gleam in her eyes of quiet calmness. She was ready to go. He was glad for that, to have his sister beside him during this.

After all, what if they were trying this by themselves? With just three people, no way would it have worked, and something could have happened to Karina. He wished that he'd been able to convince himself as much as he seemed to have convinced her that everything would be fine. He was glad they talked about the situation first, so he knew he wasn't the only one worried, but now those thoughts just didn't want to go away. He gripped his hand tightly before spotting Emma, Mitchell and Andrew standing back a bit, hidden by the shadow of the building. They would be coming in later. Part of him wondered why there weren't any adults around. After all, Madeline did say there were some outside the city. So, did Madeline try to restrict the plan to just her comrades? That didn't seem likely, so, where were they?

Maxwell shook his head and headed toward the door, Karina's footsteps sounding solidly in his ears. He needed to get his head in the game. As such, he really needed to stop thinking of all these things. The doors opened with a whoosh, exposing the interior to the elements, but not for long.

They stepped inside, and Maxwell noticed how quiet it was. Well, quiet compared to during the day. He could see a receptionist off to one side, yawning as she worked at the computer. She looked up, then nodded to Maxwell. "Your sister?"

"Yep, I'm giving her the tour."

"That's fine, you know the rules though." She let out another yawn before looking back down.

He grinned before he hurried off to the left side, through the doorway and down the hall. Karina stuck to his side, looking around in curiosity. This was her first time here, after all.

After some time, passing the now familiar doorways, they reached a set of double doors. He could tell that Karina already looked a bit lost. It took him forever to get the layout of the place. That's how it was designed, to be confusing in order to waylay intruders. He could hear the hum of machinery and the sounds of conversation. He sent Karina a look and she nodded, taking a step back. He opened the door and stepped inside, quickly analyzing the area. He could see two people off to the side, sitting at a table. They were away from the loading dock doors and probably wouldn't even notice the doors opening. They looked to be playing a card game.

Maxwell gestured for Karina to follow as she stepped inside.

He hurried to where he knew the lever and buttons which controlled the gates were as she looked around the large room in surprise. He glanced toward the room with the two workers before spotting the gate buttons. With a quick press, he heard the sound of the door grinding open and noticed as the two workers perked up, curious. He glanced at Karina who grinned, doing a quick wave before moving closer to the two men. They stepped out of the office and Karina moved.

That self-defense training helped. She took them out in no time, quickly striking into the nerves at the back of their necks with an ease that almost made him jealous. Almost. He turned as he heard the sound of running footsteps and he looked over to see Mitchell, Andrew and Emma slip inside. He quickly pressed the button again, closing the door as Karina lugged the men to one side, behind a set of canisters that he knew, from experience, held dirt. He shook his head and headed over as the others joined him.

"Good start." Mitchell grinned before he looked around. "So

where to?"

"This way." Maxwell gestured, heading toward a little doorway hidden behind the canisters. They passed by the men and, after Maxwell swiped his key, stepped inside. It was a long hallway that led to another doorway with a keypad on it. Emma stepped forward, looking around. She seemed to be waiting for something before she moved, hurrying down the hallway and squatting before the keypad.

Unfortunately, they only had one working communicator. So, Emma received it since she was the one who could move the fastest of all of them and was also the one who would be unlocking the doorways.

Maxwell waited quietly, noticing Karina's impatience as she twitched her fingers, occasionally shifting her hand to her right side before quickly bringing it forward. He ignored it as he heard a click and looked over as Emma covered her nose, turning the handle. She gestured for them and they hurried over.

The smell that reached them put the city's smell to shame. Maxwell almost threw up, scrambling to plug his nose as fast as Karina was. The others only grimaced before stepping through. Maxwell wished he was more used to this type of smell, so it did not affect him so severely. Karina seemed to agree, if her disgusted expression was any indication.

They slipped inside, and Emma closed the door behind them before looking around. They were in a surprisingly pristine upper level. Down below was another floor with sewage and other things sitting like a calm sordid lake. A thin walkway on either side. He spotted large pumps and wondered what they did but pushed it off as he noticed the others already moving down the metal walkway. It clanged as they moved, sounding loud in the quiet tunnel-like enclosure.

Eventually, a set of stairs were the only way they could go. They descended, reaching the walkway that led to the reservoir. Dim lights shone overhead, showing the squalid liquid, sloshing right beside them. Maxwell felt Karina squirm next to him and he didn't blame her as they walked down the path. Eventually, the lights grew dimmer and the area became less maintained. He could see splashes on the walls that he didn't want to know about and heard creaking up ahead.

"There are tracks," Andrew's voice caught them off guard, surprising them. Maxwell glanced over, noticing Andrew staring at the ground in quiet contemplation. "Something heavy is regularly transported through here, and see those spots?" He gestured to either side. "It's dried blood."

Maxwell stiffened alongside Karina. Emma's eyes narrowed as she reached one hand up to her ear and spoke quietly, explaining what Andrew found. Karina appeared more than a little uncomfortable as she quickly turned away from the now menacing-looking splotches. Maxwell felt bile move up his throat and quickly swallowed, forcing himself not to throw up. He shook his head and moved ahead once more, Karina beside him. The others followed behind, wary.

Only for all of them to stop when a golden gate cut off their path. It speared up into the ceiling and even cut across the goop to the other side, cutting off the entire passage. Maxwell spotted something off to one side, against the wall and gulped. There were chains. What were there chains for?

Emma scanned the walkway before spotting a doorway. She stepped over to it, examining the simple key lock. Maxwell could tell almost instantly it was to be opened on this side only. He exchanged worried looks with Karina as Andrew clicked his tongue. Mitchell frowned, watching their surroundings with unease. "Would it be possible that this is how they transport things to the gated community? Things that they didn't want others to see the official way?"

"What do you mean?" Karina asked, voice wavering just a little bit.

Mitchell frowned before he shrugged. "Well, we know people are taken into the gated community, and it's not legal, so—"

"This is an underground trading area." Andrew looked around.

"That's what I presume." Mitchell nodded before they all turned as a click resounded around the hallway, ringing off the metal.

"Got it, let's go." Emma stood up, wiping her brow as she opened the door, a lock pick dangling in her hand.

Maxwell wasn't sure he wanted to but pressed on anyway.

Finally, after some walking, they reached what seemed to be a maintenance doorway, no handle or even lock visible on this side. He looked around as Emma drew to a stop with a frown. "We're in the gated community. Leon is trying to access the cameras right now. Call your friend. See where he is."

Maxwell nodded and reached for his phone, he stared and then sighed. "Damn. There's no signal down here."

"Not surprised," Emma only seemed slightly deterred as she tapped her earbud, muttering quietly. "Even our connection is weak."

Maxwell slipped his phone back into his pocket and stared at the door. What were they supposed to do?

His question was answered when Emma tilted her head, hand up to her ear in a perplexed expression. "Are you sure?"

Her words faded as they waited for Emma to finish listening. She turned to the doorway and sighed. "Fine, just let me know—" she stopped, then huffed before stepping forward. She pounded on the door, causing Maxwell to jump. What was she doing? Getting the entire areas attention?

He gulped, shifting next to Karina, whatever they were planning with that approach, he hoped it worked.

~ * ~

Lex stared down the long hallway, moving swiftly past the entrance people and pressed his hand to the door. He felt the familiar pinch of the needle before the door swung open.

He was just descending the stairs when he heard three sharp bangs, startling him and a few other workers. They looked over toward him before shaking their heads and getting back to what they were doing. Of course, he wasn't sure what it was they were doing, but thankfully, there were only a few around because of the late hour. Night shift?

He shook his head and walked over, glancing at the camera for a moment to see its red light blinking instead of steady. He tapped once on the sewer door and kept moving.

As much as he wanted to just get this over and done with, his mind raced with thoughts of his father and Caym. Where was his brother? Considering their deal was practically nullified two days ago, he figured Caym would just swoop in. That was the other reason he wanted to just get this done and out of the way. For fear that he wouldn't be able to help the twins, not because he wanted to run from Caym, but…his hand drifted to his pendant as he knocked on the right-hand lab door and waited.

No, it was because he didn't think he would have any leg to stand on if he didn't go with him. He didn't want to hurt Caym anymore and he did want to know why he was so cold the last few times Lex saw him. His thoughts were cut off as the door opened to reveal the man he met the other day, looking tired.

Richard spotted him and grinned. "Thanks for helping me the other day. What brings you around here?"

"Is anyone in?"

"Anyone? Oh, you mean the head." Richard gestured, and Lex stepped inside. "No, she and the others left a while ago. Me and a few others are the only ones left here. The others are all working on our main project. 526-0034, have you heard of it? Your father must have mentioned it once."

Lex furrowed his brow. Main project? "No, I do not recall."

Richard blinked, seeming surprised. "Oh, I figured you would know since the subject did use to work with your father's company…"

"Ah, that." That was enough confirmation for Lex. "Where is she being studied?"

Richard perked up and then waved to a right-hand hallway. "It's down that way. Oh, as for the exit, it's down the left-hand side. I figured you should know since I could tell that was your next question." The man grinned. "It's mostly so the upper and lower parts of the building don't interact, safety precautions. Anyway, so the two sides intersect at the end, so either way works, you just don't have to worry passing by all the experimental labs on the left-hand side."

"Oh?" Lex hummed, curious. "Can you show me where she is?"

It seemed the man was working so much lately, he hadn't heard the news. That worked to Lex's advantage.

"This way." He gestured, leading Lex along. They moved through the circular room off to a path on the left side.

Alarms rang through the building and Lex jumped, glancing up in surprise.

"Intruder detected. It seems an intruder has infiltrated the complex. All hands at the ready, I repeat, all hands at the ready." The voice blared through the once calm speakers.

He cursed and looked over to the confused man. Lex pursed his lips before muttering a quiet apology under his breath. He moved swiftly. He opened a nearby door and shoved, causing the man to call out in surprise. "Stay in there if you want to survive." He spoke sternly, then slammed the door and locked it.

He heard scrambling and heavy pounding from the other side, followed by yells. He grimaced. "Do you want to be found by the intruder? Stay quiet."

Richard stopped, and Lex shook his head. He hated to have to do this, but he was now under just a bit of a time constraint and it was true, he didn't want the man hurt. He turned and hurried back the way he came. He didn't have much time. What even set the alarms off? He opened the door, quickly shoving a chair he grabbed on the way under the handle to keep it open as he hurried down the hallway. He could hear talking and sirens blaring but ignored it. He spotted the door and opened it without a moment's hesitation.

Chapter Twenty-four

Karina jumped as the door slammed open to reveal Lex. The shrill screech of the sirens grated at her ears as they hurried inside. To think the knocking actually worked. Guess she would have to thank Leon for keeping an eye on the cameras. After all, that was the only way she could think that Emma was able to time it properly.

"I do not know specifically where your mother is. There wasn't time to find her. I do, however, have a general location."

"That's fine." Emma looked around, spotting the line of labs. "Andrew, Mitchell, check those rooms, let's go." She gestured before heading toward the open doorway.

Karina noted the dead camera and sighed in relief. At least the gated community didn't know where they were. She noticed Lex glance at Emma curiously before looking ahead. She threw the observation to the side. It had been a while since they saw each other. Their footsteps rang out as they entered a large circular room with way too much white and surrounded by metal-lined doors.

"There are two hallways that I know of. We'll search them and see what we can find." He turned. "Emma and I will take the left-hand hall, Maxwell, Karina, I want you two to take the right." He gave them a look of hesitation and frowned, as if he wanted to say something else, his gaze flickering to Emma.

Maxwell blinked before he nodded. "We'll be fine. Speaking of..." He glanced around. "What about Mitchell and Andrew, shouldn't they be—"

"They're helping get the scientists out, who knows how long that will take." Emma smoothly cut in. Maxwell frowned, but didn't argue.

Karina watched the exchange in silence, wondering for a brief moment before shaking her head, hands on her hips. "Well then, why don't we get going? We already have our pairs and since that stupid alarm is ringing, it would be safer than going alone."

"True." Lex's lips twitched up into a subtle grin before turning to Emma and gesturing for her to follow.

Karina blinked, confused as her arms dropped to her side. What was that look about? She glanced between Maxwell, who held an expression of confusion and wariness, and Lex, who seemed a bit stiffer than usual, and not just because of the situation, as he disappeared around the corner. Did Lex suspect something? Did Maxwell? Karina didn't argue, quickly running after Maxwell, who was taking her advice and heading out. They opened the door, exposing a long hallway. She could see it curve near the end. They separated, glancing through each doorway as they passed. At least, each doorway they could see through. The name plates on the side helped as well. Karina could see most of the rooms were empty, but a few held some people that she could see were either dead or on the verge of death. She quickly looked away as she spotted one older man digging at his throat. They heard footsteps and looked up just as a guard rounded the corner, gun raised. Karina's eyes widened, and she quickly dove to the side, pushing Maxwell down as bullet's ricocheted off the far wall. She looked up as the guard walked down the hallway. One hand pressed to his ear. "Two found in D district. I repeat, two found in D district."

She could hear Maxwell quietly curse next to her, his words too soft to hear, but the meaning was quite clear.

"You two are coming with me." He pointed his gun at the two of them and Karina gulped before glaring. She wasn't going to be taken prisoner so easily. She reached her hand back, keeping her position away from his sight. She would only get one chance. She better make this count.

~ * ~

The walk down the hallway was quiet, yet tense as the sirens blared above their heads. Lex glanced toward Emma as she perused the place with a sharp look. He spotted the door Richard was hidden in and pursed his lips. He glimpsed someone peering through before disappearing. So, he'd seen them. Lex sighed. There wasn't much he could do about that.

"Why did you want to join me?" Emma's voice caught him off guard and he glanced over, expression even.

"I could ask the same to you. Why did you have your comrades break off when it was clear that I, your informant," he tried hard not to roll his eyes at that comment, "was leading you to where your objective is?"

Emma bit her lip and shrugged, looking away. "Contingency plan. Just in case…"

"Just in case what? I threw you all to the wolves?" Lex found himself unamused as he returned to moving down the hall, keeping half an eye on Emma as she followed after. "I could have done that any number of times, including at the end when you idiots decided to just bang on the door like it was nothing."

He didn't miss the way Emma winced as he glanced up at the sirens. "Let me guess, those sirens are your doing as well?"

Her jerking to a stop and staring at him was all he needed to know. "How?"

"It's the same reason you had your friends split off earlier. You have another reason to be here, one that, while I'm not particularly thrilled about, the twins would outright have your heads over."

"Oh, and what is that?" Emma's voice was cold, filled with such ice as to drop the temperature in the entire wing.

Lex brushed it off, continuing on his way. After all, they still needed to make some semblance of searching, even though he knew the hallway he sent the twins down was the one that would have their mother. "The fact that you used our invading of the underground as a means of gaining entrance into the gated community for not just the five of you."

"What's wrong with that? You're from outside the community as much as us, don't you want to get out of their shadow too? Or is it that you've grown so used to living here that—"

"You have no idea." Lex's expression was frigid, causing Emma to snap her jaw shut. "Why do you think my earlier statement stands? I don't care in particular what you do, but the twins do. The last thing I want on their minds during all this is that it's their fault if something happens to this community..."

"It won't be! They'll be heroes for—"

"For what? For helping to..." Lex shook his head, dismissing the thought. "Come, let's hurry, we don't have time to waste here arguing."

Emma narrowed her lips into a downright thin line before hurrying up to him, fingers twitching. He peered sidelong toward her, fingers clasping the cool leather of his knives, hidden away as usual. He had a bad feeling about this.

~ * ~

Karina flicked her thumb, jerking the safety on her gun as she gulped, staring at the guard before her, dressed in black, but without the medallion. Her mind flipped back to home for a brief moment before she shook her head.

"Where are the other prisoners?" Maxwell grabbed the guard's attention, voice steady, but legs trembling in a way that showed he wasn't as calm as he appeared.

Karina didn't think too much about it, recognizing the opportunity for what it was. She pulled the gun out of the holster and, forcing herself to think of the target, she shot. The recoil sent a small spasm up her arm, but she heard the guard cry out and crumble, falling to the ground. Maxwell whipped around to her, shock on his face. She quickly shook her head, hurrying up to the guard, grip tight on her gun. She quickly kicked his away as the man gripped his upper leg tightly. He glared through the visor.

Faster than she realized it was possible, he lunged forward, tackling her and reaching for her gun. She yelped, pain shooting up the back of her head as it made contact with the cement floor. Her grip loosened, and she heard the gun clatter to the ground. A heavy arm dug into her throat and her hands darted up, clawing at the thick muscle pushing into her windpipe. She stared up at the guard as he dug into her throat with one arm while the other reached for her fallen gun.

She heard movement and watched as Maxwell swiped the gun, backing away as he shakily aimed it at the guard, expression scared. "Let her go."

The guard stiffened but didn't let up. Darkness pulled at her as she scrabbled, nails digging into the skin, causing the guard to bleed. She couldn't breathe, no voice left her throat.

"Let her go! Now." Maxwell's voice sounded in her ears.

She felt the man shift and she could just barely see Maxwell move as another shot rang out. *Wait, did the guard have another gun? Shit.*

She opened her mouth, trying to say something, anything.

She felt something shift and heard a thud, followed by air flowing into her raw throat and lungs. She gasped, surprised to find the weight gone. She twisted upward, looking around in time to see Maxwell straddling the guard, struggling to keep him down. Karina scrambled forward just as Maxwell raised the gun and slammed it down on the guard's temple.

She froze, along with Maxwell, as they watched the guard slump. No movement or sound invaded the area except for their shattered breaths and pounding hearts. Karina could hear rushing in her ears as she stared at Maxwell in shock, spotting the blood spattered over the gun.

Maxwell stared at the gun before his fingers uncurled. The gun clattered to the ground as he tentatively reached forward, touching at the guard's neck with two fingers. She pulled herself forward, unable to speak with her raw throat.

Maxwell was trembling as he quickly stood and stumbled back, as if trying to get as far away as possible. Karina pushed herself to her feet and quickly grabbed Maxwell's arm, stopping him from running. He looked at her, mouth opening and closing. "Kari, he's... I..."

"Focus." She placed her hands on either side of his face and quickly pulled him to face her, ignoring her burning throat. "We need to rescue Mom. We can think about what happened later. You can't fall apart now, all right?"

She was saying that to both of them as she forced herself to not look at the guard Maxwell had... She was unable to... She glared as tremors ran up Maxwell's body before he placed his hands up to hers, tears barely on the verge of being shed.

Karina leaned forward, quickly pressing her forehead to his. "Come on, let's find Mom and get out of here. Now."

He nodded, and she pulled away. He turned, looking away from the dea...dead guard. Karina squatted down and, after a moment of indecision, picked up the gun she was given. Her gaze briefly moved to the other gun. She shuddered, deciding against grabbing it, even as she watched Maxwell hurry away without a backward glance.

The metal felt even colder in her grip, even though she knew it was probably warm from being manhandled and fired.

They continued down the hallway, turning another corner, this time more carefully. Karina kept her grip firmly on the gun, not wanting to put it away again. Maxwell was avoiding her, his expression stoic and face forward.

She heard it before she felt it. A loud explosion ripped through the building, causing it to shake. She looked up as dust shuddered and another explosion sounded above. What the hell was happening?

"Did you find her?"

Karina turned to see Emma at the other end, Lex beside her, a frown on his face. Karina shook her head as another explosion sounded and she stumbled, bumping into Maxwell, who quickly caught her.

"Well, that answers that question. Can't really hide it now, can you? Do you mind letting them know what is going on now?"

Lex's voice was cold, and it was only then Karina spotted the knife positioned warily in Lex's grip. Lex's gaze shifted to the gun, but thankfully, he didn't say anything. Though she did notice the way his fingers twitched, his lips pushing downwards into a deeper scowl.

Emma peered over her shoulder before she let out a sigh. "It wasn't my decision." She shrugged. "You know how much Madeline hates the gated community and, well, Andrew looked up to the Suicide Arsonist. You can probably guess what's happening above."

"Wait, what?" She found herself only slightly pushing away from Maxwell. "Do you mean?"

"They came here to get into the gated community, not to rescue your mother. As we speak, they are probably making their way out of this building and—" Lex cut himself off as Emma looked away.

"How could you?" Maxwell's voice whispered, filled with pain. "You lied. You said no one would be hurt. We would do a quiet in and out. That's why you had so many people, yet no adults. I thought it was strange, but I never said anything." Maxwell shook his head.

"They're doing what the Resistance tells them to do," Emma said, her voice curt as a sad expression crossed her face. "Both knew the costs and did it."

"Come on, we don't have time for this," Lex interrupted, expression neutral, just as it was when Karina and Maxwell first met him. Emma nodded.

Karina felt the grip on her hand tighten so much so that her fingers were numb, but she didn't say anything, feeling the same way. She would think of this whole situation later. Still, she was surprised she noticed the numbness in her fingers when she was so numb herself.

She shook it off. Maybe it wasn't that bad, after all, how far can two boys get? No, it would be fine, she told herself as she took the lead, heading down the rejoined path into another area. She heard Lex mutter something, the confusion heard clearly even though the words were more muddled. Still, this hallway was filled with high level security doors. She examined the hall, only to start when Maxwell tugged her to one side. She looked over to see a doorway with a small nameplate that read 526-0O34: Veronica Elifer.

She darted forward and examined the door thoroughly before spotting a keypad. She turned to Emma. "You can open this, can't you?"

Emma nodded and squatted down, staring at the pad. Karina

watched her warily, only to blink as Emma's fingers flew over the apparatus. In no time, they heard a click and the door hissed open. Karina hurried inside, Maxwell at her heels, and looked around.

The place was barren of everything except for a toilet, basin and bed. The bed was occupied. It didn't take much to spot her mother's brunette hair, cut short in ragged strands and her thin frame, made to look even thinner in the oversized hospital clothing. Her mother turned her head, and, for a brief moment, Karina found her breath caught in her throat, surprised to see such warmth even after all these months. Her mother's mouth formed words before she sat up. Karina couldn't figure out what she was feeling, seeing her mother, but Maxwell did. He moved forward, letting go of Karina and hugging Mom firmly, downright quivering. Mom jumped and quickly pulled him into a tight hug before pushing away.

Lex stepped in. "I'll help you up."

Mom looked up and, after a moment of hesitation, nodded, taking his proffered hand. Maxwell let go and Karina found herself grasping for his presence, this time for comfort rather than to stop him. He glanced at her before turning back to Mom, who seemed to be weak. Mom shook out her legs and gave Lex a grateful smile.

"Let's go," Emma called from outside and Karina had to agree.

They needed to move. She found herself hovering behind her mother as Lex helped lead her out the door. She seemed weak, but not overly so. Karina realized she wanted to just run forward and sob into her mother's chest. She also knew that she couldn't, she couldn't break just yet. They needed to get out of here.

~ * ~

Lex looked over his shoulder as he supported the young-looking woman beside him. He hadn't realized just how young their mother was until now. Even with the beginning signs of the disease and the obvious experiments she endured, she still held a certain youthfulness and tenacity he often equated with the twins. He pulled from that thought, watching Emma out of the corner of his eyes. He knew something like this was probably going to happen. The opportunity to take out the gated community was prime. No doubt others were up above, invading the place as they walked. To have Andrew and Mitchell go toward the area that obviously led to the upper areas, he should have said something.

In the end, that was not his issue. He just hoped things worked themselves out. His mind briefly flipped to Richard before he shook his head. The man would be fine down here, but he did wonder why the man lied about where the children's mother was. Did he not know? It was possible he was lied to as another means of defense. After all, you can't be too careful. Lex shook his head and looked ahead as they hurried through the hallways.

"Who are you?" The woman's soft voice invaded his thoughts and he looked over. He spotted Karina and Maxwell hovering behind, gaze firmly on the woman more often than not. He turned away from her curious expression as he spotted an elevator up ahead. So that was the exit Richard was talking about.

He heard the pounding footsteps of approaching guards behind them and waited until they were in the safety of the elevator to speak. "My name is Lex."

The woman waited, as if expecting more. He glanced toward the twins and Emma before he continued, "I'll explain later, for now, we have to get out of here."

The woman scrutinized him with a fairly familiar gaze, and he dimly noted it reminded him of Maxwell before she nodded and stared ahead, pushing away from him with the same stubbornness as Karina. "Yes, let's."

Lex shook his head. She was definitely an Elifer just by how similar she and the twins were. He turned and waited until the elevator shuddered to a stop. The doors opened. A long hallway set only with a door at the end stood before them. He could see a light that did not look like moonlight seeping through the window of the door as he hurried forward and thrust it open. They stepped outside, and he could see the twins stop, horror flashing over their faces.

The gated community was up in flames. He could hear cries and hollers and the screeching sound of sirens ringing off the sweltering air. Smoke could be seen in black strokes piercing toward the sky.

"How horrible." The woman at his side gasped, the sound filled with a mix of sadness and pain.

For the first time seeing anything above ground, this was probably not what she was hoping for. He felt sorry for the woman, to put it bluntly.

"How could you?"

Lex looked over just in time to see Karina grab Emma and whip her around, holding her by the collar as Karina practically throttled her. "You knew this was going to happen and you let it? Those are people dying in there."

"No, they're not," Emma growled, pushing her off and glaring. "The things on this side are monsters, we're eliminating them before they eliminate us."

Lex stopped himself from wincing at the malice in the normally kind girl's voice. It seemed the stress of the situation and his earlier statements hadn't helped in the slightest. He heard footsteps and looked over just in time to see a familiar figure step out from behind a set of trees.

"Caym?" He couldn't stop the strangled sound from escaping his throat.

His brother was standing there, as if unaware of the flames and screams behind him. His gaze was solely on Lex's.

"I found you. I can't believe I found you in all this." The words were so faint and soft, Lex wasn't even sure if he caught them, but for a brief moment, he could see a surge of relief and a small smile on Caym's face before it just as quickly disappeared.

Lex felt a shiver run down his spine as he noticed something off in Caym's expression. He seemed different and Lex couldn't quite pinpoint why. "What are you doing here?"

"It seems my guess was correct." Caym's voice came out cold and slightly hollow, the relief replaced by a clinical and dangerous edge.

He grinned, a bit too wide. "Lex, were you about to renege on our deal?"

"Deal?" Maxwell called softly, and Lex brushed if off, focusing on Caym.

They didn't have time for this. Why was Caym here?

"The deal was reneged when Father died. I have—"

"Nothing to do with it? Well then, what about this?" Caym glanced to one side before he grinned and turned back to face them. "It seems like you've teamed up with the Resistance. I wonder what they will do to you if you go with them."

"He'll be fine. He isn't—" Maxwell exclaimed, only to be cut off as Caym glared at him before letting out a sigh, gaze flicking briefly to Emma.

"So, they won't do a thing if they find out he's the son. No, brother of Enthrope's head chief?"

Emma gasped, and Lex suddenly felt daggers digging into his spine, but ignored it. "Caym, what are you playing at?"

What is he doing? Lex stopped himself from biting his lip, but was unable to avoid his fingers digging into the skin of his palm.

"I want you to come home, where you will be safe." Caym's expression softened and, for a brief moment, the look in his eyes disappeared to be replaced with a pleading scrutiny, a sadness. No, that wasn't nearly the right word to use, whatever it was. It stopped Lex in his tracks. As fast as it was there, it was gone, Caym's voice returning to its slightly off tone. "Father is gone, and Mother will be too…soon. If you come with me, I'll let the rest go. After all, I have a fire to put out, and while I understand that some people might be important for our continued survival." His gaze flitted to the twins, who stiffened. "That is not my concern right now. After all, you took care of them, so there's no doubt that they won't hoard that special talent of theirs, now is there? Remember, I'm not Father, I'm not inclined to hoard it either, you know."

"What is he talking about?" Emma voiced quietly. Everyone ignored her.

Lex stared at the proffered gesture, thoughts swirling. Part of him wanted to go home and yet part of him was afraid. He felt his arm move up to the pendant hidden under his shirt. Caym examined Lex with a moment of hesitation. Only for understanding to flash across his face.

"You still have it?" The words were pained, but almost hopeful.

For a brief moment, Lex could see that familiar kindness under his older brother's mask. He was still there. The Caym he knew was still there and Lex wanted to know why he changed, what happened, and yet...

He heard movement before, to his surprise, Karina stood in front of him, glaring at Caym. "This is complete and utter blackmail. Lex is coming with us and that's final."

Caym stared at her in silence before he tilted his head up. It didn't take much for Lex to notice where Caym was looking. Yet, even so, he found himself unable to say anything. After a moment, Lex sighed. "No, Caym, I can't come home, not yet. After all, we all need to get to safety. That was the deal. Once I get them out of here, I'll come back, all right?" He hesitated before looking at him, dead in the eye. "I promise."

Caym stiffened, before he regarded the crowd. He looked away, obviously deep in turmoil.

Lex felt a hint of hope as he watched Caym, even as he gestured for the others to start moving. Karina gave him a hesitant look, only to help Maxwell with their mother as they started to hobble away.

The sound of movement seemed to catch Caym's attention and he turned to look once more. "Why?" His voice was quiet, barely heard over the raging fire, which had been ignored up until this point.

"Because you would do it too in my shoes." Lex stared at Caym, who winced. "Isn't that why you stayed behind? To make sure nothing happened to me? You know you could have escaped then too."

"No."

Lex froze at the quiet word that seeped from Caym's mouth as his face suddenly contorted into anguish. "You know why they never came after you? Why it was that you were seen as returned back from the dead? Why even Mother was somewhat happy to see your return?" Lex hesitated, and it was all Caym needed as he spread his arms out, grin widening just a little too far. "I lied. I told them I saw you die, and you know what? When you came back, they didn't care. Even Father just wanted to use you. I couldn't allow that."

"Wait." Lex felt his heart stop for a second. "What do you mean? What did you do?"

"What was necessary. Now we don't have time, are you coming or not?"

Lex opened his mouth when he suddenly let out a yelp as two hands grabbed his. He glanced back to see Maxwell and Karina. Maxwell's gaze was on Caym, his expression indecipherable. Karina looked like she'd swallowed something unpleasant. "Come on, we can't stay." The encroaching fire held their attention, along with their mother and Emma, who were waiting off to one side, ready to flee.

"All right, just one moment." The twins hesitated, exchanging looks before letting go. Lex returned his attention back to his brother. "Caym. I don't know what happened to you, and believe me, I want to know, but now isn't the time or place. Let me make sure we all get out of here alive, then I'll come back, okay?"

Caym's scrutiny shifted to the twins for a brief moment, his expression contorting, emotions flashing wildly, before a smile, this one completely wrong, sprang onto his face. Yet the next words were cold, as if something had snapped. "As usual, little Leo. You are much too kind-hearted. Fine, have it your way."

Lex stiffened. "Wai—"

"Men," Caym spoke up, gesturing to a few people, hidden in the trees. "Capture those two children and Leonard, alive. You may kill everyone else."

Ice slid down his spine at the words. No, what was he doing? "Didn't you hear me at all?" Lex felt his voice crack, startling the twins as much as the previous words from Caym had. "I want to know what's wrong with you! I want to help, I promise—"

"I know." Caym spoke, voice soft and expression dim before returning full force. "This time, I'm making sure you keep your promise."

"You misundersta—" Lex's words were cut off as a loud

explosion ripped through the clearing, startling everyone.

He saw Caym stumble as he spotted the men from earlier, scattered from the explosion. He gritted his teeth, gaze on his older brother once more before he turned and fled. Caym didn't leave him a choice in this case. Why? He'd said he'd come back, did something in Caym just…snap?

They moved through the trees as he led them to where he knew the gates were located, barely able to see or breathe through the clogging and dense smoke. The heat from the fire felt like an oven in the moonlit night.

He could barely see guards hurrying to and fro, trying to help the fleeing community people. He frowned, wondering about Richard. He hoped the man was all right. He looked over just in time to see the gates burst inward with an explosion, causing the fleers to stumble back.

He quickly covered the twins' eyes as those too close to the gates got ripped apart by the explosion. Emma barely gave it a glance. Maxwell and Karina both reached up. Instead of pulling away, they moved to replace his grip with their own. He took their free hands, grateful. He quickly led them past the bodies that littered the ground, ignoring the screams and cries as a group of people in masks came through the gates and into the community. They seemed to spot Emma and moved around their group.

Out of the corner of Lex's eyes, he spotted Richard's wife, Lanie. She was off to one side, hurrying with a baby and a young child at her side away from the chaos. He almost sighed with relief. They would make—

He heard another explosion and quickly looked away as the trees were decimated. Fire leaped into the sky as bloody and twisted corpses lay over the ground in heaps. He must have bitten his lip at some point because he could feel blood trail down his chin. He shook his head and focused back on his main task, even as a part of him felt heavy. After all, it wasn't just the twins who let this happen. Still, he couldn't lead the twins forever like this.

"Open your eyes. I can't keep doing this."

Karina stiffened as Maxwell shuddered before they both took a deep breath and dropped their arms, focused on the gates, as if knowing not to look behind them. Smart.

They moved through the blown-apart gates, hearing gunshots start to sound behind them.

They quickly moved to the left, away from the onslaught and the twins stopped as their mother crumpled, breaths ragged and legs shaking. He had to give the woman kudos, for not having walked much in months, along with probably being starved and experimented on, she was doing very well.

"You're…you're Leonard Askren. Aren't you?"

Lex could feel the heaviness, lashes fluttering from resignation as he turned toward Emma, who was quivering where she stood. Her eyes were wide and filled with hatred that he both understood and couldn't refute. "Yes, why?"

"Why are you here? Are you trying to make fun of us? Is this some sport to you? You lied to these two and made it look like you were helping, didn't you? You would have gladly gone with that man back there if Karina hadn't stepped in, or Maxwell, for that matter. You wouldn't have cared. Would you?"

"Stop," Karina spoke, voice shooting up in frustration, once more stepping in front of Lex. "He helped us. He's the reason you were even able to get in in the first place."

"So?" Emma's expression was murderous, to put it mildly. "He's still one of them. You saw the underground area. I and the other two know for a fact that it was a slave depot. I bet your brother was also on the menu, if not for that man keeping an eye on him."

Lex grimaced; so that was what the sewage system was. His employer was telling the truth.

"She's lying, right?" Maxwell looked at him uncertainly.

"I thought it was a lie too. My employer once made a comment on it, then passed it off as a joke. I didn't reali—"

"Didn't realize?" Emma asked. "That's rich."

"There they are. Stop them!"

Lex jerked around in time to see men barrel into the small clearing. He spotted the gun, aimed at Karina, at the same time as Emma. Maxwell, who was facing away, turned.

Emma reacted quickly, faster than him and pushed Karina aside as gunshots rang out. Lex jerked Maxwell and Karina back behind him, wrenching the gun from Karina's grip and firing. He wasn't particularly used to guns, but he had still used them before. With rapid succession, he took out the four men that followed them and dropped his arm, breathing out heavily. He could feel his mind on the verge of shutting down and quickly shoved all those thoughts, everything he wanted to worry about, into a side compartment. He needed to focus, and emotions would do him no good at this point.

His attention drifted toward Emma and he grimaced, spotting the already forming pools of blood decorating her body like swiss cheese. That thought quickly forced him to look away. After all, she never had a chance.

He turned to Karina, who was staring at the body of their former friend, breath caught in her throat. Maxwell looked like he was about to break down.

Lex heard more footsteps and shouts and he grimaced. "Come on, let's go." He grabbed the twins 'arms and pulled them forward while sending their mother a look. Their mother pushed herself up and hurried after in quiet silence. Lex was glad their mother was so accepting of his presence, even with knowing… He shook his head as they hurried out of the few trees and through the back alleys of the surrounding buildings. The fire lit up the sky, as bright as the sun, casting them in deep shadow. He walked down another alley, spotting police cars ahead.

He noticed Arik, standing there impatiently, worry radiating from his whole being. He seemed to spot them and sighed with relief. "There you all are." He spoke as they hurried up to them. "Andrew and Mitchell came out earlier…" he trailed off, turning toward the community with a sad expression his face. "Why did it have to happen this way though? Why do such violence?" He let out a heavy sigh and shook his head. "Come, this way. I'll lead you to their safe house."

He turned and led them through the police brigade's barrier. Lex could see Arik's father at the head, quelling the cheering crowd. The pedestrians hung at the other side of the barrier, barely kept at bay by the police brigade as relief shone on their faces, glimmering in the light of the gated community that burned behind them.

Chapter Twenty-five

It had been a long time... a long, long time since she had breathed fresh air and seen her children. She only wished it hadn't come with so much pain. Veronica pulled her children close, startling them. Two pairs of eyes looked at her, filled with so many emotions that it broke her more than any of the experiments. They were scared, tired, happy, angry, upset, a plethora of emotions and there was nothing she could do for either of them except hold their hands as they walked through the streets. Her observations shifted to her other savior, the young man who helped her. The young man her children desperately wished to come with them.

Leonard Askren. So that was her employer's son. She never met him before, but she'd heard of him from when she still worked with Enthrope, him and Caym. She knew from the stories that the two were close, but... She pulled from that thought and examined him quietly. He was tall and held himself in a way that spoke of quiet confidence and world-weariness. Right now, though, she could tell that all the death and destruction was weighing heavily on him, his face set in a solid mask that would impress a world-renowned poker player.

She shook her head again, still she was glad that her children were alive and well... somewhat.

"So, where's Emma?" The boy who introduced himself as Arik turned to them with curiosity shining. "She was with you, right?"

Veronica found her thoughts shifting to the pained young girl. The desperation and despair in her voice. The anger at both herself and the situation.

The way she didn't hesitate to push Karina out of the way, at the cost of her life.

She could see her daughter stiffen, shaking. Maxwell glanced over to Karina, worry clear on his face.

"She didn't make it," Veronica found herself saying quietly to the boy, causing him to freeze. "I'm sorry."

He stared ahead, stopping in front of a building. He looked like he was in shock. "What… what happened? How… How did she…"

"She was shot," Leonard spoke, staring straight at Arik. "She was protecting Karina."

Veronica noticed the door open at the same time as Arik whipped around, tugging at Karina's shirt as pain and anguish flared over his face.

"You promised. You promised to keep them safe. Didn't you say what was one more?"

"I tried," Karina cried out, startling Veronica as her daughter reached up and threw his grasping fingers to the side, tears shimmering and just barely contained. "I said I WOULDN'T promise! I said I would try and I did."

"Obviously, you didn't try hard enough. How could you let her die?" Tears flowed down the boy's cheeks as he quickly rubbed at his face.

Veronica's attention was caught as a young woman stepped out of the doorway. She held herself in a way that demanded attention and obedience. She glared over the group and quickly pulled them inside. Veronica wasn't actually sure what happened, but they found themselves in a living room. Arik was off to one side, shaking. Karina sat on the couch, head in her hands as Maxwell sat beside her, holding her tightly and whispering something into her ears. Veronica stared at her children, surprised at their strength.

"You are safe now." Veronica looked over to see the woman who brought them in step up to her. "So, you are those two's mother, Mrs. Elifer? My daughter told me of your situation. It is good to see you are out of their clutches."

"Thank you." She wasn't sure what else to say, but it didn't seem that she needed to say anything else.

The woman nodded and turned to look them over before glancing over to another boy with Asian features and short black hair. "Leon, status update."

Leon looked up. "There is a lot to peruse over, however, the general statistics show that we've managed to occupy L. J. Fox Inc. as well as the surrounding buildings. Our main force has managed to infiltrate the gates and have gotten rid of most of the Enthrope police. The police brigade is suppressing the crowd from joining in, but they probably won't be able to for much longer. We will need to finish quickly."

"Understood, let Team A know to hurry along. Team B has rescued the people, correct?"

"Yes."

"Good, make sure they are out of the danger zone, then let the police brigade know. We can't stop the people from having their revenge, so we might as well let them have it."

"Wait, what do you mean?" Karina spoke up, voice hesitant. "Aren't you supposed to help the people?"

The woman turned, giving Karina a stern gaze. "We are. In this way, they won't turn on us. For many, it will be cathartic. We're just making sure they won't be killed in the meantime."

Veronica closed her eyes, her thoughts flickering. Her husband was right. To think things were in such turmoil. She could only imagine what was happening...will happen in the gated community.

She highly doubted there would be any survivors and it made her feel sick.

"What did you expect?" Arik spat.

Veronica opened her eyes to stare at the emotionally injured boy. "My father can only do so much. The people's hatred is too great to have the Resistance be the only ones to go in there." He shook his head. "Not that you would care."

"Shut up." Maxwell spoke, teeth grinding as he glared at Arik. "I get you are upset, but my sister...we both tried. Don't think you're the only one affected."

"Maxwell is right. Calm yourselves. We have other things to worry about." Leonard turned his gaze to the woman. "My name is Lex. I am to assume you are Madeline's mother?"

The woman smirked. "You presume accurately. My name is Wilma. It's a pleasure to make your acquaintance. I am to assume you are the confidante?"

Lex nodded, and Wilma smiled, this time, a somewhat warm smile. "I guess I must thank you. For helping in our cause." She turned toward another boy with brown hair and nodded. "Mitchell, would you bring them to the spare rooms? I think they need some time to rest."

Mitchell nodded and stood. Veronica hesitated before gently pulling her little...well, not so little anymore, twins up with her. They barely hesitated, thoughts far away. She stared at them quietly. She heard footsteps to one side. She turned to see Leonard...no, Lex, step over and lean down a bit to examine both of them. "Come on, you two. We did all we could. Your mother is safe now, so why don't we get some rest."

"But..."

Lex reached his arms out, ruffling their hair. "Idiots." The word was said in a fond tone.

Karina huffed and looked away but didn't protest. Maxwell put his hand up, catching Lex's fingers.

"Thanks."

Lex snorted and stood. "Thank me later, get some rest now."

Veronica examined her son and daughter. She pushed them forward. "Your friend is right. I'll be up in a minute, all right?"

Her children hesitated before Karina nodded. She took Maxwell's hand and they hurried after Mitchell. Veronica watched them go before turning to Lex. "Thank you."

Lex scrutinized her for a moment. "I'm not sure why you are thanking me."

Veronica chuckled. "Then there is no need to worry."

She glanced over to Wilma, who was waiting patiently as her people worked. Veronica spotted a couple older folks flit in and out, but all of the youngsters seemed to be here, at the safe house. She turned to

Wilma and asked. "So, what now?"

Wilma waved in time to grab a paper from a bustling worker to look it over. "Now, we wait. There is nothing left for you all to do. However, we are going to have to leave the city soon. If we aren't careful, the other communities could come down on our heads, plus this city is going to have enough problems as it is, now that part of its infrastructure is destroyed."

"You're not going to help rebuild?" Lex asked quietly.

Wilma sighed. "As much as we would like to, we just don't have the means. Not yet anyway. Still, that is not for you two to worry about. Just know that we will be leaving in a few hours. I'll be bringing you all to our base so that you can recover."

Her gaze flitted to Veronica. "We also might have to ask you to let us know what exactly was happening down there. I do hope you don't mind."

"It's fine." Veronica winced, feeling herself shaking against her will. She forged ahead. "Thank you for taking care of us. Still, I guess that means we need to rest while we can, and we had best not intrude any longer."

"Of course. I will see you in a few hours."

Veronica took the dismissal for what it was and headed out the door, Lex close behind.

"You don't really want to talk about it, do you?"

Veronica chuckled weakly, though there was no humor in it. "No wonder my son and daughter look up to you, you're quite sharp."

"You can only live so long out here without knowing something." Lex's voice was quiet and almost as weak as hers.

Her gaze flitted to him and she noticed his shoulders were slumped over, and his feet dragging. He seemed all the world like a tired soul. She knew why. He wasn't in a good spot right now. "Your brother..."

"I would rather not talk about it," Lex said, sending her a look before he sighed and ran a hand through his hair. After a moment, he reached into his pocket and, after taking a good long scan of the surroundings, pulled out a pack of cigarettes and a lighter. Respecting his privacy, she turned away as she heard the click and whoosh of flames. After a moment, the air was filled with a faint acrid stench. She finally turned back to see the cigarette hanging between his shaking fingers as he let out a breath, staring at the ceiling. Considering his clothes hadn't smelled like smoke when she first met him, he either had a good means of cleaning, or he didn't do this often. Yet now, smoke was the only thing she could smell, and it wasn't just from the cigarette.

"There you are. This way." Mitchell's voice startled her as she noticed him walking up to them with a small smile.

His smile dimmed slightly when he glanced toward Lex, before returning a little weaker, but in understanding. Veronica followed after the boy, Lex behind her, lost in thought. It didn't take long before they arrived at the spare room. "Unfortunately, we only have so much space here, so you'll have to share, not that anyone here would mind, right?"

Lex shook his head and slipped inside. Veronica quietly observed Mitchell. "Thank you. Let us know when we're heading out, all right?"

"Can do. Now if you will excuse me."

Veronica watched him go before turning and stepping into the room. Her twins were sitting close to the window, staring out at the slowly dawning sky, their expressions lost. She could see them starting to stand and shook her head. She walked over to them and squatted down, pulling them both close. "I'm glad you two are all right."

She heard a sniff, from whom, she wasn't sure, because the next thing she knew, they were both holding her tightly, faces buried in her chest as their bodies trembled in a heaving mix of emotions. She pulled them both into a tight hug, glancing out the window at the dawning of a new day.

She wished she could say this was an end. That she no longer had to worry. That her little twins no longer had to worry, but… Her gaze flickered to Lex, who was watching both them and the rising sun with an unreadable, perhaps lost expression. She knew, without a doubt, that it wasn't the case. As much as she hated the thought, her son and daughter were still in the thick of it, and she knew it was only a matter of time till their friend was in danger too.

After all, she knew organizations like this. Though Emma was dead, it didn't mean that they wouldn't still find out about what happened.

When that happened, what would they do?

What would she do?

Still, those were thoughts for another day. For now, she just needed to be here, in the present. Maxwell and Karina needed her, and if she was being honest, she needed them just as much.

Even if it was just to erase the dark memories and thoughts that were invading her mind as she sat there.

A new dawn, to a new day, and she couldn't find it in herself to care. She almost found herself wishing that the sun would never rise again.

If only so she didn't have to worry about what the future would bring for all of them.

About the Author

Julie Boglisch is a twenty-seven-year-old woman with a penchant for writing and artwork. Her first book was published in 2017 and since she's been working hard to get her foot into the author arena. She is someone who is proud of the journey she's been on and looks forward to writing and depicting more of the worlds in which she had the pleasure to create.

Also by Julie Boglisch
at
Rogue Phoenix Press

Epidemic
The Elifer Chronicles Book One

It has been forty years since America closed its borders and separated from the world following the Vietnam War. In the ensuing years, the country has developed in incredible ways, or at least, that is what Maxwell and Karina, a set of twins from a community deep in the forests of New England, have been told all their lives. In a town surrounded by larger than life trees and crags, they didn't have a reason to believe otherwise.

That belief is put to the test when they find their house ransacked, their mother missing, and their only chance to live is outside of the barriers they've grown used to. Barriers... that they never realized existed.

Chapter One

The soft chime of a clock resonated through the two-story house at a steady rhythm. A moment of silence ensued, only to be broken by the sharp clack of running footsteps as they pounded down the stairwell. Veronica Elifer tilted her head up just in time to see her son dart past the kitchen doorway. Her eyes caught brunet hair and a lithe frame as he moved toward the front door.

"Maxwell," she called after her son.

"Sorry, Ma, but I'm going to be late!" her son replied as he threw on a pair of sneakers without even untying the laces.

Veronica crossed her hands over her chest. "Be home by dinner, all right?" she demanded which got a sharp nod from her son, along with a cheeky grin. She rolled her eyes at her son's antics.

"Of course," he replied before he darted out the door.

The door swung shut.

"That boy."

She glanced at a single picture set near the sink. The glass frame glistened as she picked it up. She gripped the picture tightly.

"Felix," she whispered.

The picture showed two people who stood side by side in obvious joy. A tall man with sea-green eyes and a small goatee stood with one arm around a young woman. The woman held one hand to her bulging stomach as she leaned against the man. Both smiled broadly toward the camera.

"You know…he's growing up to be just like you," she said, as she gazed solemnly at the picture. "I can't believe they're already fourteen, almost fifteen. Time does fly, doesn't it?" She paused before she continued, a little softer.

"Has it really been four years since then? Since that incident? You saved them then, but…" She tried to rid herself of unwanted thoughts before she looked out the kitchen window. "I just hope neither of them has to go through the same things you did."

She stopped before she gazed up toward the crystal-clear sky. She felt her expression shift to one of determination and fierce defiance as she stared up, as if in a prayer to the heavens. "I can't let it happen again."

Never again.

She heard a soft knock and jerked up. She turned warily toward the doorway, gently placing the photo down. She walked over and slowly opened the door.

There was no one there. She looked around then peered toward the ground. A white letter lay on the pavement. She squatted down and picked it up. She flipped over the paper and froze as her free hand moved up to her mouth. Her eyes widened as her fingers trembled.

"Felix!"

~ * ~

Maxwell gritted his teeth in annoyance as he ran down the street. He couldn't believe he was actually going to be late for school. He was usually never late! He frowned as he berated himself for his screw-up. Oh, his twin was going to have such a riot when she saw this. He skimmed over cracked pavement and brown sidewalks. He could see pristine hedges on either side of the long street, hiding brilliant white but squat houses. Windows were flung open to the fresh autumn morning air as people milled about, watering plants, lounging outside on plastic chairs or lying on the bright and fluffy green grass. Flowers swayed in the early morning breeze.

Maxwell took in the quaint village landscape. *It's such a beautiful day out,* he thought.

Long bangs draped into his eyes on either side of his face. In slight annoyance, he brushed them behind his ear as he moved his pace to a walk. He got his breath back as he looked at the clothes he had hastily thrown on in his panic, a gray sweatshirt with blue jeans. He had a black bag draped over his shoulder which he knew from memory had his name sewn into the smallest flap.

"Maxwell."

He peered up at the sudden shout. To his right, heading toward him, was a middle-aged woman. She wore a summer dress and had a bright smile on her face.

"Hello, Maxwell, running late to school? I saw your sister a while ago. I was surprised to see you weren't with her."

"Yeah, guess she didn't want to wake me. So, what's going on?" he asked as he finally took notice of a line of people behind her.

The woman glanced back and chuckled, a sheepish expression on her face. "I'm taking a quick break. I need it, considering how busy it's been, what with winter coming in a few months and the harvest festival a little before that, everyone's doing last minute preparations, just the usual."

"Ah, I see…must be pretty hard," he replied.

"You're right, it is a real strain sometimes, but at the same time, it's quite nice. That reminds me, are you available this week? I need some help with the store and it seems like everyone else just wants to enjoy the last bits of summer," she stated with a frown.

Maxwell, hesitating for only the briefest of moments, nodded.

She beamed. "Great. I know with school having only started a few weeks ago you're still getting in the swing of things, but I'm glad you're willing to help." She glanced at the watch on her wrist. "Oh boy, I have to get back, my break is almost over. Actually, shouldn't you already be…"

Maxwell blinked in confusion before he squinted at the watch the woman held out to him. He stared uncomprehendingly, before he yelped. *Crap!* he thought as he felt his eyes widen. "I'm sorry! Thank you for reminding me. I'll see you later. I'm going to be late," he exclaimed and with a quick wave, dashed down the road.

He noticed the woman return to her post outside her home to take care of the crowd gathered there.

The town had a population of around three thousand people and most residents had their own shop right outside their home, just like that woman. Each specialized in specific things, such as carpentry, clothing or food.

It isn't really odd though, Maxwell thought, as he ran down another street. He skimmed around a corner, just in time to avoid an elderly woman heading rather briskly in the other direction.

"Sorry," he shouted toward the woman, who only held a look of bemusement.

He let his thoughts continue where they left off. Considering the town was completely surrounded by trees, trees and more trees, each tree, according to scientific calculation, was easily over ninety feet tall. They cast long shadows over the houses and roads, even in the morning sun. Many people thought it was peaceful and quaint.

Of course, there were always exceptions.

He thought of his sister right off the bat.

Maxwell passed more houses and heard people call out enthusiastically from stands and windows alike. He waved before he continued on. His breath came in shorter and shorter gasps. Unfortunately, he couldn't take another break, considering how late it was getting. He gripped his backpack tightly so it wouldn't fall off, annoyed that his home was so far away from where he needed to go.

It was only a few minutes later that he reached the heart of town. A cobblestone plaza lay in the middle, surrounded by pavement. Right in the center of the plaza was a fountain with an eagle spreading its wings wide. Water spouted out of its beak, which was pointed upward toward the sky. On one side of the plaza was a church. Its steeple soared over the plaza. Granite steps led up to double doors made of oak.

The bell rang. It chimed over the town in a sweet melody. He peered at the steeple as he waited for the final chime. The final note rang out beautifully for a moment, before silence took over. Maxwell stared solemnly toward the bell tower before he let out a resigned groan. He turned to examine the rest of the plaza. On the other side, parallel with the church, was a school. It was a small one-story-tall building that filled up half the square by itself. He could just barely see people dart in the doors. Next to it was the convenience store. It was the go-to for anything that couldn't be made by hand.

Maxwell took in the crowded streets before he spotted a familiar figure. He hurried over to the figure.

Standing by the school was a girl about the same height as Maxwell. She leaned her back against the brick wall of the school in a nonchalant, and slightly annoyed posture. Her raven-black hair curved around her face, and fell just a little past her chin on either side. The rest of her hair was pulled back sharply and tied up in a high ponytail.

She wore a blue halter top with short tan shorts. Her arms and fingers were clad in black fingerless gloves that reached comfortably to her elbows. Worn but well-used hiking boots covered her feet. Long black socks surged up to just below her knees, finishing the ensemble. She also had a backpack draped off one shoulder.

Her face expressed boredom as Maxwell stepped in front of her. His sister seemed to sense his presence. Sky blue eyes opened to acknowledge him as he leaned against the wall beside her to catch his breath.

"Took you long enough," she stated.

He felt her gaze on him before a grin crossed her face.

"I was starting to wonder whether you were going to skip. Of course, personally, I would be happy to do that."

Maxwell huffed in annoyance before he pushed off the wall. "You could have at least woken me up, Karina," he stated with a shake of his head. "School only just started and we're going to be late for the second time."

Karina raised her eyebrow.

"Don't say the first time wasn't your fault. You thought it would be funny to steal my alarm clock and replace it with a freaking spider! Who does that?"

Karina pushed off the wall. "It was only plastic."

Maxwell's shoulders drooped. "Anyway, let's get inside."

"Yeah, because you are oh so excited for math, right?"

Maxwell groaned. He never was going to live that one down, was he? "Oh, shut up," he muttered as they walked quickly down the wooden hallway to reach the first door on the right.

Of course, he didn't have to worry too much. Math, thankfully, wasn't till the end of the day, but still. They knocked and stepped in, just as Karina's name was called.

Karina waved. "Here," she shouted as she took her seat.

Maxwell groaned audibly at his sister's antics.

The room was a normal classroom with blackboards and rows of desks set up neatly in aisles. The teacher, a balding man in his thirties, glanced up with an unsurprised look. "Maxwell Elifer? Can you try to make sure you and your sister actually get here on time?"

Maxwell took his seat, but didn't comment. *I'm just lucky that we both even get to class,* he thought in annoyance as the teacher finished his roll call. *If it wasn't for the stupid alarm clock, I would have gotten here on time, along with Kari...* He mentally sighed once more and slumped in his seat.

Only to perk up as the teacher said, "Okay, class, pop quiz time."

Maxwell glanced around as a groan vibrated around the room, filled with about twenty students around his age. He dug into his bag and pulled out a pencil. He tapped it onto the desk as he waited. He could see Karina. Her eyes were closed and she was leaned back against the chair. An unenthused look sat on her face.

"Kari," Maxwell hissed under his breath, soft enough for only her to hear.

Why couldn't his sister at least try to look like she was paying attention?

Karina opened her eyes before she sent him a glare and let the chair fall back into place.

It was then that he received his quiz.

He quickly wrote down the answers and passed it forward. After another five to ten minutes, the teacher collected all the quizzes.

"All right, let's see how you did. Question one, what was the second name of The Great War and what followed?"

A kid near Karina raised his hand and spoke. "After the conclusion of the Great War, they renamed it World War I and shortly after came World War II, promptly followed by the Eternal War Era."

"Good. Now, question two, what caused the name changes to occur?"

This time, another kid spoke up. "The name of the Great War was originally changed because it was easier to distinguish, after the second 'great war' started, which was which. The name of the time following World War II was changed because they noticed a connection between each successive war after the fact regarding certain superpowers, including the United States."

"That's correct, because of U.S. involvement in most wars post World War II, they deemed to call the entire period between that war and the Vietnam War the Eternal War Era, in order to more easily group them together. Now, final question, what was the consequence of that time?"

Maxwell raised his hand. "There was a depletion of goods, and as a result, they wanted to find more efficient ways to preserve society. As such, they created this place, so that people could learn about nature and grow in it. After the movement, the U.S. closed all borders officially and turned in on itself. It focused on recovering its own problems and, as a result, ended up booming in private businesses…" he trailed off as the teacher gestured to him proudly.

"That is correct. As a result, they didn't need this town, so now we just learn and live in peace."

Karina tched. Maxwell smirked toward his sister who had her arms crossed over her chest. He could see one leg jitter against the table.

"I hope everyone did well. Now, turn to page two hundred and fifty-four of our textbook and we'll get started on the Industrial Revolution…"

~ * ~

Maxwell sighed as he stepped out the door of the school. He saw Karina beam with joy as she ran down the steps in the direction of the forest right past the convenience store. "Come on, Max, I want to show you something. We can go home after, 'kay?"

Maxwell's eyes narrowed as he walked down the steps as well. The afternoon sun shone down over them as the school doors opened to the rush of students leaving classes. "Kari, I'm tired. Why don't we just go home and you can show me this weekend?"

"Max, come on, it won't take that long." She frowned as she faced Maxwell with sharp blue eyes, as if to dare him to argue.

His sister could be…interesting at times, but she did mean well. "Fine, what is it?" he asked as he hefted his backpack more comfortably on his shoulder.

"You'll see," she said, sounding relieved, as she went to walk away.

"Kari…it better not be something stupid, like trying to find wild animals, or racing through the trees again…didn't you almost break your ankle last time you decided to try to swing between the trees?"

Karina shrugged. A nervous grin sat on her face, which betrayed her nonchalant posture.

"Come on, Maxwell, it won't be THAT bad…please?" she begged.

Maxwell had to mentally reiterate to himself that his sister did mean well, even if she was a bit on the hyperactive side.

Karina started to usher Maxwell forward.

Great. I don't even know HOW she finds half the things she does. I always end up caught up in them…and usually not for the best. He let his thoughts trail off with a shiver. He remembered one too many times running for dear life while his sister would grin widely, even as she muttered apologies.

He could see Karina smirk and stick her tongue out playfully before she spun away. She seemed to pause before reaching an arm backward. She grabbed Maxwell's wrist and darted toward the surrounding forest. Maxwell yelped as he followed after the energetic girl. Karina was fast, much to Maxwell's consternation, as she ran down the road without a care, plunging right into the tree line. Maxwell stumbled behind her and yelped in frustration as he tripped over another root.

"Hey!" he shouted as his backpack slammed into his back.

Karina ignored him as they darted into the trees.

"Kari. Will you slow down?" Maxwell gasped out between wheezes, as he struggled to keep up with Karina's harsh pace. *Where the heck does she get all this energy?* he thought in exasperation.

"Heck no, come on, little brother, you should be able to do this much," she called back as she swerved around another tree. Maxwell barely managed to avoid it as he let a curse slip through his lips and under his breath the whole time.

"Karina, this is ridiculous! You're running way too fast. How do you have so much energy after a full day of school?" He yelped as he managed to scramble over a fallen tree limb that his sister practically jumped over. It didn't help that she gave him no warning she was jumping anyway which made him stumble over it.

He saw Karina frown as she tilted her head to look back at him. He felt her glare even as she faced toward the deep woods. "Stupid little brothers," she muttered under her breath as she leaped over another small fallen sapling.

"You're only about two minutes older than me," Maxwell replied curtly as he followed up her leap. This one he could actually make, even as his breath caught in his throat.

The two ran through the forest with rapid speed. Occasionally, they slowed to give Maxwell a break before Karina dragged him off again. The afternoon sun shone down brilliantly, as branches shifted in a light breeze. Fallen leaves coated the ground and crunched under their feet. Maxwell followed, somewhat unwillingly.

Finally, Karina slowed her pace down to a walk. Maxwell felt his lungs gasp for air as he forced himself not to lean forward and rest his hands on his knees like he wanted to. Why did his sister have to be so athletic compared to himself?

He heard wind whisper through the trees as he felt his sister's gaze on him. He tilted his head up enough from its drooped state to see her sheepish expression.

Sorry, she mouthed as he glared at her. Really? His sister was too hyperactive for her own good.

"So…um…how was your day?" she asked tentatively after he caught his breath and they moved on, thankfully much more slowly.

Maxwell put a hand to his face before he dropped it and spoke. "Just…great…I really just need a break," he muttered as his sister dropped her pace enough to walk beside him instead of in front of him. Her gaze was even, if a little confused.

"Break? From school? From the run?" she asked.

"Well, yes, that too…" he trailed off as he suddenly remembered why he woke up so late. To be more precise, why he hadn't gotten enough sleep to actually hear his alarm properly.

He noticed Karina's eyes on him and once more looked toward his sister. It only took a moment for understanding to flit across her face. "Dad…"

"It was four years ago today after all," Maxwell responded vaguely.

He felt Karina bump into his shoulder. "Come on. If we go at this pace, it'll take all day," she said, as she gently grabbed his hand once more. Maxwell nodded, grateful for the distraction as he followed after her at a faster pace that was still much slower than before.

It was only a couple minutes later, however, when he once more thought of it.

Maxwell's lips tightened into a thin line before he forced himself to relax. He looked to see his sister and cringed. The smile on her face was weak. He instantly recognized it as a fake, one only used when she didn't want to worry others.

Sorry, Kari, he thought as he noticed the grip on his wrist tighten. *You're still trying to forget as well.*

A long low sigh slipped through his lips before he found himself jerked to a halt.

He peered up to see a rocky cliff edge surrounded by trees. the rock wall seemed a lot more intimidating up close. Maxwell saw it from a distance through the trees for a while, but since his mind was preoccupied, he hadn't really thought about it. Not until it was in his face. He tilted his head up to take in the fact that a tree lay against the rock face precariously, looking ready to fall to the ground at any moment.

He saw his sister's smile widen as she let go of his wrist. He rubbed his wrist gingerly. "So, was there a reason why you dragged me out here? This is a nice rock wall and all, but that's about it."

"Geez. THIS isn't the spot. It's just on the way. Now come on. I can't wait to show Mom as well, if I can ever convince her to come with us."

Maxwell noticed his sister's eyes glimmer as she stared up at the rock face, her expression shining with the prospect. He peered down at the ground and felt his bangs fall into his face once more. He brushed his bangs back, looked up and said, "You do realize she wouldn't have the time, right? She's the only doctor and scientist in town. This morning was one of the few times she actually had off."

He saw his sister's expression falter for a moment before she seemed to steady herself. A glimmer like determination flashed through her eyes as she looked at Maxwell.

"It's worth a shot. She's been working hard ever since…" She paused before she sighed and continued, "I think it would be a good chance for her to take a break so that we can be like a family again. As you said, she rarely has time lately, so it would be nice."

Maxwell eyed his sister. He breathed in and slowly exhaled before he looked up at the rock face with a glare. He really wasn't looking forward to this. "I hope you don't expect me to climb that, because, you know, there's no way I'm going up that thing," he said.

He saw Karina shake her head as he continued to stare at the rock face. A cloud slid over the sky to dapple it in steely grey. "One day you'll be glad to have a chance. Anyway…" He finally pulled his eyes away from the treacherous, in his opinion, rock face to look at her. He noticed her eyes gleaming with an unidentifiable emotion. She flung her hands out to either side as she exclaimed toward Maxwell enthusiastically. "Don't you want to see what's beyond these trees? Beyond this place? In the past fourteen years, we have never been away from home, ever. Mom has, and so did Dad, when he was around. Don't you want to go into that world outside and see what else is out there?"

"No," Maxwell replied with a deadpan look. "I'm quite content with staying home. This town has everything we need. I don't see the point. Plus, what about Ma? We can't just leave her."

Karina closed her eyes and seemed to debate with herself for a moment before she opened them, and said, "We'll all just go together, I think that would be more fun anyway."

Maxwell stayed silent as Karina turned to face the rock face. She reached both arms forward to give them a good stretch. "We get to the top of our rock and you won't even have to worry about it anymore. Come on, it's easy."

Maxwell gave her a deadpan look as he felt his eye twitch. Karina noticed his expression and huffed. "Fine, I'll show you," she stated.

Maxwell scrutinized her. He tilted his head up as he noticed that everything seemed a shade darker. What was once a beautifully clear late-afternoon sky was now gradually being filled with dark, foreboding clouds. He frowned as an uneasy feeling settled in his gut. His sister seemed to sense it as well. Karina looked around once before she shook her head, as if to rid it of thoughts, and stepped toward the rock face. She pushed herself up with quick and efficient movements as her hands flew up the rocks with ease.

She reached the top and dangled her legs over it to look down. "You coming?"

"No way," he called as he tried desperately to hide the nervousness that seemed to want to slip into his voice. Heights…why heights? He blinked and glanced up once more as a low rumble sounded in the distance. "Um…how about we go back home? Ma is probably waiting for us." Maxwell said.

Karina tilted her head up to the sky. He heard a small, noncommittal noise from her before she frowned. "It does look like it's going to rain, doesn't it?"

Maxwell nodded. Karina slid over the edge and began to climb down. She took slow steps even as Maxwell felt something fall onto his cheek. He jumped as a yelp came from the rock face. He turned just in time to see Karina skid down the side. His eyes widened as he stumbled forward. Karina stopped only a foot or two below where she lost her footing.

His sister leaned against the rock face, still having a way to go. Her expression was a mix between stunned and slightly scared. Her clothes were ruffled. Her knees, elbows and hands were scratched up from trying to stay close to the rock face. A light stream of blood slipped from her fingers as a tremble racked up her spine. His sister let out a shaky breath as she took stock of any injuries. Both teens stayed in silence before Maxwell cautiously called up to her.

"You okay?"

"What do you think," Karina snapped back, her voice harsh.

Maxwell cringed as Karina stared at the wall face. Was she nervous?

Maxwell saw her grip the stone more tightly before she finished her descent, jumped to the ground and brushed herself off.

Maxwell muttered a quiet, "Show off," even as he let himself smile, relieved.

She gave him an annoyed look before she coldly walked past him. "Hurry up, slowpoke. We're going to be late."

Maxwell raised an eyebrow as he followed after her. *Wasn't that my line?* he thought in bemusement.

Karina ignored him as she walked determinedly onward.

Maxwell pursed his lips. Shadows fell over the tree canopies, as the sun's rays struggled to shine through the now completely darkened sky. "It looks like a big storm," he muttered as he eyed the horizon, feeling the apprehension well up more as he watched the fast-moving clouds.

The two continued back in an awkward silence. They kept their slow pace through the trees even as Maxwell tried to bring up a conversation. Sometimes, he made comments on the impending storm silently urging her to go a little faster, other times, he talked about how lazy the math teacher was, which was making learning the subject even harder, since it was also the last class of the day. Yet other times, he would bring up their mom.

He could see his sister glance at him, conflicted between her want to stay moody, and her wish to chat with her brother.

Moodiness won out even as a low rumble sounded once more in the distance.

"Well, this is more peaceful than I thought," Maxwell said as they slipped around another tree. *The times I don't want to talk, she annoys me to no end, the times I want to talk, she's as silent as the freaking trees...* He put a hand to his face as he quietly chuckled.

He never could understand the way his sister acted most of the time, even though they were practically inseparable since birth.

The clouds steadily grew darker as they walked. In the distance, they could hear the chime of the church bell, which signaled that it was around six, even though the dark clouds made it look like it was closer to midnight.

"Well... It looks like we're going to be late again," Maxwell muttered under his breath as he glanced at his sister's back. Karina gazed ahead steadily as she kept up with a firm pace.

They made it into the village center about five minutes later. Maxwell's legs shook from exhaustion as he stumbled tiredly after Karina. His stomach growled and his throat felt dry.

He noted how dark everything was. He could see windows that were previously wide open to the sun, shut tight, only a hint of light seeping through the panes. Plastic coverings sat over some of the plants and most of the stands, prepared for the storm. The streets were empty, to the point of it being almost eerie for both teens.

With each step, they picked up their pace as they passed house after house with barely any light peeking through. Occasionally they caught a flicker, the flutter of a curtain or the gleam of a back-porch light. Shadows weaved through the dwindling sunlight and cast tables, sheds and buildings in ominous textures. Trees and branches began to sway back and forth in the wind that started to pick up around the town. A low whistle could be heard as it swept through the houses, trees and vegetation. A groaning rumble sounded a distance away. With each moment and sound, the twins' steps grew faster until they ran, full speed, down the street. There was another low rumble in the distance that grew longer and louder. Street lamps flickered disconcertingly on either side of the road.

Soft pants could be heard over the incoming storm. An uneasy pressure filled the air as the smell of salt and water wafted toward their noses. A low rumbling boom sounded once more, suddenly a lot closer, which startled them.

Karina's eyes were narrowed in concentration as they sped around the final corner. Their house stood ahead, three down on the left. Its windows were opened with not a single light seen.

"Something's not right," Karina said as she slowed down to a cautious walk.

"You don't say," Maxwell replied, as he slowed himself down, his own thoughts in turmoil as he scrutinized the empty streets.

The storm's pressure seemed to grow, as if it begged to be let loose and break over their heads as another, longer, rumbling sound vibrated around the town. Wind blew stronger. It pulled at their hair and clothes. Maxwell breathed out. He hadn't even realized he held his breath to begin with.

Karina ignored him. She put a finger to her lips as she walked up the front steps. Her eyes seemed to zero in on the front door as she moved.

Maxwell eyed her in a mixture of annoyance and confusion as Karina purposefully held up a hand toward him before she stepped to the doorway alone. She hesitated before she thrust the door out of the way with a jarring bang.

Also by the Author
At Rogue Phoenix Press

Demon's Song
Requiem of Stone Book One

Alex always wished to see the Overlands, a place of sunshine and freedom. However, as a slave in the far corners of the Underlands, it was all but a dream. That is, until he's framed for murder and is forced to flee during a demon attack.

Searching for the answers to why he was framed and seeking a chance at the fleeting freedom he's always dreamed about, he journeys to the capital, meeting friend and foe along the way. But the Underlands are both beautiful and dangerous. Having a demon hunter on his tail and a witch whose sole desire is to become the high Seer around him, he's in for quite the journey.

Coming February 2021

Demon's Call
Requiem of Stone Book Two

Having escaped the city of Raynout, Alex, Rita and Milos find themselves journeying in search of Alex's mother and the answers she can provide. Their search leads them to the dangerous and unknown region of the north, where legend tells tales of its perilous waters. Along the way, they learn not only more about the Underlands, but about themselves as well as they struggle to come to term with who they are and where they belong. Meeting interesting new allies and a dangerous new enemy, the three of them must learn how to fully rely on each other... before the waters of the north tear them apart.

FOR THE FULL INVENTORY
OF QUALITY BOOKS:
http://www.roguephoenixpress.com

Rogue Phoenix Press
Representing Excellence in Publishing

Quality trade paperbacks and downloads
in multiple formats,
in genres ranging from historical to contemporary romance, mystery
and science fiction.
Visit the website then bookmark it.
We add new titles each month!

www.ingramcontent.com/pod-product-compliance
Lightning Source LLC
Chambersburg PA
CBHW051059030726
47504CB00006B/1697